LOST IN THE NEON NIGHTS

THOMAS RAI

SORA PRESS

To My Family...

PROLOGUE

04:46am - 24th Day of the 1st Month, Imperial Year 44

A tall young woman hastily gripped the rim of a wet porcelain sink in-front of her and tried to steady her shaking hands. She was shaking nervously, her twin hearts were racing in her chest, as if they wanted to burst through her ribcage, she couldn't focus, her vision blurred, leaving her nauseous, and lightheaded. Something was wrong.

She thought about the drink she'd been given, thinking it had tasted a little peculiar . What had been in that aperitif that he gave her?

She stood there, struggling to breath, her breathing was now shallow, erratic and laboured, every breath was a challenge as if she was inhaling through dense fabric. A tingling sensation travelled down the two sets of scales that ran down the sides of her spine as she gripped the black sink harder, her knuckles turning white as she tried to stand; her legs becoming weaker as she steadied herself, she staggered in her dark blue high heels, in a barely lit bathroom.

She wasn't safe here. That's all she knew at this point. She had to get out, but how? She could remember vaguely that she was on the twelfth floor, in a private suite. No idea of whose apartment it was, it definitely wasn't his. It couldn't be, could it? She couldn't recall how she got here, the journey down to this level was a blur.

Her memories from the soiree she attended on the 232nd floor were whizzing around her mind, she needed to find the others, hoping that they hadn't all left the party, but it seemed like a lifetime ago, since she had seen them, she had drank quiet a bit but not enough to be this tipsy.

She stood staring at her reflection in the restroom mirror, which made her step back in shock. Her blonde hair was now a mess, her makeup smudged and her lipstick faded in places, and smeared to the side on others.

The bathroom was dimly lit on one side, by a ornate hanging light which cast the rest of the room into the shadows. She struggled to find the switch for the lights and the automatic system wasn't responding to her calls for lights. Her expression changed as she tasted a metallic residue on her tongue, causing her to spit into the sink. The slightly metallic taste in her mouth was vile, her thoughts turned to thinking if her drink had been spiked. Had *he* spiked her drink? She thought. She shook her head. It couldn't have been him, dismissing the notion as quickly as it came to her.

Her once perfect makeup was a complete mess, her mascara had run down her cheeks, Her hair dishevelled, she tried hastily to fix it as she reached up and felt the side of her head, which pounded with pain, wincing as she touched a sensitive area on the right side of her skull, pulling her palm down quickly and recoiling in dismay at the sight of blood covering her hand. Had she hit the edge of the table upstairs that hard? She thought to herself;

trying to remember, it didn't feel as if it was that serious when it happened. She was a shocking sight.

Looking out of the edge of her vision she saw a movement, her instinct was to dart towards the open door on to the balcony, falling to the floor as she approached the platform unable to stand properly in her heels, grabbing hold of the railing as she struck it face first, the impact causing her to become disoriented, everything started to spin.

She sensed something dribbling on her bottom lip, instinctively licking the corner of her lip, wincing at the pain, recognising the bitter metallic taste of her own blood, before wiping it away with the back of her hand as she tried to stand up. The cold air catching her off guard as she got outside, she staggered forward as she became nauseous. She had drunk way too much that night.

"I told you it was over last time" she screamed out into the darkness of the bathroom hoping it could hear her, as a shadowy figure paused at the doorway, She could barely make out its appearance as it kept itself just out of the light, making her second guess if someone was there, it knew it was being watched.

"It's over. I'll tell them the truth…. please don't come any closer…" she exclaimed as she steadied herself, turning towards the railings. Her fear of height causing her hands be become clammy, feeling even more nauseous. It was too high up and she didn't like it. She spun around as she noticed two hands grab her forcefully by her hips, lifting her onto her tiptoes, unable to stabilise well in these six inch heels. Struggling to stay on her feet as she tried to get away, holding onto the figure as she felt herself loose her balance.

"Stop it, please, I beg you…" she helplessly cried out before his icy hand smothered her mouth, drowning out her cries for help. The lights of the transports below lit up the lower levels, but the twelfth floor was plunged in to darkness from the shadow of the immense building which towered beside it.

She struggled as she felt its body push against hers, pinning her against the railing. The young woman cried out as she felt his hand find its way up the slit in her skirt, before shifting her attire over, exposing her to the cold air. She had a horrifying feeling that she knew what was coming next. She panicked even more, causing her to be able to feel her hearts racing in her chest. She kicked out violently against him, before noticing his fist move to grab her hair and right ear, causing her to freeze in fear.

"Ceres, I told you this isn't over until I say it's over..." his voice caught by the wind, as he pulled away his finger ripping the golden hoop earring from her ear as she struggled against him, loosing her footing as she fell backwards, falling into the darkness below, screaming as she fell.

CHAPTER 1
"HEY DARLING..."

6 Hours Earlier...

"So, who are we supposed to be seeing again?" A young woman remarked nervously, glancing over her bare tanned shoulder, expecting someone to be close by, but was met by silence, as she shyly walked into the club's foyer. Her black leather knee-length coat being swiftly taken by the clubs maids of every possible gender who were dressed in barely anything, some wearing nothing at all, others wearing nothing more than high heels and lingerie, much to everyone's distraction, she expected the extreme here, but not this.

"So this is what it's like at one of her soirees," she murmured to herself as she ran her fingers of her left hand through her luscious light blonde hair.

While she was mesmerised by her surroundings, the entire place was elegantly decorated, opulence was in fashion here, she felt utterly under dressed for such an occasion. Her athletic and physique was covered by a deep blue figure-hugging dress, with a neckline that plunged wide to reveal her moderate cleavage, ornate copper toned swirls exquisitely embellished the deep blue fabric.

She stood, taking in her surroundings, a total change from the minimal living quarters she was used to at the dormitory. Her shared room was small and basic, with few luxuries. Knowing she hadn't spent much time at home over the past six cycles.

She stood admiring the opulence of the place, with its ornate sculptured statues, gorgeously shaped ice sculptures of varied people in compromising poses, perfect specimens of different races within the empire, they sparkled as they reflected light in every direction as well as lowering the ambient temperature, sporadically being cold enough to cause her nipples to stiffen in the icy air, but she didn't care, it got her the attention from the media which she craved 'at least they'll be acknowledging me' she thought to herself.

She pondered how the semi naked members of multiple species who held silver trays kept themselves warm while they wandered around with trays of either Dhaamyr wine in tall glasses and the silvery vials containing the refined, tremendously addictive and sort after narcotic Kalita, sort after by many of her species. The cold air could cause some compromising situations, which caused her to chuckle to herself. She could deal with the random chills herself, but what about them?

For an instant her thoughts shifted to the possibility of picking up a vial of Kalita, before remembering she was ordered not to unless offered, All because of an agreement with management, an agreement she hesitantly agreed to, she could have done with its calming nature, specially on a night like tonight, the pressure was already getting to her.

"Who?" she asked again, hoping for but still getting no response. She nervously looked over her shoulder repeatedly. Where was she?, she thought.

The foyer was heaving, there wasn't a single space free, no where was empty, at the entrance were the media, with their micro drones flying around, to the highest levels of society, All the social aristocracy were here, specially at a Soirée hosted by Lady Centych Kalidral Vale. The socialite daughter of Lord Hysio Vale, one of the twelve ruling members of her people's aristocracy. Her validation meant everything to her, and she couldn't mess it up. Not here. It would cause the end of her career.

See excitingly looked down at the delicate silver band around her left wrist, surprised to have received an invitation like this, a summons many would have killed for, and here she was. One of the final twelve and personally invite by Lady Vale herself.

She tried to take in all in, her palms sweating, her stomach in knots, here she was with the who's who of society, the social elite, those who unquestionably made things happen, as long as you were willing to do them a favour, a favour she has been aware of since she was younger. She hoped he would be there tonight; she had a proposition that he would confidently jump at. He had to be here, being at Lady Vale's debutante social appearance here on the imperial capital planet of Prim. It was almost a dream come true. An event that could make or break her career. An audience with her was practically impossible to get, yet her ladyship had requested this meeting.

Her mind ran wild. All she knew was that she had a 60 second audience with her, at an unknown point during the night, she felt the fear bubbling in her stomach, so she better be prepared for it to happen at a moment's notice, any failure would cause her dismissal from BYL Entertainment , or worse total social rejection.

She repeated her question, this time getting a whispered response from behind, causing her to jump, her hearts skipping a beat for a moment before beating normally again, a sensation she didn't enjoy, causing her to take a deep breath to steady herself.

"Hey Darling..." the whisper said seductively.

Before feeling a quick kiss on the back of her neck., causing her to shiver, as goosebumps to briefly appear on her arms as the sensation cascaded quickly down the two rows of scales that ran down her spine. They progressively changed from her rose hinted porcelain skin tone to a light blue, before hastily returning to normal. She struggled to ignore the overwhelming thrill; her hearts beating erratically once again, she had to control herself. Hoping that her pheromones weren't that easy to notice, she needed to focus. Tonight was judgement night. She couldn't fail now. The last six cycles boiled down to tonight.

"Hey, not here..." she scowled. There was a time and a place for that, and this wasn't one of them.

"We gotta be on our best behaviour, that's what management said unfortunately" Ceres added before she turned around, stopping just as she was about to speak, distracted by what she saw, which was Nyxcerra handing her knee-length black leather coat to a maid., who scurried it away, into a hidden wardrobe behind a mirrored door.

The flashes of the media's cameras went into overdrive as she revealed her outfit for tonight's soiree. She was the one that everyone wanted to see and she knew it and experienced enough in how to flaunt it; it was all a game that she knew the rules of. She was the visual and would play for the crowd.

Ceres found herself lost in thought again, mesmerised, finding herself casting her own gaze at every inch of her, unable to hide her own infatuation with her, taking all of her in. From the black high heel boots, which glistened in the light of the lobby, up her toned legs to an exquisite and figure hugging dark red dress, which left nothing at all to the imagination, contrasting with her gentle and warm tawny toned skin, all topped off by her deep red lips, completely matching her long deep red hair which transitioned to a light orange as it reached her bare shoulders. As she turned towards the flashing cameras and hovering drones, knowing the media wanted more.

She smiled a devilish smile as she caught Ceres' gaze, realising that she was staring at her light green deep-set eyes, trying to get her attention, Nyxcerra winked once as she beamed, before chuckling to herself, causing her to casually wrinkle her nose.

Knowing precisely what she was doing to her, and didn't genuinely care if anyone recognised it, she continued to play to the crowd. It would get the media gossiping. That's all she wanted. She knew the worth of an excellent story could do for her career; she had always walked the fine-line between what was appropriate and what wasn't, notably with Ceres, much to the chagrin of the other girls.

"Fine..." she hesitantly replied, before adding,

"I'll be good, as long as you are..." she purred before grabbing Ceres' hand and walking beside her, knowing this would make her blush, which was done instinctively. As well as stir the interests of the media in attendance, a girl from the Artreia - Dasho - tribe holding hands with a Valari girl, it would cause scandal back on Jalan II or the other predominantly Impiri worlds, but it was a novel concept here on Prim, the multi-millennia old rivalry between the twelve Impiri tribes was always simmering to the surface, but Nyxcerra didn't care for it.

"First, Thebus, head of promotion at Tamek PR," she began listing the important conversations she would have that night, pausing as she tried to remember.

"Then sign off with Aeryth," before clutching her hand tighter, the tightening causing Ceres to pause she knew what was coming.

"Then you will be summoned to meet with Lady Vale, you will be told when at a moment's notice," she paused

"Then Casotta DeVri, she's the lead designer at the Dasé DeVri fashion house. They want us all to showcase her latest collection... as long as she considers you graceful enough," Nyxcerra's tone sounding surprised.

"If she considers me graceful enough, I'm gorgeous... haven't you seen me?..." Ceres exclaimed playfully, gesturing at herself before she smiled and embraced Liex, after noticing him, dropping Nyxcerra's hand. He was going to be the one introducing her to the mover and shakers. Without their support, the group wouldn't stand a chance of competing against the established artists across the industry.

Liex was young, confident, handsome in a generic sense, specifically for a Thetan, his forked tongue still creeped her out though, Ceres thought to herself, causing her to shudder as she thought about it, But she couldn't stand his duplicity, all smiles and hugs one minute, then.

"Fuck them, hate having to be pleasant to them" the next second when they were just out of earshot., she didn't know if she could trust him, but she had to fake it, it was the only way they could get anything done, he was known to be ruthless and highly skilled in negations, constantly thinking about the perception of every action undertaken by any member of the company.

Out of the corner of her eye she saw three young women being escorted to the exclusive lounge, she sighed a sign of relief, the tension finally releasing from her shoulders, as Syala, Jysell and Tiiona had managed to get ready in time for the second transport, not missing it and had arrived here on time. Syala was stunning in a conservative but elegant dark green skirt with a lighter green blouse, touched at the shoulders. Tiiona had as she expected turned up in a shirt, waistcoat and dinner jacket, all in yellow, paired with a long trailing yellow skirt, 'you go girl...' she thought to herself, while just managing to glimpse the dark maroon dress that Jysell had worn, the cream coloured ribbon tied at the back was borrowed from Ceres, she smiled, realising that she had managed to use it.

She thought they might not take it on time, as they missed the initial transport to the event. Even though she hadn't seen them arrive, they had been fast tracked to the upper floors, while she and Nyxcerra were still being wooed by the media, constantly asking for more photos and holo's. She wondered when they would be taken up using the secret elevators to the 232nd floor where the actual party was.

She was anxious to get there, stuck between wanting to get there, but also wanting to delay it as much as possible, this is where Lady Vale would be, she didn't want to make a mistake, anxiously sighing before posing for more photographs, she turned towards them and posed, smiling for ever photo, casting her gaze over at Nyxcerra who was doing the same, laughing and joking with the media, Nyxcerra was defiantly the visual, they loved her elegance, but they adored Nyxcerra's unbridled sexuality and wanted as many photographs as they could get in the building's lobby, their drones weren't allowed any further.

CHAPTER 2
"IT'S ALWAYS ABOUT THE EYE CONTACT..."

Two hours Later -12:42am

"So, have you two grown accustomed to the social life here on Prim?" Aeryth asked at a break in the conversation between Ceres and Liex, she took a small sip of her drink, taking a moment to savour the taste and aroma, the sweetness followed by the kick of the alcohol.

Aeryth was a glamorous older female, her blonde hair was now tinged silvery white, her expression was calm but firm, she stood there watching them engage in conversation with her, being on their best behaviour. She knew the power she had over them.

She was dressed elegantly, her red lips matching the red blouse she was wearing, finished off by her black leather trousers. She stood there tapping her finger on the glass she was carrying, anticipating a reply, noticing and enjoying that it caught Ceres by surprise. Causing her to chuckle to herself. The sign-off was due later Ceres thought. But for Aeryth, having this power over them was more enjoyable, so she would do it now. There was no point waiting, no need to keep them on edge. She grinned devilishly.

Ceres looked at her, beamed a beautiful smile, trying to calm her nerves and her mind, which didn't expect the sign off right now. Aeryth was it, head of talent at BYL entertainment, with a list of accolades that made her the most influential executive in the industry, across the entire empire, everyone knew who she was, from here on Prim, to the distant worlds of Maxia II and Tallos Prime. Hundreds of billions had heard her artists, and there she was, a meter from Ceres, the woman who would decide her entire future.

Ceres took a deep breath before replying, her hands shaking, a lump in her throat. She had been rehearsing this since her first day, almost six cycles earlier. Notably when in conversations with men. But she realised Aeryth took more than just a slight interest in her, and she'd hopefully use that to her advantage. Anticipating that Nyxcerra would join in soon, raising her voice and overacting, laughing at any joke Aeryth made, just enough to force Nyxcerra to join in.

Nyxcerra was talking with Nabil, her dance instructor, before excusing herself when she could hear Ceres laughing at the jokes Aeryth was telling, and knew what was going on. They had talked the night before and promptly fell into the practiced rhythm. They flirted, teased and peppered Aeryth with questions and answers, making submissive comments thanking her for her care and guidance over the turbulent six cycles.

A young, fresh-faced girl stood behind them, over-hearing the conversation. She sighed. She knew exactly what Nyxcerra and Ceres were up to and they knew that Avéline hated the calculated nature; of it, after they discussed it on the transport over, she was against it morally, but knew it had to be done.

Avéline was engrossed in her own conversations with Vyna, their vocal coach and producer. He had been instructing her on how to get even more out of her voice, telling her to not be afraid of standing out. She shook her head, her silvery grey hair tied up into an elegant bun. She was the youngest of the six girls. She looked it and at times acted it. She was naïve and unaware of the things the others were aware of.

"But I'm not sure I can do it..." she stuttered anxiously as she nervously fixed her black dress. She'd gone for a simple black number with black knee-length boots, in her mind a classic look.

"I mean Nyx' has a better low end, and Ceres, her highs are light, mine are just too shrill," she added as she tried to deflect his attention, dropping her shoulders resigning herself to her own limits.

He laughed at her and smiled.

"Well, my sources say she's going to keep ya. I mean, the instructors from the label had come close to dropping you, remember that..." he replied as he grabbed hold of a drink from a passing server and downing it hastily.

"But they didn't. Remember, they listened to me, especially when I told they about your potential," he added boastfully.

"Trust me, you know I got your best interest at heart..." trying to calm her down, seeing that she was getting nervous. He knew her range, and that's what made management excited, notably when she got to the whistle register. She knew her range was vast, from the low E2 to the dizzying heights of G7. Far exceeding the range of everyone else in the group, but it was her control of this voice was what they wanted, her pleasing texture and ease of manipulation, this alone cemented her place in the group, even after six cycles she still felt like she was an imposter and was going to be found out at any moment.

————

Meanwhile, across the club...

Nyxcerra carefully watched how Ceres' pale yellow eyes —barely flicked away from Aeryth, even when her gaze shifted to her or an aide who handed her another drink. They were always fixated on her. Even though she was skilled at getting the attention of others, she usually used her physical assets to get what she wanted, if that failed she used the methods which Ceres was an expert at, she got into your head, and you ended up doing her favours.

Remembering the time when they had ended up sleeping together, she used all of her physical assets to get her interested in one of the parties that the girls on her floor had thrown during the Renio festival at the end of the first cycle. They were both quite drunk and had ended up embraced in a passionate kiss that ended up with them in bed not much later. These thoughts made her hearts race. She had a job to do tonight, 'don't get too distracted, she murmured to herself, trying to put the illicit thoughts away for a moment.

'It's all about the eye contact', Nyxcerra remembered Ceres telling her, it was the first in many lessons she had told her, usually as they fell asleep late at night, things she'd overheard from her mother, but more from her father, the legendary Luca-Tal Soobaks. He had worked with Aeryth when they were both in the group of Eternity, more than three decades before Ceres was born.

It was the first lesson in what he called the art of seduction and domination 'Look directly into their eyes until they can't look away from you. Capture their gaze, always keep them interested in you', she remembered her father saying, 'the occasional glance elsewhere to play it coy, but it's you who is in charge.' Her mom regularly added, causing Ceres to be unsure of who was actually in charge at home when she was growing up, her father or mother?, to them it was how they acted with everyone, constantly about the power play, sacrificing one thing to gain leverage over the other in something else, shed grown used to the power play and used it with everyone, except Nyxcerra, it never worked on her.

"Maintain eye contact, don't let her out of your sight," Nyxcerra whispered to herself, before repeating it another time.

———

Meanwhile...

"As you can see, only you six were invited here tonight. I'm sure you know what that means." Aeryth asked, letting the words hang, shocking Ceres, surprised by the remark at a break in the conversation. The revelation that the other six girls wouldn't be there tonight, she knew that meant the other group of six girls would be gone when they got back to the dormitory.

Aeryth gestured for a young Casperian waitress with long dark green hair to stop, before taking hold of two glasses full of wine from her iridescent tray, pausing for a fleeting moment to admire her light green skin before sending her on her way, with a single glance, discreetly watching her hips sway as she walked away. She was young, petite with a sway which caused Nyxcerra to glance over for a second, trying to not get herself distracted. She looked away looking back towards Aeryth, Ceres shaking her head as she caught them both looking.

Noticing Ceres and Nyxcerra standing in-front of her brought her back into the conversation. She blushed lightly, realising they had caught her.

"... Sorry about that.." she chuckled.

"I was obviously distracted..." she paused again to get a second view of the waitress.

"But you both know what I'm like.." she freely laughed,

"These are for you two. Take a moment to savour the taste and aroma. You've made it this far..." her voice trailed off as Ceres looked at Nyxcerra and smiled, trying hard to control her building excitement. Her skin tingled, her hearts stopped for an instant before the adrenaline caused them to beat faster. Before taking the two high fluted glasses from her, containing a sparkling pink liquid.

"We won't fail you, we promise, all six of us..." Ceres added as she took a sip, Dhamyrr wine, with a hint of Kalita, she swallowed it gently, feeling it gently travel down her throat, leaving a familiar sweet aftertaste, everything seemed heightened, she could sense her twin hearts beating so fast they caused her to get lightheaded for a moment, not a good combination with the wine now making its way through her body.

"You better not. I've taken a gamble creating an Impiri girl group, but we identify potential in all of you, and billions have been watching you, and they can't wait to witness the final reveal," Aeryth added, her voice tinged with arrogance.

"I'll let you tell the other girls. I've got someone to see," before adding.

"We'll discuss this more in the coming days. It's going to blow the minds of your fans. We have an interesting first cycle planned," she added as she glanced over at her side, who casually gestured that she needed to go. Ceres looked at Nyxcerra before gulping the entire drink in one. They had actually done it, the six cycles of hard work, from the hundred and six at the beginning, down to the last twelve for the past cycle.

Now the other six had been dropped. She saw flashes of the past six cycles, a rush of thoughts and memories. All of this had been in the public eye. BYL entertainment had broadcast the entire creation of the group across the empire, with tens of billions watching every week, peaking at over sixty billion during the now infamous 'suicide month', where six of the girls committed suicide. Even with this, the audience were interested, the content restricted to adults but still bringing in over a billion viewers a day.

The audience saw everything, the tears, the sacrifices, the moments of joy, the heated arguments, some scripted, or carefully edited to focus on a particular narrative, all of this watched by billions who were waiting for the final reveal. The media, who followed and supported them, had dubbed them the 'final twelve' for the past cycle.

"Nyx, we've done it..." she exclaimed, nervously shaking, as she took shallow breaths as she pulled her close and embraced her, feeling Nyxcerra's hearts racing, she looked down, catching Nyxcerra's gaze, she had been staring at her, lost in her own thoughts, a massive smile on her face, grinning from ear to ear, her eyes sparkled in the overhead lighting.

"No.... You did it Ceres, without you we wouldn't even be here.." she purred as she grabbed hold of her hand,

"But we must find the others, give them the news,"

hastily pulling Ceres toward Avéline, who had wandered over towards a nearby open door leading out onto the balcony after her conversation with Vyna.

————

01:37am

Ceres felt someone's gaze on her as she stood talking to a waitress, causing the scales on the back of her neck to shiver. She had a canny knack for being able to notice this. Even if they were across the room, there were times she could sense the emotions behind the stare. She was a ' dark seer'; she recalled her mother calling her that once, cycles ago, a throwback to her family's past. It had been generations since a seer was born in her family line, but it was nothing more than passing glimpses and an overwhelming sense of emotions.

She looked up to see a young woman staring at her; she stood in a group of what Ceres presumed were socialites, the others in the group were busy talking and laughing, while the young woman was still and kept looking at her, she smiled and nodded, but didn't take her eyes off of her. Giving Ceres goosebumps, the young woman was more than beautiful, looking in Ceres' mind as a real life interpretation of Amathia, the goddess of beauty.

She was tall, her caramel brown hair cascaded down onto her bare shoulders, but it was her eyes that caught Ceres' attention, a rich emerald green which seamed to flicker in the light. Ceres smiled and bowed elegantly. She intuitively knew her place. That was no normal woman staring at her, something she had grown used to. That was her lady, Lady Centych Kalidral Vale, the head of her tribe. She continued to bow before being startled by Leix tapping her on her bare back, recoiling slightly at his unexpected icy touch.

"She would like a word with you..." he whispered over her shoulder, emphasising who he was talking about, hoping that Ceres would understand.

"Don't turn around..you've got less than ten seconds before she's here, now don't you fuck this up.." he cursed through a smile, before Ceres even had time to reply, he anxiously added as if they had just come to mind.

"Remember, one - answer the questions she asks you, two - don't maintain direct eye contact, three - agree with what she says, and four - show your respect, if you don't we are both absolutely fucked, she could have us both killed and no one would even notice."

"I'm not so naïve," she reminded Leix as she lifted her head, amazed by what she saw in front of her.

Lady Vale looked as gorgeous as ever in an exquisite dark blue and gold jacquard dress with a cascading layered skirt which stopped midway up her thigh, revealing her long legs and her golden high heels, knowing that Ceres was looking. She could certainly pass as a fashion model, anywhere in the empire, every part of her was toned, not a single hair on her head was out of place, what caught Ceres attention was her hairstyle, the glow of the lights in the room picked out silver threads interwoven in her hair. Her devilish smile drew her in. Without even trying, she had enthralled her. She blinked rapidly before widening, staring at her, taking a shuffled step back.

Lady Vale stared strangely into hers, as if waiting for her to speak.

Ceres didn't for a second think of herself as a coward, yet at this moment she was completely lost for words, as if her entire thought process was overwhelmed, she wanted nothing more than to turn and run—anything to avoid making direct eye contact with the woman who she had admired for cycles, the ruler of her tribe.

She bowed her head slowly at Lady Vale in a silent gesture of subservience, understanding the etiquette for such a situation, as she sucked in a deep breath, not being able to believe this was happening to her. After a second, Lady Vale stepped forward and embraced her. Unexpectedly, Ceres stiffened as she anxiously stood there, unable to respond.

"My... my lady," Ceres managed to get before she released the embrace. Knowing exactly what she was doing, people would assume they were friends, or casual acquaintances, a sign of her own social circle, being associated with the highest viewed group in the empire would expand her own influence.

"So, finally I get to meet the Valari who's capturing the hearts of our people," Lady Vale enquired, awaiting a response, enjoying the silence she had caused.

"My, my Lady," Ceres stuttered again.

"Maybe just one of them" she paused, trying to think of how to answer it.

"The other is totally yours, your grace, I would never..." she added, catching Leix by surprise, as he stood back, listening to the conversation, the surrounding crowd stopped talking, everyone tried to get within earshot of what was happening.

"Good Save..." Ceres heard Leix murmur behind her, causing her to finally relax her shoulders.

"I'm glad to know that it's one of us who is leading this endeavour..." Lady Vale replied as she slowly looked Ceres up and down, knowing it was making Ceres feel awkward, but she was carefully scrutinising her physique before adding.

"And such a perfect example of our kinds superior genetic beauty, wouldn't you agree Nez?" She proclaimed, her words hanging before a pale skinned young woman with light red hair appeared behind her, anxiously holding a digital pad, she was dressed in all black, her shoulders bare, an intricate black circular tattoo on her right shoulder signified her status as Lady Vales indentured servant, she kept her gaze downward at all times before casually lifting it from looking at the pad, glanced at Ceres for a moment, smiling for a second before dismissing her, as she cast her gaze back down again.

"She's a beautiful example, My Lady, ambitious of course. Surely she'll tow the line...?" The young girl spoke. A group of bystanders glanced over, trying to determine Ceres' expression. She felt her hearts racing. She glanced over at the exits before closing her eyes as she tried to overcome her nervousness before opening them again. How could she answer that? What line was she supposed to be following? She thought, noticing that Nez was glancing at Lady Vale. Their eyes met before cutting intensely toward Ceres. They seemed unaware of the silence which had descended on the area. Or was it all for show, to manipulate her and show her power over her?.

"You will lead my lady, and I will humbly follow...." she trailed off.."

"Of course," Ceres added peacefully, hoping that she had said the right thing in the right way. Was her silence a give away to her fear? She thought, before bowing her head at Lady Vale in another silent gesture of subservience, causing Lady Vale to smile briefly before gesturing at Nez.

"See...." she gestured with an open palm at Ceres,

"I told you she knew her place and was loyal" she stopped as a thought came to mind.

'She's got a spark in her, you know, the same spark that I see every day when I look in the mirror, wouldn't you agree?" she mocked, Nez instantly spoke up. 'Of course My Lady, she'd definitely got some spark, she must have taken inspiration from you, that's for sure.", Lady Vale looked at Nez, shook her head playfully before tutting, "That kind of flattery is going to get you into my good books again isn't it.."

She glanced over at Leix.

"Leix, you know my aide Neziphera, she's loyal, and frequently surprises me with flattery like this, let Aeryth know she needs to get an indentured aide, she can obviously afford one, it would do wonders for her...." she laughed, before realising.

'But that would obviously put you out of a job..., wouldn't it'. She mocked openly, causing Leix to nod his head, knowing that he couldn't say anything in return. A smile was his only recourse.

Within a heartbeat ~her smile changed in an instant to a frown, her demeanour changed, now this was purely business, he knew what was coming, her feedback, this could make or break his own career.

"You were right again, Leix, much to my surprise and disappointment.." she mocked, being surprised that Leix had instructed her well enough as a commoner to greet her and respond to her line of questioning. She playfully smiled at Leix, who smiled nervously back. He'd never had a compliment from her before, and was taken back, laughing nervously at a higher pitch than normal. Cause Ceres to place at him,

'You've instructed her well, she's polite, no eye contact,

that's a plus, she answers with great concern to my percep-tion of her... so that's what I would call a success..' she paused, this paused sent a shock through Ceres, her lips trembled, feeling as if she couldn't move, there was no escaping what she was about to say next.

"However..." she spoke, as she emphasised the last word, Leix's nervous smile dropped. Ceres gasped, she'd done something wrong, wrong enough that Lady Vale was going to use it against her, she nervously grabbed at Leix's, holding onto his arm, She tried to speak, but all that came out was a shrill tone, followed by a gasp.. The music stopped, the atmosphere was tense, conversations stopped, and others turned towards them. Whispers travelled through the club, awaiting the next words on her lips.

"She didn't show the right level of respect, a simple bow, honestly?," she hissed, turning her gaze away from them. As Leix heard this, he reacted instinctively.

"Oh Fuck," he blurted out angrily, unable to hold it, loud enough that Ceres heard him. The floor went silent. She'd made a mistake, just as she instinctively fell to her knees, genuflecting immediately, lowering her gaze straight to the floor, her hearts racing, her whole body shaking uncontrollably, beads of sweat forming on her forehead, unable to control the fear that was running through her mind, what was Lady Vale going to do.

"My Lady, I never meant..." she sobbed, her emotions overwhelming her instantaneously, before sensing Lady Vales' hand on her shoulder.

"I'm messing with you my dear..., you are going to have to get used to it, if we're going to be friends..." Lady Vale added, as Ceres lifted her head,

"My Lady...?" Ceres stumbled over her own words.

"And drop the 'My Lady'. Kali is what I prefer..." she

remarked as she was ceremoniously ushered away by her assistant Nez.

"We'll keep in touch. My people will liaise with your people..." she added, without turning around as she walked off, laughing, with Nez hastily following behind her.

Leaving Ceres standing there, her hearts racing, trying to understand.

CHAPTER 3
"READY AND WILLING..."

Later That Night - 03:02am

Ceres caught sight of him again, casting her mind back a short while to when she had first seen him in the lift to the VIP lounge, he'd been talking with a friend, unable to make out his words, a language she didn't understand fully, the words nowhere near any of the four languages she spoke. He fascinated her. Just thinking about him caused her hearts to race and her scales to tingle, and she knew he had noticed her. The conversation he had was about her, she was sure of it.

She roughly perceived the content of his conversation, as one of his acquaintances had noticeably looked her up and down as if she was a prize before making what she presumed to be a derogatory comment, causing him to glance at her and laugh.

All she understood was it was about her being 'ready and willing' that was the only thing she understood of the language they had spoken.

She tried to ignore it; she felt tiny compared to them. They towered over her, their suits barely fitting their muscular physique. Did she dare confront him?, Ceres looked at her reflection on the base of a silver tray left beside the bar, she felt confident, Lady Vale had complimented her, which caught her off guard, at least someone other than Nyxcerra thought she looked great, still reeling from the brief audience with Lady Vale not five minutes earlier.

She'd had time to reset her look, carefully reapply her lipstick. And eyeliner, her hair still looked great. She knew exactly how to get what she wanted from him, remembering what Lady Vale had whispered to her, as she passed by a moment earlier, by surprise, this message was a private one, not for anyone else to hear, not even her aide Nez, the content of the whisper causing her to chuckle to herself.

He wasn't on the list of those she needed to see that night, but if she could get a favour from him, it would be great for her and the others, she knew those who he represented in other ventures rose to the top quickly, and she would not wait for success to come to her, remembering her fathers saying 'go out and get what you want, no one's going to give it to you...'

She walked off towards the VIP bathroom. Give him some time. Before she had to work on him, she had something to do. She didn't need long; she thought to herself.

She just needed to make this recording, she thought to herself. Then he would be hers, at least for the moment, shed get what she needed, if he got what she knew he wanted.

CHAPTER 4
"I MISSED YOU..."

A Few Minutes Later...

Ceres delicately tapped onto the holographic screen in the restroom. Before stopping, she made sure that she was alone. She looked around, making sure that no-one else was there. This had to be private. The restroom was opulent; the walls covered in dark wood; the floor was covered in black marble tiles and the large mirror which filled one wall surrounded with gold decoration and jewels.

Off to the left side of the room were four cubicles, doors closed but empty. While she stood looking at the screen in front of the mirror, tapping a small pebble sized device on the counter.

She frowned as she looked at her hair, trying to fix it, as she made sure her makeup was perfect. It had to be. When a knock sounded at the door. For a glorious, terrible instant she thought it might be Nyxcerra. She needed to get this done, she only needed a minute, if it was Nyxcerra shed have to delay her for a few minutes, but what excuse could she use that Nyxcerra would believe, she panicked before remembering that Nyxcerra's knock had always been more rhythmic.

"Yeah?" She turned around, looking towards the door.

"Just security ma'am, checking to see if everything is ok..." a husky voice called out. Ceres sighed.

"I'm good, no issues, can you just keep guard on the door for a couple more minutes, just gotta record a message, I need a-bit of privacy."

"I'll be here until you leave..." he called out, reassuring her. She just wanted to make sure that this was private. She didn't want its contents being released. It wasn't the time or the place. She winced in pain for a moment, as the pain quickly overwhelmed her, the shooting pain radiating down her legs before quickly subsiding, to her relief, knowing she didn't have her medication with her, she stood supporting herself against the sinks, trying to catch her breath was got gradually easier as the pain subsided.

———

A few minutes later....

"Aeryth has officially left the party, and now we can play..." Nyxcerra purred as she opened the door,

"Don't let anyone in here please, I need to have a private discussion with her..." she turned her head towards the hulking security guard who just nodded his head in acceptance, just as the door slowly closed, Nyxcerra turned for an instant and pressed the lock button on the door, waiting for a second, with a smile on her face, before turning back with a spring in her step.

"Dasé DeVri is officially using us for their next season's fashion line. We got the job..." she proclaimed, unable to keep the news to herself.

"Aeryth and Casotta negotiated the basic details, and have to go back to Aeryth's to... finish the negotiations," Nyxcerra exclaimed with a wink. She gave a little laugh, as if the idea of the negotiating was going to happen over an actual meeting. She had left the party, arm in arm with Casotta from Dasé DeVri, both obviously and openly flirting with each other. Ceres knew that they had been life-long friends. Some believed that they had at one point been more than just friends, but no one dared ask.

"You did it, Ceres. You got us all to this point, and I've never been as proud of you as I am now." She beamed with a gleam in her eye, wanting to see her reaction, as she fixed her dress while glancing briefly at the expansive mirror.

"I missed you and wanted a little private time with you..." Nyxcerra stated, giddy from all the Kalita and alcohol she had consumed that night.

"Really? Here?" Ceres pressed, but Nyxcerra just smiled at her, unfastening her dress at the shoulders, causing it to fall, as usual for Nyxcerra she didn't wear a bra to events like this, she said earlier that she wanted to tease the holographers and media with glimpses of her physique, but truthfully she wanted to tease Ceres and she was powerless to stop it. Before stepping forward, embracing her, planting a slow and sensual kiss on her lips, for a moment time stopped, slowly arching her back, before breaking the kiss.

"What's going on?" Nyxcerra inquired as she broke the kiss, looking at Ceres, causing her to smile seductively back, as she trailed a finger towards her cleavage while maintaining eye contact with her.

"So what's brought all this on?" Ceres inquired, as she felt her own scales tingle, as she glanced at Nyxcerra's lips, causing Nyxcerra to coyly smile, without taking her eyes off of her; knowing the effect

this had on Ceres..

"Nothing much. Just wanted to celebrate with you, you know. It's not like we've only signed to the biggest music label in the known galaxy." She playfully answered, biting her bottom lip.

Before she was able to reply, a scent caught her attention. The aroma of Nyxcerra's pheromones, Ceres looked at her.

"Really, here, now..." Ceres pressed again. She was risqué but never in a bathroom, especially when there was a full club outside.

Despite the late time, the public nature of the location Nyxcerra was aroused, not sure if it was the alcohol, the adrenaline running thought her system, or just her rampant libido she wanted her right now. She didn't care if anyone noticed, at this moment, as long as she could playfully deny it.

Nyxcerra smiled.

"What were you up-to in here.. anyway?" She enquired before going in for another kiss. As she lifted Ceres onto the marble sink top, causing Ceres to hitch up her dress, her long legs now fully on display.

"Just a diary recording, you know, with all that's happened and all. Then I've got a little negotiation with someone from Tanek PR to get into, just a little preliminary work of course" She knew Nyxcerra would understand what was happening and that this would pacify her for a while, she'd be back home later for their own fun. Luckily, the pain in her legs had faded. Her hearts were now racing for another reason.

"I love you, you know that..." Nyxcerra added, gone for a moment was her playful side. She meant this and knew that a Ceres would understand.

'I know you do, and I love you too. Can't believe we've been together for nearly five cycles...." Ceres smiled, blushing momentarily. She'd said it before, but today was the beginning of their future, so it seemed to mean more today, she thought.

"I know, five cycles with this naughty minx...." Nyxcerra laughed as she playfully looked at her, lost in thought.

She smiled as she thought about something before giving a low guttural purr, which vibrated within her chest, causing Ceres to look puzzled for just a second, before being pulled towards her.

Nyxcerra kissed her again, pulling her close as she kissed her, the adrenaline from being this intimate in an opulent bathroom in the club of the 221st floor drove Ceres to kiss back, pulling Nyxcerra close, running her fingers through her hair: luckily this bathroom had no exterior windows, as it would have provided an interesting show for anyone outside, but it worked perfectly for their needs, the dim lighting, techno music thumping in the background which would mask any noise they made and especially the low-slung sink tops, being conductive to the acts she wanted to do.

"And I love you too, more than I can ever explain.. I can't be in here long, we can have more fun back home, I won't be more than an hour," Ceres replied during a break in the kiss, Nyxcerra carefully drew her fingers up Ceres thigh with a devilish look in her eyes,

"Then I won't keep you too long, just a little fun to keep me happy before I go," she purred as she gently hitched Ceres' legs akimbo before dropping herself low, resting on her heels with a devilish look on her face.

CHAPTER 5
"SHE'S GOT YOU WHERE SHE WANTS YOU..."

Twenty Minutes Later...

There he was standing with several friends, Ceres was not exactly sure of who they were, but they were familiar, she'd seen them around the studio a few times usually grinning at something he had said, then he looked up as someone pointed out into the crowd and saw her as he carefully brushed his dark hair away from his face, revealing his chiselled features, his light blue eyes, in stark contrast to his matte textured almost onyx toned skin, a telltale sign of his kind, he was an Eczack.

She was partially lit by the pink and orange neon lights of a huge art piece which filled the corner of the club. She loved how she looked in this light, the light from the artwork casting a shadow across her right side, her yellow eyes flickering in the light. He knew it was her by the way she walked, her hips swaying as she got closer, and those eyes, the way they glistened in the light, it had to be her; he thought to himself.

A few spectators approached, but Ceres waved them off. She knew what she was doing; she wasn't going to stop until she had spoken to him. He was Toraji from Toraji & Emnis PR. She'd initially noticed him months before when the media had done a seminar on public image, a session she remembered well. She didn't say a word as he stood up from the sofa to greet her. She just ignored him before perching herself on the nearest available space in front of him.

Which was a low-lying glass table. She crossed her legs to better reveal the slit in her dress, revealing her long legs beneath. Tempting him, she watched him stare at her. She now had his attention, and she loved it, it was all a game to her. He gestured for others to leave them be. They hesitated before he waved them away with a hiss and a stern look and a few words she didn't understand.

She looked at him sternly, her lips pursed, not really paying him much regard, casting her gaze around. Waiting for him to make the first step, Ceres never made the initial move. That's what her parents had told her, to give him the pleasure of wooing her, that it would be his idea for something to happen, even though she was confident enough that she could get what she wanted from him.

'They are all the sam....' she thought to herself, noticing his glances and knew the way he sat, trying to hide the reaction she had caused him physically.

At least, not with his kind, public relations. She'd understood that they thought they were in charge, when they were the ones that picked you, and that you should be grateful and compliant , willing to do what they wanted

"So, I hear congratulations are in order?" he asked when she reluctantly cast her gaze at him as he carefully made her look in his direction with the back of his right hand. He wasn't from here on Prim, that she realised.

"Well, thank you, I've worked hard to get to where I am, as you know, so I'm not afraid of putting my back out to get what I wan....' she playfully replied, hoping that he could read between the words she had said,

"I'm sure you can' he added, looking at her body, casting his gaze along her legs, down to her high heels. She smiled, knowing she was getting her attention she wanted, and that he had understood her playful innuendo.

His accent was broken, hints of the multiple languages he probably spoke. That was good, she thought to herself; He looked down at her left arm, taking a quick glance at the dark blue tattoo which made its way around her wrist and up her forearm, a symbol of her tribe, and her place in the social hierarchy.

She wasn't anyone important, not in her tribe, not really. She was a daughter from a family of new wealth, but beyond that she was no one a fact she actually enjoyed.

"So, Balashoi - 'little one'", he muttered as he placed his hand on her knee, she shivered, not out of surprise, but he was physically cold to the touch, but that wasn't the only astonishment, he spoke her mother tongue.

She could pass for any of the main Impiri tribes, but she always preferred being one of the few outside of the Jalel and Kasik systems who could speak Tyuri; She loved that most in the industry were usually fascinated by that melodic, calm and sexy accent. He laughed a deep set laugh as he saw her realisation that he spoke her language.

'How are you doing?, are you enjoying tonight's entertainment, was thinking of leaving, it's a bit tame for me...."

"Not doing too bad, it's a-bit tame, but I'm sure it's not that bad.." she paused, " thought I better get to know you better, since..." she replied, but was interrupted by him placing a finger on her lips to shush her, leaning forward as the music got louder.

"Not here to talk work... can't you see that? I'm here for fun tonight," he remarked, shaking his head lightly, with a devilish smile.

"But neither am I ....' she playfully retired,

"Just looking for a few favours, you can appreciate that, I do something for you, and you do a little something for me..?" she purred, as she gently positioned her legs, causing the dress to reveal her entire right leg, up to the hip.

"I see..." he muttered, as he caught her gaze, watching his glances up her legs and body to her face.

"So, not wanting to dance tonight?" He remarked, letting the words linger in the air.

"Not with anyone who's asked me so far," she replied, raising one eyebrow and smiling seductively, she knew what she wanted.

"Dance with me." There it was. She'd given him permission to do what she wanted him to do. He was playing her game, and didn't even realise it. That's what she hoped as she leaned closer to him, grabbing him by the jaw , placing a slow solitary kiss on his lips, before pulling back. Just as one of his acquaintances returned from the bar,

"Tora, it looks like she's got you where she wants you." He mocked, as he patted him forcefully on the shoulder twice before sitting down with three vials of the narcotic Kalita in hand, passing one to Toraji and offering one to Ceres. She didn't shift her gaze from Toraji, reaching out with her right hand, grabbing hold of the vial, taking it from his hand with a mouthed.

"Thank You", flicking open the cap with her thumb in

one fluid movement. Before pouring a small amount of the bioluminescent blue powder onto her underside on her fingernail of her little finger, and without hesitation, raised it to her nose and inhaled it. Closing her eyes slowly, as it hit, only then taking her eyes off Toraji.

"Seems like this girl wants more than just a little favour, am I right?" Toraji's friend exclaimed as he poured his Kalita into a drink. He laughed again as he banged on the table. Toraji looked over at his friend and smiled.

"A favour and a good time, that's what it looks like..", he laughed as he took in a deep breath, before stopping puzzled, before a smile slowly appeared on his face.

"And she's really up for it. Can't resist these Impiri girls, those pheromones, though. She's definitely game for a good time." As he took another deep breath.

This took Ceres by surprise. First, he could detect them, and second, yes, she was aroused, but not by him. The quick embrace with Nyxcerra in the bathroom elevated her arousal, thus releasing her pheromones. But if that's what it took to get a favour from him, and for him to buy it, then she had nothing to lose.

'Didn't you know us Eczack can sense them too, you're almost as appealing as my two wives...., almost.."

Even though he was married, this was business, not personal.

"So, when are you going to take me to dance?" She enquired, feeling the effects of the Kalita taking work. Her vision blurred slightly, her heart rate dropped, and her body tingled, an enjoyable experience, which would be heightened by any kind of arousal.

"Somewhere, a little more private." She joked as she got up, holding him by the hand.

———

Moments Later...

As she closed the door to the suite behind them, she chuckled to herself before smiling at him playfully, holding his hand, growing accustomed to his icy touch.

"So, you know what I'm after, don't you..." she added, out of nowhere, wanting him to realise this was purely business, nothing more, nothing less. Toraji stared at her without blinking, he knew exactly what she was saying, he smiled, feeling his own heart race. She was beautiful, and she was throwing herself at him, all for a little exposure, expose that he was happy to give, any of the girls from the final twelve would bring a huge amount of work to is business interests. He laughed playfully, realising she had come to him, instead of him having to approach Aeryth first, then her.

"You're going to have to work for it, you know that, don't you?" he replied playfully. He pulled her close, feeling her hearts racing in her chest. For a second she flinched, not sure if she could go through with it, before ignoring it.

She was overwhelmed by her emotions, her lust for him, her breathing increased in speed, sure that he could hear her breathing, she ran her hand over his arm, wanting him to take her there and then.

She could live for a moment in this charade where she was being intimate with him, but it was purely a step to better things, she'd done things like this before, usually to get a little favour, but never at this level, somewhere not so private that someone could catch them in the act.

"You know what, Toraji, you know the things I want, and I'm willing to give you a good time." Ceres added, her breathing shallow, unable to take her eyes off him.

"Since that class months ago... don't think I didn't notice you," he replied as he ran his fingers through her hair.

"Sorry for embarrassing you in front of your friends. I had to show you I could play at that game too."

She pulled him forward, his hands tangled in her hair. Ceres felt like her whole body tingling, as she was full of static. She tried not to make any noise as she stumbled onto the bed in the suite, but it didn't matter; no one knew they were there, and no one would expect her to be with Toraji, other than Nyxcerra. Feeling the effects of the drinks, she stumbled forwards onto his chest; he hesitated.

"I know this is only work, but I can't resist you. Maybe it's this beautiful dress," he told her. His dark eyes locked glances with hers. She reached behind her back to unfasten her dress, wanting him to take her then and there.

"Like I said before, it's just work, you and me, so shut up, and fuck me," she told him, and kissed him before he could respond.

She felt the cool response from his skin, in contrast to the warmth of her own, she could feel his hearts racing as she felt his hand helping her remove the dress, she turned towards him, dropping the dress off her shoulders, exposing herself to the hot summer air.

Before she embraced him, saying nothing, she was enjoying the dangerousness of this encounter, knowing the reaction she was getting out if him, she played with the buckle on his belt, causing him to hastily undo it, before revealing himself, this is when Ceres stood up, and stepped carefully out of the dress, revealing herself to him.

"We haven't got much time," she paused,

"and I'm in need of a good time", she added with a naughty smile and she got down onto her knees, looking up at him with her brilliant shining yellow eyes, glistening in the light, reaching up to his belt, all the time not taking her gaze from staring him in the eyes.

'It's all about the eye contact' she thought, maybe her mother was right that time.

CHAPTER 6
"WE ONLY JUST FOUND OUT AN HOUR AGO..."

3 Hours Later...

Nyxcerra knocked on a huge closed door, half asleep, still feeling the effects of the Kalita and alcohol she had taken only a few hours before. She wanted, no she needed sleep, her stomach rumbled, food would cure this hangover, but here she was, standing outside the management office just as the morning sun crept into the darkness of the corridor, casting elongated shadows across the dark wooden floor. The echo of her knock reverberated across the hallway, bouncing down the corridor before dissipating.

There was no response. Her thoughts turned to this being a prank by Aeryth, remembering the pranks that she loved to pull on the girls, usually calling them up to the offices or the rehearsal space, just to reward them for progress or to give them words of encouragement, especially those known to be in her good books. Casting her mind back, she had never been in her good books, more likely in her 'naughty girl book'.

A list she was, at times, proud to be on. She liked to push the buttons of others, usually because of her upbringing and lax attitude to the rules, especially if made her happy. Her stomach rumbled. She was hungry but couldn't stomach anything, not after all the alcohol she had drank the night before.

It had to be a prank, knowing how she'd be the one with the worst hangover. But Juble', Aeryth's assistants nervousness and demeanour, made her worry. This was something serious. She could feel it, didn't know why, but she could feel it.

She raised her fist to knock again, hesitating for a moment, stopping an inch from knocking, before deciding against it, she turned nervously, pulling her long purple hair away from her tawny toned skin, gathering and twisting it with one hand, while fiddling with an elasticised band on her other wrist and trying to tie her hair up. It was the easiest thing to do when it looked this way. She hated not being presentable, but Juble, didn't give her time to get ready.

She took a step forward before being stopped by the sound of the door sliding open and a voice calling out,

"Nyxcerra." the voice called out, echoing through the empty wood clad corridors. The corridors were sparse, especially on this floor, the upper administration suites. Her mind was full of thoughts. Were they unhappy with the neck kiss on Ceres the night before? Had they seen things she had tried to hide from them? Was she being dropped?, all she knew was that Aeryth wanted to see her, not any of the other girls.

Something was wrong. Why was she the one alone facing the head of talent? She wasn't the lead. That was Ceres' role.

Why had Juble, her Odian personal assistant, been nervous and upset around her on the lift journey from 20th floor to the 272nd floor, brushing it off as being still tired from the night before?, this confused and worried her even more.

Odian's being known across the empire for their calm and emotionless demeanour. So why was she upset? Her thoughts being interrupted by the voice calling out.

"You can come in... close the door behind you," Aeryth called out.

"Ye... yes," Nyxcerra replied nervously as she stepped into the room, as she nervously rubbed the back of her neck. She had only been here once before, Ceres had been here multiple times, usually at the bequest of management, she remembered waiting outside with the rest of the girls as their fate was being decided in a management shuffle, her hearts raced, why wasn't Ceres here?, unless she'd already been called up.

"Ma'am, you asked Juble to tell me to come up to your office. All she said was that it was urgent..., but where's Ceres? She's our lead..." she replied nervously, her voice trailing off, not wanting to look at Aeryth directly, as she felt her palms getting sweaty.

Nyxcerra turned shyly towards her, her hands behind her back, clutching her hands together. She turned as Aeryth wiped her eyes with a silken cloth before hastily stuffing it into her pocket, her eyes puffy and full of tears. This caught Nyxcerra by surprise. Something had to have happened last-night, something important enough to have her here just after six in the morning, only two hours after they got back from the soiree.

· · ·

"So I guess you saw what happened last night?.." her voice trailed off as she folded her arms, holding one arm at the elbow.

'I'm being requested to leave the label... aren't I?" Nyxcerra coyly asked as she gently lowered her gaze as she expected the answer, resigning herself to her own thoughts, there couldn't be any other reason why she alone had been called to come up to this office, the nervous glances by staff members, the awkward expressions by security. She had never liked this floor. Never.

Casting her mind back brought up some tough memories. She'd been up to this floor multiple times before over the past six cycles, usually when others had been let go. The broadcast reactions downstairs to the billions of viewers watching were always staged, knowing in advance that they were being let go, except for the single time they let someone go publicly, with no prior notice.

"No, definitely not. I didn't ask you here to talk about your choice of indiscretions last-night." Aeryth snapped.

"They are not of our concern. We honestly couldn't care about who you fucked." She paused, sighing before she spoke, annoyed that she had snapped at her. This pause sent a shock through Nyxcerra.

"I'm sorry for snapping, it's just" she stopped, struggling to find the right words to express herself.

"There was a serious incident last-night. We just found out an hour ago..."

Nyxcerra almost choked on her sip of water from the small glass she had picked up from the side of the desk.

"I'm not, I mean I'm not following, why am I the only one here, I'm not our lead, where's Ceres" she finally got out, the relief of her own indiscretions being ignored was replaced by the fear of what was being mentioned

"Actually, it's Ceres, she's.." she stuttered, stumbling over her own words, as if her thoughts were flowing faster than she could communicate.

"They found her body in the early hours. It seems she fell from the balcony of one apartment... "

Nyxcerra took a step back, staggering for a moment as her legs buckled beneath her, before steadying herself on the back of a chair, even though the office was tiny compared the other offices in the building, it felt like a vast distance grew between them; she felt small and lost. Not knowing how to react to this news.

"We didn't want the information coming from anyone else, the police are keeping silent on this for now..." the words from Aeryth's mouth rang out, but to Nyxcerra it was just a murmur, her mind trying to fathom what she had just been told. A torrent of thoughts and questions all bubbled to the surface.

"She was supposed to have come home with us, but she said she'd be along soon enough, just had to see an acquaintance. She wasn't supposed to be there..." she flustered, stumbling over her words as her mind went into overdrive, tears welling in her eyes, before streaming down her cheeks,

"Now you brought me here alone? What am I supposed to do?, tell the rest?" She demanded through a clenched jaw, unable to look at her straight in the face. She was trying to push back the tears that were welling up.

"I'm sorry, we thought it would be better if it was coming from you, we wanted to get a head of this before we have to make a statement to the media," Aeryth said resentfully, she had wanted to save herself from the overwhelming emotions, annoyed that Nyxcerra had seen through this, made it harder to keep her own emotions in check. She wanted to say it all, but couldn't. How could she, if Ceres had told them, she wasn't sure, she couldn't risk it.

"I just couldn't deal with having to tell you all. I know selfish of me," Aeryth finally broke down, deflecting her own pain.

"Seeing you all grow up so much over these six cycles, the news of this horrible incident..." she paused

"You're not the only one finding this hard..., you have no idea, she is......'

"Was. My niece, she was my.." she stopped. As she fought against saying something more, stopping herself at the last moment.

"She was my family, to you she's a friend, to me, she was family, I've had to make the difficult call before you came in, telling my brother-in-law that his daughter, my niece is dead...."

"To be honest, telling you girls is an afterthought, and of course I realise I'm asking you to do a lot, but...."

'Of course I realise she was your niece, I'm not that naïve." Nyxcerra snapped in reply, and the matter-of-factness in her tone made Aeryth sit back in her chair. Nyxcerra's emotions were running wild, her thoughts were a mess. How could she tell them, the girls, that Ceres was dead. From being afraid she was going to be losing what she had worked towards, to instead being told that her closest friend, lover and group member was dead.

"I thought we had done something wrong, and I was in trouble, but here you are telling me that Ceres is dead. I can't... I can't deal with this, she was my...". She paused a split second before wanting to confess her deepest feelings that she and Ceres were lovers, but a tiny voice in her head pulled her back. As she spoke, she sank to her knees before crying out.

"How am I supposed to..." she got out as she began to hyperventilate, her chest tightening, her breaths become loud and shallow.

"Why am I supposed to be the one..." she cursed through a clenched jaw, trying to stop herself from screaming out at the top of her lungs.

"I can't, I can't..." she sobbed between shallow breaths as she hyperventilated before finally finding it too hard to keep it in, feeling as if she was going to burst. She screamed out., a scream which took her own breath away, catching a member of Aeryth's assistants by surprise as she walked past the office, wiping a tear from their own eye, having been already told.

Nyxcerra's scream dying out as she struggled to take in oxygen while screaming out, her muscles tensed.

Aeryth sat crying, unable to hold her own tears back, the scream reminded her of the one she gave after she was told, understanding the anger Nyxcerra was experiencing as well and the inability to make sense of it all, when a scream felt like the old way to express herself.

"I thought it would be simpler if it came from you, you knew her the most, and you were so close." She stopped.

'We, no I thought it would just be simpler...". Aeryth spoke as she got up and made her way over to Nyxcerra, her voice close to breaking as she passed a silky cloth to Nyxcerra, before hesitantly crouching down beside her, wanting to embrace her but knowing it wasn't the right time.

"I'm here, you know, if you ever just want to talk..."

She stopped, unable to hide her own emotions, before

crying into a silken handkerchief, sobbing openly in front of Nyxcerra who couldn't take it, hastily rushing out of the room, slamming the door behind her, before breaking out into her own fit of tears as she sank to the floor, crying out into her own hands, muffling her screams.

CHAPTER 7
"IS LITTLE MISS STILL ASLEEP..?"

Later That Morning...

It was still the early hours of the morning after the soirée and Nyxcerra still couldn't make sense of it; She sat on the large sofa in the living room of their shared apartment, staring up at the delicate clouds that floated outside the window, the sun had risen, but the other girls were still sleeping, and here she was sinking into the chair she was sitting on, her legs tucked underneath her. Wanting to be absorbed by it. She looked a mess but didn't care. A steady stream of tears made their way down her cheeks, running onto her light grey pullover, turning it darker as the tears soaked in, but she didn't care.

It had been over an hour since she'd been told to see Aeryth in the upper office; it still made no sense. How could Ceres be dead?

She tried to keep it all in. She'd come home to find Tiiona in the kitchen, wearing a huge jumper, getting herself a drink, but she couldn't say anything, just lied that she had been out for fresh air, though she couldn't forget what she had been told. It was burned into her mind with such force that she never thought she could ever forget.

Her mind wandered, remembering the last time she had talked to Ceres. It had been just before she caught the transport back. Ceres said she would only be an hour or so and would be back before she knew it.

Even though she knew she was gone, when she got back to the room she had expected to see her asleep in her bed, the shock of not finding her caused her to break down.

She had managed to hold it together for the last hour. But every so often she'd collapsed into her clothes, savouring the warmth of the jumper, Ceres had given it to her. It still smelt like her, a light floral scent which gave Nyxcerra comfort.

As she looked out, Avéline and Tiiona startled her by walking out into the living area, still wearing pyjamas.

"Morning Nyx, shouldn't you be in bed? We got hungry and wanted a snack before..." Avéline stopped as she saw Nyxcerra's face. She looked different; there were circles around her eyes and a dullness to her skin, but it was more than that.

Something had fundamentally changed about her, as if she was no longer the same Nyxcerra that she had been the night before. As if something had taken all the joy from her. Her eyes were raw from the crying, and as she spoke, her voice buckled under the pressure.

"Hey," she said simply. Unable to muster anything else, not knowing how she was supposed to let them know.

"Hey, what's up" Avéline replied. Her eyes searched hers, but she just returned her stare. Something was wrong, Avéline thought to herself.

"Is everything okay?" Avéline asked.

"I... I need you to get Jysell and Syala...., we have got to talk..." she managed to get out.

She nervously shook as Avéline wandered down the corridor towards the bedrooms.

Avéline was surprised that she was being asked to round up the other girls. It took a moment for Avéline to process what was happening. Something was wrong, and it was something big.

After knocking on the door to Jysell and Syala's room, she slid the door open. After a while, they woke up and begrudgingly made their way to the living room.

Jysell, still rubbing her eyes, wrapped herself in a light green silken robe, shivered as she sat down on a chair near the kitchen, Syala wrapping herself in a long fluffy dressing gown, sliding her feet into equally fluffy slippers.

"brrr, a-bit cold this morning..." she glanced around, noticing everyone was there, except one.

"Where's Ceres, is little miss still asleep, I'll go and get..:," she added, standing up to go before being gestured to sit down.

"It's about Ceres..." Nyxcerra pleaded. The tone in her voice caused everybody to sit up and pay attention.

"What do you mean?, has something happened??" Jysell enquired, as she grabbed hold of a nearby pillow and hugged it.

"There's, there's been an accident, our beloved Ceres is." she stopped, unable to bring herself to say it,

"Is she okay??" Tiiona chipped in, gone was her confidence, her voice breaking as she spoke.

"She...." she stuttered, struggling to get the words out, as if she dared not speak them.

"She died in the early hours of this morning...", with that Avéline broke into tears falling to the floor, Tiiona stood silent, staring into the middle distance, fighting back her own tears.

"What... no, we saw her only a few hours ago..." Tiiona added, walking over to Nyxcerra, reading the sadness in her face,

"How..." she whispered, as if the breath was sucked out of her lungs.

"All I know is she fell from an apartment balcony around 4am this morning..." Nyxcerra replied, as she cried.

Jysell gasped and covered her mouth as she began sobbing. Syala embraced her as they both cried into each other's arms.

Avéline just sat awkwardly on the floor, shaking while she cried, in between silently screaming out, baring down against her own urges. She didn't know what to do or to think, or what to even say. Nothing made sense.

Tiiona crouched next to Nyxcerra, grabbing hold of her, not saying anything, just holding her as she screamed, muffled by Tiiona's shoulder.

CHAPTER 8
"JUST BEFORE THE FALL..."

It was early the next morning and Nyxcerra still couldn't fall asleep; she felt drained, the constant bouts of breaking down in a fit of tears as Aeryth updated them on the police investigation. Every time she stopped crying, more information came in and brought her to tears, a seemingly never-ending loop.

She kept flipping restlessly back and forth on the bed, unable to rest her mind. The persistent turning caused the duvet cover to bunch up, cocooning her inside. She sighed as she rolled over and looked longingly out into the apartment. Staring at Ceres' empty bed, three meters from hers, the bedside lights cast a warm glow across the room. The room was sparse, a few personal effects, a few photos from home, but not much more, even less on 'ceres side of the room.

Ceres' silken pyjamas were still neatly folded on the bottom of the bed, awaiting a return which wouldn't happen. Tears cascaded down her cheeks onto the bed, soaking into the green sheets, turning them a darker shade of green, almost black. Nyxcerra sobbed silently, trying not to wake Jysell, who was barely a meter away, sleeping on the floor, slumped over a long cushion. Jysell was fast asleep, her tightly curled hair acting as a second cushion. She didn't want to wake her up with the sound of her crying, but knowing Jysell had always been the one who could sleep through anything.

Nyxcerra recalling the moments she'd slept through storms, through moments when Ceres' was drunk and was playing music loud, singing at the top of her voice. These moments made her smile, remembering the best occasions, before she crashed out of those memories into reality, causing her to cry again.

Avéline, Tiiona and Syala were all asleep, having taken turns looking after her. Tiiona had come up with the idea earlier, but was the first one to sleep, Nyxcerra hadn't paid attention to who was there, she had spent an hour just staring into the distance, lost in thought, between bouts of crying uncontrollably or times where she just screamed at the top of her voice, cursing the goddesses for what had happened, her throat so sore and damaged that barely a sound came out anymore. The others tried to console her, but it wouldn't work. How could it/ she thought.

She just couldn't forget the details they had been told.

"There were signs of sexual activity, high levels of alcohol, Hydroprexin and dangerously excessive amounts of the narcotic Kalita in her body, all consumed in the last hours of her life, just before the fall," that's what the police investigator had told Aeryth, who had advised them, after her own insistence that they be notified.

Nyxcerra could not comprehend it. Many things made little sense; why was Hydroprexin in her system? She'd used it before as a muscle relaxant after hours of dance practice. Who had done this to her, and why was she there on the balcony, knowing Ceres had always hated heights, a fear that she had mentioned to her one night cycles ago.

After the news that morning, she had asked to see her body, seeing Ceres in that state, lying motionless on the cold metal surface in the mortuary. Shocked her to the core, gone was the warming glow of her skin, replaced by an ashen tone, her yellow eyes fixed at a point in the distance. Gone was the golden sparkle. They were hollow now and dim.

The sound of the other girls crying down the hallway and worse, the inconsolable expression on Ceres's father's face right there in front of her sitting beside her body, stuck in her mind, seeing it every time she closed her eyes.

She wanted to say something, but knowing that nothing would make a difference. She couldn't say anything to anyone. No one really knew how she felt. How could they? She thought to herself. There was no way she could tell them the truth about their relationship. They had hidden it from the other girls out of fear of hurting them and their chances.

Everything was overwhelming. She didn't want to deal with anybody, not to mention dealing with the fans, who had correctly worked out where Ceres's body was lying in state and had begun a candlelit vigil. There was another gathering five floors below them, still being able to hear the chanted invocations of thousands singing. Prayers for protecting the rest of the girls, including some songs which Ceres had sung over the past six cycles during the auditions.

She knew they meant well, but she couldn't dare to face them yet, but resigning herself to knowing she had to at 8am, she had to give a speech outside to the media, on behalf of the group.

· · ·

Her ill-planned impulse to want to speak for the group in a meeting had struck a tone with Aeryth, causing her to admit that she wanted her to speak on behalf of the group permanently, as lead, but the decision was still up in the air, one other member was also in the running, but Aeryth thought it wise not to tell her.

A role she knew she never wanted. She'd always been a follower. She'd partnered with Ceres occasionally during projects as part of the auditions—Ceres was always the one to speak.

Nothing fazed her, even when she hadn't felt up to speaking during auditions. After her mother died, she still put those emotions aside and spoke on behalf of the group. Nyxcerra knew it would be difficult and too soon to act in any way as lead, but she knew she didn't have a choice, she had to fill in until a lead was decided by management. Aeryth had mentioned that they wouldn't delay the first release.

The song they would sing would change, which was now in the process of being fast tracked, but it would still release forty-eight days from now. How could they still do that? Rang out in Nyxcerra's mind. Right now, she couldn't think about anything else...

CHAPTER 9

"NYX, IT'S TIME..."

The Next Day...

Nyxcerra stood behind her bedroom door, dreading the walk, outside of this room she feared she would be questioned, 'are you okay?' they would ask, she knew the girls meant well, but she couldn't tell them the truth, she wasn't okay. She'd lie to them, of course, pretend she was fine, fake a smile, but she didn't want to fake it, but she had to. Leaving the apartment was one issue, going to the media briefing was another. She wasn't sure which she feared the most.

She'd done the walk from the apartment to the elevator, that was 37 steps, a 47 second trip on the elevator, 87 steps to the conference chamber. She'd done the route during the night before, whilst the others were asleep. Only a member of security had seen her out during the dead of night.

Here in her room she was safe, but reminded constantly about what she had lost.

Losing someone you loved was shocking enough, but

having to give a speech to the media, the barrage of questions, that part she couldn't fathom.

Part of her still refused to believe that this wasn't a nightmare, that she wouldn't wake up and everything would be back to the way it was. Ceres would still be alive. They would all be preparing for the debut.

Her thoughts were interrupted by a sudden loud knock on the door. "Nyx, it's time... are you ready?" Jysell's voice called out. Jolting Nyxcerra back into the present, she looked at herself in the mirror, her hair in an elegant up-do style, the simplistic look mirrored by the muted tones of her outfit, dark grey trousers, simple black shoes, and a loose fitting cream blouse. A departure from what she would normally wear, a lot more conservative than anyone was used to.

"I'm coming..." she called out, accepting her fate, she had to do it, her stomach twisted as she felt nauseous, her fingers and toes tingling, she took a deep breath, resigning herself to coming as she slid the door open.

Twenty-Five Minutes Later...

Aeryth had finally finished speaking. The media were shocked by the announcement, a barrage of questions followed. She'd said what she could, that the investigation into Ceres' death was still in progress and that the Capital Police service would be the ones releasing any further information.

They then asked about the group, whether they were still a group, would they be put on hiatus, or would they fail to debut.

"Well, to answer that loaded question would give you something to write about, but how about I tell you this,

Aerrea are still a group, they will be taking a five-week hiatus to allow them to deal with the grief from the loss of our beloved Ceres, but they will be back within 6 weeks...." she stopped, waiting for the crowd to ask questions before speaking over them, a tactic she loved doing.

"Our amazing team of talented writers, music producers, and holo-producers are busily working behind the scenes to craft their debut, a debut to remember, a lasting memory to Ceres.". Aeryth added, playing to the crowd, knowing how to spin it, getting them talking about the debut, hoping that the talk of it would last for the forthcoming six weeks.

Nyxcerra stared straight ahead, still reeling from the announcement being made. It was official. The entire empire knew now, if they didn't know, they would know within the next standard day. She was absorbed in thought, a wave of whispers travelled through the room, journalists leaned forward, hoping she would say something. Nyxcerra sighed heavily, as if a heavy weight was placed on her shoulders, a curse she alone had to bare. She carefully put down the pad she held in her hand, still keeping her gaze fixed on the cameras, before pushing it away as she dropped her gaze to the crowd in front of her. Staring at her hands, lost in thought for a moment, Tiiona looked over at her, whispering,

"Nyx, you've got this..., take your time... we're here", loud enough that it caused her to smile as she heard it. For a moment, there was clarity in her mind, knowing that the girls would support her.

During this silence, the crowd of journalists got restless, shuffling in their seats, before murmuring again.

"Is this over? Is she going to say something more? Not what I would expect from a lead?" the whispers travelled through the crowd. Nyxcerra kept her composure not wanting to respond to their comments, Normally the murmuring got under her skin, annoying her, but not this time, she didn't care, She had read what the company wanted her to say, but she couldn't do it anymore, she had said enough.

The words that Leix had written for her felt hollow, insincere, lacking the actual emotions that she had wanted to say. She slowly raised her head and looked straight ahead, the cameras and drones capturing every moment before beaming it across the empire, being broadcast to over a billion viewers at any given moment.

Without thinking, she began to speak. The words flowed from one to the next, its melodic and dulcet tone resonated, silencing everyone almost instantly.

"Ceres, níoorbh ía mol cholea amdháin ía, bai ía mol dhaeirfiúr ía, bal dhaeirfiúr dúinna ar fad ía. leatnfalimid orainne Marl ghrúpah a méid al these astaigh ul aithi al bhai sont al mach. Del beidh síl inár gocu imhní cinneh gol deoha." She stopped as tears welled up. She began flicking her eyelashes, trying to force them back, but it was becoming difficult. Not realising she had spoken in her native tongue until she finished, the look on the faces of the reporters explained enough that she knew what she had done.

"I'm sorry... I didn't mean to," she nervously added, before she tried to smile, her voice close to breaking. She could feel her lips trembling, her hands clenching nervously.

"It, it was just easier for me to say this in my language, you know, but I'll translate to Imperial standard..." she added, trying to get the eager crowd of journalists on her side.

"Ceres, she wasn't just my friend, she was my sister, she was our sister, we will continue as a group to achieve what she wanted us to. She'll be in our memories forever" her voice trailing off, feeling the stares of the crowd, before bowing gracefully. Her use of her tribe's primary language 'Shabik' came as a complete surprise to the crowd of journalists, not expecting her to speak in this tongue. They fell into an awkward silence. But not to the other girls. They had heard her speak it occasionally, usually in broken form while talking to her family.

They turned to look at her, before lowering their heads, just as Nyxcerra rose up from her bow.

"Please, will you give us time to grieve? We will not be giving any further interviews until the debut." Before bowing, her arms at her sides, hands open wide, as she held the bow, the other girls one by one stood up and stopped their bows.

"Thank you for believing in us, from the depth of my hearts. Especially at this difficult time for us," Nyxcerra added as she raised herself from a final bow.

Just as one journalist was about to ask a question, Leix stepped out in front of the cameras, clearing his throat with a small cough before speaking. His mannerism was a surprise to Nyxcerra as she looked at him, his usual brashness replaced with sincerity and emotion.

"Please, we know you have questions, but this is a tough time for us all, there is nothing more to add at this time" she had never seen him use this formal tone before, the was lost in thought before being startled by the aide from the company gesturing her to leave the room by a side door, the other girls gestured for her to hurry. As she walked off, she heard Leix speaking again.

"Our girls need time, to express their grief, to find it

within themselves to produce the best work you have even seen, we here at BYL Entertainment will give them that time, but don't worry... as Aeryth has previously told you, you'll hear more from our wonderful girls as soon as possible... with a tribute to Ceres,"

CHAPTER 10
"YOU DECIDED TO START THE AFTERLIFE WITHOUT US..."

Four Days Later...

Nyxcerra stood looking out into the congregation, her hands trembling, chewing the inside of her cheek, trying to distract herself. This congregation filled her with dread. Everyone in the audience was the who's who of the industry, the influencers, were there, as expected. Having to grieve openly, on camera to those watching made her feel sick. She hated the negativity of it all; it was against her way of life; she was used to celebrating the life of someone, but her ways were seen as too brash and too focused on the perception of not caring.

She looked out into the crowd, seeing who was there. She didn't recognise all of them; she fought back the urge to tell them to leave. This was a private matter, but it wasn't, not anymore, for the past six cycles everyone knew who Ceres was. There wasn't a single free space left in the temple as far as she could see. Every nook and crevice was filled. Ceres' family and friends were at the front, followed by management, then almost all the original 106, as well as established artists at the company,.

Even though it was packed, it was reasonably silent except for a melody coming from outside. The faint singing from outside was by innumerable fans that were singing songs that Ceres had sung during the trainee cycles. This brought a smile to her face as well as others. Including Ceres' father, who was seated in the front row.

Nyxcerra smiled at a time when she wanted to just curl into a ball and cry. However, the fans made it bearable. They eagerly awaited the ceremony being projected on to large displays outside the temple.

At the back, she saw the temple's famous spiral art piece which reached up eight floors. The main hall's ceiling reached up twenty floors. The focal piece was an ancient tapestry hanging from the rafters. It was an enormous vertical tapestry that began on the ceiling of the hall, making its way down to sixteen floors, a showpiece in the largest imperial centric temple in the entire empire.

She glanced at the clock that hung off on the far left side of the hall. She made sure to keep it just in view on the top left of her vision. 16:50 it read, the ceremony was close to starting. She could feel her hands becoming clammy, her breathing becoming shallow, was she strong enough to go through with it, her train of thoughts were interrupted by the sound of the other girls walking out to stand beside her, Avéline and Tiiona to her left, Jysell and Syala stood to her right.

They were all dressed in black, minimal makeup, no jewellery, a dark blue satin ribbon tied on their right wrists. In remembrance of Ceres tribe, at a time like this, tribal differences meant nothing. They were grieving. The crowd stopped their murmurs. They knew what was coming. The procession of the coffin into a space in the centre of the hall, she resisted the urge to run out and hold on to the coffin as it was put into place.

In the centre of the long hall, Ceres' ornate coffin now lay behind it row upon rows of flowers were laid by those in attendance leading up to the great fire pit, which crackled as the slight breeze caught it. Her she would be cremated in a private ceremony later on.

No matter how hard she tried, she couldn't take her gaze off the coffin, knowing that she was there. Her hearts ached as she glanced at the clock. Her time was up. This was happening, and it was happening now.

"Almost five p.m" she muttered to herself, realising that the drones were focused on her. Nyxcerra decided to resign herself to the fact that she would have to speak in front of them all. But nothing she could say would be enough.

"A great writer once wrote, 'it's not about what you said, it's not about what you did, no one will forget the way you made them feel…'" the youthful priestess spoke as she lifted back the white hood of her gown. Finally revealing herself to the attendees, she was youthful. She couldn't of had more than a few cycles in the temple, but she commanded the crowd with her presence and voice, the crowd hanging off every word.

"Hayli Ceres Soobaks was one of those individuals who always made everyone feel loved and welcomed." She paused, gesturing towards the girls who bowed solemnly to the crowd, Nyxcerra holding her bow for longer, until standing back up as the priestess spoke again.

"I'd like to hand over to those who knew her as close as her tribe would, her professional family. The girls from Aerrea," there was a respectful clap from a few in attendance.

Nyxcerra cleared her throat and slowed her breathing before speaking.

"Ceres, what can I say about her? She was always willing to step up and help those in need. She made everybody feel not just good, but also important and valued. We all are reeling from her sudden and unexpected passing. But glancing out at everybody here today, I see so many people Ceres loved." She hesitated for effect. She didn't want to rush it.

"And I realise that even in death, she is watching out for us. This makes me think of a conversation we had cycles ago..." she paused, momentarily chuckled to herself before continuing.

"You'd always said you'd be the first one to do anything... a trailblazer, brake down the barriers that our people faced,... and you did that, and now you did another original, you decide to start the afterlife without us, Ceres?" Causing a mild chuckle from some in the audience, she immediately glanced at Ceres father who laughed, she sighed as long as he was still in good spirits she was doing well.

Nyxcerra closed her eyes, allowing herself a brief moment of relief to grin. She couldn't stay where she was. She took a few steps forward, down the stairs towards Ceres' coffin.

"You know," Nyxcerra said looking down at her feet, unable to raise her gaze to look at the casket which was mere feet away, she told herself she wouldn't be able to take it, to see the closed casket, knowing Ceres was in there. She cleared her throat before speaking, raising her voice, trying to project it. The pause lingering before she spoke again.

"Even though we weren't really family, all of us being together felt like some resemblance to a family. You had been there for me when I couldn't take the pressure anymore, usually the pressure I put on myself...." she stopped before continuing, trying to stop herself from crying, looking down at her empty hands, before clenching them.

"But you were always the one that made us all..." she paused, searching for the right words, which finally came to her, the only thing which made sense.

"You made us all fit," rang out across the gathering. The crackling of the fire in the centre of the great hall broke the silence. She took a long deep breath, trying to keep herself together, her mind wanting her to sink to her knees and cry out. She could feel her knees weakening, but resisted the urge. She had to be strong for the girls.

"I might have told you how much I cared, how I appreciated you, I did love you, we all did" She raised her head, as if a weight had been lifted from her, and gently a put her palm on the casket, running her fingers across its cold black surface, Before walking past the coffin towards the fire.

"Now your not here, I'm going to be strong, for them, for us, the way you showed me", she heard the sniffles of some in the crowd, most of the other girls from the 106 were handkerchiefs in hand, sobbing quietly.

"You're the only one who knows what I'm going through. How to push aside the negativity and seek out the positive..." she added.

Ceres father stood up, as he gestured for her to stop, as he stood up on the front row, the sound of his chair creaking caused her to stop, he stood there, stoic, fighting back his own emotions, his eyes wide as pools full of tears., moments from crying/ Seeing him like this caused Nyx to stop, her hearts racing. Had she said too much? Her thoughts became erratic.

"You need not say anymore. The praise you bestow on her, my daughter, no matter how much you think she deserves it." He paused, sighed a breath he didn't know he was holding, becoming overwhelmed, fighting his own urge to cry.

"She was only strong because she had you, all of you. She told me this a few cycles ago, and I promised I wouldn't tell anyone."

"Promise," each of the girls whispered. Ceres had made them all promise to look after each other, and she was extremely disappointed if you broke one, a standard she held everyone to.

"And yes, I shouldn't be telling you this, but under these circumstances, I'm sure my darling daughter would have allowed it. That's the woman she is... was," he stuttered at the end, painfully correcting himself while fixing his collar.

Nyxcerra smiled, and without thinking rushed over, breaking all that she had been told not to do and embraced him, giving him an enormous hug and whispering,

"I won't forget what she did for me. All I do from now on is to make her proud," she cried. Ceres' father hugged her and whispered,

"Thank You, for making her happy...".

"I can't... imagine how you are feeling, but I would want you to feel proud of the individual she was..." she broke the embrace and made her way slowly to the lineup of the girls.

Nyxcerra turned towards the rest of the girls, Jysell and

Avéline in tears, Syala close to tears and Tiiona as usual fighting hers back. The priestess stepped forwards holding a small device in her hands. She placed it on the floor.

"I have a message here, from someone who wanted it played... Ceres herself..." she pressed a button on its surface and stepped back. Within moments, Ceres appeared as a hologram. The sight of this caused Avéline to cry, and the crowd to quieten.

"Hello girls, I recorded this the day we found out we got through the six of us. And I've never been prouder of all of you... I don't have long, gotta get back to this gathering, our party," she said as she giggled, that infectious type of giggle that got everyone smiling, especially Nyxcerra, who smiled almost instantly, even though her hearts were close to breaking.

"Got a meeting with Lady Vale soon, and I'm as nervous as I've ever been..., but I'll be brief. If you are hearing this, things haven't gone... to plan." She playfully shook her head, as if things like her death were something to mock.

"Either some freak accident or the Kafda Syndrome has returned and taken its revenge upon me, or simply I've died of old age... Hopefully, by now, we've been together as a group for cycles, achieved all we wanted to." She paused.

"Despite our obvious differences, I hope we still talk to each other... If I haven't told you recently, I love you all, my sisters..." she broke her flow, becoming serious, a devilish smile crept onto her face.

"Tii, stop frowning, back straight..." she mocked, causing Tiiona to break her frown and stand up straight. Knowing that Ceres knew exactly what she would do, she knew her too well.

"Avéline, my dear Avéline, you are as much of a mystery

to me today as you were the day we first met... and you know I love mysteries. Never change my girl, never change." Causing Avéline to smile before bowing. Holding back her own tears, Ceres had always appreciated her differences in opinion.

"Jysell, you amaze me every day. Always pushing, Syala, stop trying to be what you aren't, just be yourself, screw what you think others want you to be, just be you..." she looked over her shoulder, as if listening to what was going on around her.

"and who am I forgetting..." she mocked before winking.

"Nyx, my darling Nyxcerra. What can I say, that I haven't already told you countless times before? Even though I'm the oldest of us, I've always looked up to you." she paused, her smile becoming genuine and relaxed.

"I sometimes put a lot of pressure on your shoulders as we were growing up, but it wasn't because of jealousy, it's because I wanted to have someone I could rely on, an equal. And that's you, my darling, my equal. The light to my darkness," this broke Nyxcerra's fragile hold on her emotions. She bowed her head and slowly sobbed. Avéline placed her hand on her back and slowly rubbed it, trying to soothe her.

"It's okay, we've all got you..." she whispered.

"Dad, I hope I've made you proud. If I've died and gone straight past rebirth and into the afterlife, I'll tell mom that you miss her, as we both know she's there..."

She paused as the sound of Nyxcerra's voice echoed out from the holographic projection.

"Hey Girl, you better not keep me waiting..." her voice called out. That's when it hit her. Nyxcerra knew exactly when this was, during the party, just before she met up with Ceres. Now it all made sense, what she had been doing in the private bathroom. Why she had told a guard to keep wait at the door and to not let anyone but her come in.

"As I said, love you all..." Ceres exclaimed as she reached towards something just as the hologram ended.

With this Nyxcerra broke down, turning toward Avéline, who embraced her.

A few hours later...

The ceremony had now ended; the priestess had recited the words from the ancient texts, offerings had been made to the deities Idara and Ishara (Goddesses of Life and Death) for her rebirth through reincarnation, "a good life loved for a good life in return." The priestess mentioned at the end of the sermon.

The hour of rebirth had occurred where Ceres' coffin had been placed on to the fire-pit, which was then covered by a huge metal cover, to aid in her cremation. Hymns had been sung, with Nyxcerra, Jysell and Syala leading the hymn, a hymn that Syala started signing unexpectedly, catching everyone by surprise, with Jysell and Nyxcerra joining in later, bringing some of the congregation to tears, including Aeryth, and surprisingly Leix, much to Nyxcerra's amazement, he wasn't as heartless as she thought.

Ceres' father had mingled with those in attendance 'appeasing the beasts. Against my better judgement' he called it, this had brought a small smile to Nyxcerra's face, understanding that he had to do it, to keep up appearances with those who made things happen.

She had been introduced as 'my daughter's closest friend', this made Nyxcerra nervous, what had Ceres told him about her, this concern was alleviated shortly after when he told her the tales that Ceres had shared with him, stories about the moments they had experienced during the trainee cycles, the highs and the lows.

Before pulling her aside to tell her he had ideas about Ceres and her relationship, and that he didn't care, who it was with, as long as she was happy, his brought him to tears when he said that he'd never seen her this happy as she had been over the past 5 cycles since they had gotten together.

This revelation Nyxcerra couldn't deal with. She didn't know whether to cry or to go out and do something to keep her mind off the situation before deciding on the latter. Something her belief system supported, much to the distaste of some in Impiri society. Even fringe elements in her own tribe having shied away from over the cycles.

At least that would keep her mind occupied for the time being. She didn't want to think about Ceres not being there. Wondering what she had done in life to deserve this in her life, but knowing full well that this wasn't her doing, it was the goddesses of fate which had done this to her, an authority which she submitted herself to, without question, she had to deal with it, in her own way.

She'd left Ceres' father to speak to others in attendance, greeting them with a smile and reverence for the occasion. She had been upfront about everything, which had surprised some in attendance, especially the senior members of the Impiri community. Traditionally she should have been wearing a dark veil, shielding her from view, as all young female Impiri were supposed to do, and to have all skin covered while in the presence of Impiri males for three days after the funeral. Syala had covered her head in a black veil, as was her customary right, but the rest had chosen to forgo the antiquated traditional idea.

Nyxcerra had used nanotechnology to change her hair colour to black, and wore minimal natural looking makeup, just enough to even out her complexion. Out of all of them she wore the most revealing, a knee-length black skirt, a black silk blouse, tanned stockings and black patent leather shoes.

Compared to most of her kind, who usually refrained from expressing themselves in such a forward manner until they had reached the age of 26, the traditional age of adulthood for Impiri, Nyxcerra was 24 and was forward in her conversations, causing some of the congregation to dismiss her as brash and uncouth, but she didn't care. Her tribe has always been the one to push against the norms of society, and to push against certain traditions.

Some of these traditions weren't followed by her tribe, a huge majority in her tribe followed the teachings of Anthara Typhe, which focused upon the importance of pleasure and self indulgence as a way to enrich life and support emotional and physical expression. Seen by some as pure pleasure seeking, but to Nyxcerra she just saw it as the avoidance of pain, a stronger driver in her life.

For Nyxcerra she had been outwardly this confident since reaching the age of ascension at 18, the age of adulthood in her tribe for the last twenty thousand cycles.

After stirring up some conversation with Ceres' extended family, she politely excused herself. Nyxcerra had noticed someone she had wanted to talk to. She'd seen him during the ceremony, and vaguely remember seeing him the studio. He was a Carpathian; he was average height, slightly taller than her, athletically built, his black hair cut short, a delicately sculpted goatee graced his ashen skin, he was easy to notice in a place like this.

She scoured the temple looking for him, before finding

him in a temple's alcove toward the back of the main hall, where it was quiet.

"Not a tan of this gathering?" Nyxcerra purred as she looked at him, glancing him over once, noticing his nervousness. He looked at her and immediately lowered his gaze.

"No... not really; had to come Aeryth said I needed to attend, all staff on active projects have to be here... so I'm here." He replied nervously, still keeping his gaze looking at the floor,

Nyxcerra stepped closer, as he backed himself against the wall, causing Nyxcerra to smile.

"It's okay, I'm finding it difficult being here too. I'd rather be doing anything, but you know, I can't..." Nyxcerra added, trying to get him to look up at her.

After a while trying to strike up a conversation with him she had managed to get him to look up at her, he was shy around women, which tickled Nyxcerra's sense of humour, she'd found out he was another artist at the label, Rhysio Daaren, at least a decade her senior, an excellent songwriter, he bragged, listing the awards he had received over the cycles.

He was a creative type which Nyxcerra found intrinsically attractive. As she talked to him she curled her long hair around her finger, gently playing with her hair, every so often she bowed to a member of the media that walked past, with each bow she revealed more of her leg through the side split, with glimpses of her stocking tops being seen, she couldn't help it, her upbringing had thought her to push the boundaries and she was happy to do so.

She smiled innocently when anyone had noticed them; she knew exactly what she was doing. Even at a time like the present, she had always been the one to push the boundaries, much to the embarrassment of others.

Jysell had left the rest of the girls to search for Nyxcerra, finding her talking intimately with Rhysio in the alcove towards the back of the temple,

"Nyx, Aeryth is looking for you..." she called out, her voice laced with disdain at having to do this.

Nyxcerra laughed, gesturing at Jysell, surprising Jysell at this laughter during the ongoing funeral.

"I told you Aeryth would send her, always sending the obedient one to find me...," as she spoke, she looked directly at Jysell, and with her eyes fixed on her she leaned over and kissed the cheek of Rhysio, leaving him surprised, he seemed as if he would speak. But before he even had the chance, Nyxcerra had placed her finger against his lips, causing him to step back, startled.

"Don't speak Rhysio, we'll talk about that proposal again soon" she paused, looked him up and down, admiring him, knowing the reaction she was getting from him

"You can be assured of that... its got my thinking lots of naughty things, it's going to be something playfully seductive" she whispered, at the same time she placed her right hand on the back of her collar and sighed as she rubbed the edges of the scales on the back of her neck, this cussed her to shiver as a wave of sensations cascaded down her spine.

"Always spoiling my fun..." she quipped as she sauntered away slowly, fixing the length of her skirt, which had ridden up slightly during her time leaning against the wall of the alcove. She reached down and wiped the dust off of her stockings as she stepped away.

"He's quite the catch, don't you think?" she asked, not waiting for an answer before adding.

"In purely a professional manner, of course," she added

jokingly. Jysell wasn't sure if she was being rhetorical, but she replied anyway.

Jysell glanced back at him for a second before turning away.

"Nyx, really, even here...?" Jysell proclaimed as she walked past, noticing Nyxcerra's action.

"Oh..." she hesitated and stared at him,

"Oh, not that, definitely not, not with him, too much of a by the books type, handsome..." she hesitated before shaking her head.

"Maybe good for a bit of fun, but no, we were discussing something professional, something that he had written for me, He's a songwriter, don't you know..." Nyxcerra purred, as something he had said had got her interested, and thinking of something positive, taking her mind for a moment from the emptiness in her hearts and mind.

"Of course he is, that's Rhysio, he wrote for Mystix, great at writing some dark concept songs..." Jysell mocked, surprised that Nyxcerra wasn't planning on luring him back to their apartment to 'discuss' his songwriting.

"Well, I told him I wanted to read some lyrics he's written recently. Maybe Aeryth will allow him to work on something for us. She said that she'd be tapping the talent pool at BYL for us."

CHAPTER 11
"HEY NYX, HAPPY ANNIVERSARY..."

Nyxcerra woke up to the bright morning sunlight streaming through the bedroom window. Sighing as she had forgotten to close the blinds the night before, she tutted to herself as she stretched before turning over, expecting to see Ceres beside her.

Instead, there was nothing. That's when it hit her. It had happened again, expecting Ceres to be there beside her, before reality set in. It had been like this for weeks.

For a moment, she was confused. Ceres had been dead for a few weeks, but it still felt as if she was still there. Nyxcerra rolled over before sitting up, noticing an envelope underneath Ceres' bed. Her hearts raced. What could it be? How she hadn't noticed it before was beyond her. She got up, made her way over and clambered under the bed, grabbing at the envelope with an urgency she hadn't experienced in a while. The cream envelope was barren except for three characters written on its front. She knew these characters; they were the character ideograms for her name. How Ceres had remembered them flashed through her mind. It was cycles ago that she had even mentioned it.

Hastily opening the envelope, pulling open the flap, revealing a small folded note inside, which she proceeded to pull out, opening it out in to a small page.

"Nyx, Happy Anniversary my darling…" she read out loud. Tears started to pool in her eyes as she realised the date, this note was written for today. It would have been five cycles since they agreed to be together, and not just for fun. They had promised on that day five cycles before to be together always. Nyxcerra's hearts sank, longing to hold her close, to stay awake at night and watch her sleep, a memory she cherished.

"Goddess Illarai, this must be your doing. Today of all days…" she whispered, not expecting a reply.

She looked back at the note, her eyes welling with tears as she read every word, hearing Ceres' voice in her head.

'I've got a present for you, it should be delivered today, something we saw when we were out that day, you remember, that day when we got caught out in the rain, came home soaking wet, I was certain we'd get sick, but you made me that sweet Halu tea and wrapped me up in my duvet, you looked after me, before looking after yourself. I love you, you know that. This gift is just a little something from me.'

As she read the end of the note, she let out a breath she didn't know she was holding.

'All my love, Always…' she continued to read until the end of the note.

"Always," Nyxcerra whispered before placing the note beside her, hearing a commotion happening outside and the sound of the front door being closed.

Nyxcerra jumped out of bed and ran to the door, opening it so fast that she nearly tore the door off of its track. Startling Avéline, who was standing beside the door, carrying a small box.

"Nyx, hey, you, your up...? this..this came for you..." she stuttered, surprised to see Nyxcerra hurtling out of the room., nearly knocking her over.

"Ave, what's,... for me?" she managed to get out, her hearts racing.

Avéline held out a small box, within an instant Nyxcerra had grabbed the box and was unwrapping the black silken ribbon, the box was small, no bigger than six inches square, she nervously opened the box, tears welling in her eyes as she revealed its contents, nettled in the box was a gold bracelet, causing them both to gasp.

"Wow, Nyx, whose is it from...?" Avéline enquired, thinking Nyx had already gotten a secret admirer.

"Ceres, it's from Ceres... she'd..." she spoke before going quiet. She sank into herself, her shoulders dropping, breathing a deep breath, trying to fight against her urge to cry. She shook her head, trying to snap herself out of the situation.

"We'd seen it a year ago, during a day out, we'd gone down to the old jewellery quarter out near the old hyper-space port" Nyxcerra recalled, the memories of that day flooded back. It was a happy time. On a rare day off, where they were allowed to go out, no cameras, no drones, actual freedom. Something that Nyxcerra longed for, especially now.

"It's beautiful Nyx, must be an antique. Look at that design..." Jysell interrupted as she overheard, glancing at it as Nyxcerra studied the design, releasing the clasp, allowing the bracelet to open.

"Look at the artisan skills, it's beautifully engraved..." she added. Nyxcerra looked at it, studying the design, the intricate engravings on its surface, the morning sun shining on its surface casting a golden glow.

"I can't believe she ordered this." Nyxcerra added, this would have cost a fortune, five or six thousand credits, far beyond what the prince the girls would have realised.

Nyxcerra carefully closed the clasp around her wrist and lowered it, allowing the bracelet to hang just above her hand. It fit her perfectly, causing her to smile as a tear ran down her cheek.

CHAPTER 12
"TAKE A SEAT, TRY AND GET COMFORTABLE.."

The Next Day...

After the sight of Soka crying profusely as she left the therapy room, not even noticing Nyxcerra, she ran straight past her. Nyxcerra's hearts raced, her hands trembled. What kind of individual was he? She was perched at the end of the sofa in the waiting room, her hands in her lap, dressed in all black, her skirt just below her knees, grasped tightly in her hands was a small charm, a gift from her mother when she was a child, she glanced at it as she waited; it acted as a way to calm her down.

This floor was far, not one of the floors she'd been on, floor 197, one of the three medical floors. She'd gone to 196 for a pulled ligament, and for a bloody nose after getting into a heated argument with one of the other 106 girls cycles before.

The waiting room was flanked by large windows allowing her to look out into the city below them. She had glanced at the view for a moment before sitting down. A mixture of thoughts cascaded through her mind, 'Why was Soka here?, why was she crying so much? Wasn't the therapist supposed to be helping them? What questions would they ask her? She didn't want to be there anyway, but she didn't have a choice, a feeling she hated. She wanted to get out of here, but she couldn't go.

The crying flagged in her head as a bad sign. What questions would he ask? Rang in her mind repeatedly, she thought to herself, as she was lost in thought, before being interrupted by a voice echoing out into the room.

"Nyxcerra... you may go in..." a voice called out through the hidden speakers in the room. Startling Nyxcerra as she had just got herself calm after seeing Soka crying. The sight of this burned into her memory. She didn't move. The voice repeated again.

"Nyxcerra... you may go in... Dr Anwat is waiting for you" the voice called out this time, this time it was more formal., she sighed as she heard the voice again.

She nervously stood up, straightened out her dark blue pinstripe skirt, and made her way towards the frosted glass doors, the sound of her high heels clicking on the cold stone floor, as she got closer to the doors they opened, for a moment she froze before she hesitantly stepped forward, entering the threshold with trepidation, her palms sweating as she rubbed her palms with her fingers.

She was startled to see Doctor Anwat standing there; he was young, his light blue skin caught her by surprise, a Venite, she had heard that they were a race of extremely gifted listeners, but she didn't have time for psychiatrists, she wanted to not talk about the bad things in her life, but they always wanted to talk about them.

"Nyxcerra, follow me, if you please..." he spoke, his voice nasal and intellectual, peppered with an air of arrogance. She looked at him. His dark blue hair shone in the early morning light before nodding her head in acceptance.

The room was spacious, plants grew everywhere. It was more of an arboretum than an office. She never expected it to be like this. Others had mentioned it, but she thought they were joking about it, much to her eventual surprise.

As Nyxcerra walked behind him, she was taken aback by the beautiful flowers and plants growing. She clenched her hands into fists as she walked. She didn't want to open up to him, especially after seeing Soka crying as she left the room, what had happened, surprised to see Soka here. She had been let go a cycle ago, but she was here. Even though it was against her belief and way of life, she had to do this. Aeryth said she wouldn't be allowed to sing if she didn't see him, at least once. So she would do as she was told. She would see him once, and only the once.

She didn't want to, but she would do as Aeryth had asked, just to talk to him, it was part of her contract, a section she remembered thinking would never be forced upon her.. She was following him through a winding path into an open space surrounded by flowers, as he walked into the centre he directed her to sit down, on one of the four chairs in the space.

"Take a seat, try to get comfortable, if you see me making notes after you speak, it's normal I'll be taking a few notes during your time here, it's what they require me to do" he spoke as he gestured at the chairs

"Okay, I'll try to get comfortable," was Nyxcerra's response. As she chose to sit across from him, he creeped her out. As she spoke, he glanced at her lips before glancing back at her eyes. She picked an opposing chair from him, liking the fact that a small cuboid table was placed between them. Something made her fear him. She didn't know what, but she feared him, at some instinctive level.

"So, are we expecting someone to be your support while you're here…" he'd asked, but she just sat there for a moment, before she shook her head as she replied.

"To be honest, I don't need anyone…" was her simplistic answer, which he had chosen to make a note of. Dr Anwat felt Nyxcerra tensing up. Her answers became short, not letting much of herself out, not allowing herself to actually grieve.

"What are your thoughts on what happened…?" He posed a question, trying to get more from her.

"I'm dealing with it the only way I can. It's shaken me, more than I would want to admit, but I'll get through it in my own way, in accordance with my faith and way of life…." she answered, Dr Anwat noticing she was gripping the sides of the chair she was sitting on, trying to steady herself as she glanced continuously at the golden bracelet on her right wrist.

'She didn't want to come here, he thought. 'Why's she staring at the bracelet, a possible gift from Ceres, must make a note? He thought.

Despite giving off the air of being in control and actually grieving, she wasn't. She didn't want to talk about it, not now, not to him. There was something she wasn't saying.. this made him stare at her, making her feel even more uncomfortable.

He glanced down at the screen on his lap. As she glanced over its screen, he paused at a point of information, a brief smile crept onto his face before disappearing.

"So, how was your relationship with Ceres… did you two ever argue.?" He asked, wanting to get some sort of response from her, some sort of emotional response. He hoped it brought back some memories that would make her react, causing Nyxcerra to crane her neck back, surprised by his line of questioning.

"We...., I thought we got on well, as you would expect. We'd spent the last six cycles living together, so yes, we argued at times...."

"About?" He added as he glanced at her lips as she spoke, before quickly looking at her straight in the eyes. This made her uncomfortable. She grasped the charm tight until she realised that he was staring at her hand which contained it. She stopped grasping it as she replied.

"Stupid shit usually..." she paused, thinking of the stupid things they had argued about.

"You know, we were a lot younger then..." she nervously replied, hoping it threw him off, not wanting to answer too many more questions.

"We were either too tired and things wound us up, or we disagreed about something, but it never lasted. She'd apologise,..." she paused, considering what she had just said, thinking he would read into it.

"or I would..." she added. He looked at her and smiled before writing more notes.

"Okay, thank you Nyxcerra, I'm going to ask you a few more questions, don't be concerned about them, they are just routine questions to judge your mental state at this difficult time...just for the record," he added, as Nyxcerra began nodding. Wanting this to hurry up and end.

"First, how many times have you cried over the past twenty-six hours? roughly..." he asked without any emotion.

"Not sure, a few, more previously, the shock of it all, but it's getting easier to not cry..." she replied.

"Okay, that's good to know, so since you both lived in

the same room, have you managed to clear out her personal effects..." he stopped and watched her, seeing her calm demeanour chance, she was flustered, her eyes started to fill with tears.

"So, what's it been like living in that room? I'm sure it's difficult at times, especially with the constant reminders," he added.

"It's difficult, But I come back there, to the room we shared for those cycles he added., to our place. To the place we spent so many hours talking... you can't imagine what it was like there, when she was gone." She sobbed as the tears finally came flooding down her cheeks.

"I couldn't be there, the emptiness was overwhelming, but when I wasn't there, there wasn't anywhere else I wanted to be except there..." she cried, covering her face nervously, she couldn't control herself now, she didn't want him to see her like this.

"No matter how hard I try to pack her things away, I can't bring myself to do it.."

"Are you afraid that if you pack her things away, that you'll get over it, her death..."

"Get over her..." Nyxcerra stuttered as she replied.

"No, yes, maybe, I'm not sure, but I won't be able to get over her, I just won't..." she replied, sobbing into her hands.

"Of course you can't get over it, not when you loved her..." he added, causing her to sit up straight as he finished, fighting back the rears.

"What... what..." Nyxcerra stuttered, as she continued to force back her tears.

"Well, you loved her, didn't you..." he added, watching for her reaction, a sly grin appearing at the corners of his mouth.

"It's quite easy to see, actually. It says it right here in the information Leix gave me. He looked down at the notes before looking up.

"We, we were..." Nyxcerra replied, shocked that the others might have known about them.

"Lovers...?" `Doctor Arwat added.

"Friends, she was my..." Nyxcerra added hastily, trying to hide her response. They knew, was it that noticeable that she loved her, that they were lovers? If Leix knew and Dr Arwat, did the rest of the girls know? What did they know, and how long had they known? All these thoughts ran through her head, her breathing becoming shallow and rapid as her scales tingled. She was petrified., she wanted to get out of her, she didn't feel safe.

"Well, I don't think I can help you with get over your grief, if you don't truthfully tell me what was going on..., were you, or where you not lovers..." he spoke, he dropped the calm nature of his voice, he was demanding and stern.

Nyxcerra looked down at the floor, resigning herself to the truth.

"Yes.." she whispered, barely audible.

"Can you say that again..." he replied, his tone cold and calculating.

"Yes, I said, yes we were lovers.." Nyxcerra admitted.

"And how I can help you, help you find peace and move on..." he replied without taking his eyes off his notes as she sat there in tears.

An hour later...

. . .

He didn't speak to her until they'd arrived at the centre of the room. On the floor were two large intricately embroidered cushions, gone were the four chairs, replaced. He hoped Avéline would recognise these "truth cushions", a traditional Etrui practice of being honest, with absolute candour, as was her culture. He knew he could get the truth out of her. He knew how to read her. She'd already been here before, after the incident with Kasiope, and the follow-up sessions after dealing with emotional setbacks.

"Doctor Anwat, you remembered..." she proclaimed as she noticed the cushions. Her eyes opened wide. He smiled a wry smile as she rushed over to them, touching one with her fingers, appreciating the detailed embroidery.

"Where? How did you manage to get these...?" She stopped as she felt the silk cushions.

"We never sell these to none..." she stopped, flustered.

"No offence meant by that, but we never sell these to none, Impiri. Most find them too rigid in places," she remarked, not wanting to offend him.

He bowed, smiling a brief smile, before blinking twice, his golden snake-like eyes widening in the bright room.

"I spoke to a friend of mine, he knew someone who could get me them, on behalf of my clients, I thought it might bring you some sort of comfort..." he replied, as he noticed her response, he could taste her pheromones on the tips of his forked tongue, he passed before gesturing for her to sit down, before sitting down himself, after a while of sitting quietly he spoke.

I'll go straight into the questions..."

"From what I'm told, you don't live in separate rooms?" he said, raising an eyebrow, studying her reaction. She didn't fidget like Nyxcerra. She sat legs tucked in beneath her, her delicate flowery dress resting just above her knees. She sat upright, her hands in her lap.

"We don't, two of us were paired up, me and Tiiona, Jysell and Syala, Nyxcerra and..."

She stopped just before mentioning Ceres' name.

"Ceres?" He added, causing her gaze to drop, looking at her hands.

"Yes, Ceres..." she forced back her emotions,

"It's difficult to mention her name, you know, around the others, especially to Nyx."

"Do you think you are dealing with her death well..?" He added, awaiting her response.

She sat there, still looking at her hands, "Honestly, I'm not dealing with it well. The shock of it still runs through my mind. There isn't a day in which I don't think about her. She was a big part of my life, you know??" she replied. He sat there studying her response, her lack of emotion. Was she holding herself back? She had to be. How could she be this composed? She couldn't have cycled through the stages of denial, he thought.

"You seem to have come to terms with it, Nyxcerra was sitting there in tears, but you..." he paused, letting the words sink in.

"You are sitting there like you've accepted it."

"I might have accepted it, in my head. But that doesn't mean my hearts have, we have all wept openly, but it's Nyxcerra that I'm worried about, that I'm trying to be strong for. She's a mess. If I bring her up, it hits her differently, if you know what I mean?.."

She paused, as she became emotional, thinking about hearing Nyxcerra cry herself to sleep at night. Her shared room with Tiiona being next to Nyxcerra's.

"I don't think I can help her, I want to, I hate seeing her

like this..." she started to cry, her breathing shallow and rapid, it was now too much to hold back.

" I feel powerless to help... just like I was with..." she sobbed as she pulled out a silken tissue from her red leather clutch bag which was on her lap.

"Kasiope?, Avéline, you know we discussed this last time. You weren't to blame for not knowing what she was going through..." he reached over and patted her on the hand,

"You've done nothing wrong. It's okay to care about someone else's emotions, but don't forget about your own."

A Few Hours Later...

"Let's get this straight. I'm here for one thing only," Tiiona told him as she sat on one of the two chairs in the centre of the room.

"To get Aeryth and the senior management off my back by helping me pass this stupid mental health check-in. I've dealt will loss in my life already, I'll get through this without your help, look at me, I'm fine, some days better than others, Do I feel sad, us, of course, wouldn't function if I didn't." She stopped talking before standing up.

"Do I miss Ceres, of course? It's difficult to not miss someone I've been living with for six cycles. If I need any condolence, I'll talk to the others, as we're all going through the same. So I'd like to leave, preferably with as little conversation as possible." before turning around,

"Denied...." He added, gesturing for her to sit back down?

"Denied..?"

Not just you leaving, you're in denial, like none of this effects you, well I'm afraid to tell you that it does affect you. You don't have to be strong all the time." He added.

Later that afternoon...

Jysell sat on the lowdown chair in the psych office, the afternoon was drawing to a close and the sun's light elongated all the shadows, Dr Anwat sat across from her nodding his head as he wrote down notes,

Jysell was fidgeting with her hair. She'd been there for close to an hour. She wanted to go.

"You do miss Ceres, don't you?' he said slowly.

"Don't you?"

"You don't seem too affected by her passing like the others..."

"Of course I do, you already know. I miss her a tremendous amount," Jysell exclaimed, hurt that he thought she didn't care.

"The fact that I'm dealing with it doesn't mean I didn't and don't care..." Jysell added the tone of her voice, dropping its lighter tones. She was annoyed, hating his line of questioning.

"You didn't really know her, did you" he replied, not liking her dismissive tone. He wasn't going to be talked to in this way, not by her.

"We're you surprised to know that she was taking Pathexdrose for Kadfa syndrome. It had come back in the last 6 months. She'd hoped this treatment was going to work as it had before, 8 cycles ago"

He stood up and chose to sit on the chair next to her, leaning forward to speak to her, carefully placing his hand on her knee, which caused her to fidget.

"We knew she was getting muscle pain again. We didn't know she'd had Kadfa syndrome relapse, but things like that , I would have expected her to keep some things secret, not to scare us all." She replied, looking down at his hand the entire time.

"I don't think this is appropriate, do you?" She added. I'm just here to calm you down. You know you can tell me anything..."

"Then I can tell you this is over. I'm done with this conversation, also you've done for the last hour is goad me, and now questioning my ability to care..." she exclaimed as she stood up.

"Fuck you..." she proclaimed as she walked off, Dr Anwat sitting there, smiling, knowing that he had managed to get to her, that he could recall her for further conversations due to her lashing out.

30 minutes later...

Syala sat there, motionless, on one of the two chairs in the middle of the room, staring out into the middle distance.

'So, Syala, this only works if you answer the question....' Doctor Anwat spoke, his patience growing thin, as he placed his tablet on the table between them.

'I'll be fin....the goddesses will help me through this, they've always helped, everything is always according to their plan, who am I do understand the machinations of those who gave life....' Syala spoke, in somewhat of a meditative state, her eyes closed.

"I know you have things you need to ask Dr, but they are irrelevant. Having somewhere to meditate away from the rest of the girls will do me wonders," she spoke again, as she opened her eyes.

'Then as long as you need, you can use this space, just let me know and I'll make it available to you for future use, I'll be here once you get to a place where you want to discuss it further...." he added, frustratedly as he couldn't get anything else from her, this one would be the more difficult to deal with.

Later that night...

Dr Anwat was standing outside of his office talking with Leix. He looked nervous that Leix was checking in on him. Leix stood, not moving, waiting for Dr Anwat to come to him. He gulped nervously before walking over. He'd done as he'd been told.

"So, how is our investment?" Leix enquired coldly, no real emotion on his face, to him they weren't individuals, they were figures on a fiscal report, having them not at the top of their game cost BYL money and his job was to make sure that they kept costs low and profits high.

Dr Anwar frown at him, before looking down at his tablet, displaying his notes

"Honestly, they are a mess."

"Nyxcerra, she pretends she is fine, but she cannot cope, Tiiona, she is in denial, not grieving at all, her brash and cold exterior is hiding some serious trauma, possible breakdown at some point..." he spoke, causing Leix to look concerned,

"Go on" Leix added,

"Avéline, she's dealing with it in her own way, but she's dealt wit her loss, a-bit too quickly but that's fine, Jysell and Syala are both dealing with it, Syala didn't even say much, dismissing the concept of therapy. Preferring to meditate her way out, which means I'll have some way to guide her through this. They all can be influenced , I can always keep them in line." He added, causing Leix to grin.

CHAPTER 13
"IT LOOKS SO...EMPTY"

Two Weeks Later

"It looks so... empty," Tiiona said aloud as she wandered into the room, struck by the divide in the room, everything on what had been Ceres' side of the room had been boxed up and was ready to be sent away to her father.

"Mm-hm" Nyxcerra replied as she sighed, as she placed a box in front in front of her, before perching herself on the side of the bed, her gaze fixated at Ceres side of the room. It was empty. She couldn't disagree. Then again, everything seemed empty to her these days. She felt hungry but didn't want to eat. Nothing could fill that void inside her. Even though she tried, she had to get on with life again.

"Without Ceres, no matter what I put here, it will always feel empty..." Her voice trailed off as she lost herself to a thought, remembering the good times spent there.

"Six cycles together in this room..." she stopped, laughing out loud for a moment at the times they had drunk Khamyr wine while telling each other stories, having to try and cover up the next morning their lingering hangovers, failing most of the time.

"You remember those times, don't you..." her mind wandered to the happier times, the giggling they did when hungover, trying to make each other laugh, especially when they couldn't stand properly, their balance being affected.

"You remember, don't you when she tried to be sober when we were clearly drunk and they punished us for it? Those dance practices were torture, especially when hung over. I was barely able to keep awake..." she exclaimed, with a sense of joviality in her voice.

Tiiona wandered over, crouching down near Nyxcerra, who was still sitting on the side of her bed. She looked around, making sure that none of the other girls were there, not wanting to expose her own emotions.

"Yeah, she always had that facade, especially when the cameras were rolling, but she never had it with you..." she paused as she placed her hand on Nyxcerra's, who sighed gently, knowing Tiiona in her own way was trying to help.

"She was completely candid with you, none of us had that same openness with her, I'd always hoped she would open up more to us in time..." she stopped, fighting back her own emotions, she'd seen glimpses of Ceres opening up to her, but most of the time she treated her like the disruptive little sister, always scolding her for arguments which started, even though she wasn't the cause of them, sometimes she was, but not always.

"...won't get to experience that..., but I miss her too..." Tiiona candidly added.

Nyxcerra's eyes began welling with tears. She sniffed, trying not to break down,

"See, I'm normal you know, even I cry sometimes, I'm not completely heartless." She mocked, trying to deflect her own sadness through laughter.

"I know, I do too, so much you won't believe..." Nyxcerra replied, as she sighed deeply.

Tiiona looked at her, tried to force a smile, but knew Nyxcerra could see through it. She had terrible at hiding her emotions, any of them.

"You can tell me..." she hesitated.

"if you want, you know I'm here,... we're all here if you need to talk..." Tiiona added,

"You remember the time when we managed to surprise her, for her birthday, pretending that we had forgotten, by the goddess's name, she was upset..."

Nyxcerra lost herself to her thoughts again, Tiiona was still telling her a tale from cycles past, but to her it was nonsense, nothing made sense, just words. She nodded her head in acknowledgement, but didn't comprehend anything.

Her entire world was empty. Her room, her bed, and first and foremost, her hearts. She had the nightmares again, waking to realise that Ceres was gone. Every one of these was as if she was finding out about her death for the first time.

She'd spent the last few weeks moping around, not eating, the long nights crying had taken their toll, she didn't look her best, her eyes red, dark circles under her eyes but she honestly didn't care, she'd cry to herself while in the shower, drowning out the sound of her cries. She had barely eaten more than a few half meals in days, she couldn't stomach it, she had tried to be strong, but after Aeryth had given them a five-week hiatus to come to terms with their loss, she'd fallen into a pit of despair. She knew she had to get on with things.

Nyxcerra decided it was time to move on. She began to get dressed properly, had taken middle of the night gym training sessions, coming back when her muscles ached, pushing herself more and more every night. After much procrastination, she had finally begun to pack up Ceres' things. She'd gradually packed Ceres' things away over the last few days. It had taken longer than expected, having told her father that she'd get to it when she felt she could.

Tiiona placed her hands on the box before lifting it up, causing Nyxcerra to get startled.

"Hey..."

"Can't let you do this all by yourself. I'll put this over with the rest...." She smiled, trying her hardest to give Nyxcerra the chance to deal with that was happening.

A Few Days Later...

Nyxcerra's eyes caught on a message from Aeryth, its subject causing her to pause 'Line-Up of Aerrea- Confidential'. Before she had time to think about it, Tiiona hastily gestured for it to open. Even though the message was addressed to each of them, she didn't want to open it, dreading its contents. She was calm as Tiiona started to read it out loud, jokingly mimicking Aeryth's tone and delivery, causing Jysell to laugh, only to flush with anger when she read the contents, her tone changing back into her own low register tone.

"And for the lineup, after careful consideration of all prior evaluations, Ceres' place as lead will be taken by Tela Nyxcerra Jaeihai..." her voice trailing off.

"Well, fuck me, I wasn't expecting that..." she exclaimed before walking off with no further comments, slamming to door to her and Avéline's bedroom just as she got inside, the reverberation causing pictures near the door to rattle on the wall.

"Congrats, Nyx..." Avéline jumped in, hating the silence which had descended on them all.

"Give her time. She'd gotten herself psyched up for getting the lead. Leix had told her she was being considered." She added,

"What the hell..." she thought in outrage, swiping the message away, before gesturing for the holo display to disappear. She sat down quickly, sinking her head into her hands as she gently shook her head.

Leix had told her she didn't need to worry, she was the visuals, her look was her main selling point.

"Female fans want to be you, male fans want to be with you." That's what he had said. It kept repeating in her mind, She was happy with that place. Her mind was now full of chaos. Nothing made sense anymore. As she sat, she started to gently sob. Syala and Jysell both looked at each other, unsure of what to say, relieved it wasn't them.

Avéline stood up from the high-backed chair she was sitting on before walking quickly over and perching herself next to Nyxcerra on the sofa, settling herself as she sank into its soft cushions.,

"Trust me, it's just her pride. She'll get over it. I'll chat with her." She paused, contemplating her words as she patted Nyxcerra on the leg.

"Come on, Nyx, for Ceres..." she paused.

"She'd have wanted you to do it..."

Nyxcerra leaned back, resting her hands by her side as

she exhaled. She was upset and more than a little confused. 'Why had she been picked, she wasn't cut out to lead? She spoke her mind a little too often and had been reprimanded for her overtly sexual nature.

That's what Leix had always told her, she'd been reprimanded a few times, being unable to leave the building during a free day, she knew her mouth got her into trouble, her sense of decorum lacked finesse at certain times, especially when talking with senior management.

She wasn't sure why she was slightly angry, except that Leix had lied to her, maybe to pacify her need to know what was going on. Her thoughts listed, her own reasons why she wasn't the right choice.

She was a twenty-four-year-old home schooled girl from the Artreia tribe. She'd grown up on the moons of Corellia, which had made her street smart, but lacking real confidence. She thought about her journey so far, through some miracle of fate, or some gods practical joke on the universe had ended up not just beating over a million applicants for a spot in the final 106, but to be whittled down to the final six.

She knew she was beautiful, but that's all she had. She thought to herself, thinking her life would be easy,

"Aeryth's gotta have seen something in you, Nyx," Adeline explained, trying to support her, knowing that she was already doubting herself.

Nyxcerra quickly stood up, leaving the girls to talk, she had to say something to Tiiona, and she had to do it herself, she nervously made her way towards the bedrooms, knocking on Tiiona's and Avéline's door, expecting a verbal tirade of abuse, frustration and disappointment.

The knock on the door fell silent. Nyxcerra hesitated before putting her hand on the door handle, before slowly pushing the door open. Tiiona fell silent, trying to hide her tears as she looked out the window on to the bustling city below. They wouldn't know about this until a press release came out, and then it would be official. She sat trying to make sense of it all, being betrayed by Leix. She clenched her fists and was silently contemplating what to do next. She was angry, but not with Nyxcerra, but with herself for reacting the way she did.

Nyxcerra allowed herself a small smile. She never thought anything would get to Tiiona, she was always the tough one. When people pushed her buttons, she pushed back, but she had never seen her looking this lost.

"Tii," Nyxcerra enquired, awaiting a response, leaning forward, still half heartedly expecting a rage filled outburst.

"I never expected them to pick me, you must know that... I was happy being..." she was interrupted my Tiiona who turned around and spoke, noticeably pushing back her own emotions.

"Yeah," Tiiona said slowly.

"It's not you I'm angry with, it's that bastard Leix... he..."

"Played us against each other, probably for his own twisted games."

"I think so? I really thought she'd pick me. The dynamic would work, just like Mystix. but..." she trailed off halfheartedly.

"Tii, you'll always be my rock, but it's not about us, is it? It's about all of us. I promise I'll try to do Ceres proud, you know..' she paused,

"Get that album of the cycle award that she wanted for us. As long as I've got you by my side...." She stopped. "We're okay; aren't we...?", Nyxcerra enquired, hoping she hadn't ruined their relationship. She needed her strength and determination now more than ever.

"I'll be fine, just give me some time, I am happy for you... just a bruised ego..., you know.." Tiiona added, trying to mask her hurt, gradually unclenching her fists, as she took a deep breath.

"Time, I just need some time....' she repeated.

CHAPTER 14
"AND WE'LL GIVE IT TO THEM..."

A Few Days Later...

"How was practice Ave?" Tiiona asked as Avéline walked through the door of their apartment, she was dressed casually in a light summery dress, it was midday and Avéline was snacking on a bright orange Lucoz fruit, with its soft furry exterior, all the while carrying a large plastic cup with the other hand, filled halfway with a light brown milky liquid, a thick straw popping out of its lid. She leaded over the straw and took a sip.

"Don't know how they get this recipe right every time, just like they make it at home, even down to the bitterness of the tea..." she spoke to herself, her throat still tingling from over stressing it while in practice.

"Fine," she said curtly, it had been good, but had to rush back to the apartment, not having time for a proper lunch break, taking a bite of the fruit, Avéline looked as if she wanted to speak, but kept herself quiet, she looked around, as if she was trying to find someone else.

"Where's Nyx?" she enquired urgently.

"She should be back soon. She went to speak to Dr Anwat. Just a follow up she said..."

Tiiona replied, Avéline's mannerism made her curious, what was so urgent that she needed to talk to Nyxcerra first.

"It's okay you know, you can tell me, we both gotta be open with things, that's that Dr Anwar said for us to do..." Tiiona added, well that was what he had said, as a condition of her getting out of the therapy session, she hated him with a passion.

"Your right, everything in the practice was great, Although, there was a new producer at the practice studio... seems like things are changing in the production team, company wide. We've been..."

"Who've they given us? Better be someone who can deal with our different styles..." Tiiona interjected, cutting Avéline off before she could finish.

"I was trying to tell you, his name was Ryx. Everyone was fawning over him. I'd heard of him before, but nothing major." She lied. She had stood there in awe of him. He was handsome, tall and confident. She hoped that he had noticed her glances at him.

"Ryx, Ryx Ardashan, he's worked with the best in the business, a very distinct style, did you know he worked with Mystix on their last album, you know the one "Ain't nobody waiting for the night to end..." she added enthusiastically, before realising and quickly blushing.

"Aeryth wants him to work with us. She said that he had a great concept for us, for the first album." Her voice trailing off. Now she was unsure of what she knew.

'I thought we had a concept..." Avéline added, her tone laced with doubt. ,

"But you've seen his work. Mystix did a great concept

last year, that's one of his..." she paused, thinking about the concept, and how to explain it.

"It's a dark girl crush concept, but that's what the audience in the core want, they're sick of that cute look, they want more..., and we'll give it to them..." Nyxcerra added as she walked in, surprising them both.

The room fell silent, Avéline hesitated before speaking again, how much of this did Nyxcerra already know about, she'd been in a meeting with Aeryth since 6am, and had only come back just before 10, just as she herself was going upstairs to the practice rooms. Why hadn't she said anything before, if she knew?

"That's why I'm back early. She wants us to have a word with him." She paused, unsure of how they would take the news.

"... Today... he'll only be here for the next hour or so. He wants to show us his vision for Aerrea. They got rid of Vyna..."

"What?" Nyxcerra responded without even thinking.

"Yeah, Aeryth said he's been let go, that he'd been under investigation for a while, that's why Ryx is coming in to take over our production..."

"What did he do?, I saw him only yesterday at the studio, we were working on a demo of a song, you know the one I told you about.." Jysell enquired, puzzled by the chain of events, remembering that Vyna didn't seem to be having any issues the day before and was acting as if he was working on their album, but now they had all changed. She ran her fingers through her hair, muttering to herself 'what have you done Vyna'

"What's that Jys??"

"Nothing, things just seemed fine yesterday.." Jysell replied, not wanting to make anything out of it.

"I know. I saw him being escorted from the studio earlier. That's when Aeryth told me she wants us up there asap." Avéline added hastily, a sense of urgency in her voice, this surprising the rest of the girls.

"Then we better be going..." Nyxcerra spoke, gesturing for the rest to follow. Jysell went to get Syala from their room. She knocked on the room door before slowly pushing the door open. Tiiona fell silent,

"As long as he gives me some great verses, I'm fine with it..." she explained.

Nyxcerra allowed herself a small smile. She never thought Tiiona would smile so quickly after yesterday's leadership news.

"Tii," Nyxcerra enquired, awaiting a response,

"He's good, you know. Mystix did a great job on that last album.."

"Yeah, Jiyeo said he'd pushed him further than other producers.."

"Jiyeo...Jiyeo." she stuttered, not expecting Tiiona to know him. Thoughts of how she knew him ran through her mind.

"Yeah, Jiyeo, don't you remember? I did that uncredited vocal work on his solo., at his request...."

"Oh yeah, I forgot, so you still keep in touch..."

"Yeah, he'd told me to keep this quiet. Ryx had casually dropped that he'd be working on two albums, Mystix 3rd album and a concept 1st album for a girl group..."

"And that's us..." Nyxcerra sighed. Now it all made sense.

"Yeah, it would seem to be.." Tiiona smiled,

"I'm actually looking forward to it, Ryx has an amazing work ethic, even for that one day doing an uncredited, he pushed me to be better, to not be afraid of what I can deliver, a-bit of a perfectionist..."

"Likes to brag. Be prepared for that." Tiiona added.

Up on the 100th floor an hour later...

"So that's the idea, a dual concept," he interrupted Nyxcerra just as she was about to speak, after taking off her headphones. He was a young Kamarian, no older than thirty, known for their ability to hear subtle nuances in any sound, far beyond the auditory reach of most imperial citizens, he stood arms folded smiling a gentle, confident smile and arrogantly looking at all of them as they stood in the studio, Tiiona and the rest were still listening to music, while Nyxcerra was holding the headphones in her hand while she talked with Ryx.

"So, what do you think? It's different, edgy. A light and dark concept,... it brings balance don't you think, it's what Aeryth said the demographic wants."

"I'd say more of a leather and lace concept, if you think about it. A nice light synth pop vibe, followed by a raunchy seductive girl crush, pushing the narrative." She stopped as she thought of the right word.

"That we are..."

"Unpredictable..." Ryx added, at the same time Nyxcerra uttered it, causing Nyxcerra to nod her head in acceptance.

Their conversation was interrupted by Tiiona who turned around and spoke. As she put down the headphones, she hadn't heard their conversation.

"Ryx, love it, I can work with this, gotta tweak the lyrics slightly for my intro, good but they don't have my," she paused to think of how to politely say her honest opinion.'

"Signature flow, close enough though, but otherwise, a nice dark vibe.." she proclaimed with a wide smile on her face as she fixed her hair after removing the headphone and putting them on the mixing desk.

This caused Nyxcerra and Ryx to break out laughing, while Avéline, Syala and Jysell were still listing to the demo tracks.

"What's up?" Tiiona said slowly.

"It's just I've not seen you this excited about a project before," Ryx added.

"But it's nice to get your feedback, what did you think about Boudoir?, it's perfect for Nyxcerra don't you think..?" Rex added, already knowing it was perfect for her, Aeryth already green lighting the song for the album.

"I think so. Definitely got potential for her signature vocal range, very suggestive lyrics. Who wrote these?"

"Rhysio, he said he'd mentioned this to you Nyx, at the funeral, but you hadn't had time to get back to him on it.."

"Thought it was him, he'd said that he'd wanted me to listen to it, and wow... I'd definitely like a chance to sing it..." Nyxcerra smiled, as it all made sense, Rhysio had mentioned that he'd been approached to work on some songs for a new producer, but he'd been terrible with the name."

As they had all removed their headphone, Rex had a question to ask a question that the girls didn't realise would be the beginning of their career,

"And 'missing you', what did you think?, still got a bit of tweaking to do but it's pretty much done, your thoughts?" He enquired. At that point, the room went silent. There were a lot of thoughts running through the girls' heads,

Nyxcerra nervously played with the bracelet she had

received from Ceres, Tiiona stood there and folded her arms, Jysell but her bottom lipas she fixed the zip on her dark orange hoodie while Syala nodded her head, they were all waiting for someone to say something, but it wasn't long before Nyxcerra took a deep breath,

"I really thought that it was perfect, those lyrics, just perfect, how you've managed to write that, it's so," Nyxcerra replied. She lost her trail of thoughts. The lyrics had hit her hard.

"Fitting. Ceres would have loved it, it's going to..." Avéline added, finishing Nyxcerra's sentence.

"Be a fitting tribute to the legacy she has already gained...", Aeryth interrupted as she walked into the studio, she'd been watching them from the doorway for a few minutes, wanting to interject, but also to watch Nyxcerra step up as lead, which she hesitantly did, causing Aeryth to smile.

The girls went silent, as Aeryth glanced at Nyxcerra, who by now knew she had to follow the line that she set for them.

"The feeling it gives will work, and the fans will lap it up," Aeryth added,

"I've had Ryx working with Rhysio for the last week, coming up with it. That's going to be your debut."

"Our debut..." Nyxcerra proclaimed,

"I thought we were singing..." Nyxcerra spoke before thinking, realising what was happening. Their original debut song was being shifted in favour of this tribute to Ceres.

"Never mind..."she added at the end.

Aeryth gave her a stern look before faking a smile.

"This will be better. We'll do her proud. You can trust us..."

"I know I can. We wouldn't have spent the credits on this last-minute change if we didn't think you, or the girls, could do it justice, just don't prove me wrong." Aeryth added, trying to crush the questioning from any of the girls.

"Take a rest, your going to need it, I want you all to be rested for tomorrow, Ryx will send you over the lyrics later, but you'll be recording it tomorrow..." Aeryth announced, it was happening if they liked it or not.

CHAPTER 15
"YOU COULD SAY SOMETHING LIKE THAT..."

6 Cycles Before Debut...

"To be honest, I'm just here because they dared me to apply. You know one of those stupid dares? My parents dared me. I didn't think I'd get through the first stage... but here I am," Avéline admitted, which elicited a smile from Tiiona, meanwhile shaking her head gently.

"I bet your parents didn't mind, did they? My parents didn't want me to apply, but I begged them.." she paused.

"For month and months, put in my application on the last day, without their permission..." her voice trailed off

"Which definitely wasn't a good idea...". She looked down at her feet, remembering the heated argument when her acceptance communication arrived. Only then did her parents finally give in begrudgingly.

"And I'm guessing it was a simple thing for you...!" Tiiona asked, awaiting Ceres' reply, who just shrugged it off,

"You could say something like that,", cutting the line of

questioning. This response caused Tiiona to pause, she was put off my Ceres' demeanour.

Ceres had been the one asking Avéline and Tiiona what had caused them to apply. But didn't want to add her own thoughts, she just wanted to know how to get the most out of them. Her father had told her it was the easiest way to get what she wanted, 'understand them, their motives and use it to better yourself'. The words ringing out in her mind.

The instructors had grouped together them as a three, a simple task. Sing a cover of a song as a three piece. She needed them to listen to her, and the best way was to get them on her side.

"So what's, what's your range?" Avéline nervously asked, but to no response. She held onto her plait of hair, nervously fidgeting with the ribbon tied at its end, she was hungry, her stomaching rumbling, causing her to gently rub her stomach for a second, feeling its emptiness, she had skipped breakfast again, drinking an energy drink, that's all she had, she looked down at herself, unhappy with her appearance, Ceres and Tiiona were slimmer, Ceres was slender and athletics while Tiiona was slim, out of them all she was the shortest and looked the youngest.

Tiiona and Ceres were busy discussing what sections of the song to sing. It had to be an easy song, something from a group.

"All of us, by Tay-lal, it's a perfect choice..." Ceres proclaimed, much to Tiiona's disapproval

"Great for you, but it doesn't fit my style. No one's tried to spit those verses." She proclaimed. Both of them ignoring Avéline. She was used to it. She was quiet. She began humming, the hum becoming a murmur before becoming clearer. She didn't enjoy arguing.

"But then again, it doesn't manner what they say,

because I'll do it, anyway. Why does it come down to this, there isn't just me it's always been the three of us" Avéline began singing to herself, lost in her own thoughts, repeating the lyrics, ignoring Tiiona and Ceres' ongoing argument, not realising that they had heard her singing, until she finished.

"What?.." Avéline spoke as she noticed them watching her.

"Did, did I do something wrong..." she stuttered.

"No, definitely not, just wasn't expecting that tone... not from an Etrui," Ceres remarked flippantly.

"We're not just about the traditional songs, you know. I've loved that song since I was old enough to try and sing it. Mother said it was a classic..." Avéline replied, with some small amount of conviction in her voice. Her people, the Etrui, were an old people, the oldest of the Impiri species. Their population was small, genetically distinct from all other tribes. Most Impiri could go a lifetime without ever meeting one.

"So they put a Valari, Etrui and Helaycu together in the same group. I don't know about you, but I think they are stirring up the tension for the viewers." Tiiona added as she overheard an argument occurring in the small rehearsal room next door, the muffled raised voices before hearing a door being opened and be slammed shut.

"Can't believe that Artreia bitch, telling me I'm out of tune, who does she think.." a voice exclaimed before walking off, causing the girls to break out into laughter.

"Well, we all know who she's talking about. What's her name? Nya?, Nyxla...?" Ceres added as she cracked the door open, peaking out. Her own curiosity getting the better of her. Knowing that once outside of the room, everything was being broadcast to billions. Drones caught everything, knowing she didn't want any scandals to ruin her chances, getting into the final hundred and six from the million girls who applied was easy, her father's connections helped her, but she hadn't been told anything more, much to her dissatisfaction.

"Nyxcerra, I met her last week during the induction, she's got a good voice, she sings with amazing mixed voice, really connects with the emotions of what she's singing" she paused, thinking if she should say what was on her mind.

"She's an Artreia, a typical Artreia, overconfident, not just in her abilities and especially with how she looks... what should we expect? She's a pleasure seeker." Tiiona added, but her words fell on deaf ears. No one responded to her comments.

"Well, they said they wanted a diverse group of girls, I mean there is at least four from each of the dasho, except Etrui, and that's where you come in Ave'." Tiiona added, causing Avéline to smile, they were only just three weeks into the program, and she was already being called her nickname. Tiiona was the complete opposite of her, something Avéline never expected to be able to get on with, lost in, though Avéline just nodded her head.

"Thanks Tii, I know,

CHAPTER 16
"SORRY, LITTLE ONE, NO VISITORS..."

6 Cycles Before Debut...

It was a scorching hot summer afternoon, the air shimmering in the heat, the streets were still busy, most citizens kept themselves to the shade, the breeze moved the air at a delicate pace, just enough to take the edge off, the heat, but for some it was still too hot. The main parade was busy. The low-rise buildings off the Safuu district gave way to Byni Avenue, the most exclusive area in the capital.

Standing as gatekeeper to the avenue was a huge building which towered high into the clouds, some people gave it a wide birth, others stood in awe, a young girl waited nervously at the corner of the building, looking around, passers-by glanced at her as she occasionally bumped into others, sometimes dropping the small suitcase she carried in hand, it wasn't big enough to carry more than a few days worth of clothes.

"Is this a bad idea?" she murmured to herself, watching

the flow of people on the sidewalk that passed the entrance to the building. Tourists wandered around, taking photos of everything, tour guides pointed out key buildings in the district,

"And here is BYL Entertainment, rumours are that the latest batch of trainees will start later, maybe we'll see some today, a truly special surprise on today's tour..." the tour guides voice, high pitch and playful, even on a hot day like today, she was still positive.

A group of girls across the street made their way across the busy thoroughfare before walking straight past security while periodically shooting glances at her and giggling., before looking away, occasionally pointing at her.

"Is she a trainee? She's a-bit mean looking, I mean look at that style, hopefully she's just a..." one girl spoke, as she glanced at her, scrutinising everything about her.

"Doubt they'd pick a Helaycu girl, especially one that low?" Another girl joked before laughing as she saw the young girl's orange tattoo on her wrist. It was a basic design. She was a daughter of a low level Helaycu house. She nervously pulled down the sleeve of her white blouse, which was tied up in the middle, revealing her taut stomach. When people made comments like that, she hated it. 'How dare they, they don't even know me...' she murmured to herself.

Casting her gaze at herself in a reflection in a window, she was of average height. Athletically built, light blonde hair styled with an undercut, the tips of her hair dyed a dark orange, with a single intricately twisted braid at the back, running down to the middle of her back. She looked like most of her tribe, thin, athletic, street smart, her tribe having found it easy to base themselves in the inner cities across the empire, usually in security or the medical field.

She sighed as the heat got to her, sweat beading on her head. She reached back and pulled the back of her blouse, allowing the slight breeze to cool her back. She hated the heat; she longed for the mild summers back home, nowhere near the scorching temperatures here, shaking her head as she saw a young Hakanarian couple, who casually strolled through the street, in full glare of the afternoon sun. Wishing for a moment she had their ability to deal with this heat, she wondered how they could deal with it until it hit her. This was their home world, not hers.

They were used to it; it was their empire that brought all the races together, the great Hakanarian Imperial Empire, an empire of trillions, and here she was, on Prim, the capital world, in the city of Anox, second city, to the capital of Caspria, she was giddy with excitement but also with nerves. She stood there in awe for a moment looking around, in comparison to her home planet, this place was perfect, immaculately clean, beautiful walkways and pavilions. She missed the park she had visited that morning, the beautiful trees, the mixture of different species who were wandering around.

She hadn't seen this many species before, not being able to name more than thirty of them. As she thought about things, reality kicked in. She didn't have much time; she needed to go in; she had to register; they were expecting her.

She waited, looking at her watch before deciding to walk closer to the building, she glanced up slowly, feeling nauseous, she'd never stepped foot into the city of Caspria before, everything was a new experience, this was it, the headquarters of BYL Entertainment, it stood pride of place on the corner of the main avenue, surrounded by the head-quarters of the major businesses in the empire.

The building stretched high into the sky. It was huge. She remembered seeing pictures, but never understood the true scale of the building. She looked at the sign above the main doors, BYL Entertainment, before being stopped by a well-dressed member of security.

"Sorry, little one, no visitors..." he gruffly spoke, catching her by surprise.

"I'm here for the auditions. Wouldn't be here otherwise," she replied sarcastically before pulling out a small device and tapping twice on its surface. She held her breath, hoping they would allow her, otherwise she had nowhere else to go.

A small projected screen appeared, hovering just in front of the security guard. After a moment of glancing at the screen he gestured at the display, swiping it away, which caused it to disappear instantly. He stood himself to attention before gesturing for her to go in, the door opening just as she got close.

"Make your way to the reception desk, give her your name and she'll tell you where to go..." he called out as he returned to duty.

She nervously stepped through the entranceway, the lobby was busy, countless individuals were sitting in small clusters, as she walked through the different languages being spoken clicked into place, these were some of the other trainees, she could recognise Parshia, Thamu and Sokath, languages closely related to Parthi, her own language.

She could understand seventy percent of what they were saying, she sighed realising she wasn't the only one nervous about being there, before she'd the chance to think about it she was stopped by someone, she was slightly taller than her, her long auburn curly hair bouncing off her shoulders as she bumped into her.

"Oh, so sorry about hat, I'm a-bit clumsy, too nervous in this place.." She stopped talking as she realised that se was rambling.

"Im Soka and you are..." she asked nervously.

"Tiiona... that's me..." she replied.

"I don't know if you know. Am I in the right place?"

"BYL Impiri 106 trainees..." Soka replied, looking around, before turning back

"I hope so, otherwise I'm lost as well" she playfully laughed, causing Tiiona to chuckle,

"At least no I know someone here, So Soka, do we know when we're going in?" Tiiona enquired.

Minutes Later...

It was a vast, dimly lit space filled entirely with monitors and spotlights—the kind that cast beams of light harshly against you, you were there to be seen, there were golden statues placed at random throughout the hall, an occasional coloured statue broke up the barren space, yet they were featureless, elegant female forms but the artist that had created them had painted them in a solid colour.

The girls already knew what this meant, these were not just cheerful colours, each of these was a colour associated with the twelve Impiri tribes, turquoise for the Artreia yellow for the Zouliku, candy-apple green for the Thebasus and a dark rich blue for the Valari among others. In society here on Prim it meant nothing, but among the Impiri, it meant a great deal and their people would watch. Any misstep would reflect badly on the tribe.

As the girls nervously progressed through the space, holo projections of current and recent artists appeared, as lifelike as if they were really there, catching some by surprise.

CHAPTER 17

"YOU CAN JUST CALL ME NYX"

6 Cycles Before Debut...

"... Some of the other girls have arranged to meet for dinner at seven. Of course, the cameras will be there. Aeryth said that no audio recording would be allowed, so we better look the part." The young girl mocked, before continuing, without dropping a beat.

"It completely optional of course, can't believe some girls are still reeling from the first stage of the eliminations, even though it's only been three weeks" she paused as she thought about it, her playful manner dropping for a moment, her brow furrowed before realising. 'Can't be doing that, gonna give you wrinkles, she thought to herself before she started speaking again.

"Resume recording... Even though its only been three weeks, some of us had created some strong bonds, I'm afraid to make any more bonds before they are broken, well it's almost six so I better be getting ready, gotta look the part for the cameras," she stopped speaking as she stood in the sunlit room, feeling the warmth of the sun on her back, before pulling off the low-cut beige top she had been wearing, casting it carelessly onto her messy bed before making her way to the bathroom,.

Just as there was an unexpected gentle knock on the door, followed by another. She didn't turn back or hesitate, let them knock again or wait, she thought.

After another knock, the door slowly opened, sliding effortlessly into the wall, allowing a cool breeze to make its way into the room, before being followed by a young woman, tall, and athletically built. She walked in into the streams of sunlight which shone through the small single window in the room, her long blonde hair cascaded onto her shoulders, her walk was effortless, seeming to glide as she walked before pausing in shock as she surveyed the room, a far cry from the luxury she was used to. It was minimal, not even aesthetically minimal, it was clinical., sparse with no character or hone comforts, at least on one side.

The two beds in the room were spaced four meters apart. Between them lay a dark black rug on the polished wooden floor with two tall and thin wardrobes at the far end of the room with a narrow floor to ceiling window between them.

Off to her far left was a closed door, with the sound of someone riffing off a melody, a tune which made her chuckle, knowing exactly what song it was, a melody her father hummed most days, one of the songs he had written cycles before she was born, before she shuddered nervously.

That was her roommate, realising that was their shared bathroom. Sharing with someone was acceptable, but only just. Gone was her privacy she thought, she'd asked not to be treated differently, not to use her privilege to gain better treatment, but didn't expect this.

She cast her eyes around the room, looking back towards the door she came through, out into the living area, shared between the six of them. They were a puzzling bunch; she thought to herself.

All she knew she was sharing a room with the young Artreia tribe girl, Nyxcerra. She hadn't got to know her properly. They had been sleeping in a vast hall, sleeping on makeshift beds, with no privacy for the past two weeks. At least now anything said in the bedrooms was away from the prying eyes of the viewers, and scrutiny by the media.

Thinking about it, she realised that she had only talked to her once during the entire three-week induction. Nyxcerra had already gained herself a divisive reputation, confident about her singing abilities, beautiful, with an already infamous s-line, staunchly proud of her heritage and position within the hierarchy of her tribe, being the younger daughter of the next in line, but was known to have a-bit of a temper.

Ceres hoped that this wasn't the case. That this reputation was unfounded, that she would be easy to get on with, that she wouldn't overshadow her own ambitions, that she was pliable and would bend to her own needs.

She didn't really understand why the label had put this group of six together. 'maybe it's driving ratings. This eclectic mix is bound to cause some drama, which the viewers will enjoy. ' she thought.

Moments Later...

Nyxcerra wandered out of the bathroom into the shared bedroom, her long dark red hair bounced on her tanned shoulders, wearing nothing but lingerie much to the surprise and amazement of Ceres, who was still standing in the middle of the room, coming back late from a meeting with the executives. Ceres stared in amazement. She hadn't expected to see this, unconsciously whistling on an exhale, catching Nyxcerra unaware.

"Ah, finally you're here..., Ceres? Isn't it? I still can't decide on what to wear," she pouted, standing in her lingerie and stockings in the shared bedroom, standing between the two single beds.

One side of the room was lived in, made to resemble some kind of personality, a dark turquoise throw on its surface, a potted lily near the window, and the mild smell of Kalita tinged the air. While the other side of the room was bare. The pillow, duvet and a black towel lay folded on the bottom of the other bed.

Compared to the dark grey room Nyxcerra's white lingerie added something to the room, even more of a contrast was her tanned skin, which looked even more golden in the golden light of the sunset, the bright turquoise tattoo on her right wrist which signified her tribe and status reflected the light.

Ceres stood, glancing at the tattoo, before looking down at hers, its dark blue ink making its way up her fore-arm, before casting her gaze back at Nyxcerra's. Unaware that Nyxcerra herself was staring at her, watching and trying to understand her, she paused for a second before snapping her fingers playfully.

"Attention, my dear, can't keep daydreaming. We have to get ready for this evening's meal, and I can't be going into any old thing. Not if I want to be kept in the labels' good graces." She playfully mocked, standing there with her hands on her hips, with a curious look on her face. She knew exactly what she was doing, she liked she look of her, but knew of the difficulties it would cause, not just with the label, but with her parents, a girl from another tribe, what would they think, her own thoughts chaotically danced in her head.

"... and you... and you must be..." Ceres stuttered unusually, still taken aback by Nyxcerra's brazen attitude to nudity. The body confidence of the Artreia was known across the empire. The most famous Impiri models were all from the Artreia, even though they had a small population.

"Nyxcerra, Tela Nyxcerra Jaeihai... if we are being formal, but since we will be living together for the foreseeable future, you can just call me Nyx" she bowed playfully, casting her own gaze at Ceres, she was smaller than she expected, a perfect figure, her bright yellow eyes caught her attention, causing her hearts to race, she was as stunning as she had expected.

The other girls had called her "the legacy", on a count that her father was a legend in the industry, having been signed to the label for over fifty cycles.

"I thought you'd be taller...?" She mocked as she cast her gaze up, taking in what Ceres was wearing, her dark blue pencil skirt, clung to her hips, and a rich black blouse finished off her outfit, adorned with a thick gold necklace hanging close to her neck. Ceres' reply catching her off guard, causing her to drop her small tan leather bag to the floor.

"What do you mean, taller... well I..." she was interrupted by Nyxcerra's laugh,

"I thought you'd be taller, but then again, compared to a Artreia like me, you're more than tall enough..."

She caught Ceres' gaze, which was glancing over her. This caused her to smile a devilish smile.

"So, what do you think? This white one," she added as

she gestured to her white silken bra, playfully trying to distract Ceres,

"or this one..." she added, reaching over and grabbing a turquoise one from the bed.

"Then it's what to wear. That's a whole other situation. We'll get to that later." She hastily added.

"Does it really matter at this stage? It's not like it's that important this early on. The stylists will take charge of that at the later stages..." she spoke, as if reciting something she had been told.

"Well, that's what my father said..." she added, with a hint of arrogance lacing her voice.

"That's all well and true, but an insider source tells me she is observing tonight, and this being so early on, I want to make a good impression," she quipped back in a matter-of-fact way.

"Aeryth?, Tonight? I'm sure she cares right now. We are still so far from being useful that we're probably not even on her radar; yes I know she oversees everything. She'll just probably send an aide or junior exec..., I'll just..."

"Well, you can't be going to dinner dressed like that, not when they will be watching," Nyxcerra pleaded, shaking her head, loving how uncomfortable she had made Ceres.

"You should know, we gotta look the part..."

"Well, I'd originally ended up deciding on the all black number, always a good option don't you think..?..." she laughed with a wink, gesturing for Ceres to follow her as she turned and walked towards the two tall wardrobes at the far end of the room, spinning on her tan stockinged heel.

"This much stuff?" Ceres exclaimed as she saw the amount of clothes that Nyxcerra had brought with her.

They were told to only bring essentials. Ceres exclaimed as she saw the full wardrobe of clothes, with more stacked at the bottom, neatly folded. The room was lit by the light of the setting sun, still bright enough, but the shadows were quickly growing.

"This is nothing, just a small selection. I'm going to have to switch it out at the end of the season, get the autumn and winter clothes shipped from home, get these sent back." Nyxcerra proclaimed innocently.

Ceres glanced over and noticed another bra cast on the corner of the bed, followed by a large black towel piled on the floor near the bed.

"Sorry for the mess. Got a little carried away, lost track of time. You know, heat of the moment stuff," she purred, as she looked around before she reached into the open wardrobe.

Ceres standing behind her, watching, arms folded. Her nose wrinkled in a frown. This wasn't the same girl she had met before. Then she was stern, emotionless, cold and spoke with a level of arrogance that she couldn't stand.

Especially when she was herself cold to most, and was unapologetically arrogant. She thought of her as competition. But not now.

"This isn't the same girl, she is playful, confident physically, and is somewhat flirtatious" she thought along with the list of things she needed to do, unpack her bag, take a bath and relax for the evening, eat a small dinner and get a good night sleep. Her mind thought of food and immediately her stomach rumbled.

Her mind wandered, as Nyxcerra searched in the wardrobe, talking to herself

"Not that. I'd end up looking like ... and definitely not

that. I don't want to be that distracting ..." she mumbled, but all Ceres heard was a mumble.

"Of course not" she replied as if on autopilot, her concentration lost as she stared at Nyxcerra, the elegant curve of the small of her back, leading up to her shoulders, the twin rows of scales which travelled up her spine, were still a shade of blue, still aroused by her previous activities but slowly returning to their usual olive skin coloured hue.

"So what was Kami doing here, this floors off limits to the 2nd's..." Ceres enquired, catching a whiff of the same cologne in the air, the same one she caught from the embrace with Kami, as she walked into the apartment.

"He's a good one, he, he... he came to," Nyxcerra nervously stuttered,

"You know, he came to give me some support..." she added, unable to hide it, as she blushed slightly.

"I must give my thanks to Niejen when I see her again. Did you know she's his younger sister?" She murmured, Ceres completely ignoring it, still lost in her thoughts as Nyxcerra came out of the wardrobe, carrying two new dresses, one a deep turquoise, in stark contrast to the deep red of the other dress.

"Come on Ceres, you know more than anyone, what the Industry wants, we gotta show them we are serious, I thought you'd be the first one pushing us, I mean, it's you and me who....." She joked, startling her.

"What, what did you say... "she mumbled before apologising

"Sorry Got a lot on my mind, vocal practice tomorrow, gotta rest the vocals, can't be out late this..." she was just about to finish when Nyxcerra interjected

"We know what's really going on out there, Come on, let's all go out there, the others are getting ready, let's make a memorable impression..." Ceres looked at her, knowing she was right, her father would have told her to do it, it was one of his rules

"There's never a bad time to make an impression..." just thinking about it she could hear his voice echoing in her mind.

"Just put on something classy...." Nyxcerra replied instantly, still holding the two dresses.

"Now onto something more important right now, the turquoise or the red..." Nyxcerra proclaimed proudly. Ceres looked at them. Both were exquisite and modern, the turquoise one catching her attention.

"Well,...." Ceres got out before she interrupted.

"I know what am I thinking, Red, but it's a bit brash. Might cause a few enemies with the other girls from the other dorms, might cause me more harm than good. "

"Then again, that wouldn't be too much of a bad thing... lets the label know the girls here mean business," she purred again with a devious smile.

"The turquoise, I'd say, it will draw everyone's attention, not just mine, and I think I know how much you like to be the centre of attention..."

Nyxcerra stood there, contemplating the decision, before casting them onto the bed, the covers still a mess.

"Then it's settled, but it won't go with this..." she snapped as she reached around her back and, with a quick finger movement, unclipped her bra, before removing it in one swift movement, casting it onto the bed.

Ceres cast her eyes across the room. Not wanting to be distracted, she couldn't come to terms with Nyx's overtly flirtatious attitude. Nyxcerra looked at her as she reached into her wardrobe and pulled out a bright red lace bra.

"This will do, don't you think..?" she inquired playfully, as she put on the new bra, noticing that it made Ceres feel uncomfortable.

"Come on, it's not like its something you've never seen before..." you need to be confident in your body, like me... I mean, I'm 100 percent sure there is a nice tight little body under that well-dressed exterior." She mocked, knowing exactly what to say to make her blush, hoping it would break down her stern demeanour.

Ceres blushed as expected, her hearts raced and a strange tingling sensation travelled down her scales, flustered she took a deep breath.

She'd never admitted to anyone her sexual preference, but she couldn't take her eyes off her, she was stunning, average height, but all of her proportions were perfect, she glanced at her s-line, wishing she had the same, compared to Nyxcerra's curvy hips and ample cleavage, she was tall, athletically toned, her hips were narrow and her breasts were little more than a handful.

She instinctively let out a breath she didn't know she was holding, shaking her head slightly to focus on herself.

"I've shown you mine. Now show me yours," Nyxcerra laughed, trying to make Ceres laugh.

Ceres wrinkled her nose again, trying not to laugh, her arms tightening their fold, gripping her sides.

"Come on, just a peak..?" Nyxcerra exclaimed wistfully, causing Ceres' stern exterior to break, as she let out a little laugh.

"No, just get ready and I'll try to throw something on, as you said classy..." she laughed as she turned to search the room for her suitcase, which was standing at the foot of the bed.

CHAPTER 18
"YES, JUST HUMOUR ME"

6 Cycles Before Debut...

Ceres slowly walked down the hallway. The sound of her bare feet sticking to the floor in the summer heat disturbed the silence of the hallway. As she nervously made her way to the communal kitchen, she didn't want to accidentally wake anyone; the kitchen was her only destination. She desperately needed a glass of water, something to soothe her aching throat. It still ached after that evening's dance practice.

It was late and the rest of the trainees were asleep. The cool breeze of the air conditioning in the hall way permeated through her loose green silken nightwear, causing her to shiver. The soothing sound of a piano stopped her midstride. Her first thought was that it was a recording. It was perfect, its tone fading into nothing. She knew the sound of a live instrument when she heard it.

Curiosity got the better of her, Ceres followed the

sound of the music, following it past the kitchen, after pausing, thinking that she would get the drink of water later. She followed it down a long corridor to the practice rooms.

She found a young girl there, sitting in front of a small piano in a practice room, its door open, her fingers moving gracefully across the keys. She hadn't noticed Ceres as she gingerly entered the room, hoping not to disturb her. The room was barely lit, only a single side light lit one corner of the room, casting a warm glow on a single wall, enough that she could see the piano, the doorway still partially shrouded in darkness.

Ceres stood listening, not knowing what was being played, but could tell they filled it with emotion. The young girl's slender fingers easily reached the keys as they glided across the piano.

"You play?" Ceres asked, cutting through the calm atmosphere of the room.

The young girl's playing ceased abruptly, turning around to face her as she stopped, with a surprised look on her face. She hadn't been expecting anyone else to be up this late. It was close to 3am.

"Yeah, I'm sorry if I woke you, just needed to get this melody out of my head," she answered, running her fingers across the smooth, white keys. Ceres smiled as she stepped toward,

"It was beautiful, such emotions, and no, you didn't wake me. I was just sneaking to get a drink. I won't tell anyone if you don't..." she whispered, hoping she would keep a secret.

"I decided to play today on a whim, I haven't played in a few cycles, just to see if I still had it in me, you know, make sure I haven't lost my touch... that I could still get a melody out,"

"Well, I can tell you that you definitely still have it," Ceres told her, as she walked to stand by the old black piano. Resting her arm on the piano, she smiled slightly, staring at the keys,

"I'm Hayli, by the way..." Ceres exclaimed.

"Syalette, most call me Syala." Syala added, nervously, her voice calm and melodically, she wasn't used to others, preferring to be by herself.

"Can you play that again?" Ceres asked.

"Are you kidding?" Syala enquired, not sure about the music herself.

"Yes, just humour me, just for a moment... I wanna try something..."

She began to gently rest her fingers on the piano keys; the melody starting delicately. After a few moments, Ceres started to sing quietly, her voice full of emotion, just following her own instincts.

"But don't you leave me here alone? Can't stand these feelings now you're gone. I can let you leave without saying goodbye..." she sang along with the melody before being interrupted.

"Well, what do we have here..., you're the piano player whose been playing at night..." a voice called out at the door, startling them both, as a young girl , petite with long blonde hair down to her waist stepped forwards into the light, dressed in all black casual wear. Causing both Syala and Ceres to stop what they were doing, Syala smiling in recognition.

"Nie-Jen, quit it. I told you I was going to go and practice..."

"Yeah, yeah, but I couldn't sleep. It's way too hot tonight..." before she stopped as she noticed Ceres.

"So who's your new friend...?" She enquired sarcastically before stopping in her tracks as Ceres turned around. A look of amazement flashed across her face, followed by a look of fear.

"Hayli Ceres Soobaks..." Nie-Jen whispered in awe as she realised who was standing in front of her.

"Do... do I know you...?" Ceres replied, shocked and taken back by being called her full name, Hayli her given name was used by those who she didn't know, Ceres the name used by family and friends, as was a tradition amongst her species, the single common trait amongst the twelve differing tribes.

Nie-Jen stepped back and lowered her gaze reverentially, which puzzled Syala, who stared up at Ceres.

"I'm afraid you don't, but I sure know yours, Maha'kh..." she replied as she lifted her gaze. As she caught Ceres' expression, she smiled nervously, her hands behind her back.

"Maha'kh, (Older Sister).." she whispered in confusion. Why had she called her that until she noticed Nie-Jen's tattoo? A dark blue basic tattoo made its way around her wrist. It was basic, a symbol of her lower status within the tribal structure. There they were, standing at the opposing ends of its structure.

"That is fine..Dothaka- little sister," Ceres replied before gesturing for her to come closer.

"Haven't been called Maha'kh in a while. Most have forgotten the old ways, but I do appreciate your terms of endearment and awareness of status." Ceres replied, not expecting to be called this, especially on Prim.

"It was the least I could do, in respect of the daughter of

Luca-Tal Soobaks, it's such an honour..." she nervously gushed, stepping closer before realising she was rambling and stopped, nervously laughing before Ceres stopped the awkwardness.

"But we're all the same here. We are all trainees, aren't we? Status means nothing here, and it shouldn't. Management at BYL knew they'd have trouble with this many of our kind here. I mean 106 Impiri girls from the twelve tribes. I mean, there is an Etrui from what I hear.." she exclaimed.

"Really an Etrui....?"

"I've never met one before. I didn't think they approved of the way we live life, a bit conservative from what I hear, and that's in comparison to me." Syala added.

"Yeah, she's still a bit conservative, had a brief conversation with her, she's good friends with Soka, you know, the ditty one from Salvi III"

"I didn't think an Etrui would be a risk, but her voice, she's got range, like epic range. I think it's true about Etrui having a 7 octave range." Ceres added.

"I just hope they don't put her forward to fill some demographics and equality nonsense. It should be purely on merit," Nie-Jen added, before realising who she was talking to.

"I didn't mean to insinuate anything," Nie-Jen back tracked, trying not to put herself against Ceres,

Ceres paused for a moment, deciding whether to have fun with Nie-Jen, to give her the cold treatment, or just to forgive and forget the simple slip up, normally she would have been cold and calculated, but was it worth it here, she needed as many allies as she could get.

She smiled a gentle smile, shaking her head slightly before speaking

"No offence taken, its all down to who's the best, some of us are just gifted more than others, I mean did you hear Vilna's voice, its good but she strains it too much, if she keeps doing that she's going to lose her voice, then she's done for."

CHAPTER 19
"THEY WERE GOOD TIMES..."

6 Cycles Before Debut...

The room was silent as she went into the verse. Some clapped gently, while the instructors stood quietly, tapping on tablets. She was already being scored,

"Let's fall in love, but don't know each other that well yet," she sang, clenching her fists tight, shaking gently., as she went into the next line of the song.

"Actually, I'm a little frightened., I'm afraid this is something new." She poured her heart out into the words, the timbre of her voice rich and emotive. She stepped forward, finding herself in the music.

"Let's just be together now, let see how it goes" she let the last word hang until she dropped into an innocent sounding tone for the next lines

"Keep it free, keep it easy, no strong words for what this is. Let's just be easy, go with the flow., But these words are frightening me. I just can't say it now." She stopped, her hearts racing in her chest, she let out a deep breath, bowing to the instructors, before stepping back and turning towards the other girls, the rehearsal room was packed with girls of a similar age, she picked at the right curls in her hair, as she walked back to the other girls she had been practicing with.

"I hope they liked it...." she asked, the other girls patting her on the shoulder.

"Of course they did 'Jysell, even she's writing notes...." one of the girls said as she pointed at one of the instructors, who was taking notes.

'Well, that's a first' 'Jysell quipped in return, having never seen her write notes on anyone's performance int he last ten days..

An hour later....

She lay motionless on her bed, her hands behind her head, staring up at the ceiling, staring into the middle distance. Imagining the delicate clouds that would be floating above the building, knowing they were there without actually seeing them.

It had been ten days since she'd come here, things were still so different, she still fell out of place, but so did all the rest of the other hundred and forty-four , they all came from different Impiri backgrounds, from all tribes at all levels in the society.

She had only just settled into the pace here on Prim. The leisurely pace of back home was replaced by a constant need to keep busy, as expected on the core worlds. Her mind wandered. At least for this hour they could do what they wanted, but all she could think about was that this hall was different from what she had expected.

It felt more like a prison than a makeshift dormitory for

an entertainment company, this space was usually reserved for small parties, public relation events or album launches, but not for these three weeks. The small micro drones controlled by Empire Entertainment Broadcasting flew around, usually just out of sight, as it was broadcasting the entire trainee experience to billions cross the empire. Not much was censored, just a few minutes of delay to allow for careful editing. To forward the narrative BYL had set up for certain members, setting up rivalries when there wasn't any, always thinking about the viewers and crafting an engaging story.

She could hear them flying around the main hall, which was just rows and rows of minimalistic beds, a single pillow and a thin duvet, with just enough space under the bed for her belongings, was is the only thing they all had in common. The promise of privacy in grouped apartments danced in her mind. Lost in thought, absentmindedly prying her long slender fingers into sections of her tight spiral curled black hair.

She'd left home expecting more, but finding less. As she stared into the distance, trying to find some peace in a hall full of Impiri girls, she'd never seen so many of her own kind before, having lived in a remote research colony far from the empire.

The discordant mixture of sounds in the room over-whelmed her, she was used to her own thoughts and the occasional voice, not the voices of a hundred and 5 others, unable to pick out a single voice she understood, no one spoke Aburesh, her native tongue. Much to her disappoint-ment, she'd hoped at least one of the Zouliku tribe girls here did, so she wouldn't feel as alone. She missed the conversa-tions. Without them she felt in a small way that she was losing part of herself.

"So Jysell..." a young girl's voice called out inquisitively, inflecting upwards dramatically at the end

"Where did you say you was exactly from again?, can't really work it out..." a young girls confused voice interrupted her daydreaming, within seconds she was sitting up and swinging her legs to the floor before stood up, to find the young girl, with long luscious auburn hair staring at her confused and sweating in the afternoon heat.

"Soka, you know where Peliar II is, right?", Jysell resigned herself, she couldn't sleep anyway, it was not just hot, but the air was still, typical Prim summers others had said, hot summers and cold winters, she could barely remember the summers on Kalas II, her home when she was little, but she could remember that they were hot and humid.

"Yeah, not far from the Kestral colony..." Soka replied excitely. Finally, she knew something, as she nervously twisted her auburn hair with her fingers. As a breeze from the air conditioning blew though the hall, elevating the summer heat. Both of them sighing as they felt the slight cooling breeze.

"It's about time. It's so dry in here. My throat has never been this dry..." a girl across the hall exclaimed. Causing others to cheer in agreement, causing Jysell to chuckle, before answering.

"Well, you get to there, then take a difficult journey from there to the Petrax system, then keep going past the Keshut Nebula, past the void of Tellax, out towards the Ambrosia system, once there your about another three weeks from Maxia II, which is where my dad is posted for research, been there for ten cycles, I know it's the furthest reaches of the empire. So, yeah, that's home. , took fourteen weeks and thirty-seven jumps to get here..."

. . .

"Geez..." Soka exclaimed as she tried to work out the distance. She was terrible at figuring all this out, but she knew it was far from here on Prim.

"I've never known anyone from that far out, my family's from the 2nd moon of Proxima Segis II, so it took less than a day to jump here... I even got jump sickness from that small trip..." she laughed, trying to make light of her inability to travel without feeling rough. She smiled nervously. Causing Jysell to laugh,

"Of course it did, you and your always sensitive constitution..." she mocked, which got Soka laughing as well, a question rang out in Jysell's mind, she had to ask it, surely Soka would know more she thought, she got on well with everyone, knew the gossip which circulated around the hall.

"Soka, did you hear that singing last night...?, way past lights out..." Jysell asked. Curiosity compelled her to find out, it's tone, even from this distance, was impressive. Someone was hiding an impressive voice, but hadn't shown it during the practice sessions.

She knew who it was. It couldn't have been anyone else. She had hoped that the EEB hadn't heard about it. Between lights out at 10pm and 5am they were alone, no drones, no instructors. If the EEB heard about it, then they would want to broadcast everything all day. She didn't want this. None of the girls did.

Soka looked at her, thinking back to when she had woken up during the night.

"Yeah, barely heard it, was dealing with a muscle cramp at the time..." instinctively rubbing her thigh,

"I really don't know how you heard it, it was so feint,

Could barely make out the distinct voices..." she jovially replied, her right thigh still winged with cramp.

Jysell laughed openly. She knew it was feint, but she'd grown up honing that skill.

"When your the only Impiri family on the forest planet of Maxia II you learn to hear well , so many potential dangers out there, Castil wolves, winged Petras, not to mention the forest Xanti, all really easy ways to get yourself killed, so having good hearing is a life saver...literally." She joked, As she thought about the night before, recalling the voices she had heard, while she pretended to be asleep.

"There was three of them, couldn't you tell, definitely one of them is Miss Soobaks, distinctive voice, grew up here on Prim so she's Imperial standard, but still has a Vaski twang in her voice, especially when she sings." This causing Soka to think about her own accent and how they could tell where she was from.

"You can tell she's trained, best of us so far in my opinion, but that's expected, but not so sure about the others., possibly Syalette or Medusi, but there both from Keshian III, so similar tones.." she added.

"That's amazing Jysell, you definitely have a skill, but now that you mention it, you can hear Syalette's Kaloi accent when she's nervous, never realised it , which is despicable as a Kaloi speaker myself..." casting her gaze down to the basic blue tattoo which made its way around her wrist, unlike Jysell's bright yellow tattoo which circulated midway up her forearm, designating her as the second daughter of a Zouliku tribe minor house,

"How are you getting on with what the Kaleb (derogatory name for a psychiatrist), asked you do? Soka commented, as the thought came to her.

Jysell looked at her, smiled a half arsed smile, not really pretending to be ok,

"Yeah, a little, it ain't working too well, keeps me up at night..." she added.

"Are you okay?, if you want to talk about it, I'm here to listen? If you need me, my kind are good listeners", a voice faintly asked as she tapped Jysell on the shoulder. She had been sitting on a bed to the other side of Jysell's and had been meditating to calm herself, but had overheard everything.

The feeling of the tap on the shoulder surprised Jysell. She closed her eyes for a second, picking out her voice from the noises in the hall.

'Avéline... Avéline.... Avéline' she whispered to herself, repeatedly, trying to remember some of the names of the girls in the hall, failing miserably, but Avéline's name came to her quickly but she wanted to be sure. Avéline was an Etrui-Impiri, her distinctive silver grey hair and purple eyes, the telltale traits of her tribe, a rarity, having only ever met one in her entire life.

Jysell turned around, seeing Avéline looking at her, trying to force a smile. She was smaller than most of the other girls, petite, her distinctive long silver grey hair in two braids one either side on her head, Jysell looked at her, puzzled by her sense of fashion, even in this heat she was wearing a long sleeve blouse, and a skirt which stopped just above her ankles. 'Even in this heat she's still so conservative...' Jysell thought to herself, before forgetting she needed to answer.

"I'm good, you know?, taking day by day... as it comes,

but what about you?, you knew Kasiope from before didn't you?" Her words hung in the air like smoke before dissipating. Avéline looked at her, exhaling gently before speaking. For a second, her calm facade broke down, overrun with grief.

"Yeah, we were on the same cruiser from Vedris, those three weeks onboard, we'd grown close, never expected to make a friend so easily, but now she's gone..." her voice trailed off, as she tried to stop herself from crying.

"They were good times, we were from totally different upbringings, I'd lived in a Etrui commune in the mountains of Venar, with my grandparents while she'd lived in the capital city, we were so different but she treated me well, she was a good friend..." Avéline spoke, the more she spoke the more she was overwhelmed by her emotions, tears began running down her cheek, which she hastily tried to wipe away.

Jysell tried to lighten the mood by stepping forward to give Avéline a hug, feeling her sobbing into her shoulder. Crying out before gradually subsiding. But Jysell couldn't hide her own hurt, her own urge to cry out. She hadn't talked to Kasiope much, but she was a friendly girl, but that night still scarred her.

She had found Kasiope in the shared kitchen that night, staring at her arm, with a knife in her hand, sobbing, crying while mumbling, nervously shaking, so locked into her own state of mind she didn't even notice Jysell's arrival in the kitchen.

"They can't do this, they can't... what do they mean by not suitable" she mumbled before violently slicing open her wrist, even though Jysell had tried to stop her by dashing forward trying to grab the knife from her hand, but failed to get there in time. As she frantically tried to stop the bleeding, she screamed out for help. Within a few moments, others arrived.

Luckily for Kasiope, she survived the suicide attempt; she had been quickly removed from the lineups. Some thought she would return later, but a few days later, her things were gone. She had been dropped and sent into rehabilitation. Jysell couldn't shake the image from her kind. They had offered her counselling, though she wouldn't ever forget the image. It was burned into her mind for all time,

She cast her mind back to the day of the incident. She and Kasiope hadn't spoken since that morning over breakfast, where Kasiope had been called to have a word with the senior instructors. She hadn't seen her in the hall after the health and fitness checks. Some of the girls had called in the weigh in. But they all knew it. If they put on too much weight, to what the label called their 'ideal' at three consecutive checks, they would be released. Jysell should have realised something was wrong, but was focused on her own advancement. Now the bed beside hers was empty. She tried to not think about it. Avéline had been supportive. Her bed was a few across from them.

Out of know where someone started singing, the melody carried through the air, causing some to sit up and see who was singing, others stopped their conversations to glance over, others hook their heads when they saw who it was.

"And then again, long may the pastures grow, singing words that only we know...." She sang, her long dark red hair bouncing on her shoulders as she bounded through the hall, with a smile on her face, weaving her way though the rows of beds, on her way towards them, before slowing down to remove the black hooded jacket she had been wearing. Revealing her toned physique, her tanned and toned midriff exposed to the air. Her white crop top is in stark contrast to her rich, tawny toned skin.

"Afternoon, Jashul, Monel and Sabul. (Afternoon in the three languages she knew the girls spoke in) instructor Caria asked me to have a word with you three, she wants us to work out the harmonies on 'Hurt' by Namis for this evenings performance review... our grouping for the rest of the show rests on this performance" she spoke melodically as she came to a standstill, her eyes sparkled as she smiled,

"It's going to be nice to work with you girls. I'm Tela Nyxcerra, by the way, but I'd prefer Nyx, short and sweet, just like me...." She playfully added.

Jysell looked at her fiercely. She folded her arms as she spoke. She could feel her hearts racing.

"Jashul - afternoon, Nyx, it's been a while" she spoke through clenched teeth, appreciating being greeted in her native tongue but not showing it. They had argued on their first pairing together, back at week-one, now they were on week-three, the crunch week.

They'd both made themselves scarce lately when, in similar circles, they had agreed to a cooling of their conversations for the sake of the program, a drama like that would overshadow any support from viewers they had gained.

"Jysell, I think it's time I owe you a serious apology. We got off to a bad start... which was my fault," Nyxcerra's smile dropped, as she read Jysell's expression.

"You said that I was being stupid for singing it that way, that the style wouldn't work..." Jysell barked back, remembering the heated argument they had a few weeks earlier.

"I know. I'm trying to make amends for that. I got it wrong, especially when you scored higher than me in last week's observations"

She shouldn't have been surprised that this song had been picked, but two groups performing the same song, that had shocked them. It took a moment for Nyxcerra to process what was happening.

She'd been longing for this opportunity to show her range, yet she'd been dreading it too. She glanced over at Jysell, who nodded her head in acceptance, smiling a slightly nervous smile.

"Tonight we will be performing Hurt by Namis, arrangement by Nyxcerra, Jysell, Soka and Avéline," she proudly proclaimed. As she walked over to the piano in the room, Jysell had just sat there ready to play. The lights in the auditorium turned off, plunging everyone into darkness before the spotlights picked out Nyxcerra and Jysell, the others just making it into view. The crowd of the rest of the girls fell into the darkness.

The instructor stood there. The other girls in the room grew quiet as he stood there. He scared them. He looked different; there were circles around his eyes and a pallor to his skin. His expression was emotionless, which caused everyone to be uncomfortable. When he spoke they listened.

"Can we start?" she said simply. Let him give the go ahead; that was all she needed to hear right now.

"Go," he echoed. His eyes searched hers, but she just returned his stare, cool and level.

"Be prepared for a different arrangement," she added, before taking her place, the drones getting into place. She could hear them in the distance but couldn't see them, thankfully.

"There's no excuse..." Nyxcerra sang, her voice rich and full of emotion, with just a hint of chest voice, resonated out into the crowd, taking some by surprise, gasping in amazement. She wasn't just a visual, she could sing equally as good as anyone else here, and now she was proving it.

"The sight of you out with another Whispering in somebody else's ear" Avéline stepped forward out of the darkness and into the light, her voice was different, fragile, every word sang as if her own hearts were breaking, as she stepped back Soka stepped forward.

"The things that happen when you're alone, I didn't think I needed your love...." Soka took a short breath before adding, "anymore...."

"Why did we do this?" They all sang in harmony, except Jysell.

"Making everything complicated, I'm not over you completely. Still got thoughts of you in my mind..." Jysell added, her sultry tone complimented by the arrangement she played on the piano.

"Memories I wish you could erase them, I don't need those thoughts anymore" they all sang Nyxcerra and Jysell taking the lower tones, Soka taking the mids with Avéline taking the fragile top end.

Jysell's style on the piano changed. The melody became powerful, just before all of them sang.

"Used to adore you. Now I see you out with her.

My heart breaks a little deep inside, Yet I don't show it, I got my pride. Every time I close my eyes, when I'm dreaming". All of them stopped allowing Nyxcerra and Jysell to finish it off, the rich and sultry tones of their voices full of sadness and regret.

"Now I wake up, and I'm weeping, I want to cry, kick and scream your name"

A Few Minutes later

All of them stopped again, allowing Nyxcerra and Jysell to finish it off, the rich and sultry tones of their voices still full of sadness, regret and pain

"Now I wake up, and I'm weeping..." before they all came together again to sing the first line

"I want to cry, kick and scream your name" "

Letting their voices carry until slowly quieting to nothing. Nyxcerra bowed almost instantly as she finished, first to the instructors before bowing at the crowd, just as a round of applause started at the back of the crowd. Avéline stood there nervously before bowing, Jysell bowed lowest after standing up from the chair by the piano, before glancing at the instructors who were busy whispering to each other, before of them caught her eye and nodded.

They had done well, she thought, but was it good enough? She had other performances to watch now, nervously awaiting the results at the end.

Jysell lay motionless on her bed, her hands behind her head, staring up at the ceiling, staring into the middle distance. Imagining the stars that would be above the building, knowing they were there, without actually seeing them. Staring into the ceiling comforted her. Sometimes she'd count the panels in the local area of her ceiling, sometimes wondering what was happening on the higher floors, the deals being done behind the scenes. Hoping to one day catch a glimpse of Isool, he was a young Hyalui male, one of the writing staff, she'd seen him in an interview with Mystix, and already had a crush on him, he was quiet and charming, hoping to bump into him at some point, knowing that he lived on one of the higher floor apartments.

Jysell had managed to hold it together during the showcase. Even though she had apologised, she thought that Nyx was arrogant and condescending, but she dealt with it. That night she collapsed into her bed, covering her head with the pillow, and let herself erupt in hot, bitter tears.

They hadn't been eliminated. Four of the girls from the hundred had been told to leave that night. Her hearts raced, partially from excitement and partially from anger. She's been grouped together in a grouping of six to live with and perform with, until she was eliminated or she succeeded. She grouping had surprised her the most. Casting her mind back to the grouping which has been announced openly, to the girls and to the press and billions around the empire.

"And our final group. Hayli Ceres Soobaks, Tela Nyxcerra Jaeihai, Carmiya Tiiona Delste, Sella Jysell Karaay, Shasherm Syala Janrand and Wini Avéline Scori... you have been grouped together as group 12" Shaya announced, with a smile on her face, and with her voice laced with sarcasm.

"And our wildcard group, your mentor until you leave here will be the artist Namis, he picked you as a group..." his voice ringing out in her head, already resigning herself to having to work with Nyxcerra again, but now until their were eliminated or they succeed.

Ceres looked over at Aeryth, noticing she was laughing with Namis, which infuriated her, were they talking about her, had she done something wrong to be put into a group with such a varied tribal history, causing her to walk off in anger, trying to find somewhere to cool down.

CHAPTER 20
"TOOK YOU LONG ENOUGH..."

20 Minutes Later...

Namis opened the door to his office on the floor above, surprised to see Ceres standing there, causing him to freeze, for a second, reading Ceres expression, she was angry, staring at him, pouting her lips, her arms loosely folded, he had to walk past her to get further into his office; Ceres stepped aside and Namis walked past her, shutting the door.

"Took you long enough," she muttered, her arms folded even tighter as she stood there, letting out a vast sigh.

"I had a lot to think about." He added sarcastically, as he wandered over to his desk, slid open a drawn and took out a small and a half empty bottom of whiskey. He then ignored her and poured himself a small drink into the small glass before taking a small sip. The lights in the office were sparse, they plunged most of the office into darkness. He thought she'd finished bitching, But Ceres wasn't finished.

"I assume so. Really, putting me with these amateurs? Is

it to support me or punish me" she bitched back sarcastically. She'd had enough of his attitude.

"Humility Ceres…" he paused, as he slammed his palm against the desk, "and teamwork, skills you severely lack," he remarked with a smile.

"I'm sorry, I lack? Don't you hear yourself? Picked us as a group to teach me a lesson! They better be up to scratch," she added through a clenched jaw.

"You know full well that Nyxcerra has a voice we can work with, and the looks that I'm sure will win votes and viewers, you'd better get with the program, and I can't always protect you.."

Ceres felt oddly pleased to have made him explain himself before what he said sank in.

"Tiiona can deliver bars and verses like no one else in this batch of trainees…" he added, pausing in thought, "Jysell, she's got the potential to be a solo artist, if pushed the right way, Syala, a bit too conservative, stuck with tradition, hopefully you can make her see things from our point of view, otherwise she's gone…" he stopped, glancing at her,

"You have the instant appeal and confidence to be a lead… if your good enough, and that is up for debate, Nyxcerra she's a runner-up for lead in my opinion, Avéline, she's our wildcard, she lacks confidence but has a range larger than all of you, I'll make sure our Producer Vyna and our vocal coaches get the best of them,"

"What about me? Is my progress being scrutinised as much as the others? I want to know…" she pleaded, in an almost childlike fashion. She'd never been left out of the loop before, not with who her father was. He'd always been straightforward with her, but now she was unaware and this frightened her.

"I've not been told anything. Aeryth has been silent on that. You need to speak to her..."

"I don't know anything anymore. I wish I could do more, as I promised your father," Namis replied, with a bitterness that surprised her.

Ceres stood there, fuming, unable to understand why Aeryth hadn't come to see her, to make it clear what was going to happen, she was her aunt after all, her mother was Aeryth's older sister, having married her father forty cycles before.

They were standing beneath an enormous lighting display hanging from the high ceilings on this floor. She stood utterly still. Ceres nervously didn't want to go. She wanted to stay there until this was resolved. She wouldn't be able to sleep until she knew.

Ceres bit her lip nervously, wishing she'd rehearsed some kind of speech, not just lashed out at someone who was trying to protect her on behalf of her father.

"Look, I'm sorry okay... father said it about be easy, but you're saying that this can't be fixed in my favour..." she asked, the tone of her voice annoyed him. She sounded spoilt and entitled.

"I know how I reacted when Shaya announced the groups. I saw you laughing with Aeryth. It was stupid and immature of me to storm off." She replied, realising how childish it was.

"I came her now wanting to tell you I was sorry—but then my emotions got the better of me, just like my father, I get a little hotheaded," She blinked back an onslaught of tears.

"Definitely like your father. I can recollect some very heated arguments over the cycles, and the occasional drunken punch up." Namis replied while he rubbed his jaw jokingly.

"Namis, just promise me this isn't punishment, I can't fail him, not this time, the solo audition failure at the last hurdle was hard for him to take, but even harder for me, you can't imagine the look he gave,"

"It's not a punishment. I think Aeryth wants there to be no question of your abilities. That's all I can think it could be, but that's just my opinion. As I said, you need to speak with Aeryth. I'm sure she'd make some time to see you. Just make it discreet. Don't want to start any rumours of favouritism."

CHAPTER 21
"HENCE I'M NOT THERE WITH YOU..."

6 Cycles Before Debut...

My dear Ceres, it read, she had hand written this, her eyes widened as she began to read, she hadn't called her by that name in cycles; she had been calling her by her formal name, something which caused her hearts to ache every time she called her it.

For an instant she paused as she tried to calm her nerves, a written a letter like this was rare, even more coming from her, it was still perceived as being used for important correspondence, even in this age of holographic recordings, a physical letter carried gravitas, She tilted the beautifully crafted paper, into the light to be able to read it clearly, the dark blue ink shone as the sunlight struck its surface, she carefully examined the strokes of the words, every word elegantly placed on the page.

'I know you will find this letter and the way in which you receive it, totally out of character, especially for me, if your reading this, I'm not doing well, the cancer has returned, hence I'm not there with you on this important day.' Ceres stopped, trying to push back her emotions. She'd wished she had been able to come, but the journey would have risked her health.

I was not always the way you think of me, cold, ruthless, heartless. Names which hurt every time we argued when you were younger, and if I'm being honest, I deserved them, but hopefully this letter will explain why I was that way.' Ceres paused, glanced over at her father who was busy sitting on the chair in the transport waiting patiently, he looked up, feeling Ceres staring at him.

"I can't believe mom wrote this," she whispered before being drawn back to the written page.

'There are things which must be said, on this day, the day I've been getting you ready for your entire life, your first real step into the industry that I love', and at times I feel I make you feel second to, that was my fault. She continued to read, her eyes dancing over the words, quickly leaping from line to line, the urge to complete the letter overcoming her.

'You might be reading this thinking that you aren't ready. We'll I've done as much as I could. Hopefully, by now you have grown into a confident and powerful woman and a reflection of me.'

"Always about you, wasn't it mother" she whispered through clenched teeth, causing her father to lift his head again before realising he wasn't being spoken to.

'I write this letter for your father to give you, on a day of his choosing, for me, it would be a day that you'll do me proud. I love you with all of my hearts, your loving mother.
"

CHAPTER 22
"I MISS YOU SO MUCH..."

3 Weeks Later...

The song faded from the crescendo, fading into Nyxcerra's solo, ebbing and flowing as it built to a slow roll that crashed like a great wave into the souls of those that listened. A silence descended over the eager audience; the ability of the members mesmerised them, much to Aeryth and Leix's delight.

The lyrics grabbing their attention, each of them fixed to their seat as if held captive by the intoxicating somber tone coming from her, a far cry from her usual tones. From the depths of her soul, the lyrics rose and swelled around everyone in the room, before ending with.

"I miss you, so much," her voice cracking at the end, as she struggled to keep herself from crying. This had been the first time she had sung it to an audience that wasn't in the recording studio.

The audience was silent, an eerie silence, the atmosphere was tense. The silence hung in the air like a fog for a while, as if all in attendance could feel her misery. In this moment, her pain was their pain. Reporters and influencers looked at each other, some wiping their own tears away, others wanting to say something, but afraid to be the one to break the mood. No one wanted to be the one who interrupted this outpouring of grief, who would be the first one to clap or ask questions.

Avéline was glad now that Nyxcerra had agreed to the performance. Yes, it was difficult. She struggled to fight back her own tears. But it meant a lot to her. She had spent the night learning it, Ryx and Rhysio had to keep working tirelessly on it for over a week, and now the media and influencers had heard it. They were now officially a group.

She looked over at Tiiona who smiled nervously, gesturing that it went well, as she bowed to the crowd. She had hoped a performance might relieve the pressure they all dealt with, her hearts racing in her chest, everyone was bowing except Nyxcerra.

She stood there, grasping hold of the microphone, her knuckles cracking as she held the stand. She kept looking at the floor, awaiting the response from the crowd of journalists and influencers. It was a gamble singing a song like this, but they had no choice. This was the debut single. It eased some of her fears, but not all. She waited for the hopefully positive response that was ended by the gradual applause, which started softly before filling the entire room. As she lifted her gaze, she saw members of the media clapping enthusiastically while wiping away their own tears.

The applause from the crowd had ended, and Nyxcerra took a small step back, grabbing a silken cloth off of a tray being held by a member of the studio staff, before wiping the tears from her eyes, That was when Avéline realised how hard this had been for Nyxcerra but it was something she had needed to do.

As Nyxcerra exited the broadcast suite, she cast her eyes over the crowd of journalists, busily conferencing with their studios, influencers live broadcast their opinions. She smiled at them and bowed gracefully, replying with thanks and that she hoped she did them proud, but it was all a blur, she didn't care about their opinion, Aeryth's was all that mattered, she caught sight of Avéline's light silvery hair before noticing, the rest of the group.

They were standing on the far side of the bar, Aeryth was leaning back on her elbows with a relaxed smile—a smile that Nyxcerra didn't see very often, a smile she had seen while she talked with Ceres, except now the smile was tinged with sadness.

She realised with this simple gesture that they had done well, Aeryth was searching through the media streams, in between conversations, checking the demographic information and trending topics on a projected display before stopping as Nyxcerra got closer, all of this while Leix was talking animatedly, making little flourishing gestures with his hands, whilst Aeryth smiled, nodding her head before replying

"Well, it was a gamble, but it initially looks like you were right, this response was what our girls demographic wants, it's only been 30 minutes, but we are trending across seventy-five percent of the usual platforms, the girls are favourable across the genders, it's going to be days until we know the true effect." Aeryth replied as she fixed her low-cut blouse, which skimmed shockingly low over her cleavage. She'd kicked one foot behind the other and laughed.

"It was worth the gamble..." causing the girls to nervously smile. Before they realised Nyxcerra was there,

Aeryth looked over, straightened herself up and embraced her,

"She would have been so proud of you, I'm so proud of you..." she whispered, causing Nyxcerra's bottom lip to tremble.

"I'm proud of you all. You've done yourselves proud, you've done me proud, the company proud, but most of all you've done our beloved Ceres proud..,"

It might be been foolish and juvenile, but Avéline wasn't paying attention, just smiling. She couldn't help instinctively taking her eyes off of Ryx, he extruded confidence, in a way she wished she could, especially in her conversations with Aeryth and the other executives.

Especially Aeryth, given what she now knew about her time in the industry and travels with Ceres' father cycles earlier. She felt herself drawn to him in every way. He made her feel completely at ease. He made her feel more comfortable that Vyna had made her feel.

He comforted her when she needed it, encouraged her to sing the more troublesome parts, even though she doubted herself.

He never did. She still resented Vyna their first instructor for getting himself dismissed, her thoughts gradually returned to Ryx, how he made her feel, she smiled at him, hoping he would notice her in the way she wanted, she looked at him again, this time catching his gaze at her, smiling.

CHAPTER 23
"THIS WAY GIRLS"

A Month Later...

Padros Bulso had carefully spent the early morning carefully herding the girls into the perfect place for a range of holos to be taken. He enjoyed putting them into the strangest locations, at points throughout the canyon. These places would get him the best shots. He knew it would be difficult but worth it. She glanced at some of the shots already taken on a small display, smiling while he swiped through them.

He had scouted the location the day before while the girls were on an off day, marking its co-ordinates on his map, knowing exactly what shots he was looking for at each of the locations. They all knew the brief, not just photos for fans, but a range of images for 'key marketing partners' Nyxcerra remembered Leix telling them.

These partners would get them everywhere, from bill-boards to adverts on the social platforms, Nyxcerra was giddy, knowing that one would grace the pages of 'Vocal', the leading music publication across the empire, still being printed traditionally, adored by fans and collectors.

She knew they needed enough images and holos for a range of different media outlets across the empire. Nyxcerra sighed as she stood partially shaded enjoying a brief cooling breeze which whistled through the canyon, briefly shivering as the breeze traveled through the thin fabric of her long length silken dress. It's dark turquoise surface detailed with darker turquoise flowers.

The dress fitted loosely in places and hanged perfectly in others, fitted to emphasise her hips and breasts.

"Finally, a breeze..." she murmured, as she posed while he took his shots, carefully following his instructions, by know she had gotten used to the poses he enjoyed her making, so she began reeling off the poses, with Padros snapping the holos in rapid succession.

She wanted to get this over and done with. Especially here. She knew they had to be quick. The morning sun was still rising and within a few hours, the heat would be an unbearable 135 degrees. She could feel her skin drying out already. She glanced over, watching the other girls mocking her poses, trying not to laugh herself. She knew she looked stupid, almost robot like, moving from pose to pose, but she wanted to get it over and done with.

It wasn't the best she could stand the heat, but it was a dry heat, and that she despised. Remembering the cool sea breeze all year round back home on Corellia.

The spiral walls of the canyon gave the holographer the perfect place to take a barrage of holos, before clambering away onto a higher ledge, looking down. Every few moments, breaking the serene silence of the canyon by his incessant shouting.

"This way girls", much to the girl's chagrin. He clambered his way to the ledges closer to the top of the narrow canyon, had enough of an angle to block out a huge amount of the sun. Before calling down to the girls, allowing him to focus on luring the girls into shots where they were partially lit, but also equally shrouded in darkness. These shots took a while, and an hour later they were still having the shots taken, and it was getting noticeably warmer. They struggled not to sweat in the heat, the drones with cooling fans only making it slightly bearable.

A stone path made its way through the twisting canyon. Avéline sighed after they were finished with her closeup. 'How many more of these do they want' she whispered to herself. Knowing that at some point they would want all the girls together to get an artistic group shot, he had mentioned a perfect clearing at the entrance to the canyon.

Nyxcerra couldn't wait to get this finished with, the sole purpose of this three-day excursion into the Desert of Myria on Coria III was to get shots, from the dunes of the Palatina desert, which was a nightmare because of the unexpected onset of a sandstorm, which had destroyed a few of the drones being used.

Nyxcerra enjoyed the shots of the girls in white taken to the old ruins at Lockestall and Balronto. It was eerily quiet there, but for once, she found peace. Her mind remembering just sitting on the dark red sand of the Locke desert, looking into the night sky.

She was intrigued by how the ancient city of Lockestall had been reclaimed by the desert since its abandonment thousands of cycles before. She began laughing to herself, thinking about the rides on the backs of Kaminan camels.

"Come on Nyx, can you stop with the laughing, it

wasn't that funny," Tiiona exclaimed as she saw Nyxcerra glancing at her and laughing to herself.

Nyxcerra's infectious laugh got Jysell and Syala giggling, which made Tiiona frown, trying to hide her own want to smile.

"Girls…" Padros tried to calm the girls down, sighing to himself, 'typical….' he mouthed.

"You gotta admit it Tii, it was funny, never realised you were afraid of animals…" Avéline joked.

"I'm not afraid of them, honest, they just don't like me…" Tiiona replied before cracking a smile, trying not to laugh herself. The holographer, realising they were happy, started taking shots, catching their spontaneity in their actions.

Nyxcerra's laughing ended at last. She needed this release. The heat in the canyon started to increase, hoping these next few photos were the end of it.

"Jysell, Syala, just got to get one more shot of you then we'll move on, for this part…" he called out, Avéline signed, she was glad, but what more did he want, they had been out for the past four hours,

"Padros?, are we any closer to the end of this? It's hotter than Ataaione out here, and they have two suns…" Syala exclaimed, as she took off the silken shawl covering her. She hated the dress she was wearing, too revealing for her taste. She sighed.

"Let's get this over and done with" she scolded, everyone knowing her distaste for her outfit.

CHAPTER 24
"I MISS HER TOO YOU KNOW..."

7 Months Later...

The early morning sun forced its way through the clouds in streams, cascading over the mountains, breaking up the darkness which had plagued that morning. The rains had finally died down as the transport touched down. The landing area was empty. No one was here, not this time of day, especially in the colder months.

The sun appearing just as the girls readied themselves before getting out of the transport. Nyxcerra stepped off the transport first, looking up at the clearing sky.

"Thanks Ceres.." she mouthed, hoping in some way that she'd asked for the rains from the stop, from her place in the afterlife. The cold breeze whistled though, chilling her quickly causing her to gasp as she tried to pull her navy coat tighter around her shoulders as she stepped down from the transport, followed by Avéline, who was already wrapped up warm, her silvery grey hair almost all covered by a maroon beret, her eyes sparkled in the morning sun.

"Come on Tii, it's not that cold..." she mocked as she gestured for Tiiona to follow her. Tiiona pulled the collars of her black jacket up, before hastily wrapping a scarf haphazardly around her neck and covering her mouth.

"Really Avé, it's freezing..., it's the middle of winter..." she wished it was somewhere between this temperature and the temperature from seven months before during the deserts on Coria III. She liked stability, the middle ground. She sighed, half smothered by the scarf. As she stepped out, Nyxcerra began the walk up to the Impiri Cemetery, ignoring the lone drone that had followed them from the capital. She knew who it was. Aeryth had said she'd keep an eye on them, especially today. She told them she wouldn't be able to attend herself, that something personal kept her away, hoping that they believed her, knowing she wouldn't be able to cope.

The drone detected her movements and began to float alongside her, before pulling back, as if it had understood her need to be alone.

Nyxcerra needed the walk right now, to be alone, to clear her own thoughts. She hadn't expected the rest of the girls to want to come. She had to, especially today. She'd woken up this morning feeling lost and hollow, her pillow soaked with tears, the same as most nights. No matter how hard she worked at it during the day, every night she would break down and cry.

The rest had seemed to forget that this day was coming, or had just hoped that she wouldn't remember. How could she forget this cycle? It was so different to the last? She smiled as she thought about the surprise, the lying about forgetting. It was childish, but the look on her face was priceless. Nyxcerra longed to see that face, just one more time, before remembering the cold harsh truth all over again. She'd never see it again, not really.

She felt isolated and lonely, and worst of all, she couldn't even talk to anyone about it. She'd thought briefly about talking about it with Avéline , but she'd ask her to see Dr Anwat again. Just thinking about that made her hearts race. She'd seen him that one time and refused to see him again.

He had put her through the darkest parts of her psyche. She couldn't trust him, he knew too much. She worried if he enjoyed knowing more than he let on. She wanted to discuss it with anyone, any one of the girls. But right now it was till too raw for Nyxcerra to discuss it with anyone.

On a day like today, she would have turned to Ceres, she thought. She'd always find a way to bring her out of herself, from thinking the worst. She missed that positivity endlessly.

As she walked slowly, Avéline caught up to her, putting her arm through hers and pulling her close.

"I miss her as well, you know..." she whispered, resting her head on Nyxcerra's arm.

"I didn't think you would want to do this alone, that's why..." she stumbled over her words, trying to not make excuses.

"Why you all came..." Nyxcerra added, without looking down at her, but gently placed her gloved hand over Avéline's.

"I'm not sure I could have made it even this far..." Nyxcerra remarked, as the sound of approaching footsteps from the rear as Tiiona, Syala and Jysell hastily walked up behind them.

"Thanks, for coming with me today" "

"You know why we've ended up here, at the Kayvul - 'Impiri cemetery, on a day like today."

"You know if she'd been here, and it was one of us that had... you know." She smiled as she looked at all of them. They were dressed well. They owed Ceres that, to make an effort for her, especially on her birthday.

"You know, even with this weather, she'd be wearing her heaviest coat, leather trousers and knee-high boots—you remember the brown ones that she loved."

They passed the main front gates. A drone hastily made its way out from a small shielded area, causing them to stop in the tracks, just as a hologram was projected onto the area directly in front of them. It was an elderly gentleman, well dressed, long gone was any remnants of his hair colour, his white hair glistening in the sunlight.

"What brings you.." it paused

"Lovely ladies here today?, to see one of our obelisks of mourning, which dasho- tribe are we requiring to see today..." he spoke, awaiting a response.

"He looks so real..." Tiiona whispered to Jysell, over the sound of the wind howling past her.

"Valari Dasho, Soobaks, Hayli Ceres..." Nyxcerra broke the silence.

"Valari dasho, down the winding path, take first left, Soobaks family obelisk, row 26, number 175." The hologram replied after looking lost in thought for a few moments.

"Thanks, I think I can remember the way..." she bowed instinctively to the hologram, before it disappeared and the drone flew off.

"I know the way..." Nyxcerra gestured for the others to follow as she walked arm in arm with Avéline.

They carefully made their way down the gravel path

until she found the Valari section, looking out towards the sculpted and managed gardens of the cemetery. There were innumerable obelisks as far as you could see.

Nyxcerra hadn't been back here in the months since her ashes were interred here. After the funeral service , the privately held cremation, Ceres' father had asked her to join him on that day.

She remembered standing in the rain and wind, watching the priestess lower the crystallised cube that had become of her remains into a box below the family's obelisk.

She picked at the obelisk. A leaf had stuck itself to the surface. It came off easily as she cast it to the floor. The surface was smooth on three sides, but on the nearest facing side it was inscribed in a language she could barely comprehend.

"Here lies the honoured remains of the Soobaks family, may their remains lay here as a reminder to their family and friends that nothing is eternal, except the everlasting soul, which shall be reborn in the fires lit by the goddesses to be reborn a new." Nyxcerra whispered as she read the inscription.

Tears welled in Nyxcerra's eyes as she stood there, wishing more than anything that she could tell her things, that she missed her, that she couldn't go on without her.

She felt stupid. She could talk, she wouldn't listen, maybe she would, but inside she believed Ceres would hear her from the afterlife, or from the life she now lived reborn into another body. She thought. There was no one around to hear. The media weren't allowed. At least here she could say what she wanted, within reason. She shook out her scarf, spread it over the cut grass, then sat down and cleared her throat. She felt a little foolish,

"Hey Ceres. It's me, Nyx." She imagined her friend sitting there, her flecked amber eyes wide with amusement. "We've come to see you, all of us. I wanted to tell you a few things. But you know them already, can't say them anyway..." she whispered as she noticed the other girls looking.

"I miss you, you must know that. I miss that smile. I just wish you were here to tell me what to do, how to do this..." she gestured at the other girls.

"I'm still working on getting us that award you know, the one you wanted for u...." Nyxcerra added, trying to keep her emotions in check

"How we can..." she stopped as Jysell placed her hand on her shoulder.

"She'll guide you, you know that, from the fire, she'll make sure we'll be fine. That's what I believe, anyway."

CHAPTER 25
"YOU REMEMBER THE TIME SHE...."

A Few Days Later...

Nyxcerra stopped mid laugh with Jysell and sighed.

"You know she would have been okay with all this, don't you...?" Jysell added as Tiiona carefully passed her a Vebiarula fruit, which she carefully glanced at, checking its smooth purple and orange skin for blemishes before slicing it finely with a knife, revealing its dark orange interior being careful to cut around its seed.

"Nyx, you...", she was cut off by Nyxcerra's reply, "Yeah, I know she would have, it's just..." she stopped as she laughed to herself slightly, before realising they were staring at her.

"Every time I think about her, it's difficult, every time we do something, it's something she would have told me about in our private late night chats..." she looked up while slicing Kreon fruit, pausing for a second to savour its sweet and floral scent,

"I, we just don't want you to be..., you know.." as she struggled to contain her own emotions.

"I know, and thank you. It will just take time. I'm getting there slowly..."

Jysell laughed as she picked a few Emio dates from a packet and slowly cut out the seed from its sugary exterior, as she remembered a conversation cycles past.

"You remember the time she made us think of how we would have answered questions from Zhalba Muqadam, on his talk show...?" Jysell laughed as she recalled the memory.

"Yeah, it's just an eerie feeling that he's interviewing us tomorrow, and she's not here for it..., she would have gotten such a buzz" Nyxcerra laughed, a smile crept onto her face, her eyes widened, for once she was happy and Jysell knew it, lifting the mood in the room.

"She'd have us rehearsing the answers all night..." she laughed as she picked up an aarhoo fruit and sliced it quickly, without even taking her eyes off Nyxcerra. This caused Nyxcerra to laugh. Even more though she wanted to cry, the memories still hurt to be remembered.

"Until sunrise..., then I'd get more of it before she would finally fall asleep" The laughing was interrupted by Avéline walking into the kitchen carrying a basket of aish bread she had ordered, stopping as she got in, realising what was going on, they had talked about this the night before, while Nyxcerra was asleep, and immediately fell into the practiced rhythm.

"Hey Nyx, can you help me with this?, think they sent over a few too many loaves. I think the guy who runs the bakery has a thing for you, he said the hulwayat one is espe-cially for you." As she picked it out from the basket and threw it underarm towards her, Nyxcerra putting down the knife carefully and catching it, breathing in slowly. It was sweet smelling and still arm.

"I mean, even without that, I can't eat that much aish, not if I'm to keep to this weight." Avéline mocked, Even though she loved aish bread, and could have easily eaten another loaf, her stomach never truly felt full, not when she had to keep to her ideal weight. Nyxcerra chuckled to herself.

"Ave? Really, you have nothing to worry about, I gotta be careful with my s-line, gotta keep this body in check" she laughed as she looked at Avéline's petite frame, her delicate curves, her elegant neckline, leading to her even narrower waist, a perfect inverted triangle, a figure she envied, she was a typical s-line, curvy in all the right places, but would quickly gain weight if she didn't look after herself.

"And what do you mean? Khabaz is just being nice..."

"Oh, Khabaz is his name, is it? Think we have the beginning of a beautiful..." she stopped as Nyxcerra blushed,

"Oh, definitely got a thing for him. Someone check her scales??" She laughed, trying to glimpse the scales as she walked behind her carrying the still warm bread to the kitchen table, its smell wafting through the room.

Syala walked in, carrying a cube shaped cargo container,

"Nyx, someone just dropped this off for you. All they said was its an urgent priority delivery from Corellia ". Nyxcerra looked at the container before rushing over to take it from her. It was heavier than she expected, before she carefully placed it on a chair.

Nyxcerra opened the container cautiously. What had her parents sent her? She thought,

"The shipping must have cost a fortune, all the way from Corellia" Avéline remarked, gasping at the sight of the senders address, as she opened the clasp after placing her finger on the scanner, the container processed for a moment, before sending a beam of blue light which scanned Nyxcerra before it hissed, causing Avéline to be startled before laughing at herself.

"What, I just didn't expect it...", Tiiona looking at her, mimicking her startled expression, before jokingly shaking her head.

"Come on Ave, really..."

"7 days express courier, premium jump gate priority, hand couriered from Corellia to here" Nyxcerra read off the docket attached to the container, realising it normally took 3 months for a one-way trip from the outer worlds like Corellia to the core worlds. "Sending this would have cost thousands of credits, and at least different 30 jumps. Why would they have sent this?" She puzzled before it hit her, as she noticed the family crest sealing the box. The realisation hit her. She collapsed to her knees and immediately started to cry, causing Jysell and Avéline to rush over to her, trying to comfort her.

"What's the matter Nyx, what's happened..." Avéline spoke calmly, trying to coax an answer from Nyxcerra who lemon mumbling, "Can't be, can't be, she never said, why hadn't they, it's too soon..."

Jysell crouched down in front of her, and stared straight at her, "Come on Nyx, what's happen, what's too soon...?"

"My seinothoir - grandfather, he.. he's dead..."

CHAPTER 26
"SAY OUR GOODBYES..."

"These were to be sent in case of his death and father's assent within my tribe," she looked at Avéline, who was standing still, not knowing what to say.

"I thought you said everything was okay at home?" Avéline added, trying to find something to say. Feeling like anything she said wasn't enough.

"Yeah, mom said seinothoir - grandfather was close to the end. He'd been suffering from seanaois syndrome, as can be expected. He's approaching 397 cycles." She paused, remembering the last time she saw him.

"Saw him via holo last month, say our goodbyes..." she'd just been pushing the thoughts of its inevitably out of her daily thoughts.

"It was good this time. He still remembered who I was, which made it all the more... " she stopped, trying not to cry.

"Just didn't expect it so soon. He'd been having a good spell recently..."

As she slowly lifted a few things out of the box, one

thing caught her eye, lifting out the separator placing it to the side as she revealed a folded jacket made of dark turquoise velvet, its surface intricately detailed with the golden embroidery, its weight surprising her as she slowly lifted it out. The other girls gasped as they saw it.

"In the goddess's name, Nyx, it's beautiful…" Avéline added. On top of it was a necklace encrusted with gemstones. They hadn't seen anything like this before. Nyxcerra looked at them, then down at her own wrist, for the first time in cycles she felt drawn to look at her bond, the tattoo that most Impiri had, hers was a brilliant turquoise, it stood out against her skin,

"Didn't think this would happen so soon, thought it was always cycles off, I'd be retired from the industry by then…, well… nothings been as I had planned it…" she painfully mocked.

"So what's the precedent with something like this?, Tiiona enquired,

"Do we know have to address you as Lady..?" She playfully mocked bowing gracefully before giving a devilish smile, knowing exactly, she knew her own place in her tribe, she was '80 from the top' she remembered her mother saying once when she was young.

"Well, technically yes, it's complicated, but Yes…" she joked, not wanting to explain the exact nature of her lineage, all they knew was that she was close to the top of her tribe. Now, after his death, she was third in line. Her Great Uncle was Lord Flearann ua n-Dúnlaing Jaeihai, the new head of her tribe. A fact she tried to keep hidden.

27 minutes later…

Nyxcerra stopped mid laugh with Jysell and sighed.

"You know it's not fair that we're sitting here eating dinner, Syala's not broken fast yet,..." looking over at the clock having in the kitchen.

"Sy, isn't it time..." Nyxcerra called out down the hallway,

"Yeah, I'll be out in a minute" Syala called out as she sat legs folded in the middle of a dark green embroidered mat on the middle of the floor in her shared bedroom. In front of her a small candle sat in a bowel of water, the candle lit and gently flickering.

She sat motionless, hands placed on each knee, her eyes closed, her breathing shallow, her head covered in a white silk shawl.

"Everything is nothing and nothing is everything, maybe I live truthfully through their guidance..." she whispered before opening her eyes, as she opened her eyes she carefully took the shawl off of her head, spending a moment folding it neatly before placing it into a small wooden box on her left side, before carefully leaning forwards to blow out the candle, which gave off a tiny amount of smoke as it was extinguished. Her legs aches after prayer, but that was normal. She carefully licked her lips, her throat dry. She'd been awake since before sunrise and had eaten breakfast, as was customary. Now the sun had gone down and now she could eat.

After putting things away, she walked out into the kitchen, seeing the girls were still there talking, but had set out a plate for her, an energy and protein packed dinner. She smiled as she noticed.

"You didn't have to girls, I could have got it ready"

"But then it wouldn't have been fair. You've been

fasting all day. At least we could do would be to help you get ready for food after a busy day." Jysell added as Tiiona carefully passed her a Vebiarula fruit, which she carefully glanced at, checking its smooth purple and orange skin for blemishes before slicing it finely with a knife, revealing its dark orange interior being careful to cut around its seed.

"Nyx, you...", she was cut off by Nyxcerra's reply, "Yeah, I know she would have, it's just..." she stopped as she laughed to herself slightly, before realising they were staring at her.

"And we got you some fresh Kobali nuts, for breaking the fast"

An hour later...

Nyxcerra stepped out from the bathroom, her hair almost completely dry, except for the ends of her hair. She looked at herself in the mirror; it was the dress she'd been sent by her mother, worried about if she'd sent the right size. It had been over a year since she'd seen her in real life; The dress covered her shoulders halfway and flowed down into a stylish sweetheart neckline. Something her mother had always told her fitted her frame, and as she stared at him, she smiled. It was a close fit which put the focus on her figure, but in a graceful manner.

Her arms were only covered at her shoulders. Which not only helped accentuate her gorgeous skin, it also kept the focus on other parts of the dress. The dress reached to just below her knees, something she never expected. She was always the fan of showing a bit more, but in this instance, she didn't care,

She barged her way through the bustling crowd, her jacket collars up. She kept her head down. She needed to get out of the apartment. The shipment from home brought back too many memories, and not the kind she wanted to remember. she shock of the news of her grandfather's death still ran through her mind.

She nervously scanned the street, but not trying to catch the eye of anyone in particular, wanting to ground herself in the environment. She stood in the middle of the promenade, listening to the sounds of the streets, savouring the smells, the faint sweet aroma of Kalita caught her attention, the smoke trailing its way down the promenade, casting her mind back to the times she collected Kalita tea from a small boutique back home on Corellia in an Impiri district.

The Impiri district here felt the same, various languages, the mixture of all the tribes. She needed to get to the temple. She knew it was around her somewhere; she remembered taking a detour on the way home on one of her free days, but it was different now, she stood there glancing around, trying to soak in the atmosphere of the place, these were similar to the streets where she grew up, where she was happy, long before becoming a trainee, before the rules, when she became of age, a simpler time., a time when she was free to be who she wanted to be, no pressure.

A strange sensation struck at the depth of her stomach, causing her to pause her slow, meandering walk. She actually missed home. She had left home to get away from the pressures of her family, only to miss the familiarity of her own people.

For the first time in over six cycles she wanted, no needed to be home, she loved the hustle and bustle, remembering the times she walked through the streets back home as a young girl, by herself, longing to want to do that again. The sights, the smells, bittersweet memories.

The family's summer apartments were only a few streets away from the marketplace. She remembered fondly the summers spent amongst her people. The stories she heard from members of the community, everyone knew her grandfather. She missed him dearly; he had always told her not to be afraid of what other people think, as long as you were being true to yourself and your people. Even on a late night like tonight the streets were packed, some getting on with their business, others she noticed, her own people, the Artreia in a show of respect, their bond shown proudly, dressed in their finest attire, showing their respects to her grandfather. Nyxcerra staggered forward, her emotions getting the best of her. Even this far from her home planet of Corellia, Artreia everywhere was still in a state of mourning.

"Bandiúc, Bandiúc - my lady, my lady," a voice called out, ignored by many on the street. A few stopped, looked around before ignoring it and continuing what they were doing. The occasional member of her own tribe stopped, looked around, before catching sight of her, and graciously lowered their gaze, they knew why she was there, it was the last day of Kalgan Shiv- the mourning, a 7-day period after the death of a family member when a visit to the temple was customary, especially on the last night.

Nyxcerra wondered who had called out her name, the voice familiar but not enough that she instantly knew who it was, before seeing Khabaz the baker making his way urgently towards her. He was tall, broad shouldered, carrying himself well, Nyxcerra looked at him, she'd never seen him in civilian clothing, he was dressed in a dark blue suit, detailed with beautiful turquoise and black embroidery, she'd always seen him dressed in his baking attire, his sleeves were now rolled up.

"My Lady...! You shouldn't be out here, not with the rest of us common folk..." he proclaimed, gesturing for her to follow him.

"Let me take you back home ..." he pleaded, noticing a crowd gathering, realising who she was.

"Not to that place. I just wanted to get out, to be here, with our people. The familiarity will do me good" she insisted, wanting to keep moving, to get to the temple through the back alleys.

"Young miss Avéline was worried about you, she was frantic, she'd seen you sneaking out, so she let me know, I don't know how you can stand such..." he remarked, stopping as he saw her expression change, her eyebrows furrowed, her lips pursed. She staggered forward.

"I'd mind my manners. I won't take you..." Nyxcerra replied, her voice losing all its playfulness.

"I mean no disrespect, all I meant was, how you can deal with such over protection, but I know why you're here..." he added, trying to reassure her.

"Kalgan Tir, - 'mournings end', he paused, as she placed her hand on his chest,

"You, you knew, I never suspected..." she stuttered, taken back by his use of Shabik.

"That I was kaol- kin" she looked down at his wrist, his turquoise bond proudly on show, the design basic, from a middle status house.

She grasped his hand, turning over his wrist to look at the design on his forearm, inquisitive about his status.

"Fifth, sixth, no no... Seventh son, house of báicéir" she murmured as she studied the intricate details of its design which made its way up his forearm, counting the intricate circles hidden within the design.

"Yes, there are seven of us..." he paused,

"I was about to make my own way to the temple, to pay my respects. I would be honoured..."

"No, no Khabaz, it's me who would be honoured to have your company at this time... as I pay my own respects."

CHAPTER 27
"FIND THE REAL ME"

A Few Months Later...

Nyxcerra carefully navigated her way through the bustling crowd dancing at the club, being careful not to fall over, she'd been drinking a little as her balance wasn't the best in the six-inch heels that she was wearing., she loved how she looked in them, but even for her they were high, the red leather straps on them wrapped their way mid way up her calves.

It was late, or was that early? She thought. All Nyxcerra knew was that it was past 4am, and the club was still packed, but she knew that was expected, especially now, this impromptu party had caught them all by surprise, this floor was the only social place to relax in the entire BYL entertainment building. They had worked hard and any chance for a party she would have normally enjoyed it; it was where everyone expected her to be, even though she didn't feel like it.

Ornate water features cascaded water delicately down

the back wall of the bar. The bar was still packed, even at this hour. Usually this place was quiet, a hub of label staff and trainees, relaxing it was rare that as a trainee you were allowed out of the building, unless on assignment., the entire process carefully protected.

Even now as a signed artist Nyxcerra felt like she had to stay inside the confines of the building, occasionally before now making trips out, but never straying too far from the building and usually with a security escort, but now it was for her own safety, no more unsupervised trips out, unless in disguise, a concept she enjoyed, having occasionally snuck out to some of the clubs, while in disguise, having learnt a lot from the make-up artists over the cycles. She had enjoyed changing her hair colour, sometimes on a weekly basis, changing her voice was easy, she just pretended to be Avéline, her accent was easy to do, Jysell's was more diffi-cult, her melodic voice, was the most difficult for any of the other girls to do.

The bass of the music playing thumped in her chest as she passed the DJ booth at the middle of the club, enjoying the feeling it gave her, her scales vibrated if the pitch was correct, causing her immense pleasure, any other time she could have sat there, somewhere off in the back in private and allow the vibrations to bring her to orgasm, which she thought was hilarious to have an orgasm by music. She thought about a time she had spoken to many producers about having a progressively stronger vibration in a song, which would lead to any Impiri female having an orgasm while listening to the track, an idea shot down my management instantly, much to her disappointment. But today, nothing made her really happy. She felt lost and in need of a way to find herself. But she had an image to maintain, so she stayed out, flittering between everyone like a butterfly in the summer.

Looking around, she noticed every low-lying sofa was full, some sat pitched on the end of sofas, while some even knelt on the floor. Everyone was here, or on the floor below. Recent trainees were even here, much to her surprise.

She could only remember once when she was a trainee being allowed to attend a party thrown for the entire company, trainees usually had their own party, a chance to relax, there was usually at least a hundred trainees from across the empire in the building at any one time.

It had quietened down a little since the peak of the party; some of the senior department heads had left but there were individuals from all departments, from security to production, to public relations and legal, a once in decade chance to enjoy the recent success of the business as a whole.

"I mean to get an Album of a year nomination for a first album..it's... it's unheard of" Nyxcerra overheard Leix as he was still coming to terms with it, trying to figure out how to make the most of it, while talking to anyone who would listen to him. Even now he wasn't enjoying himself socially. He was socially awkward, preferring to work than have fun, something the girls constantly made fun of.

Nyxcerra paused for a second noticing Zoria in promotions was inebriated, which was easy to see on a Uvian from the flush yellow hues on her light green skin, while awkwardly flirting with Mabuus from security, who was trying to do his job, while trying to not be distracted. Zoria was usually the reserved, quiet type, but tonight she was sexily dressed, and flirtatious, but with only eyes for Mabuus.

He tried to ignore her but his skin blushed a dark blue

on his neck, in stark contrast to the light blue of his skin, a typical reaction for a Kasinite. He tried hastily but failed to hide it. She smiled for a moment, a beautiful fleeting sense of happiness for someone, when her own emotions were suppressed before her own thoughts got the better of her.

Her hearts raced as she started to feel overwhelmed by her emotions. She had to get somewhere away from this crowd. She hated being fake. She wanted to stop her fake smile and dispense with the fake pleasantries, and be honest with someone, wishing Ceres was there, she would have always listened. She carefully walked through the crowd. She kept a fixed smile on her face. No one could know how she was feeling. She wanted to keep her head down. She needed to get out of here, looking for a place to be herself.

The notification of the award brought back too many memories and not the kind she wanted to remember. Never in her wildest dreams did she expect it. Break through artist award with their first release rang out in her head.

She nervously scanned the club, smiling and acknowledging well wishers, stopping occasionally to hug someone, and have a holographic photo taken, giving her now famous perfect smile, but not trying to catch the eye of anyone in particular, wanting to get out of this environment, to somewhere where she could be herself, her true self.

For a moment she stood in the middle of the club, listening to the sounds of the music playing, savouring the smells, the faint sweet aroma of Kalita caught her attention, the smoke trailing its way through the club, a dose of Kalita would have at least calmed her. It would have helped her to cast her mind back to the times she spent with Ceres, wishing for any moment with her, even the nights they spent talking about anything, nothing important just talking about things that excited them, frightened them or just simply confused them, it would have cheered her up.

Nyxcerra recalled for an instant the time she explained how she had been brought up, the pursuit of life experience through pleasure and enjoyable acts, not focusing on the negative side of life and existence, it had taken a while but she understood it eventually, this memory caused her to smile.

The music, the sound of various languages, pulled her back into real life; the lack of familiarity with the languages made her feel isolated, listening out, hoping for the sound of her people, someone to listen to her, without having to translate it first, they would understand the loss she felt, they'd understand how to see the positive in any situation, because right now she couldn't see a way past it.

It all become too much, she hastily made her way to the farthest quietest part of the club, off towards the west-facing windows, as she hastily moved Jysell spotted her, the look on Nyxcerra's face caused her to stand up, excuse herself politely from the conversation she was in with Soka, and follow Nyxcerra.

"Just give me 10 minutes. She's having a moment; I'll just check in on her" Jysell replied when Soka asked if everything was okay, she couldn't lose track of where Nyxcerra was, but within a second she had lost her, nervously she began searching, occasionally stopping to ask someone if they had seen her, making the excuse that she needed to discuss something important with her, or that Aeryth wanted to see her.

By the time she found Nyxcerra, she was sitting on a low slung chair, which she had turned towards the window, looking out at the city and neon lights of the district.

"Nyxcerra..." Jysell called out as she got closer, but wasn't acknowledged, she was lost in her own thoughts.

"Nyx..." she called out as she startled her as she placed her hand on her shoulder.

"What's wrong..." Jysell asked, after she saw the expression on Nyxcerra's face.

"Really, I want to be completely honest with you..." she stopped, finally being able to say to someone how she was feeling. Her shoulders dropped and her false smile ebbed away, being instantly replaced by a look of despair and longing.

"It's all just too much right now. I just need some time away to find myself, still adjusting to being without Ceres..." she sighed openly, trying to push her emotions back as they bubbled up to the surface.

"To go out there..." as she began to stare out through the window, the rain cascading down the window as she lost her train of thought, looking at the neon lights of the city below.

"Out there...? Outside the building, on tour?" Jysell added in response, but not getting a response.

"Where...?" Jysell enquired, not catching Nyx's glance outside.

"Out there, in the city. You know, go and get lost out there, especially now, at night...just look at those lights." She stopped, as a tear slowly ran down her cheek, not caring that it left a trail of mascara, she was too busy remembering what she had discussed with Ceres one night, their dreams to make it, then at a time of their own choosing to spend time together, just them. To leave everything and disappear together.

To make a go of it, to have enough credits to do what

they wanted without the overwhelming pressures of the industry.

"I just want to get lost in the neon nights. Maybe find the real me, if she still exists or maybe even a new me..." her voice trailed off.

"But that's never going to happen, is it..."

"So I'm going to have to try to be the me that they want me to be, then one day... I'll go... just not yet..." she added, as she resigned herself to her current predicament. "Let's see how the tour goes next month, it might change your mind, we all know your a different person when you perform, you love that crowd the buzz that's they give you.." Jysell suggested as she looked out of the window with Nyxcerra.

There was silence. Nyxcerra just looked out the window, watching the rain trickling down the window, distorting her view of the district below, but the neon lights captured her gaze. She sighed a deep sigh, not sure of what to say to Jysell.

"Maybe I'll take it day by day, that's how she would have taken it" "

"I miss that single-minded focus. She knew what she wanted for us and for herself, but I don't."

"But Nyx, you do, we've only achieved this because of...." Jysell whispered.

"Because I'm doing what I think she would have done, but I'm quickly running out of idea...." she snapped,

"That's why I need to find myself, to find out what I want from this. I can't keep living in her shadow, you know? Nyxcerra replied, snapping at Jysell.

Without taking her gaze from the window, she spoke.

"I'm sorry Jys, I didn't mean to snap, it's just, I don't know who I really am," Nyxcerra spoke, a solitary tear running down her cheek. Jysell placed her hand on her back and rubbed it.

"It's fine. I know you are under a lot of pressure. "Jysell trying to reassure her, not sure if it was working.

"It doesn't excuse it, I'm being pulled in so many ways these days, especially with tribal commitments, I'm afraid it will take me away from what I truly love, which is us, this fucked up industry, I mean, I wish I could tell you what I know, the things that go on behind the doors of this building would shock you, they shocked me and you know how liberal I am," Nyxcerra added, as she looked out into the distance.

CHAPTER 28
"AND IF HE DOESN'T LIKE IT"

8 Months Later...

The Aerrea girls walked throughout the entrance of the small arena, it was smaller than they expected, even though it could hold 90,000 in attendance, the stadium carved into the landscape, deep inside to the surface, even with this they could still hear the chanting of the fans, it was almost deafening

They all had an aura of wealth and privilege, carrying themselves well, their assigned tour assistants carrying their drinks while hastily walking beside them, the assistants looking worn out and frantically trying to keep up.

"Tell him he's going to love the show, especially 'boudoir' "Nyxcerra hastily spoke to her assistant, who took down the message,

"and if he doesn't like it, and give a less than stellar review, tell him I'll pull the interview for next month..." she added, her voice commanding yet hollow, she was tired, the past six months of nearly back-to-back concerts, festivals and military base tours had taken its toll, Nyxcerra more than the rest.

The toll of the concerts having drained her energy. Without makeup, they all had a haunted look about their eyes, but the make-up artists were exceptional. They all looked immaculate, as the crowd expected.

"Leix has said that the auditions for 'black masquerade' have been pushed back, instead of a three-part mini series, JRV entertainment has said they will fund a big budget adaptation, at least twenty parts based on increased interest...." she mentioned to Nyxcerra as they walked, gesturing towards Nyxcerra, as she got off a conference call with Leix, swiping his projected image away as she began speaking

"They will want you to audition for the role, even though we know you've pretty much got the part, as promised by Elim. but it won't be for another cycle at least.." Jysell added, nearly forgetting to pass the message on.

"Of course, gives me more time to take more acting classes..." Nyxcerra replied.

No matter where they looked, there was the Imperial military. Their appearance at this concert, which was being hosted for the military, was an unexpected surprise. An invitation like this couldn't be turned down, upon fear of alienating a huge audience. Nyxcerra glanced over as she walked, enjoying the glances by those who lined their entrance way,

"Colonel Unabri Kasp is going to be announcing you girls to the crowd later, he's more nervous doing this tonight that speaking to the emperor himself, so take that as you will" Maribor remarked offhand, as she looked at the itinerary of what they still had to do before the concert started.

"Maribor, I just had a great idea. Randomly pick 5 seat

numbers and ask for the five in attendance to be quickly escorted to our dressing room..." Nyxcerra smiled, as an idea ran through her mind, laughing to herself.

Maribor looked at her, surprised, Avéline hearing this interjected,

"No time for any of that business......." Maribor replied as she fixed her pony tail as they walked through the crowd of military soldiers who were giving them an honour guard.

"Hey, it's not about that, no matter how much fun it would be, it's a great pr opportunity.

35 Minutes Later...

"Good Night Caspria, Good Night Caspria and Welcome to the first night...." Colonel Kasp murmured to himself as he walked towards the microphone hovering at the centre of the stage, as he walked he cleared his throat gently, he knew all eyes were focused on him, somehow feeling the glances of the crowd, he could feel the atmosphere swelling, the air filled with a sense of excitement.

He nervously clenched his fists, Clearing it again before taking a deep breath, he was to announce tonight's enter-tainment to the darkness of the arena; the atmosphere was eerie; the air was warm and dry, an occasional cool breeze caused him to savour its relief from the day's soaring temperatures.

He knew from ticket sales and scanned tickets that night that there were at least 90,000 in attendance that warm summer night. It was dark but wasn't silent. He could hear them. The faint chanting of the crowd in the distance, some singing songs from the album, even though it had only been released seven days earlier.

The lights had been turned off in the stadium. The voices of the 90,000 dropped to an eerie silence as he got closer to the microphone. The sound of the crowd carried through the warm summer air. Nyxcerra peaked her head around from behind the stage, slowly clenching her fists, before reaching over and pressing a button on the wrist controls on her left wrist. Within seconds a turquoise symbol appeared projected behind Nyxcerra, the crowd going wild, causing Kasp to stop before the microphone and turn towards where Nyxcerra was nervously standing.

He smiled begrudgingly after giving her a look of surprise. Nyxcerra looked over at the other girls who pressed the same buttons on their wrist controls, 4 other symbol appeared projected above the stage. The crowd began chanting.

"AERREA, AERREA..." Kasp's voice echoed out into the stadium thought the speakers, as he began to speak, the crowd began turning on light sticks, within seconds a twinkling rainbow of lights were glittering in the darkness.

"Good Night Caspria" he boomed, his voice echoed out, some of you may know me, I'm Colonel Kasp and it is my pleasure to introduce tonight, as part of their "Whole Empire" tour the girls of Aerrea, both a feast for the soul and a treat for the eyes as well" he gushed, Nyxcerra looked around, Jysell was standing to their left, Tiiona and Avéline to their right, with Syala behind them, with an assortment of backup dancers making up the back row.

CHAPTER 29
"DO I NEED TO HAVE THAT BIG SISTER CONVERSATION WITH HIM?..."

2 Cycles Later...

"Want to get out of here?" Tamir asked, pleading for her to come outside. He was young, tall and athletically handsome.

"Yes," Krynda replied as she ran her fingers through her long hair. She would normally do anything for him, although this time she didn't really need to be coaxed.

Tamir turned to embrace Krynda's sister, Athari, who was standing behind him.

"Hey, it is okay if I take your sister out for a break from studying, she's a-bit burnt out, oh and welcome home" Krynda watched as she laughed and hugged him back, she'd popped a crate full of food on the counter, without even changing from her work attire, she was hastily gathering things together., planning on cooking something.

"Fine with me, you got about 30 minutes, while I try to turn this lot into some sort of dinner.." she proclaimed, as she tried to think what she could make quickly and easily.

She smiled as she pulled Tulsa fruit and Kyla root out from the crate and put them on the side, grabbing a small knife from a draw and pulling out a chopping board from below the counter.

"Just give me a moment with her, and I'll send her out... okay.." she added as she sharpened the knife with a sharpened and started chopping one of the vegetables.

"Ok, Tamir, I'll see you outside..." Krynda added.

"So, what did you want me for??" Krynda enquired, looking at her sister, confused.

"He's a good one, you know?, mom and dad would have loved him... do I need to have that big sister conversation with him? Or is it okay?"

Krynda blushed as she helped her sister take things from the crate,

"Ath, I know, I'm so lucky to have him, compared to the nightmare of an exboyfriend, would never have expected him to be so... respectful, especially from someone from a house as low as his" Krynda added, trying to forget how her ex treated her.

"Do you think mom and dad would have allowed it, with someone from a house like his?"she enquired.

"Honestly, they probably wouldn't be too happy about it, but there not here anymore, so as your elder sister, I gotta do things that keep you safe, and he makes you happy, doesn't he? He's got such a big..." she stopped as she gestured about his physique, Krynda blushed again,

"He keeps himself healthy. It's that work in construction, keeps him toned..."

"Oh, so he's just toned..." Athari added as she finished chopping the Kyla root and put it on a frying pan. The oil had just reached ideal temperature.

"He makes me more than happy, if you catch my meaning...." Krynda remarked with a sly wink.

"Knows how these work..." she purred as she gestured to the scales on the back of her neck.

"Maybe he should have a word with Davir for you, could teach him a thing or two..." her train of thought changed.

"So, has he mentioned bonding yet? It's about time, it been the three cycles, hasn't it?" Krynda asked her sister.

"Four, last month..."

"We said we'd do it before you go off to the academy next cycle... but haven't said anything more about it..." she sighed as she spoke. She wanted to, but he was still note openly discussing it.

"And please, tell him to have a word. Davir's useless when it comes to the scales, spends more time turning me off instead of turning me on..." she laughed, causing Krynda to laugh out loud.

"Now go and have a chat with Tamir, shouldn't be too much longer for dinner, ask him if he wants to stay, I wouldn't mind if he stayed over tonight, just keep it down, I gotta leave for the horticulture conference tomorrow."

"Of course we'll keep it down, my rooms not a den of debauchery, not until you go to the conferenced..." she quickly added, hoping her sister missed what she said.

"Hey, just make sure he's taken his injection. Don't want any unplanned kids, not before you join the military." She added.

"Now go, he's waiting for you.." Athari added and she escorted Krynda towards the door out to the back garden.

Outside 5 minutes later

. . .

"I was thinking we'd just go to your room, put some music on, I've been listening to BYL's latest group, you know the one, the one from the 106... Aerrea" Krynda blinked rapidly, as she got used to the darkness outside the home,

"Sounds fine to me, gotta get out of this cold, a-bit of a winters snap this winter.

"A bunch of the team at work have been listening to them during the day, I hadn't watched 106, but wow, they are better than I expected, I wanted to get your vibe on them, if not, they'll be great background music for later on, Is that okay?"

"Really Tam, you didn't watch any of the 106, it was on for 5 cycles you know that, 424 days a cycle for nearly six complete cycles.."

"I didn't know you watched it..." Tamir enquired, the fact that she had been watching it completely disappear from his thoughts.

"Oh, not the main show. I caught up on the daily highlights, got a good grasp of the happenings, but in the final year, it really heated up..."

"Well, Lim at work said that tickets are going up for sale soon for next cycles tour. I can believe that they are travelling this far out from the core. It would be fun to go, if we could..."

CHAPTER 30
"I KNEW YOU'D LET ME IN..."

A tall athletic gentleman in a dark blue suit with a brilliant white porcelain half mask slowly entered the long narrow hallway. With every step toward, the spotlights above brightened until they were both flooded in light. Her face flushed as she pulled off the black mask that covered the top half of her face, as she got lost in admiration for him, she tried to tell herself he was not her type, and way out of her reach, would she risk everything to be seen with him.

Her mind went crazy. He was her Lord and bonded to his betrothed wife for over forty cycles. She'd never been alone with him, not anywhere, especially not in her apartment. Her hearts raced. She could smell his pheromones from behind the door. Even knowing it was him, she seemed powerless to stop herself from opening the door and letting him in.

His piercing green eyes behind the white mask instantly caught her attention, drawing her in like a moth to a flame. She gasped as he spoke.

"Illara, may I have a private word..." he spoke, his voice eloquent and formal, why was he here she thought, a young, none bonded Impiri girl, in a private apartment with a bonded male, over fifty cycles her senior, she stepped back, her palms sweaty, her stomach in knots, struggling to speak, until it all came out.

"Lord Arkin, what are you doing here, shouldn't you be with your wife" she whispered reverently as she shook her head gently, trying to get the thoughts out of her head. Was it a joke being played on her? Had he been sent to tease her, or to test her loyalty? The hallway leading to her bedroom was sparsely decorated, she wanted him to leave, so she could rush to her bed and lay down, and pleasure herself to the scent of his pheromones, she wanted him, and was sure that his wife knew it.

The typical thing her Lady loved doing, keeping Nyxcerra always guessing. She looked down at herself. Her all black dress was short, revealing her long slender legs. She balanced on dainty black heels. The dress hugged her figure, accented by a golden necklace, and bright red lips. She was beautiful in a slightly reserved way, a departure from her really short skirts and want to reveal more of her body. She looked up at him. He smiled nervously, biting her bottom lip, before making an effort to release it.

"I knew you'd let me in, isn't that right Illara..." he added as he glanced at her body, knowing that he was having a reaction within her, he took a deep breath, causing her to blush, if he couldn't smell her pheromones before, he could now, without a doubt.

"Lady Arkin, my gracious wife, is too busy distracted by Captain Jynl to pay any attention that what I'm doing...." he replied, his voice bitter but playful. He stepped forward, placing his hand on the wall beside Illara.

His mind casting back to how she had disregarded him earlier that day.

"Do you know what she said to me when I arrived back from the council today?"

"You've put on weight and your hair is going grey" he mocked, taken back even by repeating what she had said.,

"See, that's what I get treated to, my own wife, mistress of the house, my wife and mother to my children.... so as I said, she really doesn't care, so while I turn a blind eye, she will obviously be turning a blind eye to me being here with you." Lord Arkin calmly replied.

She knew nothing would happen here. But he walked past her without stopping, brushing past her, causing her brows to become furrowed, seaming to ignore her, stopping just behind her,

he muttered,

"I think you know why I'm here" casually, his voice caused her hearts to race. Her head was on fire, not knowing what to say. Was he attractive, most definitely? His athletic build, immaculately dressed in a tan coloured suit. Would she dare go through with it, with how she felt? She didn't know if she could let herself go. He grabbed her arm and turned her toward the wall. He brushed her hair to the side, looked at the pale scales which framed her neck.

"Seems like you need a good time," he mocked, noticing the pale tone, disappointed not to see them turning a light shade of blue as was normal for an aroused Impiri female. He lifted up the mask before casting it to the floor.

It seemed only like a second had passed. It all happened so fast she didn't know how she got there and didn't care. Lord Arkin was there, leaning against her, she could feel the heat from his body, his breath tingled her scales.

"I want to cheer you up..." he whispered into her ear.

His hand was against the wall. Nyxcerra slowly turned herself around And he was there, close, she could feel his breath on her face, her thoughts erratic, she tried to speak, but couldn't, it was bad enough that she couldn't breathe, speak, swallow or hear anything outside of her own thudding heartbeats.

Now she was having trouble with her own thoughts, would she dare engage with such an individual? He was the pinnacle example of attractive, the ultimate distraction and skilled in solely one thing, making your night one you won't forget. He sensed her nerves and leaned forward.

"You wanna let me make that beautiful face glow" he whispered in a low voice that had her hearts racing even more. She instinctively felt her head slowly nodding, surprised by her own reaction, she wanted to melt into his arms, to feel the heat from his body against hers.

Managing to swallow the lump in her throat, Nyxcerra managed to eek out a faint,

"With me, seriously?" Before her voice failed her.

He smiled at her and she wanted to reach out and caress his face, to pull him closer. But something stopped her. Her own thoughts pulling her back. She wanted someone, right now, anyone would do. The memories of her last conversation with her lady flashed into her consciousness, how she teased her, flirted even. Was the serious about it.

"I don't know if I can...it's just." She managed to speak, her voice breathy and laboured, trying her hardest to resist the urge to take him there and then.

She still didn't trust him about their open relationship. She still thought it maybe a joke, a prank organised by her lady, something so foolish, a sick example of her sometimes twisted sense of humour, but she couldn't help asking,

"Are you serious?, if she finds out about this, I'm done

for, she would never trust me again, you know that don't you?"

"It's not like I'm going to parade you in front of her and take you in our bed while she watches," he sarcastically replied, his words making sense.

"I just want to brighten up your evening, nothing more, nothing less" he said with a roguish grin that made her dizzy with her own desire, the scales down her back tingled, not all of them, but the primary ones tingled all the way down her spine, she took in a deep breath, a musky scent caught her by surprise, she felt her inhibitions start to fade, her own instincts take over as his pheromones got to work.

"I haven't had the company of someone in such a long time." She whispered. A wry grin appeared on her face as she gently blushed as she glanced at him.

She was actually going to do it, to release the tension that had built up, she looked over and saw her own hand caressing the side of his face, by her own amazement, she was reacting instinctively, her fingertips tracing their way down his neck towards his chest.

"So you've decided..." he murmured. His tone was suggestive.

She grabbed hold of his collar and pulled him close, and stepped closer to him at the same time, her lips close to his.

"I'll let you decide if I have..." she whispered as she kissed him, before pulling away nervously, letting go of his collar and stepping back. 'It was wrong, Wasn't it?' She thought, 'the Goddesses would be repulsed' she was so ashamed. She was afraid her hearts would beat right out of her chest. She couldn't go through with a lie.

"I can't...it's..." she shamefully whispered.

He carefully fixed his collar and chuckled to himself.

"Complicated…" he playfully replied. Nyxcerra nodded her head slowly.

"You could say that. I want to physically, but in my hearts I know it's not real. She's sent you to test my loyalty. I feel I've already gone too far"

"You know how to keep a secret, don't you?"

She laughed nervously.

"In my line of work, I know hundreds. One more won't make a difference…" he smiled as he spoke.

"I just can't risk it, part of me wants to rip your clothes off right now and have my way with you, the other I'm so afraid that she'll find out and everything I've worked for will be ruined, and I just can't risk it. I just can't do the things you want me to."

He reached out and with his fingers; he brushed aside her hair.

"I think I understand. It will be our little secret." He smiled graciously.

"Won't she…" Illara asked, her bottom lip trembling.

He slowly turned around and walked back towards the hallway, stopped and looked over his left shoulder.

"You were out when I turned up, no harm. She's probably throwing herself at Captain Jynl, knowing that he's unable to resist her," he smiled. Her heart rate dropped, she sighed.

"She would do that to you…? But you are bonded…" she added. Before it sank in, their relationship was open. He had picked her for a night of fun, while she enjoyed the carnal acts with another, and she'd blown the chance.

"I'm sorry…" she mouthed.

"It's fine, I'll let myself out…maybe next time"he added as he reached the door, reaching for the door handle before stopping.

"Cut..." a voice called out. Causing the lights to brighten, and a flurry of activity, as multiple people rushed into the hallway., some resetting items, others rushed over to Nyxcerra while she stablished herself against the wall.

Nyxcerra sighed, letting out a deep breath. Placing her palm on her chest, her hearts still racing, as someone rushed over to her carrying a small bottle of water.

"Here's your drink..." the young girl whispered nervously as Nyxcerra took the bottle from her. Opening it and taking a quick sip of water, she let out a breath she didn't know she was carrying. savouring the cold water, her throat had been dry and was trying to stop herself from coughing.

"Casiel..." a voice called out, causing the suited man to turn towards the voice and gesture with a thumbs up.

"Great work Cas, great work... got some great shots there..." the camera operator exclaimed, before walking off set.

Castiel turned around with a smile on his face.

"Geez, Nyx, didn't expect you to nail the lines that well... you made me feel really guilty and uncomfortable, as if I was betraying her," as a make-up artist looked at his face, adding makeup and dabbing the sweat from his forehead, continuing to talk,

"That's one hell of a scene. Hopefully, the boss likes it. I'm sure it's fine. He's probably looking at the rough cut as we speak, oh.... he's on his way."

"Castiel, Nyxcerra. Great work both of you, that's a wrap for this episode," a middle-aged man spoke, his salt and pepper hair glistened in the overhead lights. He rolled up his sleeves,

"Perfect, just perfect, Castiel, what did you think, good

or what....? He enthusiastically added, patting Castiel on the shoulder as he walked beside him.

"Reset the set for next week's episode..." he barked ordered at a gathering of crew who rushed to get the set ready. He walked over to Nyxcerra and smiled, causing her to relax.

"Nyxcerra, brilliant emotional connection, almost felt as if you two wanted to rip each other's clothes off..." he laughed, with a twinkle in his eye.

"The audience will love it. I think we have a hit on our hands..." he spoke as he patted her on the shoulder.

CHAPTER 31
"THINK ABOUT MY OFFER..."

3 Months Later...

Jysell stood conversing with Casotta DeVri, head of design at DeVri's, gathering at the "Black Masquerade" wrap party after the final day of shooting the drama. She never expected her and Syala's designs to be shown at such an event, but they had.

DeVri had provided costumes for the drama and had put on a concept catwalk show during the wrap party, she felt glamorous in her layered dark green dress and studded heels, glancing around she was mesmerised by her surroundings, no matter where she looked the movers and shakers in the fashion industry were there, Kandria Harand and Aitan Baize from Daze, Lysa Jakar the somewhat reclusive creative lead behind Valhi, Kesi Daraay and his streetwear take on high fashion, Tonor Auten from Daze and the designer to the imperial household Alsin Dangir from Maisie, they all were there.

She stood, taking it all in, feeling out of her depth,

feeling like an imposter. She shouldn't have been here, the voice in her head kept repeating, you're a singer, and a dancer, not a fashion designer. Being in the same room as the brightest designers in the empire made her giddy with excitement, but also full of dread. What if they didn't like her designs? What if they only liked Syala's designs, or maybe they hated both?

These thoughts were quickly squashed by other thoughts, realising Casotta DeVri must have seen something in her work to allow her to be shown in the DeVri up and coming junior designers category. Seeing models wear her designs brought her and Syala to tears.

They all had seen some of the outfits she'd designed with Syala. She owed Nyxcerra a thank you; she was so surprised that Nyxcerra had asked this as a condition of taking part in the series, knowing that Casotta DeVri was providing the costumes for it, recalling a conversation they had months before when she'd expressed interest in her crafting a dress one night.

She couldn't believe that it had gone so well, she was ecstatic, Casotta had loved the showcase, it was a simple showcase, but had gotten her attention, her wrist already pinging with notifications, she ignored them, knowing that the influencers in attendance had been discussing her work and it was probably flooding the social channels at that moment.

She didn't check them, not wanting to see any negative comments. Not tonight, tonight this was their night. She could answer them anyway, not during a conversation with Casotta.

"So Jysell my darling, once you've had a chance to think about my offer, It's baby steps, but you've got real potential there" she stopped smiling, knowing that this would bring a whole new audience to the fashion industry and would potentially make them millions of credits more. "have your people call my people, we'll arrange some time for you in our design lab..." Casotta added before clutching at her hand and kissing it,

"We'll discuss it more later..." she added before being directed to someone else to talk to by an aide. Leaving Jysell there to mingle with the crew and others in attendance. She carefully picked a fluted glass of wine from a passing waitress before taking a small sip.

"Ooh" she whispered, it was strong, she never drank much, and this was strong, sweet, almost syrup like in consistency.

The production company had rented out a penthouse bar for the occasion in the city of Morkiee out towards lake Sori from here. Everyone had sweeping views over the city, and over the lake towards the picturesque Draskyoium mountains and their year round snow-capped peaks.

Nyxcerra wandered contentedly through the crowds. Crew members nodded and greeted her as she passed. She needed to find Jysell, as she passed the writers' table, a table where the writers for the series were all sitting, enjoying themselves.

As she approached the table she caught the eye of someone who nudged the Individual next to him to move to allow her to sit with them, causing her to smile, She'd been pleasantly surprised by how readily the cast and crew had drawn her into their fold.

She wasn't a traditional actress. She hadn't studied at any of the schools of drama, but they accepted her. A feeling she longed for.

The twelve episodes of the drama were it 'the highest rated of the decade' she'd heard Leix tell her, when he was discussing their trend statistics in one of their weekly meetings. But at the moment, those figures meant nothing.

She hadn't realised what a bond it would create: working such long hours in such close quarters, the whole crew working to make this dramatic retelling of the famous novel "Masquerade".

"I just want to thank you all...for..." Nyxcerra spoke as she declined the seat,

"I'll come back in a moment, but I just wanted to..."

"Nyx, darling, it's we that have to thank you, you made everything so professional, I honestly didn't think you could hack it..."

"Really??"

"Yes, and much to my surprise, you nailed it. Sei'Lya and Tryn here said you'd be fine, that you were to use to the strenuous work load..." he stopped, trying to think of the right words before adding.

"With the 106..." his voice trailing off.

"I can't wait to see the last episode once it airs. I'm so nervous..." Nyxcerra added. She wasn't acting here, she had got great reviews so far, but the finale was going to make or break her none Aerrea career.

"I just hope that I'll get to work with any of you in the future... it's been an honour.." she added bowing gracefully.

It had been an incredible twelve weeks, she reflected. A luck break in the touring had allowed her to film the series. She'd worked hard during the filming hours, still getting in a reduced dance practice and vocal conditioning lesson ever week before shuttling back to the capital at the end of the week, spending two days with the girls while they were on an extended rest period.

· · ·

She was exhausted. They'd pulled all-nighters twice that week and had only finished that morning at 6am am trying to get everything filmed. She'd resorted to stim patches to keep herself going; before returning to the hotel at dawn to sleep, before being here this evening. She hoped she didn't look tired, but the team in make up had made a last-minute detour to her hotel room to do her makeup as a thank you, after receiving expensive bottles of Thaluk liquor from her as a gift for all their hard work. A tactic that Leix had told her to do. It had been difficult, becoming so far from the rest of the girls, but it had been worth it. Nyxcerra knew she'd learned more from this experience than she had in the past few cycles.

Syala looked around the venue, trying to catch the eyes of someone she could recognise, before she stopped, catching Nyxcerra's gaze as she laughed at a table not far from the entrance. Nyxcerra gesturing for her to come over, an invitation she wouldn't refuse, as she made her way through the crowd the laughter was growing wilder, as the evening had wore on and everyone kept drinking the fresh-squeezed cocktails.

"Tziu- miss Syala, it's a pleasure to finally meet you. Nyx has been telling us about you and your design partners' project. She wouldn't stop telling me about it at every free moment" he winked at Nyxcerra before continuing. Syala was shocked, Tonor Auten from Daze had seen her work, she'd loved his work for cycles, having his showcase phone-books being sent to her by her older sister, arriving months after the showcase, but she didn't care, she savoured the showcase as if it was recent, looking at it at night with Jysell on days when they couldn't sleep.

"They looked..." he stopped, frowning as he stopped

talking, causing Syala's delicate smile to fall. What had she done, she wouldn't be able to cope if he'd hated them,

"Fabulous, if I do say so myself..." Tonor Auten chimed in. His overconfident, boisterous and flamboyant personality enriched everything he did.

Syala looked at him, lowering her gaze.

"It was nothing, just a few ideas we had, for those that are a-bit more conservative than others.." she sheepishly replied.

CHAPTER 32
"IT'S BEEN A WHIRLWIND THREE CYCLES HASN'T IT..."

A Month Later...

Tiiona leaned against the sturdy prefab wall and looked at Nyxcerra, who was hastily covering her dark blouse with a long while shawl. They'd all agreed to hide their outfits until the moment they walked on stage.

"Come on, Nyx, they said we have a minute until we have to talk with her. I don't know why it's here. Thallus Perkep would be better, less gossip more..." before she could finish speak a pale green faced woman hastily interrupted her.

"Girls, on stage in 6 mins" the frantic coordinator screamed as she poked her head around the open door. She looked stressed, her breathing laboured. She glanced around the room before speaking again, making sure she had everyone's attention.

"Why do I do this" she whispered before sighing.

"I'll knock and you better be ready., 60 seconds until

Illax wants you," before she disappeared, busily organising the acts for the night.

Avéline panicked and looked at the mirror, removing a speck of mascara near her eye with the corner of one of her iridescent fingernails.

"Well, I'm done. Hope they like these..." she glanced down at the white shawl.

"Well, I think you look great Ave," Tiiona added as she tucked in the laces of her black boots before standing up. "God these heels are high, ain't worn this kind for a while... makes me look almost..."

"Tall," Jysell and Syala both exclaimed, looking at each other before breaking out in laughter.

"Yeah, yeah, both of you laugh. At least I'm ready," as Nyxcerra shook her head, she'd been ready for a while, she was always the first one ready.

"Come on, Jys, remove the hair tie, Sy, put down the food, I know you're hungry, I'm starving, we can eat after the performance, got at least an hour before our category comes up."

Just as they were ready, there was a knock on the door, "Come on girls, can't keep Illax waiting..."

At a quarter to nine, Nyxcerra pulled off the shawl that she had been wearing on top of her outfit, revealing the silken black blouse underneath. It was covered with intricate turquoise brocade, reflecting some of the overhead light which struck its surface, which shimmered. It just covered her ample chest before finishing, baring her tanned midriff, and a black figure hugging skirt which ended a little too high even for her liking, finished with black ankle boots, causing Tiiona to wolf-whistle and clap.

The sound of this whistle caused Nyxcerra to instinctively pose and smile towards Tiiona.

"Looking good boss, so I'm guessing it's time", she remarked before taking her own shawl off, revealing a similar-looking outfit, the blouse ending at her waist. This time the brocade was a light yellow.

"Make them earn any sight of skin', mother always said" murmured Jysell as she looked at her outfit, the blouse was too tight, her midriff was bare and her short skirt and knee-high boots were too much, she knew what she looked like in the mirror, before walking away, with a look of disgust on her face.

Syala looked at her,

"It absolutely sucks, way too revealing, what will the goddesses think?" She whispered once she knew they were both out of earshot of Nyxcerra and Tiiona.

"But what else do you want me to do? If we're going to keep our place, we have to make these sacrifices, you know that. "

Jysell didn't answer right away. She stared around the tiny space filled with half-eaten appetiser platters and a small bot that kept sanitised everything they touched.

"You don't know how difficult it is for me, seeing you upset, I'm not happy with it, but I can make an exception, it's fine for Nyx and Tii, maybe they're too accepting of this," Syala said at last.

"But I know it's even more difficult for you, but don't mess this up for all of us." She whispered, trying to force a smile.

Jysell resented that thinly veiled criticism. Syala had supported her, spoke to management, but now management hadn't listened, their clothing was more revealing than ever, and now even Syala didn't want to cause any retaliation from management.

"Well, well, it definitely seems like BYL are on to

another winner, it's been a busy three cycles, Madiyah disbanded at the beginning of the cycle, and Mystix went on hiatus. I honestly thought what do BYL have up their sleeves... well you all know who I'm talking about, so after a brief word with our sponsors, we'll be back chatting to the girls from Aerrea, ENB reporting live from the 493rd Adorix Awards," The young woman reported to the small drone hovering such in front of her view. The moment she finished speaking, he sighed. Gone was her smile. Everything was reversed.

She knew she had ninety seconds before the broadcast could resume. She gestured over quickly and Nyxcerra, who quickly rushed the other girls over first before taking her place at the front. Her hearts racing, all of there's were, a broadcast like this which was a last-minute deal made her nervous.

What questions who she ask?, would she mention Ceres? How would she react if she asked? These questions ran through Nyxcerra's thoughts. She stood breathing deeply to calm herself as the young woman turned herself towards the drone, instinctively knowing where the drone was at all times.

She looked down at her dark green figure hugging dress, straightening its silken fabric while she started counting down,

"30 seconds left girls, you better be ready" she quickly took out a small mirror quickly glanced at it, her eyes decorated in emerald green makeup and her lips a light shade of blue, designed to attract the view of her audience. She brushed her dark brown hair back with her fingers with one hand and closed and hid the small mirror in her cleavage as she got ready to speak again, her hair bouncing off her shoulders.

———

Moments Later...

"We have secured a few moments to ask the girls a few quick questions. For you, my loyal viewers," she added, everything she said, carefully rehearsed and on cue.

"Iellax Izen here, with the girls from 'Aerrea', currently holders of the empire's highest ranking debut single 'without you', So let's see if Ive got these names right, Nyx, Tiiona, Avéline, Jysell and Syala...", each of the girls bowed politely as they were named, without waiting any time Mrs Izen went from greeting them to asking questions,

"Thank you, girls, so much for agreeing to this quick interview before your first live performance at the Adorix awards. Last year, you gave us a special live performance during the middle of a concert at Parax IV. I wonder what you have in store for us tonight... "

Tonight you are also up most listened to song of the decade, as well as breakthrough artist award." She paused, "it's been a whirlwind three cycles hasn't it..."

Nyxcerra looked at her, noticing the drone quickly turn towards her. She knew all eyes were on her now. Everyone went silent. Even other broadcasters reporting a few meters away lowered their voices. Billions across the empire were viewing this broadcast. She stared at the drone for a second before smiling graciously, her eyes sparkling.

"As we can see this evening, you've all chosen to cover your outfits for tonight's awards ceremony until the last minute. Can we at least ask why? And which designer you've chosen, eager viewers want to know..."

"Ah, yes, right? Well..." she nervously answered, the nerves from the previous night hadn't subsided, the little drop of Nori liquor earlier managed to just take the edge off. She was still taken by surprise by the question.

"Well, us Aerrea girls want to take the industry by storm, not just musically. We have a few surprises in store for tonight."

"And for your second question, I'll leave it to our fashion conscious members, Syala and Jysell

"Well, we all loved the work of an up-and-coming fashion house back on Kestra VII. It's the work of Uvi, lead creative director of Dirvi, a new spin on one of his new season designs. We wanted to give a glimpse of the fashion back where we come from... We hope you enjoy its unveiling..." Jysell replied to the camera, as she fixed the white silken robe covering her outfit, carefully flashing just enough of the garment underneath to satisfy the viewers and Mrs Izen herself, whose eyes followed, eagerly trying to gain a glimpse of the outfit.

"My, my, my, from what I've just glimpsed, I'm sure that this is going to be one amazing season for the brand, a brand we are hopefully going to see more of..."

She looked over and knew she had time for one more question.

"Nyx, Can I ask, as eager minds want to know...how are you and the rest of the girls coping..." as she spoke Nyxcerra's demeanour changed, her smile dropped for a second.

"I, I mean, we were all shocked and saddened by the unexpected death of Ceres just before your debut cycles ago..."

"It must have been difficult for you all. We had all seen how close you all were over the many cycles we had followed your progress..." Iellax nervously added over the silence from her previous question.

Tiiona looked at her in shock, before a look of disdain

flashed across her face before being replaced as quickly as it appeared.

Nyxcerra's hearts were pounding. Did she dare speak the truth, that it was a daily struggle, that they all thought about her,

She sighed, shakily looked at the drone. She stood at the entrance to the great hall in silence. She nodded her head slowly before responding.

"We are doing well. It's a bit jarring at times, but we pulled through it," Nyxcerra replied, biting her bottom lip after responding.

"So, I take that as a yes..., it's been difficult Mhmm," Iellax said.

"If only there was a way to get more out of you ..." she murmured to herself, before she grinned,

"What did you say?" Nyxcerra enquired, only partially hearing her.

"Oh, I know more than I let on, and I think you heard exactly what I said." She accused.

"A good host always keeps her ears to the ground. A few eagle eyes have noticed a few comings and goings at the complex, in particular therapists,"

This caused Nyxcerra to stop thinking, her stomach aching, the fear setting in, 'what had she heard' rang out through her subconscious.

"Well, I've had some health concerns recently..." Nyxcerra replied, trying to stop Iellax's inquisitive strain of questioning.

"Pulled my hamstring and had a bout of patellofemoral pain during a dance rehearsal for the second legs of our tour, Syala and myself got Androgian fever for a week, so we all isolated for the required 10 days, which your loyal fans will work out is why we weren't at the festival of love last month, we've all had to keep our spirits up,"

"But are you confirming that someone has had to a speak to a psychiatrist?"

"You know what happened? Everyone does. We'd like to thank our label for making us all see a specialist..." she said in a quiet voice.

"It's okay to not be okay..." she added as she looked at the drone. Iellax arched her eyebrows.

CHAPTER 33
"FORGET ABOUT THAT NYX..."

A Few Weeks Later...

The calm in the forty-second-floor apartment ended abruptly,

"Where's Avéline?" Jysell asked curiously as she walked through the doorway of the small kitchen, which lead into a sparse but large living room. It was considerably larger than the cramped dormitory on the ninth floor that had been their home for nearly seven cycles.

It was sparsely decorated, a few potted flowering plants brought some colour to its white walls. She stood drying her now short brown hair with a colourful towel awaiting a response but getting nothing.

She sighed loudly. She hated it when no one answered. She spoke again, raising her voice slightly, why didn't Nyxcerra reply she thought, looking over at Nyxcerra who sat at the table, her blouse soaked from the torrential rains that night, but she didn't care, she was lost in thought leaning over a digital pad while tapping her fingers absent-mindedly on the tables worn wooden surface as she stared into the middle distance before she looked down at her dark turquoise tattoo.

"Nyx?" Jysell added, causing her to snap out of her daydream.

She glanced up, revealing the smudged eyeliner and run mascara lines, catching Jysell by surprise.

"Oh, Hey Jys... she's re-doing the vocals on '-' Ryx said something about..." she abruptly stopped,

"Something about not being up to Ceres' standard..."

"Forget about that Nyx, what's wrong? You'll catch a deathly cold wearing that" as she handed her the towel,

"I'll be fine, it's just..." she paused, unable to find the right words to say.

Jysell looked confused, trying to read Nyxcerra's expression, trying to take it all in before being interrupted by Tiiona who wandered in, carrying a box.

"Can't believe they've stopped the investigation... no further evidence is forthcoming," she blurted out, before noticing Nyxcerra sitting there.

"Nyx,... Nyx, I didn't mean to..." she stumbled over her words.

"It's fine, it just came as a bit of a surprise, just caught me by surprise, especially the repeat prescriptions for..." Nyxcerra spoke through the tears which started running down her cheeks.

"She never told me it was that bad. The muscle pains, I mean, didn't notice the meds, never thought she was so anxious, she seemed..." she blurted out.

"So in control, yeah, I thought the same, but it makes sense..." Tiiona added, almost completing her train of thought.

"Death by misadventure... that's what the reporters on EEB are stating, I just caught the end on the stream..." Tiiona added as she grabbed hold of a small silvery remote and tapped a few buttons on its surface.

Within moments, a large screen appeared on the far wall.

"Tii, I don't think she..." Jysell interjected, hoping to not have to relive her own emotions about that night, having only recently fully gotten over it.

"It's fine Jys, I need to get closure on this, if it was an accident then, who am I to argue with it.." she resigned herself, the thoughts in the back of her mind still calling out that it could have been a murder, why was Ceres out near the balcony, with her fear of heights.

"This is Illax for EEB. This is tonight's late news,

"VLS Entertainment group has completed the merger with ILS subject to regulatory approval, moving them from fourth in terms of viewership to third overall, BYL still ruling the roost at first.

"They have charged Janve and Exum from RKO with embezzlement., the trial is due to start within the next 30 days on Prim..

"Seems like there is a new power couple. Impiri Lady Centych Kalidral Vale has been seen out with Elim Kokad, son of the entertainment magnate Ebradir, Kokad after being seen loved up entering club Euphoria"

"In other BYL news, capital police have finally closed their investigation into the unfortunate death of Hayli Ceres Soobaks, daughter of legendary artist Luca-tal Soobaks, and star of the long running Group 106 live drama, and founding member of Aerrea."

"Her unfortunate death has been ruled as a Death by misadventure, for all those viewers who don't understand legalese, that would mean that it was an accident. We here at EEB would like to send our thoughts and prayers to BYL, the girls of AERREA and all the fans at this time. Hopefully, this brings some sort of closure."

CHAPTER 34
"WHERE ARE YOU HEADED?..."

Later That Week...

Tiiona was almost at the front door when Syala called out from the living room.

"Tii? Where are you headed?, especially this early?, thought you'd be taking a well-earned rest, especially after last nights... drinks," Her voice trailing off, thinly veiled with concern as she lifted her head from looking at the projected image of a dress.

"Hey, Sy." She turned around quickly, spinning on her heels, keeping one hand on the doorframe to steady herself. She didn't expect Syala to still be awake, she was always the last to wake up, especially this early. She had to leave. She knew she didn't have long. She couldn't miss it this time. It wasn't for the others. This time her reputation was being called into question.

Syala was sitting in her favourite corner of the room on the ageing brown leather couch, she had been busy sketching something on her tablet, then modelling them into holograms, She looked down at her sketches, she'd been designing elegant clothes and listening to an article on traditional clothing design, she frowned before sighing; she tutted to herself in annoyance, before letting out a long agitated sigh.

She wasn't happy with the way the holographic projections were coming out. Glancing down, she looked at a design and swiped it away, her fingers lingering above the delete button for a moment before pressing and glancing back up. 'Never going to get this right,' she murmured.

"Hey, Sy, has Jysell seen this one? Jys showed me the last one you both worked on. Beautiful, not my style, but I can appreciate it. Just don't purge this one. Let me see it when I get back. Remember, a fresh set of eyes... as Ceres used to say"

"Jys said this one's up to me. I'll try to keep it, but I can't guarantee it..." wanting to change the subject, she switched the conversation.

"So..." she hung on the word for a moment, trying to think of what to ask.

"Where you off too??" she added quickly, as she placed the tablet in her lap,

Syala wanted these designs to look good, to show them to the designers at Daze. They'd asked to see some more designs. She ran her hand through her hair. Her thick but shortcut hair was almost now entirely dark blue, which was in contrast to her russet, reddish-brown skin. She had finally let her natural colour grow out. Tiiona stood there thinking, trying to figure out a reason which had just slipped out of her consciousness.

"I'm going to Jorans club, might get some inspiration by going to Jorans... he's having an open mic session, night give me something to work with," she stuttered, trying to convince herself of her actions.

"Yeah and I know, sit at the back, don't let anyone know it's me, I'll be fine Joran knows me well enough to sneak me in... we don't have anything to worry about, remember?, I told you last night over dinner," she explained.

Syala glanced over at her outfit.

"Do you really need a bag that big for just practice" gesturing at the large bag beside her, and she realised a second too late that she could see the concerned look in her eyes.

"Don't worry, Sy, going to get some things washed before I go out. I'll pick them back up on my way back." She spoke, glancing at her watch. She had an hour to make it,

"Don't work too hard, oh and send my regards to Shara, her mom).., would you," she added.

Tiiona smiled.

"Of course, Sy, you know he's still single? I should set you two up?" She playfully added, sighing as she realised she had finally got herself to a place where she could even think about something like that. She had rarely trusted people outside of their small circle.

"He's a friend, that's all..." Syala replied sternly, seeing the look of hope in Tiiona's eyes. She sat staring, noticing Tiiona resign herself to his rejection.

"Tii'..." she called out as she finished putting on her knee-high boots near the door, causing her to turn and look back at her,

"It would do me a world of good, to spend some time with someone, so..." Tiiona smiled instantly, interrupting her before he finished.

"I'll sort it out..., something simple. I've got your diary so I know when to arrange it for... leave it to me..."

———

The young man clambered out of the transport, singing along to the music which was still blaring out,

"Ain't nobody better, it's just me against them all, I paid the price, I ain't no fool. Soon they'll see I was meant to rule..." he sang out of tune, not caring if he was disturbing the silence, before the music stopped abruptly.

"God, love those AERREA girls, those verses, can't stop myself" he said to himself as he pressed a button beside the door of the transport, before it lurched to the side, It was barely keeping itself hovering, an old pre-redesign Correlian city hopper.

Long gone was the bright, striking red paint, which had faded into a rusty pink hue over the cycles, marks from countless touch ups which had failed to restore her to her prime. He had the option of taking a taxi to the event, but changed his mind at the last minute, for a moment he thought, 'maybe I should have taken that taxi, better than turning up in this' as he pressed a small button to close the door of the transport, he sighed.

The landing was rough, not as smooth as it could have been.

"Damn thrusters," he cursed as he smiled at a friendly face rapidly approaching him.

"Don't give me that. It ain't the thrusters; not when you're too heavy on the throttle, she purred like a Theban kitten when I sorted her out for you last month"

"Well, maybe that's true, maybe I am too hard on her, probably because I just lost my job and Valisa broke up with me; so, I might be a little inpatient with her..." he mumbled in reply, slamming his hand against the closed door.

"What's the matter? You ain't yourself, Myla said anxiously.

"Valisa broke up with me," he repeated nervously, this time clearer than before.

"What a bitch. Today was supposed to be your big day too, wasn't it?" enquired, in response, Corr nodded gently.

"Hey, come on, we got a downhill through the Konor mountains, and we're here at the bottom of the mountain with a few hours to kill" she paused, as she ran her fingers through her purple hair, Let's sit inside your transport and get warm, and you can tell me all about it..." she insisted.

"I don't know," he said shyly, not sure whether she was being genuine or just wanting to get out of the cold.

"Don't worry," he said, leaving the block,

"We'll have a good time. I promise, I've got a good shot this time." She exaggerated. She knew he had a shot, as fair as anyone else, as long as 'they' didn't arrive. He tried to forget the last race, he was beaten by them. They had stayed back until the last mile, then within moments they were 400 meters ahead, easily winning the race.

Moments Later...

Corr and Myla were sitting on the floor of his transport, the old bucket seats in the back had been pulled out and retrofitted with a makeshift bed, great incase you wanted to stay there for a few days instead of paying for a hotel pre-race.

Myla rubbed her hands.

"at least it's warmer in here than last time, so you

managed to get the heating working." She looked at Corr, he was still lost in thought. She sighed openly.

"Do you think i have a chance this time?" He asked as he looked up at her. She smiled the moment he looked at her, before casting her gaze away nervously, bushing as she looked away.

"Is that what you really want to ask me? Corr?" she asked, as she felt her heart racing.

"What...?" He replied, not taking the hint. She clambered closer to him, putting her hand on his knee, looking at him straight in the eye.

'Ill have to do it myself...' she thought, usually not wanting to make the first move, but if he wasn't going to, she would.

"You've got me here, wearing very little, in your transport all alone, and all you can think about is the race..." Myla playfully remarked, somewhat hurt by his inability to recognise it.

"Do I have to spell it out for you? I like you... like really like you." Myla spoke, blushing, casting her gaze to the floor, being stopped by Corr lifting her gaze with his finger under her chin,

"And I like you too..." Corr whispered, before leaning forward and kissing her gently on the lips.

CHAPTER 35
"SO, YOU READY TO GET CRUSHED AGAIN..."

3 Hours Later...

The mountain retreats air was heavy with damp from the fog from earlier in the day, which had been clearing slowly but still clung in places, especially this high up in the mountains, the city of Murl could be faintly made out in the distance, on a perfectly clear day you could just make out the towering skyscrapers of the prefectural capital, over 30 miles away.

Hovering by the side of an old road was a transport shuttle, its back doors open, out of the transport hopped a masked figure, clothed in all black, they looked out into the distance, their face covered in a matte black mask.

The mask was a polygonal representation of a face, its surface lit by two orange strip lights on the edge of the jacket. After a few moments it shrugged its shoulder before It bounded down the street, with a spring in its step, carrying a hover board in a vertical sling on its back, the board sticking out past its knees.

The finely tailored and fitted jacket it was wearing was damp with moisture, the moisture clinging delicately to every surface; It reached towards its mask and pressed a small button below the chin, the mask hissed, jettisoning air before they spoke, their voice distorted, artificial, masking their true voice.

"So, you ready to get crushed again", it spoke, its voice distorted and gravelly as it walked towards a small group of individuals gathering around the transport drop of point beside a closed mountain hotel.

As was expected this time of year, the snowboarding season was months away, no one lived up here this time of year. One of the group unwrapped a makeshift scarf from around his face, before speaking, He was trying to keep warm, but it didn't work. Not in this place, the cold and damp had got into his bones., causing him to shiver.

"Ah, so you decided to turn up this time, you know those tricks from last time ain't gonna work, your days are numbered... then we'll finally get to see who's underneath that mask..." Corr confidently bragged, causing a ruckus from those around him, some in support, some shouting in disagreement, either way he had said a controversial state-ment, but he didn't dare, he laughed to himself, before being cut off by the figures response.

"Brave, but stupid..." it responded, taking off the sling carrying the long hoverboard, placing it carefully on the floor. The board was black with yellow detailing.

"Maybe this time I'll kick your ass and send you back to that girlfriend of yours...." The masked figure laughed, this addition causing the crowd to laugh out loud.

"They got you there..." the crowd laughed sarcastically at Door, before being silenced by the masked figure once again.

"Oh, sorry, I forgot, we gotta find you a new one, you keep wiping out on the circuit and in love, bad omens... bad omens,"

The masked figure replied, before gesturing rudely at him with their hand.

He hissed in reply, a typical reply from a Thetan, his forked tongue, quickly recalled after exposure to the cold air.

"Well, well, we'll see about that.." he retorted, stepping towards them, casting his bag to the floor, standing less than a meter away from the masked figure, angry that they had brought his ex-girlfriend into this.

"Hey, leave her out of this, it's between me and you..., your lucky our sponsors want to see us all tonight, otherwise I'd knock you on your ass, here and now, get to see who is really in charge here" Corr had to talk himself down from throwing a punch, he could take them he thought, he was taller and stockier than they were, a clear foot taller than them, but a fight before a race, he'd be thrown out, all this smack talk was just bravado he thought, but at some level it hurt, especially after the ex-girl friend mockery.

"Heard we got some potential investors looking at sponsorship..." he paused,

"Heard they might try to take us professional..., so I ain't gonna ruin our chances. We'll keep this professional." He paused.

"And they ain't gonna sponsor us, without you here..." he added before covering his face again as a cold wind blew past them, causing him to shiver again. It was getting brighter, the fog dissipating more, a winding road making its way down the mountainside slowly made its appearance.

"You'll get no disagreement here...I am better than you..." the figure replied.

He was about to step forward when he was stopped by someone behind him shouting,

"Miku... Miku" as they barged past him and embraced the masked individual.

"Miku, you know what Corr is trying to say, stop being hard on him..."

Miku embraced him, patting him on the back, just barely able to reach around him

"Luca, you know I'm only fucking with the boy, too hot headed, which is strange for such a cold-blooded bastard, just like every Thetan I've met" "

Corr smiled, trying to hide his rising anger, but failing miserably, he hated being here, too cold, it was just too cold.

"Luca, it's between me and Miku..., none of your concern..."

"Well, the sponsors reached out to me, so, it is my concern, we do well, and I get paid..." he remarked.

"We all get paid..." he added as he carefully stroked his beard.

"Better get yourself ready. We ain't got much time. I managed to get a block on transports and comms for.

Corr turned around and walked off, thinking back to his homeland. The warmth of Nuyla in the summer, even the cold winters were nothing in comparison to this place, stories about this place were legends to those in the sport.

Over the winter months, there were over thirty thousand living here in the mountains, but they were all gone. Homes left abandoned, food left in storage. In a few months, it would be packed, but not today.

No one had attempted to do this track. Until now. With knowledge of this, he felt a brief twinge of unease. Now this place was even more infamous, "the end" some had called it, the last place you would ever visit. One wrong move would result in your early death.

Today was Miku"s first visit. They looked carefully at maps of the area, making sure they remembered their route down the mountain. Updated incline scans and exact measures of the camber of the track were glanced over. As Misu looked at the map, they could sense someone close by. Without hesitation they quickly swiped the holo map away.

Everyone was expected to be on their best behaviour, no fights between riders, just the usual pre-race battle of words and egos. Everyone had to be good. Sponsors from a leading investment company were watching. This race would decide if the sport went professional. Luca paced around the starting point, bouncing between taking to Yaltz on communications, and a shuttle off towards the back, which no one else was allowed to go into. He stepped out of the shuttle, nervously making his way back to the starting line, walking past everyone, not noticing anyone in particular. He had to be perfect. He nervously rubbed his hands together, trying to keep warm.

'It must be perfect,' he murmured. It had to go flawlessly

Especially him, spokesperson. He was appointed by the community itself, if anything went wrong, it would be him that would face the wrath of the community. .

———

He cleared his throat, before announcing, Luca's voice carried through the cold air, Miku slowly clenched their hands, before reaching over and pressing a button on the wrist controls, a red symbol appeared projected out of the control - warning, warning : Defence Shield Deactivated" it flashed, as Miku gestured for it to disappear. Luca's voice came through the communications channel:

"The ancient Det Than-an mountain trail is both a feast for the soul and a treat for the eyes as well" he gushed, Miku looked around, Corr was standing to their left, Darro and Grafan to their right, Jallo, Bleys and Gaa behind them, with Lacen and Reymet to the rear.

The track below them steeply defended, curving to the left before winding its way back into the forest below. "A place which had seen some of the best in our sport unfortunately meet a gruesome end..." he paused,

"Some of the bravest riders I know call it enders's path, some of the decent into madness. To me and others, it's." he paused.

"the thrill to end all thrills..." he stopped forgetting himself before adding his voice, losing all its enthusiasm and become formal,

"For legality reasons, I must stress any accidents happened at the beginnings of our sport many cycles ago, all before the introduction of defends shields," he proclaimed before falling back into his usual reporting tone of voice

"Before I became too self-conscious about the speeds going down here, I made my first mountain downhill here, 20 cycles ago. After my first time there, I was in love; the trees, the mountains, the fresh air, the trails, everything in Det Thanan is breathtaking. I thought I'd never return" he stopped, glancing over at the waiting riders, each of them then turned towards the track, climbing on board their hoverboards. The atmosphere was building. Luca looked over at Yalik who was standing at a makeshift communications hub from the back of a transport. She gestured that everything was ready.

"There are multiple ways down this course. Every one

of them offers something different; from narrow, exposed rocky ancient hiking tracks, to twisty, root-crossed forest paths to shrub-lined tracks, but they all have one thing in common..." he paused for dramatic effect

"a very steep angle of descent!, today we have an estimated decent time of 10 minutes, 43.06 seconds" he glanced over at a tablet before adding

"a time set 24 cycles ago, by the legendary Ivuur Coreen. May the goddesses treat him well" he gestured towards the sky, closing his eyes for a second, making quick prayer before continuing.

"I hope you've come prepared with a new set of brake thrusters, and a desire to yield to gravity-enhanced fun...."

"And a final welcome to our fans watching from across the empire.." his voice boomed, before he glanced at a screen, gasping and stepping back in surprise,

"My goddess, we have 865 million viewers right now, thank you all for watching, today's race is tipped to be a race for the ages, Can Miku the masked rider win their 21st consecutive downhill, or will someone step up and snatch glory from their grasp...all will be decided here... broadcasting live from Det Than-an..."

"Choosing a favourite way down this beautiful mountain would be really difficult., I wonder which way our riders would choose this morning. I love the ride down from the top of the abandoned Calissian vineyard; taking Dea Sanit, via BiaVasi But it's hard to beat the views from the top of Dimos des Javan - devils decent, just to the west of Det Thanan..."

———

They raced down the tight winding road, making its way down the mountain, leading towards the devils pass, the wind blowing past them at great speed, chilling those that were unprepared. The whistling wind echoed though the pass. A winding stretch which doubled back up the mountain to avoid the devil's mouth chasm, before taking a steep decent down through a maze of twists and turns.

Corr kept his hands back, his palms sweaty, his hearts raced, feeling like they wanted to escape out of his chest. He had never done this track before, not even the holo simulations, he gripped the braking repulsers tightly. Hoping that they were enough to slow him down during the decent. He'd seen enough footage of wipe outs during this to know that just a few feet more per second was enough to take him out.

Now was the moment of judgement. Just ahead was a small transport that blocked access to the street, he knew who was there, it was the broadcast team, a gathering of influential broadcasters who were reporting on that morning's race.

He knew he had to make a good show, just after passing them he was third, picking up speed, he glanced at the tracker on his left arm, Lacen and Bleys were interchangeable at first and second, he was third and Miku was way back at ninth, he smiled as he tucked himself in, the mountain pass was becoming narrower, the wind forcing him back, as if a natural air brake, which then stopped, causing him to pick up speed, hurtling down a path which became narrower and trickier, limiting them to single file, causing him to fire his breaking thrusters before they started smoking.

It didn't look too good. This was the third time this had happened. I really needed to hire a mechanic.

"Great,"

"Uh, Corr, I think you came too early on that one." A voice came through the comms system, causing him to think for a second, just as Miku came hurtling past him, arms behind them, they were picking up speed, within a second they were gone, carving through the air as if it didn't matter, quickly approaching Bleys on second, overtaking effortlessly before taking on Lacen at first.

As she pressed on the breaking thrusters, a thruster gave out, blowing out a shockwave which cause Miku to destabilise her balance.

Immediately Miku started wobbling and weaving, the breaking thrusters not responding as she began to panic, she wasn't slowing down and definitely not stopping, As she hurtled down the route, she glanced over at the speedometer , which was reading a constant 120km per hour she was lost in thought thinking through her options and making a choice. If she didn't want to rear-end the racer in front of her, causing a dangerous accident, he was slowing down in front of her, she could see herself gaining on him, and quickly, seconds lay between her and a crash into him.

'I could either steer left, risk overshooting the route and heading straight into the forest hoping there wasn't any spectators watching from the side of the route,' she thought, knowing any contact at this speed would kill them. They wouldn't have time to get out of the way due to the morning mist which had descended.

' I could steer right, which would give me a little space maybe 20-30 ft of grassland to lose speed before hitting old building at the end of the route. Without thinking, she turned the board into sharp left turn, causing the board to fly away from her as she came off tumbling down the route at close to 80km per hour, instinctively she tucked her arms in and hoped that she could tick in her legs enough to stop them from snapping as she headed towards the grassland.

Meanwhile, the crowd was in shock, hastily rushing to where they hoped she'd stop. She continued rolling before she skidded off the road, went about 40-50 ft diagonally, hit a rock which coughed her to scream out as it struck her in the left hip. There was the sound of her hip being broken by the impact with the rock, the pain overwhelming her, once she stopped rolling and was sprawled out in the middle of a grassy field, the world was still spinning, as this subsided she managed to turn onto her back, she lay still, frozen in shock as the adrenaline rushed through her system, masking the pain from the accident. She cried out a little as Bleys and the others arrived; she began to panic, the adrenaline still rushing through her veins at the same time the realisation set in, her breathing became deeper as a medic attended to her, after sliding her on to a stretcher and supporting her neck, they carefully removed her mask, the cold air rushing in, chilling her face. The sound of gasps being one of the last things she heard,

"That's Tiiona, from Aerrea....she's Miku..." Luca exclaimed as he realised who it was as the rest of the mask was removed., before turning towards the drone and gesturing for the feed to be cut, within moments the drones fell to the floor.

CHAPTER 36
"SHE ISN'T GOING ANYWHERE QUICKLY..."

6 Days Later...

BEEP! The ventilation device sounded, its high-pitched sound reverberated within the small brightly lit room. It beeped again as Tiiona's chest rose and fell slowly, in perfect rhythm.

With every exhale, the air quickly escaped from a small ventilator. She looked a mess, her hair disheveled, the skin on her left cheek still bruised from the accident, the skin on her lips dry and cracked.

The ventilator occasionally misting up from the warm air as she exhaled. A small pebble shaped device on the top of the mask flashed multiple lights with every exhale. Again the device beeped loudly, this time the tone of the beep changed, the pitch was higher.

Within moments, Tiiona's eyes opened quickly as she inhaled deeply, as if startled. Her thoughts were chaotic, 'where am I, what happened...' she thought, not understanding where she was.

The ventilator beside her began beeping repeatedly, the beeps ringing out. Within moments, she quickly closed her eyes again, wincing against the bright light. She began to shiver as the cold breeze struck her bare skin as it wafted through the open window. Within moments, nurses and doctors slid open the door and wandered in, followed moments later by Nyxcerra, with Avéline, Jysell and Syala being gestured to wait outside, with them trying to make out what was happening through the frosted glass door.

A tall young doctor hesitated for a moment while he glanced at the screen beside Tiiona as she flickered her eyes open again, gradually getting accustomed to the light. Tiiona tried to speak, but nothing came out, just a gargled mumble of sounds. Her eyes opening wider again, her breathing became rapid and shallow.

"Wh, Wh…" she gargled, as tears formed in her eyes as she looked at him, yet the doctor still paid no attention to her, the nurse behind him eagerly awaiting his go ahead, as if she was in awe of him.

"Is she going to be okay??, you've not told us anything in days…" Nyxcerra pleaded as she grabbed hold of him by his jacket.

"You need to tell us something…" she threatened, her fists clenching, she haded being left out of the loop, shed always hated medical professionals, she felt they always made decisions without keeping her informed, casting her mind back to the time when her grandmother was sick, even as a child she understood what was happening, her grandmother being 397 cycles of age, she knew that she was dying, but the doctors and nurses ignored her, telling her that she would be fine, even though she knew she was dying. For a moment all these feeling came back, she pulled at his jacket with both hands, looking at him straight in the face.

"Tell me something..." she pleaded.

He tutted as he hastily pulled his jacket from her grasp.

"Fine..." he sighed

"It seems like her breathing has returned to normal. I'm surprised she's awake so soon after the reconstructive surgery... I was expecting another day or two," he spoke, before turning toward the nurse standing at the other side of the bed.

"Remove the ventilation, give her another measured dose of Kalita. 0.1% for the next ..." he paused in thought as he considered the time.

"The next three hours shall do, in the meantime., give her a session in the biotank," he added before turning back to Nyxcerra,

"She'll be fine, she will need your help and support for the next few months, her leg will be weak..., now I have other patients to see, she'll be out for the next few hours, go, sleep..." he looked her up and down, she wasn't as he had expected her to be,

"Have a shower, clean yourself up... she isn't going anywhere quickly." He said before he hastily exited the room, leaving the nurse to remove the ventilator.

Not once speaking to Tiiona, not even paying her any special attention, even though she was conscious, The nurse nervously stepped forward grabbing hold of the ventilator while picking up a small electrical device from the side of the bed placing this small cylinder the side of Tiiona's neck and gently pressed a small button on its side allowing the drugs to enter her system.

While doing this she carefully pulled the ventilator off. Attached to it were two thin long tubes, which retracted from the device slowly, as they retracted they scraped against the inside of Tiiona's throat. Causing her to gag, she coughed deeply as the tubes finally left her throat, allowing her to draw a deep breath, stared with tear-filled eyes at the nurse.

"Wh, Wh... Where..." she hoarsely coughed. Startling the young nurse, causing her to stagger backwards. Not expecting her to be aware of what was happening.

"You... you startled me. You should be taking it easy. Especially after the operation...." the nurse jittered as she put the ventilator on a table behind the bed.

"What operation." She spoke, her breathing becoming shallow and slow as the Kalita took effect.

"Don't you remember, after the accident? Your leg..." the nurse replied without thinking. Tiiona's tried to force herself to stay awake while the Kalita tried to put her to sleep.

The nurse dragged the cover open. Tiiona looked down in horror as the rest of her body was revealed before drifting off to sleep.

CHAPTER 37
"I'M SORRY..."

Forty-eight Hours Later...

"I'm sorry,..." Tiiona croaked her throat dry and sore, still recovering from the removal of the ventilator.

"I screwed up, big time, didn't I" she added as she looked at Nyxcerra, who was sitting next to the bed, her head in her hands. Nyxcerra raised her head slowly. She was half asleep, still dazed and confused.

"Wha, what, when, Ti...." she stuttered, trying to make sense of everything. She was make up less, her hair tied back, her eyes bloodshot, she looked as if she hadn't slept in ages, she tried to fake a smile as she saw Tiiona's face.

Tiiona looked around, this had to be a good hospital, the recognisable scent, the pristine white walls, the sound of systems monitoring her vitals, she knew it had been bad, her head throbbed, feeling uneasy, a little nauseous, hoping it would pass.

There were a few things she could remember, she could remember seeing Luca, feeling the cold mountain air against her cheeks as the helmet was removed, the shock of being unmasked, and extreme amounts of pain, everywhere hurt, every muscle tense, but how it happened, she couldn't remember, not really. Seeing Nyxcerra next to her bed worried her. There wasn't anyone else. She glanced around, expecting to be a ward, with other patients, but was surprised to find herself in a private room.

The morning sunshine streaming through the window, the calm and tranquil sound of the breeze blowing a small chime, added delicately to the sound of birdsong. She'd never been in a private hospital room before. She couldn't have afforded it, not at her level in society, but now she could. Her healthcare being paramount now, she got the best credits could afford. As a breeze touched her skin, she felt euphoric, 'must be the painkillers', she thought to herself, for once not feeling anything.

"It doesn't matter right now Tii, all that matters is that your okay..." Nyxcerra chipped in as she heard the door open and the other girls come in, she had to be herself and express her own concern, before acting as lead, Tiiona was her responsibility , she glanced at Tiiona who smiled back, nodding her head gently and reluctantly sighed before smiling as the other girls came close.

"That's all that matters...at the moment," Nyxcerra added as she stretched, her back aching, longing for her own bed, to be able to relax in a bath and soothe her aching muscles.

"It's nice to see you awake Tii..." Avéline added within seconds of arriving. Her mascara had run, but she didn't care, she'd been wracked with worry since they all heard, breaking out into fits of tears all night.

"You all came?, for this little accident..." Tiiona added, trying to force a smile. She couldn't remember much, just fragments. She could remember the emergency medical transport taking her from the mountainside, the bright overhead lights, the feeling of weightlessness. Her thoughts returned to the present as Nyxcerra spoke again, her tone concerned but laced with anger.

"You know full well that it wasn't a small accident, don't you..." Nyxcerra replied, as she stood up while trying to fix Tiiona's pillow. She tried to keep her voice low, not wanting anyone else to hear their conversation.

"4 fractures in your leg, dislocated wrist, broken finger in two places, three broken ribs, fracture collar bone, fracture in your pelvis, And more bruising and scrapes that I'd want to count..." she added as she ticked them off on the fingers on her left hand.

"You just spent the last forty-eight hours in a biogen tank, don't you remember??" She pleaded, her tone becoming worried, had the accident caused memory loss, did it affect her in other ways the doctors hadn't checked for?

"I don't, I don't remember..." Tiiona stuttered through the pain in her leg, as it overwhelmed her senses, the pain shooting up to her hip, before dissipating.

"I can't remember much of anything from the accident," Tiiona replied, wincing in pain as she tried to sit herself up, within moments she was doubled over in pain, she quickly grabbed hold of the bedsheet and bared down against the pain, hissing through the pain, unable to catch her breath.

"I'll be, fin...." she hissed through her clenched teeth. Seeing Tiiona like this caused Nyxcerra to rush towards the door, sliding the door open and looking outside, hoping that there was someone who would be able to help her.

"Nurse, we need a nurse over here. She's in serious pain

over here." She called out, wanting someone to come anytime, a doctor or a nurse.

"Nyx, it's fine. Don't worry, I can deal with it." She added as she tried to fight through the pain.

"Well you don't have to be the only one to deal with it, we are all here" Avéline added as she grabbed hold of Tiiona's hand,

"So I'm guessing I'm in trouble, serious trouble, with the label," Tiiona spoke as she looked at Nyxcerra. Trying to read her expression, but unable to read her, somewhere between confused, angry and tired.

"Surprisingly not...I know I'm surprised too" Avéline jumped in, enthusiastically, unable to contain her excitement.

"They, they covered it up...?" Tiiona stuttered, surprised by Avéline's answer, not sure that she heard her correctly.

She looked at Nyxcerra, unable to work out her expression.

"Well, no. everyone knows about it...." Nyxcerra added as she was passed a small pebble shaped device by Syala, after she whispered in Nyxcerra's ear, causing her to look worried, taking a sigh as he pressed on the pebble an image was projected into the room. A presenter stood outside the hospital. They had found out where she was staying.

"Hello Illax here, we are standing here just outside the gates to the Kismu Medical hospital at Silver Acres, and we still busy reporting on the current EBB headlines, the revelations that superstar Tiiona, the rapper and dancer for all Impiri girl group Aerrea was involved in a high-speed downhill longboard accident. Over the six days since the incident, we are still seeing a massive interest in this topic." She paused as the camera panned over to a huge bed of flowers and candles outside the gates to the hospital.

"Messages of support have come in from across the empire, from fans of all ages, other artists across the industry, to celebrity fans at all levels, noticeably.." she stopped as the camera focused down at a large bouquet of flowers, with an Imperial seal on its side.

"Her Imperial Highness Princess Adelphia of Alamathea, being an avid supporter, this bouquet being delivered just moments ago by a member of the Imperial Household., much to our surprise." The reporter still speechless.

She walked over towards a huge crowd gathered with small candles, the crowd was made up of a mixture of citizens from different species, of varying ages, each one of them praying, some chanting, others singing.

"We have had a crowd of devoted Aerrea fans who have camped out here for the last four days, praying and singing, hoping for her rapid recovery..." Illax added.

"What we do know it that interest in this incident has become a massive part of the daily entertainment conversation, as the news has just reached the outer worlds, currently a hundred and fourteen billion have seen the accident on replays, with three hundred and eight billion having watched the unmasking."

"In recent updates we are lead to believe that major crisis talks are being undertaken at BYL, with some stating the label are annoyed with the situation but cannot be seen to have a heavy-handed approach..." the presenter exclaimed.

With that, Nyxcerra swiped away at the projection, placing the device on the bed.

"I don't know where they are getting that information from, buts its correct. Aeryth and Leix have been busy trying to spin this, unofficially your lucky that it went that viral, otherwise you were going to be put on hiatus, amid discussions on your dismissal" Jysell looked at her,

"But don't worry about it Tii, the line that Leix is using is a work of genius..." she beamed

"You were representing the company, in a 'semi-official' capacity, the investment consortium who was planning on taking the sport professional was controlled by BYL's sports entertainment division," Nyxcerra sternly added. Shaking her head disappointingly.

"The terms of staying in contract with the label have changed, you are compelled to no longer race, however..."

"In recognition of the media attention this has brought, the consortium has requested that you be allowed to be an ambassador for the sport on an ongoing basis, in between your Aerrea duties and touring schedule."

CHAPTER 38
"YOU COLLAPSED AT THE HOSPITAL..."

A Few Hours Later

"Nyxcerra, Lady Jaeihai..." a voice called out, forcing Nyxcerra to awaken from her slumber. Still dazed, she opened her eyes. The room was dimly lit, the blinds were closed. A small light above her was lit dimly.

She couldn't recollect how she had gotta there, she knew where she was, she'd been in the buildings infirmary before, for a slip and fall, but this time she didn't know why, all she could remember was helping Tiiona across the foyer in the building, then feeling a-bit strange, the next thing she was here.

She turned towards the voice. Beside her, a young man sat on a chair. As she looked at him, he noticed her move and gradually stood up. He was young, couldn't have been over sixty cycles in his prime. His gentle expression calmed her nerves. His voice was low. He placed the back of his right hand on her cheek. She pulled back as his hand was cold, gasping.

"It seems like your temperature is finally back to normal. That's nice to see..." he added, his voice calm and reassuring.

"Where..." Nyxcerra croaked, her throat dry.

"Where are you...?" He completed her sentence, Nyxcerra slowly nodded her head, still slightly coming around after fainting.

"You collapsed in the lobby from exhaustion."

Nyxcerra looked at him, bemused. She shook her head gently.

"I'm fine, just a bit tired." Nyxcerra replied, trying to pull herself up, but unable to move. She pushed down with her right arm, and shifted up slowly. Falling to the left side as she struggled to get further up.

"Maybe I'm a little more than just tired...."

"Yes, Lady Jaeihai, your blood oxygen levels were drastically low. It was a miracle that you hadn't collapsed earlier. You need to take it easy... listen to your body when it's trying to tell you things,"

CHAPTER 39

"WHO WOULD I TELL MY JOKES TO, MAKE FUN OF FOR BEING BOSSY..."

A Month later....

The calm in the forty-second-floor apartment ended abruptly, as was normal now.

"Where's Avéline?" Tiiona asked curiously as she hobbled through the doorway of the small kitchen, which lead into the living room, a large colourful rug lay in the middle of the floor, it was no longer the spare living room from when they had moved it, the walls were covered with framed posters of their touring schedule, pride of place were the awards that they had received as individuals or as a group, all safe behind a force field.

It was no longer sparsely decorated, there were more plants dotted around the room, a small tami fruit tree grew next to the kitchen, its small yellow fruit being used frequently in Jysell's cooking, a few hanging flowering plants brought some colour to its white walls.

Tiiona stood drying her now short brown hair with a colourful towel awaiting a response but getting nothing.

She sighed loudly. She hated it when no one answered. She spoke again, raising her voice slightly. Why didn't Nyxcerra reply she thought, looking over at Nyxcerra who sat at the table, her blouse soaked with sweat from the last dance rehearsal. But she didn't care, she was lost in thought, leaning over a digital pad while tapping her fingers absent-mindedly on the table's worn wooden surface as she stared into the middle distance before she looked down at her dark turquoise tattoo.

"Nyx?" Tiiona added, causing her to snap out of her daydream.

She glanced up, revealing the smudged eyeliner and run mascara lines, catching Tiiona by surprise.

"Oh, Hey Tii... she's in the studio again, she's getting stuck on these lines again..." she abruptly stopped,

"Forget about that Nyx, what's wrong? You need a nice cold shower," as she handed her the towel.

"I'll be fine, it's just..." she paused, unable to find the right words to say.

Tiiona looked confused, trying to read Nyxcerra's expression, trying to take it all in before grabbing at a chair next to her, pulling it out and sitting next to her, wincing in pain as she sat down.

"Nyx, I think I've understood what happened, after talking with Dr Anwat...." Tiiona revealed, surprising Nyxcerra, who instantly looked at her, hating him. She couldn't trust what he said, she just couldn't. But it wasn't about her, she thought, hoping that Tiiona's time with him was more productive than hers.

"I know you'll be surprised. I was. He actually got me to think about why I did what I did."

"He suggested that I tell you, so you can help me with

my recovery, my journey to a less self destructive me."
Tiiona pleaded, hoping that she would be able to help.

"Well, I'm sure we know what is the cause of this. Her
death, it sent me to a dark place"

"I have to admit, watching the fires consume her body
was tough. I see it every time I close my eyes, every. Single.
Time." Speaking through clenched teeth. She bared down,
finding it hard to sit. The support braces supporting her
hips made it difficult for her to sit, especially the way she sat
down.

With every few moments sitting on the chair, she
winced in pain. The medication had been wearing off for
hours. The realisation finally hit Nyxcerra. Tii had buried
her own grief to help her, driving her to this, and she felt
ashamed that she hadn't noticed, ignoring the late night
disappearances, the bruises, the excuses for her tiredness.
She wanted to say something, to apologise, to let her know
she understood.

"We all know Ceres went on to rebirth, her essence
woven into another existence by the goddesses." She
paused. the tears began welling in her eyes as she tried to
force back her emotions

"Who are we to argue with goddesses plans, but I miss
her, Who would I tell my jokes to, make fun of for being
bossy..." Tiiona rambled, as tears trickled down her cheeks,
she stood up, trying to release the pain in her hip. She
sighed, her breathing shallow. She was out of breath.
Nyxcerra stood up, trying to support Tiiona, who waved
her off.

"Who would I ask for advice about everything? Who
would I pull practical pranks on? Tell me who! No one,
that's who," Tiiona cried out before sinking onto the floor.

Her body crumbled, the pain overwhelming her. Nyxcerra rushing over to help her, unable to help her stand.

"I can't be the tough one all the time, especially not now.." she cried as Avéline entered the kitchen, rushing over and held her close, carefully pulling a fabric handkerchief from out of her sleeve, offering it to Tiiona as she cried, her mascara running down her cheeks.

Nyxcerra felt lost, unable to help.

"It took this long for it to really sink in, to make me realise how much I miss her, I don't know what I was thinking with the racing maybe it was just to feel something, to feel alive" Tiiona ranted as the tears ran down her cheeks

"You know, really feel alive, maybe it was a cry for help" she paused and wiped a tear from her eye

"Maybe I wanted to join her. She understood me, she understood us all."

"But you turned off the safety shield. It's supposed to keep you safe. It can't do that when you disable it..." Nyxcerra pleaded.

"Yes, I was stupid for turning off the safety shields. I wanted to be in control of something in my life, you know. We've been told what to do every minute for the past eight cycles of our lives" "

"To me, the recognition wasn't even worth it, especially considering we don't know if I will be allowed to do it again, I've done reckless stuff before, I doubt I will survive this mess, I've caused too much trouble this time...."

Tiiona lowered her head in sadness, realising the stress, and difficulty she had caused.

CHAPTER 40
"HAVE A BIT OF FUN..."

"I have to admit, ma'am, the idea sounds worth it. I have a word with Elim and we get the potential of wider market access, and preferential treatment by casting agents" Nyxcerra added as she stood talking with Aeryth in her office,

"It's not for a while. I've got to have a discussion with Lady Vale, otherwise we wouldn't get a chance to even discuss it..."

She paused.

"I'm glad you can see this from my point of view, and what's best for the group"

"Well, you know I'm always happy to have a bit of fun, especially when it fits in line with my beliefs', which is why you're asking me of course" she smiled as she looked at Aeryth who nodded her head,.

"And if it helps us, then it's fine..." Nyxcerra was interrupted by the sound of a call coming through on Aeryth's communication system,

"I'll have to take this privately, would you mind..." she whispered, as Nyxcerra nodded her head and made an exit, shutting the door behind her. As she left, Aeryth tapped on a button on her desk and answers the call. An image of a middle-aged man appeared in-front of her, his dark hair slicked back, looking formal in a black suit with black shirt.

"Aeryth, it's nice to see you looking so well." He spoke, his voice gruff and tinted with sarcasm, his voice heavily accented, his light grey skin.

"Khedrin, Khedrin, I told you I'd get back to you on this. I've not had a chance to ask her..."

"Well, it's quite simple Aeryth, your next tour isn't going to happen, as the second your tour team transit syndicate space, you'll have your assets seized and impounded, unless we can come to an agreement..." he let his words ring out, knowing that Aeryth knew exactly what he meant.

"You know my request, a simple date with Jysell, a onetime offer. I'd hate to ruin our cycles of co-operation over one single missed opportunity. A date, nothing more..."

"Khe, I know what dates are like with you, remember? My predecessor made me have a single date with you, forty-five cycles ago, and I was young and stupid then, and you were a lot handsomer.."

"That hurts Aeryth, it does...." He playfully remarked, holding his hand to his heart.

"I'll have to have a word with her, leverage her continued work in fashion, it should pull some strings with her..." Aeryth added as she smiled at him, knowing that she had managed to get him to agree to what she wanted, she just had to apply some pressure to Jysell, which now was easier due to her none industry connections.

CHAPTER 41
"LOOKING FABULOUS TONIGHT...AND WITH RYX..."

3 Months Later...

Avéline stepped out of the transport, unsure of that the reaction would be, would they accept this, would it ruin her image, her fans' perception. She was dressed in a traditional Etrui dress, shorter than usual for the summer's heat. It was elegant and classy, fitting her physique.

The cameras went wild. Wanting to capture what she was wearing at the ceremony, she posed for the cameras and smiled, making her way towards the red carpet, with Ryx walking behind her, after stepping out of the transport.

She nervously walked onto the red carpet slowly, staggering slightly in her high heels with Ryx at her side, the music turned down almost instantly, everyone went quiet, conversations ended, influencers flocked over to their side of the red carpet, to get a glimpse of her, her dress had been hinted at, she'd carefully teased it through the social platforms, and tonight was the grand reveal.

However, her dress wasn't the reason on everyone turned to her, it was the fact that she was standing beside Ryx, her hand in his. She looked over at him and smiled. Ryx, knowing his place, lifted her hand to his lips and kissed it, smiling at the crowd, who erupted in cheers.

"Avéline, Avéline, so the rumours were true, so there is something going on between you and Ryx," a reporter asked, trying to ask over the cheers from the crowd.

"Maybe..." she coyly replied, before bowing, blushing heavily, she let out a breath. They had reacted better than she had hoped. Before looking at Ryx, her eyes sparkling.

"Can we have a comment about your relationship?, for the fans..." the reporter asked. Avéline was about to reply before she felt Ryx's hand tighten around hers.

"We are happy spending more time together to explore our relationship further," Ryx replied, smiling at the crowd.

Smiling to the crowds. Ryx spent some of his time introducing her to some of the other producers at the gala. This was her first Gala with him, they were now officially a couple. She had got sick of denying it. Nyxcerra had told her to just go out and do it. Fuck Leix and the marketing team. This was her personal life, and any publicity was good publicity.

In the past hour, rumours swirled that she was to attend with someone. This news took the outer worlds by storm, before the news made traction in the core worlds. Gone was her innocence. She looked confident, knowing that the media were going to enjoy this, and she was going to make the most of it.

She welcomed them with flashed smiles, casting her gaze over everyone, giving hugs to those she knew, knowing the drones would capture the details and the photos would be leaked to the media who would create their own narrative about what was happening, all part of the plan. Avéline knew what to do. Leix had told her who to see, who to hug, and who to ignore. If he was going to swim this, she had to follow his instructions., she'd initially hesitated about being seen out with Ryx, but he'd managed to change her mind.

Avéline paused. She had felt better than expected. Her nerves from earlier had subsided. She glanced over at Ryx lovingly as he accompanied her. She was in a gloriously expressive mood, even though she delicately embraced others to make sure that she still looked elegant as photos were being taken.

Ryx guided her towards a reporter, who was eagerly waiting for a brief comment, yet she stopped when she nearly bumped into a reported dressed in all black, in stark contrast to her dark red hair.

"I can't believe it..." the young woman spoke as she turned around.

"Avéline, daring.." she half stepped back, smiled as she looked at her,

"Looking fabulous tonight... and with Ryx..." she called out enthusiastically, her voice dancing through the air, causing Avéline to relax.

Avéline looked over at Ryx who looked at her and smiled, surprised to see her.

"Nice to see you too, Soka, it's... been a while.." Ryx replied, nervously awaiting some sort of response. It had been a cycle since he had seen her.

"Yes, it has.." Soka finally replied before looking back at Avéline, shaking her head playfully before embracing her gently.

'Well, I wasn't expecting this on my first night as a guest

reporter for BYL. Leix has some explaining to do..." she whispered into her ear, giddy with excitement.

"So sorry about that, what can I say, he's not always the best with words..." Avéline mocked, knowing that Leix had probably intentionally done this to cause drama.

CHAPTER 42

"LOOKS GOOD ON YOU..."

A Few Months Later...

Jysell dropped her leather bag on the dark marble countertop in the bathroom and blinked at her reflection. Her hair was pulled into a bun and adorned with a dark blue band, her black dress clung to her in all the right places, even managing to create the illusion of confidence, something she felt so uncomfortable portraying, especially dressed like this, in something Nyxcerra would wear, and would be confident in wearing.

A thick gold necklace lay around her neck, a present from Aeryth for all the girls a few cycles before, a rare gift, but she never wore it, it was brash, shiny, a statement piece, something Nyxcerra would definitely wear in a heartbeat, she preferred minimal jewellery.

She reached across and her fingers along the chain, feeling every single link. The gold was cold to the touch, especially having been stored in a small safe in the apartment. A rare statement piece, especially for her, as she never usually wore too much jewellery, finding it brash and uncouth. Yet tonight she wanted to look right, recalling what Aeryth had told her.

"He's expressed interest in meeting you, to help arrange for the safety of the girls when on tour, though syndicate operated space."

Jysell had known for a long time what things like this happened in the industry. That favour made things happen, but she was surprised that the sector head of the syndicate had become attracted to her, thinking she was beautiful.

For the past month, she had accepted that she would have to meet him; she thought she was cute yes, but never beautiful her features were sharp, and littered with narrow angles, her chest was painfully small, yet she still stood confidently, she never really cared about other people's opinions, especially on how she looked to any interested parties, confused on how Khedrin found her attractive.

She took a deep breath as she straightened the dress before carefully adjusting her bra, still shocked that Khedrin had gifted it to her. In the right size, it had been delivered by couriered.

Its cost was astronomical. Nyxcerra had been there when she opened it. She'd told her that they were the best that credits could buy, and she had been right, it was made of highly prized and sought after Therrian spider silk, which was divine, its brilliant turquoise silk still made her fill with joy, as she carefully tucked the straps under the black straps of her dress, in a way not wanting to hide its beauty.

She stopped, staring at herself, trying to ignore the sense of uneasiness prickling over her. It almost didn't seem possible, was she really going to go through with it, could she go through with it, with him, her own thoughts fighting within her, doing this would be a simple meeting or a meeting which lead to the bedroom, knowing subconsciously it was the second option.

Music played in the other room. Nyxcerra had returned home, earlier than expected. Avéline was out, Tiiona and Jysell were in the practise hall on the 77th floor working on a new dance routine as.

The upbeat melody of a song that she and Nyxcerra had been working on the prior night filled the air. Jysell shook her head as Nyxcerra turned the volume up. Nyx not realising she was here, Jysell had been given the day off by Aeryth, she had been at the spa for the morning, getting her monthly treatment, and a good massage to get rid of the muscle aches she still suffered from the strenuous touring..

"Jys.....Jys..." Nyxcerra called out, noticing Jysell's data tablet sitting on the table in the lounge. Her voice rang out against the music playing.

Jysell stayed in the bathroom. She carefully fixed her hair before applying. Bright red lipstick, she knew Nyxcerra was looking for her, but she couldn't face her questioning yet, she just wanted to get her explanation for looking this way straight in her head, otherwise Nyxcerra would see straight through it and not let her go, and would go herself.

"For all of us.." she murmured to herself. Jysell didn't want to talk about the real reason, she would stop her, and do it herself.

Especially not now, when the whole reason she'd got dressed this way was because Aeryth had arranged it under duress of having the tour be cancelled because of being abducted by a syndicate faction. Aeryth needed a favour and at least a date would be taken as payment, she hoped, trying to convince herself that's all he would want, ashamed to admit it wouldn't be enough.

"Snap out of it, it will all be fine," Jysell told herself., shocking herself in realising what she was going to do because Aeryth had asked her to. Well, she hasn't really asked, more threatened into doing, on the group's behalf.. She nervously reached into her bag for her lip gloss and reapplied, then stepped out into the hallway, her head held high. She contemplated what Nyxcerra's initial reaction would be.

"Jysell ?." Nyxcerra fell into step in front of her, wearing a dark fitted robe, wrapped tightly, leaving nothing to the imagination, her bare feet tapping along to the music.

"Wow, just wow, knew you would look presentable if you made the effort, but wow." Her voice trailing off, finding it difficult to control her own growing arousal.

"Cut it out Nyx, you know where I'm going, that meeting with Khedrin, Aeryth said if I did this, he'd guarantee our safety when flying through syndicate space," Jysell said cautiously. She'd always been a little unsure of herself, especially when someone complimented her.

"Though you were already gone this evening?, didn't realise you were still here?" She asked, reaching towards Jysell, who flinched for an instant, before Nyxcerra moved a strand of hair away from her face.

"Cheers," Jysell added before smiling, blushing easily, biting the bottom corner of her lip.

Nyxcerra's fingers curled to the side of Jysell's face, staring at her. Jysell nervously sighed, wondering how she could go through with it. Nyxcerra watched her, reading her hesitation, missing nothing. She raised an eyebrow in confused amusement.

"If you want me to go, I'll go. You said that Aeryth said I was his second favourite?..." she added, snapping Jysell out of her own thoughts.

"Definitely look the part, took me by surprise, nice touch with the necklace, looks good on you..., keep yourself safe..." Nyxcerra added, her voice trailing off at the end. A hint of nervousness and jealousy tinged her reply.

Jysell thought; she had never heard Nyxcerra's voice with a sound of jealousy in it. Was she really that beautiful tonight, a thought Jysell had experienced a lot, even more in the last few months, especially when Nyxcerra brought her playthings home with her. Part of her enjoyed it, seeing a weakness in Nyxcerra that she had never expected.

Hours later...

Jysell found herself sitting on the floor of the bathroom of his apartment, sitting in her lingerie, her hair disheveled, her mascara had run leaving trails down her cheeks. She sat staring into the distance, lost in thought, nervously shaking. Her shoes lay beside her as she was clutching hold of her dress.

The music was still playing loud, but from in here all she could hear was the rhythmic thumping of the bass, the vocals muffled, finally some peace. Jysell found herself as she came around from her thoughts. She wanted, no she needed to get out of here, go back home, and drink herself to sleep.

There was bound to be something strong in the liquor closet in the kitchen. She wasn't quite sure why she'd come in here, maybe to get away from seeing him. The smell of the artificial Kalita still tinged the air, even more now that she stood up.

She paused, turning on the tap so she could at least wash her face, remove the mascara, and tidy her hair. Khedrin said she could shower here, but that wasn't going to happen.

She looked beside the basin, looking at the ice chips in her empty cup, the ice hadn't melted yet, her head still spinning, she never drank that much, not in such a short time frame, but it was an easy to for her to dull her senses, and lower her inhibitions.

She sighed through clenched teeth as she gingerly got dressed, fixing the straps of her bra, before soaking her hands in the ice cold water she had run.

Khedrin was back, he had left the apartment while she sorted herself out, the sound of his voice, everything about him disgusted her. She carefully wiped the mascara away, plunging her hands back into the ice water, causing her to shiver. She stood looking at herself, hating what she had been forced to do, finally realising the sacrifices made to make it in this industry.

CHAPTER 43

"SHE'S A LITTLE TOO FLIRTATIOUS..."

Elim was busy talking to Nyxcerra, he carefully ran his fingers through his long hair, knowing that everyone was watching him.

Aeryth glanced over quickly and smiled as she talked with Leix, who was nervously surveying the room, this level of event wasn't to his taste, too many potential problems, for a second loosing his concentration. Aeryth's voice pulling him back into the conversation.

"Leix, Darling, calm down....focus.." she snapped, clicking her fingers at him with frustration before reverting to her usual tone.

"Doesn't take much persuasion for her to drum up a conversation with the most influential individuals in the room..." she laughed, even this far from home.

"However she's a little too flirtatious... as expected for an Artreia, typical for her tribe, too hedonistic for some" she added as she saw Nyxcerra grab a hold of his arm and pull it towards her waist as she whispered something into his ear that made he surprised before devilishly smiling, the sight of this caused Leix to begin sweating, instinctively wanting to get out of trouble.

"Doesn't she know he's off limits... if Lady Vale were to find out, we would be royally fucked !" Leix whispered though clenched teeth, realising others were watching him and could sense an unfolding situation, at that level everyone enjoyed watching someone else's downfall.

Aeryth laughed as she picked up a small glass from the bar, filled with an iridescent white liquid, she looked at him for a moment and laughter to herself.

"Leix, you have much to learn... and you worry way too much" she paused, noticing how worried his expression had become, she sipped gently from a small glass, its iridescent white contents glistening in the light, she enjoyed its thick slightly bitter creamy texture, which coated her throat on the way down, she savoured every drop.

"What makes you think she *isn't* acutely aware of what's happening here tonight...?" she quipped before taking another sip of the milky white drink.

"She... she knows..." he stuttered, causing Aeryth to laugh openly, she loved seeing Leix squirming, even though at times his worrying got on even her nerves.

"Of course, that's why we are even allowed in here, you know the circles I travel in, even this one would be off limits to me, we are all lucky to even be here, but she owed me a long standing... favour..." she calmly and proudly proclaimed, enjoying the fact that she was owed a favour, from someone at this level.

"Which I thought I would finally cash in..."

"She owed you..., Lady Vale owed you a favour, what for...?" Leix exclaimed before lowering the tone in his voice.

"Now that would be telling, all I can say is she might have a perchance for impressionable trainees willing to do

anything to get a shot at fame... and they did, for a time."
She laughed, knowing that some of them didn't last long in
the industry once they realised what occurred behind closed
doors.

"It was a common courtesy. I asked her if she would
allow one of our girls to 'privately discuss' a mutually bene-
ficial sponsorship deal with one of the brands which they
co-own..." she waited, letting the words sink in.

"And of course, she said yes, it's a simple business
matter she said, as long as the private discussions stay
private, and are concluded tonight..." Leix stood there
stunned,

"I didn't know you knew her that well." Leix nervously
enquired.

Aeryth ignored him as she gazed at Nyxcerra, who
stood across from them wearing a black flowery dress.,
which was ruffled up at her hip, revealing her long slender
legs,

"The latest summer fashion from the moons of Corcor-
dia" whispered someone over Avéline's shoulder, talking to
someone waitressing at the bar, She knew that Nyxcerra was
getting more than just his attention, she had attracted the
eyes of a lot of influential individuals, and that would be
lucrative for her, shed had to spend the night talking to
those who Nyxcerraa had caught the eye of.

"And Nyxcerra's fine with you, I don't know," he
sarcastically replied, "pimping her out to influential parties,
to further her career" he added, with bitterness in his
mouth.

"Really Leix, growing a conscious after all this time..."
she snapped back.

"It's not becoming of you, it really isn't,"

"and she is fine with it. She's one of the few that is

completely okay with it. We should have picked up on that cycles ago. would have helped win ver a few deals when she was a trainee."Aeryth added, realising she had missed out.

Avéline stood at the bar, listening to what they were saying, making her glance down at her own dress. She was beautifully dressed, but wasn't dressed sexily. Her dress was figure hugging in places, but didn't reveal too much. She hoped that Ryx would notice she had got dressed up for him whenever he was supposed to arrive.

She hoped that he enjoyed the surprise of having her back, having arrived back a day earlier than expected. Meanwhile Nyxcerra tipped her head back and rested a hand lightly on Elim's forearm, laughing uproariously at the jokes he'd just made, Avéline was just able to make out that he'd been told to make the most of the discussions with them working together. This caused Nyxcerra to laugh even more. If she was being fake, you wouldn't be able to tell. She was that convincing.

"Then I better make sure to dominate the conversation then..." she added. Avéline rolled her eyes, trying to keep herself composed. All this openly flirtatious talk was getting her flustered. She was getting uncomfortable, feeling her scales temperature rise as the least of her problems. She needed Ryx's company. She was all dressed up, and for no one.

Leix followed Aeryth's gaze, though he had heard rumours about Elim, he didn't particularly care for his known affiliations, all he knew was that he was an important player in the social scenes amongst the Impiri, his connections within the media industry across the empire were legendary, if you wanted to be in a movie or broadcast show, he was the one to know.

He was a known media darling, having caused a few

stirs by his openness to open relationships, having courted the daughters of some of the wealthiest business owners in this sector. But his association as the partner in waiting of Lady Vale worried him.

If they got this wrong, she could ruin them, and it wouldn't be difficult for her. It was not just her own influence, which frightened him, but now since the death of her father, Lord Vale. Her reach expanded further, He had operated a private military contractor business across twenty key systems, he could bend the ear of almost everyone at the top of society...and now all that power lay at the fingertips of Lady Kalidral Vale, an unknown quantity in any of his calculations.

"It's fine," she huffed, as she knocked back a shot, dabbing her lips afterwards with a blue silken handkerchief, before throwing the handkerchief onto the golden tray held by one of the waitresses.

"Everything will be fine. Her Ladyship allowed us this deal, as long as it serves her interest, no harm, no foul. Now we need to make this worth her graces."

———

Across the Club

The sound of music and merriment filled the club, Avéline sat at the bar. Listening to Tiiona and Soka, with some of the other girls from the company, her seniors, backup dancers and Nerys, their choreographer. She sat listening to every word, Avéline sat listening to the gossip from Tiiona, she knew everything, who was sleeping with who, the deals, the brake ups, the ups and the downs. Knowledge was power in these places, and she knew it all.

Avéline was seductively dressed, a revealing blue blouse, and a knee-length black skirt accentuating the curves of her body.

"And that's when she told me that she's had been sleeping with..." a voice brought Avéline back into the conversation.

She smiled, looking at Tiiona straight in the face, before grabbing her by the jaw and squeezed his face playfully.

"That's because you love the gossip don't you Tii" she mocked before letting her face go, as she saw Ryx enter the club, her hearts raced, ignoring Tiiona as she spoke to her, before following Avéline gaze, her jaw dropping in shock. In she walked, with another girl on his arm, looking loved up, laughing and smiling at everything she said. The girl he was with looking like Avéline made Tiiona do a double take,

"Maybe she's just a friend, you know..?" Tiiona spoke, unable to take her own gaze off the situation unfolding infant of her.

"I don't think she is..." Avéline's voice trembled as she saw Ryx stop and kiss the young woman, passionate on the lips before walking right past them, not evening noticing Avéline was there. Causing her hearts to break, Tiiona noticing this almost instantly, and turned Avéline around to face her, to distract her from what she had just seen.

Tiiona began laughing as she reached for a drink from a passing waitress, offering it to Avéline, who without taking her gaze off Tiiona, knocked back this new drink, which caused her to gasp as it burnt on the way down. Tiiona whispered in her ear,

"Don't make a show here. He's not worth it, especially

over her, really..." she added with a thinly veiled, worried tone in her voice.

"I'll speak with him later. Well, it might be a bit more physical than just words, on your behalf, of course..." she pleaded, never wanting to overstep her friendship with Avéline.

But she wasn't listening. She'd turned her attention inward and was muttering to herself, planning revenge on Ryx. That was typical for her. She was mild-mannered most of the time, except if she had been crossed. Now she was angry, no, she was furious. Her vicious side was vindictive. She couldn't let this go. How dare he ignore her when she had made all this effort, and in front of everyone, they all knew they were together, but no one confronted him about it?

It was common knowledge that Ryx was off limits. Conversations were fine, but this girl's openly flirtatious actions, in blatant disregard to the known social order.

Tiiona stepped in front of Avéline, grasping her by the hand. She could read her expression.

Avéline placed her hand on her chest, looking up at her, her eyelashes fluttering. She stared at her, trying to keep her emotions in check.

"He does this to me, in public, and what am I supposed to do about it, nothing...."

"That's it. It's over this time, no more. We are over... that fucking bastard..." her words shocked Tiiona. She'd never in all these cycles heard her get this angry.

"This bitch he's with, you know the hoe who is openly flirting with him, she openly challenges me, you know what I'd do if I could, don't you Tii'. She seethed through clenched teeth.

"I would grab her by that fake hair, drag her to the floor and..." she stopped,

"Why does he do this to me, in front of everyone else..." She cursed, glancing over at them, dancing lasciviously, they had to move to a more secluded area of the club, the erotic dancers had begun, and couples had started pairing off, relaxing in each other's arms, or making their excuses to leave early, to enjoy themselves in one of the open suites on this floor or the floor below, to possibly rejoin the soirée later on. Tiiona placed the palm of her hand gently on the side of her face, turning her gaze towards her, her hand trembling nervously.

"Then he is a fool, not deserving of your feelings, nothing but a fool," she whispered, loud enough that only she could hear, her voice barely audible. Avéline looked back at her, the realisation of her words casting into her thoughts, the look in her eyes changed rapidly, gone were the forming tears, she was livid, a cruel look flashed across her face as she stared at her, smiling a devilish smile before speaking, causing her to gasp in realisation.

"I need a minutes breather, will you join me outside for a moment..." Avéline asked before waiting for Tiiona's response ,

"Yeah, think you need one..."

———

Half an hour later...

Maybe Ryx should find out what it was like, she thought spitefully, storming back into the party after having a breathing, Tiiona had taken her out, to try and calm her down. She stood at the bar, staring at him from across the room. He deserved to see how it felt, watching her laugh and flirt and drink and get carried away with someone else.

Her eyes scanned the club, looking for someone, someone she could use for this hurtful display, someone who would be the type that would cause as much scandal as required in a short time, settling on a young Noysian at the bar, there he was standing alone near the bar, her hearts raced, he was no older than thirty, dressed handsomely in a dark green suit jacket over a black shirt, tightly fitted to his athletic torso.

His light blue skin lightened by white markings, in the same whitish hue as his eyes, a typical handsome Noysian, and tonight, he was in for a surprise. He was her date and didn't even know it yet.

"Him, really Avé, I mean he's definitely handsome," stopping to look at him, again, he was more her type than Avéline's she thought, remembering a crush she had on a Noysian boy she went to school with, before snapping back to reality.

"but a Noysian, I doubt he could handle one of us. He won't even understand the Talu -scales, no none Impiri does. How could they?..." Tiiona enquired, painfully mocking the previous relationship she had.

"and that's speaking from experience..." she laughed, her voice hinting at her experience.

"You don't know how bad it was with Zhu, trying to teach him, more laughable than pleasurable.." she added, but Avéline still stared at him, her eyes widening, her heart rate increased, she could feel her temperature rising, she wanted him and wasn't getting no for an answer.

"I know he's a Noysian, But I'm sure he's game for a little fun, and so am I, especially with how tonights going" she whispered to Tiiona who stood shocked as she took the initiative and walked out towards the bar, moments later.

"I want a drink," she announced as she brushed hastily past him at the bar, perching herself on a stool at the bar, before turning around to face him, letting her skirt slightly to allow her slender legs to be fully on show, wanting to give him a show, while leaning her elbow on the bar in a way that allowed her to support herself but keep him interested. She knew others were watching her, especially those from BYL, knowing they had seen what had caused her now out of character actions. She sighed a little sigh, knowing she was going through with this.

She couldn't care less about others perceived this, for once she wasn't coy about her self expression. She wanted Ryx to see. She wanted everyone to notice she wasn't going to take his humiliation. She didn't care about much of anything at this moment, except her new determination to let Ryx see how it felt, just a little. To show that she could play the same game.

He smiled at her abrupt greeting, before being distracted by her legs, which his eyes followed from her high heels up to her thighs.

"Bartender, a sweet cocktail for the young lady," he told the bartender after getting his attention, but Avéline was going to have none of it. Shaking her head and tutting gently.

"No, something a little stronger, if you wouldn't mind." She purred, looking at him straight in the eye.

"Okay,..." he stuttered, "I'm Rifan by the way" Rifan said slowly as he was studying her expression to gauge her mood.

"Maybe a Kaspian Sunset, double shot?" he suggested , but Avéline didn't care what she drank as long as it was something strong, something to remove the last doubts of her fear of making a fool of herself.

"I'd introduce myself, but I think you already know who I am..." Avéline added as she studied his reaction to her, the centre of his neck flushed a mild red, she playfully ran her index finger up the buttons on his shirt, feeling the heat from his body as she made her way to his neck.

"Now I definitely know you know who I am, getting a bit hot under the collar are we..." she playfully added, causing him to flush even more. She felt the telltale tingle of her scales reacting to her arousal, causing her hearts to race even more, not just from nerves but now from arousal. She shivered as she tried to focus.

"The Kaspian sunset sounds great, but make it double. I'm feeling a tad reckless tonight...and...." She stopped as she noticed the glances from others in the club, and the whispered conversations, before smiling coyly at him.

"I think I'd like to be reckless with you by my side, if that's not too much to ask..." she purred as she ran her fingers down his arm and grabbed him by the hand.

Rifan raised an eyebrow, surprised by her forwardness. She was different to what he expected, but this drew him to her even more.

"Two double Kaspian sunsets, hold the ice on mine..." he asked the bartender, who barely heard him due to the noise of the bar and the music playing, before busily getting to work, grabbing a bottle of a blue liquid from the self and started pouring. Rifan glanced at Avéline.

"So,...." He managed to speak before leaned over grabbing him by the collar and pulled him close, her lips centimetres from his.

"I hope this answers your question..." as she placed a gentle kiss on his lips, wanting a few seconds before withdrawing. The sweet taste of her lipstick lingered on his lips for a moment.

"Not... not really, why..." he managed to get out, as he noticed some of the crowd looking at them and whispering,

"Why you,... because you caught my eye, and can't a modern woman appreciate someone and think about her own needs and desires..." she replied as she smiled when she was handed a tall glass filled with ice and a mixture of yellow and blue liquids.

"So I thought you'd like to join me..."

CHAPTER 44
"YOU KNOW THAT, DON'T YOU?..."

An Hour Later...

The party was in full swing; the music was loud; the bar was packed and Avéline had just walked back into the main floor, after spending some private time with Rifan in the vip suites up on the mezzanine floor, it was late—late enough that she wasn't even sure whether Ryx was still here, she secretly wished he was there, just to wind him up even more. He'd hurt her, even worse was that he had hurt her publicly, she wanted to hurt him back.

She circled the fringes of the party, wanting everyone to get a good look at her, to start rumours, something Nyxcerra had talked about one evening. She enjoyed having Rifan in tow, holding onto his arm with one hand, clutching another Kaspian sunset cocktail in the other, sipping occasionally while laughing at jokes that others made, she'd never had this drink before tonight , but it suited her, she knew that if she drank more, she would have to revise her opinion of the stuff. It was thick, with a consistency somewhere between liquid and syrup. It was sickeningly sweet, but she didn't really feel the effects of the alcohol.

She paused, letting go of Rifan, who stopped behind her and offered to take her glass.

"Let me just fix this..." she purred.

"My Queen..." Rifan smiled,

'A Queen' Avéline thought to herself, she could suffice being his queen she thought, thinking for a moment that he must have been with an Impiri girl before, he knew exactly which scales to touch, which to stimulate and it what way, recalling the orgasm she had experienced with him, causing her to blush.

"Having a flashback..." Rifan asked coyly.

"Might be, might be thinking of seeing if you're up for a repeat performance later on..." she flirted back.

She reached up and ran her fingers through her hair, which was falling in thick curls down the back of her neck. Her scales still tingled, a sensation so long after the fact was a surprise. A look of fear washed across her face as she saw Ryx, glass in hand. Staring at her, as she locked gazes, the crowd slowly dispersed between them, the music stopped after the DJ was interrupted by a member of the crowd.

Avéline stepped forward, hesitated before walking towards him, leaving Rifan to stand back. As she walked forward, she stopped, looked at the DJ at the corner of the room, with a look of confusion on her face.

"Turn it back up, it's all ok, he was just leaving..." she mocked, causing some in the crowd to start laughing, including some who had been chatting with Ryx. She looked confident, but inside she was panicking , that no matter what she did, she wouldn't win against him, that she would never be pretty enough, clever enough, as he wouldn't have cheated on her if she had been better.

"I ain't going nowhere, but maybe it's you who should be going. This party is for the grownups, not you, your out of your depth here, and you know it..."

This cut Avéline's confidence. She had always felt out of her depth, and he knew it. But to bring it up in public, she'd grown over the past few cycles. She wasn't going to stand for it, especially from Ryx.

"And she's out of your league, Ryx..." with this, the crowd broke out in laughter. Ryx's smile disappeared in an instant, as even those around him couldn't contain themselves, much to his chagrin.

"I mean, honesty, you can have her. It's not my concern anymore. It's over between us..." she exclaimed, feeling relief at having told him.

"I just hope she can do more with the...." She mocked, raising her voice at the end, just so everyone could hear, before gesturing with her little finger in the air,

"Short comings in the bedroom," she added, with a vicious grin on her face.

She wasn't sure why she'd gotten so upset earlier, it now all made sense, the reason why Ryx had been acting nice to her, and she knew it all must be an act because the first chance he got he had been with someone else, he must have hated her. How could he not? After everything she'd done for him.

Ryx sighed deeply, his fingers twitching around his wineglass, staring at Avéline.

"My problem in the bedroom, it's not my fault that you're a frigid bitch who doesn't know how to please her, man. Why do you think I've had to get my fun elsewhere?" He replied, this taking Avéline by surprise, her hearts ached, of course she didn't know what to do, she'd never admitted it to anyone before. She was inexperienced. She'd never been with anyone before.

She had been brought up that way, not until she was bonded, but then things changed. She thought she loved him and that he loved her, too. She bared down, watching him mock her, tears welling in her eyes, she couldn't believe that he thoughts she was frigid.

"Frigid?, you were my first, didn't you realise that" Avéline replied, blushing, never expecting to reveal that in public.

"Maybe you should have had a word with Nyxcerra before we got together, to give you some tips.."

"Hey, don't bring her into this, it's my life, my situation, you're just a cheating bastard," she scowled, throwing her glass to the floor, shattering it everywhere.

A member of security stepped forward, standing between them,

"Do we have a problem here..." he gruffly interjected, making sure that nothing else happened.

"Why would there be a problem?" He gestured to the room with his drink.

"All of this is just... perfect." He proclaimed.

"As I said, she was just leaving..." Ryx sarcastically added, raising an eyebrow, looking around the crowd of onlookers.

"Don't start." She replied,

"Don't start what?"

"You know exactly what I'm talking about. You humiliated me, in front of everyone... I thought we had something" "

He masked a scowl with a smirk as everyone fawned over Avéline, having seen the events layout over the night.

"You really thought that, then you're more naïve than I thought you were..." he sniggered.

"That's enough..." security interjected,

"You two need to do this somewhere more private, I mean come on, doing this right here, in the middle of the dance floor, honestly, I couldn't care less, but our other patrons, they ain't here for this shit..." gesturing for them to follow him towards the private office. Both of them following in a huff.

———

As she closed the door behind them, she chuckled to herself before smiling at him playfully. She staggered forward. The Kaspian Sunset had taken its toll on her. She swayed slightly, enjoying the freedom the alcohol had given her.

"He was definitely a better lover than you..." she added, out of nowhere, wanting to provoke him. Ryx stared at her without blinking.

"You're a real bitch, you know that, don't you?" he replied bitterly, his hands clenching as if he was close to lashing out. For a second she flinched, he'd lashed out before, but in the mood she was in, she wanted to goad him, She didn't care, she honestly enjoyed it, he'd made her look like a fool, so she had done the same.

She was so sick of pretending she was hurt and wanted to hurt him even more. It was over between them, but she had to have it on her terms.

She could live for the moment in this charade where she was okay with him being intimate with another, doing it right in front of her, but she was no better, her liaison with Rifan had caused a stir in the club, so right now they were equal, he had hurt her and she had hurt him back. This was difficult for her to contemplate. She didn't like who she had become, but was still going through with it.

"You know what, Ryx, you know the things you've done, and I had to show you that I could play at that game too" others had seen the malice in her actions that night, and for some reason that knowledge didn't bother her.

"Congratulations, Avéline. You've grown into the vicious bitch I never thought you capable of." Her voice was low, smiling as she spoke.

"You should have known. I thought you said I was Naïve, well guess what? I know your secret. You never truly loved me, and maybe neither did I. Maybe we're the same, Ryx, you and me." She replied back, hurt but trying to mask it.

"You and I are nothing alike." He stepped close, his face right up next to hers, his breath ragged.

"Fuck you, Avéline. It's definitely over." He hissed, his hands clenched.

"It was over the minute you decided to hook up with that whore, it just took you this long to realise it..." she quipped, her hearts raced, she still wanted him, much to her own surprise.

Without warning, she pulled him forward, his hands tangled in her hair. Avéline felt like her whole body tingling, as if she was full of static. She tried not to make any noise as she stumbled into the hallway of the club's rear exit, but it didn't matter; no one knew they were there, except security, and no one would expect her to be with Ryx after that public confrontation, anyway.

When she stumbled forwards onto his chest, Ryx hesitated.

"You know it's over, but I can't resist you., maybe we should give it another chance," he told her. His dark eyes locked glances with hers. She reached behind her back to unfasten her dress, wanting him to take her then and there,

"Like I said before, it's over, you and me, but only when I say so, so shut up, and fuck me one last time," she told him, and kissed him before he could respond.

She felt the cool response from his skin, in contrast to the warmth of her own, she could feel his hearts racing as she felt his hand helping her remove the dress, she turned towards him, dropping the dress off her shoulders, exposing herself to the hot summer air, before embraced him, saying nothing.

She was enjoying the dangerousness of this encounter, knowing the reaction she was getting out if him, she played with the buckle on his belt, causing him to hastily undo it, before revealing himself, this is when Avéline stepped back, pulled up the front of her dress hastily, causing him to frown,

"What's going on...?" Ryx asked, not making sense of the situation.

"Actually, maybe not, now that was my turn to get you hot and bothered before disappointing you, as you did to me earlier with that whore you was with...and really, she looks like me, you really are imaginative" before staggering off down the corridor towards the exit, leaving Ryx embarrassed and partially clothed.

"Don't you dare leave, Avéline, you bitch, what's this all about" Ryx cursed as she continued to walk towards the door, before opening it and wandering out back into the club.

"I'd leave him in there if I was you..." she smiled, hoping the security guard understood what she meant, who nodded as he folded his arms.

"He needs some time to cool down," she mocked to

security who winked at her as he locked the door to the exist, understanding exactly what was going on.

Within moments there was a bang on the door as Ryx struggled to get the door open, with the security guard standing in front of the door, ignoring it, as he gestured for the DJ to play the music higher, drowning out the sound of Ryx banging on the door.

CHAPTER 45

"NO TII, THATS NOT IT..."

Six Months Later...
Onboard the Imperial Starliner Crystal Sunrise

Avéline staggered out into the rehearsal space, lost in thought. The pain in her leg causing her to wince in pain, trying to walk through it caused her to stop. Glancing around, she admired their rehearsal space, it still took her by surprise; it was large enough for a small and intimate concert, a familiar sight on an imperial cruise liner, but had served as their rehearsal space between Melor II and Hatian Prime.

It would easily hold a crowd of fifteen hundred. For them, it was barren except for a huge screen on one side, usually used as a holographic projection screen, used for backgrounds for plays.

The seating had been cleared away, a single piano sat in the middle of the room, set up for Syala to practice. She had been giving Nyxcerra lessons during her free time. She staggered forward, still feeling the twinges of cramp forming in her left thigh, pushing through the pain as she wandered over towards the wall to try to stretch it out. She needed a rest. The nine-day journey to Hatian Prime was supposed to be a rest. That's what Aeryth had told them.

Of course it was a lie, more rehearsals, Aeryth had said only a small amount of 'practice', would be needed, before dropping the bombshell that the promotional videos for the next two singles would be filmed soon, so they had to get the dance moves right. After the concerts on Hatian Prime, they would leave to travel to Antaria VI. They would embark on a twelve night tour across the planet, playing to a predominantly Impiri crowd. Avéline stood, thinking about where they were headed soon. The long journey to Antaria VI would be the highlight of the tour, playing for a crowd which had supported them the most, since the first day as trainees.

She tried to remember the places they would sing, but got lost somewhere after the concert at Maxia, and Farpoint station, too many nights, bouncing around the empire in a hurry. She could remember that they would go on towards the outer colonies, a few Military Support Concerts before wrapping up the final leg of the concerts in 14 months' time.

Over 300 concerts, with extra nights being added by BTL without notice, 'how will we survive', she thought, a discussion they had all had, but Nyxcerra didn't budge on the number of nights. It was a number that Aeryth and Leix had agreed to, and they had no input. She looked over at the rest of the girls. They were busy rehearsing, stretching or just zoned out in their own spaces. No more practice for the day, just a wind down.

Syala and Jysell sat there in the corner of the vast room, singing to one another, a usual sight during the tour.

Avéline looked over at them in awe. They looked perfect, even after the multi-hour dance practice. While she felt as if they had dragged her through a sauna. She admired their multi-tonal dark brown hair bouncing as they moved their heads. The refrains they sang, capturing the darkness within each of them: scornful, arrogant, quick-witted quips, the telltale signs of artists at the top of their game. They had changed so much over the past few cycles, their stage confidence was flawless. Avéline knew she couldn't match them for their stage confidence, but knew she could beat them in the solos. Drawing in the crowd, she sang emotionally, capturing the hearts of the crowd,

While they gave off the air of arrogance and brashness that was expected of them. For some artists, the brashness it was real. But truthfully, it was just them hiding wounds, loneliness, and pain. But you couldn't tell it by looking at them. Avéline knew she was too easy to read, much to her annoyance.

Avéline stood against the wall, losing herself in thought, her mind wandering as sighed deeply, trying to banish the thoughts from her consciousness. Thoughts of Ryx still danced in the darkest parts of her mind, bringing her down.

She distracted herself by glancing at the huge screen covering the entire opposite wall, scenes from the recent documentary about them caught her eye, she chuckled to herself, that blonde hair she had at the time, just a few months before, she thought it had been a good idea.

Thankfully, it was easily rectified. Memories flooded in from the countless months an outsider took a look into the inner working of the group, they couldn't refuse, it was a favour that had been asked for, in return for some exclusive marketing rights, a deal she knew had been earned by one of Nyxcerra's private invitations to events away from the girls.

Thoughts of what Aeryth had asked her to do caused her to shiver.

She shook her head in disbelief when she saw herself. The behind-the-scenes footage on the screen was always uncomfortable, strange even though she was known throughout the empire, she still didn't believe it, even after all this time. 'Aerrea', had finally made it, that's what they had told themselves, the group that had done everything in the past three cycles since their debut, according to Leix they were now at the top, captivating the audience, and with a supportive and ever-growing fan base, there was nothing they couldn't do.

Sponsorship deals, lucrative tours, countless awards, more credits than they could spend in a lifetime, even after paying back their training costs to the label. But they were never alone, always being watched. Whatever they wore was the latest emerging trend. The prime focus of the entertainment industry, especially on Prim. At times, it was suffocating. Avéline sighed, snapping herself out of her own thoughts. She looked down at her hands, noticing she had been clenching her fists, her red nails leaving deep imprints in her palms, her pale skin now red from the indentation. She shook her head, knowing she had to practice. There was no place better on board.

'Gotta make a go of it' she whispered to herself, as she ran her hand through her silvery grey hair, before she cleared her throat, rubbing its sides gently with the tips of her fingers, before trying to let out a flurry of harmonies, but seconds later stopping, grabbing her throat again. Nearly choking, she swallowed hard, before starting quieter, not going straight to the high notes everyone expected. Notes she knew she could hit, but was too tired to try and push it. She stood, hands expressively close to her chest, her hearts racing, as she slowly closed her eyes, loosing herself to the words bouncing around in her head.

"I gave you love, baby, yet you threw it back, You were my drug, baby, now all I feel is pain, You ripped out my heart, I got the scar right here, I brought you pleasure, baby, yet you brought me pain "

she paused, the words tripping out of her mouth.

"You told me lies, baby, you said you could bring me fame, you broke my heart, said I was to blame, all because I trusted you. You just stood there and let me fucking love you," she sang, her voice frantically and aggressively delivering the lines, her eyes still closed. Just feeling the lyrics as they came, rapidly and straight to the point.

That's when the room went silent, as if all time froze at that moment. Syala and Jysell stopped mid verse. Nyxcerra who had been lying on the rehearsal room floor, stretching her back out after the previous three hour dance rehearsal, sat up in amazement, her deep red hair cascading over her shoulders, confused as to whose voice had caused her to sit up she looked around bemused before realising who it was, the shock causing her to gasp; the realisation catching her completely by surprise.

"Ave...?" she paused dumbstruck.

"What in the goddess was that...it's so..." she stuttered, taken back, her mind still trying to piece everything together, to find the right words.

"Not the usual me..." Avéline replied, stopping mid flow. She stood there breathing deeply, her fingers tingling.

"Just wanted to see if I had it in me..." she stuttered nervously, realising that all eyes were now on her.

Tiiona appeared out of nowhere, standing at the doorway across the room from them all clutching a small cup, after taking a sip of water, her appearance startling Avéline.

"Nice bars angel, knew you had it in you, I just didn't..." she cried out, with joviality in her voice, as she placed the cup on the piano before taking off her jumper, casting it onto Nyxcerra's lap as she walked past, her caramel coloured skin glistening, almost perfect, in start contrast to her auburn hair.

"Don't think I've wasted these six cycles listening to you, learning. The flow, the cadence, the confidence..." she smiled as she glanced at Tiiona, who winked back as she walked over. With confidence in her walk, her skin was radiant, still moist with sweat, which floated in the overhead lights. Before standing in front of her, her expression had changed. Gone was the smile, replaced by an emotionless cold expression before smiling a wide open smile and embraced her, catching Avéline by surprise, who stood there rigidly, before sinking into the hug.

"Those words, those the words Ryx's writing, for the new album." She inquisitively asked, hoping to get a new angle for the new album, as she stepped back from the embrace, taking it all in.

"Trust him to show you the lyrics for the new album before the rest of us. That's what happens when you're Ryx's favourite girl." Tiiona remarked with a wide smile before stopping, silently shaking her head, realising her mistake.

"Sorry Av, just slipped out. I didn't mean to bring him up again.... just can't believe he...", she stopped,

"Sorry Babe..." she added, chastising herself.

Avéline's shoulders sank as she visibly exhaled, stopping mid exhale, as Tiiona turned to walk away, she nervously grabbed her necklace, twisting it in her fingers.

"Their...their mine..." the words stumbled out of her mouth, as if she was trying to stop them coming out.

"Mine what..." Tiiona replied, half puzzled, curiously stopping, her black hair whipping around, as she turned, stunned by Avéline's answer.

"The words I wrote them they came to me during those dark days, after...Ryx and I..."

Tiiona smiled, clenching her fist, pumping it into the air.

"Told you both, she'd come out with an exciting new song for us, one of these days. She's finally done it..." she exclaimed, as she patted Avéline on the shoulder. She shrugged her hand off, resigning herself to releasing this information in this way. Causing Tiiona to go quiet, bemused by her actions, and stared at her without saying a word.

"Tii, that day isn't here yet..." she nervously replied.

"These words.." she stuttered,

"When I said they're mine, I mean mine. Aeryth's finally, giving me my own creative space..." she pipped up, feeling her confidence grow.

"Giving you our own track, nice one. I knew you were working on getting her to that..." Tiiona jovially added, trying to get the others involved in the conversation. The atmosphere in the room had changed, a sense of confrontation tinged the conversation.

"No Tii, thats not it" Nyxcerra chimed in as she stood up, her words echoed out into the room, she casually dropped Tiiona's jumper on the floor, as she confidently walked over to Avéline, the pace of her walk taking everyone by surprise, Jysell expecting an argument, she glanced over at Syala, they were both expecting fireworks.

Within seconds, Nyxcerra was next to her. She quickly

placed her hand on the wall beside Avéline's head, standing quietly, seeing if Avéline would make the first move. Avéline's hearts raced, Nyxcerra made her feel nervous. This was going to change everything. Avéline closed her eyes, slowly recoiling from an expected argument, or even worse.

"Going solo...that's what she's promised ...am I right?" Nyxcerra spoke, catching her off guard, knowing she was going to have to be the one to start, knowing exactly what power she had over her.

"That's got to be it, it must be..." Nyxcerra added as she studied Avéline's expression.

Avéline's thoughts raced. How did she know? She knew she was easy to read, but was she that easy to read? What would they think? This and countless other questions bombarded her thoughts until she managed to coalesce her thoughts.

"Yes, Solo album. 'Nine Tales...', finished it in draft while we were on Prim last month, during that tour break. Why do you think I was in the practice rooms so much?"

Nyxcerra nodded her head slightly, letting it all sink in. Knowing this was an easy compromise, to allow Avéline to do this, to keep her in the group. They had all done it before, but Avéline was always a risk, she thought, too much of a risk.

"Finished..." Tiiona gasped in shock, causing her to stop tying her hair back, a grin appearing on her face as she folded her arms, her hair still partially tied back.

Nyxcerra was silent for a moment before she spoke.

"Ave, you took me by surprise there." She took her arm away from the wall. She had her own questions, but would hold them off for now,

"but why didn't you tell us.." she enquired.

Avéline turned to her, placing her hand on Nyxcerra's

chest, feeling her calm heart rate, causing her own shoulders to drop.

"Because I wasn't sure I had it in me…" she paused.

"You know what I'm like…" she replied, looking downward before laughing.

"I thought you would be angry with me…"

"Girl, you know you could have told us. We've always had each other's back, now more than ever. You know this…ever since Ceres" before being interrupted,

"Ave', those bars, nice delivery, confident… totally slaying that queen vibe, the flow.. flawless darling…." Tiiona stopped and grabbed hold of her,

"totally flawless…" she whispered as she broke the embrace.

"Just your own style," she added, nodding her head in acceptance.

"I'm glad it's not just me that can hear it, but Aeryth heard me practicing when we were in Prim. She'd given me space after the whole Ryx scenario. We had a talk. She knew that I was planning on taking a hiatus to get me back to being myself, but that was the old me." she paused.

"I'm far from that now, you all feel it, I'm different now…" Avéline stood there, everyone was now around her. Avéline recoiled slightly at the fact that she was now surrounded. She glanced around, hating this predicament.

Syala and Jysell had made their way over. They stood there listening, Nyxcerra stood there quietly, taking it all in.

"What does this mean for us…?" Jysell finally spoke. This was the question Avéline shuddered at hearing.

"I know we can sing together. You've all done your own thing, Nyx you and your acting, Syala and Jysell with your fashion label release last month, Tiiona your amazing solo work, but me… I've never been given the chance to do anything, I'm not that little girl you all knew all those cycles ago. I'm not afraid anymore." She replied, her voice laced with a growing conviction.

"So when Aeryth heard it. Scraps of it, brief excerpts of songs that make my heart ache with possibility. And for once, I'm trying something on my own, crafted by my mind. It hit me, a wave of growth and hope. Even she could see that I was finally ready to do something on my own." She stopped, realising that they were listening intently, but also nervously taking it in.

"Don't worry, 'Aerrea' will always be my priority. You know I wouldn't do anything to hurt what we've worked so hard for all this time. I just need..." she felt herself getting out of breath as her hearts raced, her pale skin became rose-tinted as she blushed.

"You don't need to explain, you've always been there for us, its time we repaid that..." Tiiona interrupted, hating the tension in the air.

Syala and Jysell smiled as they came further into the conversation.

"Always there..., you got this girl..." Syala added.

"So, what's the plans for your release..." Jysell added, her thoughts dancing around in her head. She just had so many things she wanted to ask. It was exciting.

"Aeryth's already arranged a small preview of the album while we are on Antaria VI just a few picked members from our fan community, key members of the media, and a few personal requests, that's all before starting a major advertising blitz on Prim..." she gushed, she'd wanted to tell them for weeks, not knowing how they would take the news.

"Starting in a few months, by the time we get back to Prim, even though it's over a cycle away, it's going to a double shock, Our new album and also Nine Tales."

CHAPTER 46
"I CAN'T BELIEVE YOU..."

13 Months Later...

"I still can't believe you managed to get us Aerrea tickets, I thought they were all sold out" the young Tamir said, giddy with excitement and disbelief as he and a young woman stood hand in hand in line, waiting to get into the concert, occasionally being bumped into as they got closer to entering the stadium.

"I can't believe you thought I'd forgotten your birthday," Krynda replied as she ran her fingers through her long blonde hair, after pulling back her hood, before adjusting her thin loose jacket.

"Hey, I just thought it might had slipped your mind, especially with all the preparations for going to the academy." Tamir defended himself. He smiled as he heard other fans singing 'Boudoir'

"Oh, I hope Nyxcerra sings Boudoir, it's my favourite from the album..." he added as he tapped his feet, it was one of the first songs he heard from the album.

She chuckled as she glanced at him, seeing he smiling.

"You only like it because you fancy her..." she mocked, shaking her head gently.

"So I'm not good enough..." Krynda playfully pouted, huffing out air, before noticing his serious expression.

"Oh, come on, she's hot" she added playfully.

"Did you know Rhysio wrote it after spending a night with Nyxcerra, that's what I heard. I also heard that the video was supposed to be even raunchier.. which is a surprise, it was pretty x-rated already, but they had to cut it, just so it could get past censorship..." she added and they moved closer to the front of the line.

Finally, it was their turn to be the head of the line. After receiving their scans to make sure they weren't snuggling in any contraband, and with a physical pat-down, they were in.

"We're in," Tamir whispered. Squeezing her hand, she pulled him close and kissed him, before breaking the embrace, whispering "Happy Birthday..." causing him to look straight into her eyes.

"I love you, you know that..." she blushed,

"And I might have another surprise for you later..." she purred as she uncovered her red bra strap on her left shoulder, winking at him, stopping him from going any further ahead.

"Don't get too excited," Krynda told him, grinning.

"There's still time for us to get some merchandise before making our way to our seats" she looked at her silver wrist band, on the display which ran its length it displayed, "HBI Live Present: Aerrea - The Iliad Tour - Abrasar Phx Stadium - Block 27, Row 1, Seat 344."

"Shit, you know how far we gotta walk to get there...,

block 27, we're only at 3..." she stopped, in thought before speaking again

"Let's get to our seats, then we can go the nearest merch' booth and get something..."

Meanwhile, across the stadium ...

The Aerrea girls walked through the entrance of the arena, lined by the press. This arena was gigantic compared to the concert they played a few weeks before at over ninety thousand., thus peaked at a hundred and thirty-four thousand seats, they savoured every moment, looking towards the drones, even the way they carried themselves wax elegant, they knew the media would follow every moment., their assistants still carrying their drinks while hastily walking beside them,

"Tell him he's going to love the show, especially our new single, " Nyxcerra spoke to her assistant, who took down the message,

"and if he doesn't like it, and give a less than stellar review, her knows the rest, hes a good one, if he knows where this will go....." she added, her voice commanding yet hollow, she was tired, but had to look their best, especially when they were hosting another military concert, 75 percent of the audience were either in the military for from a military family. No matter where they looked, there was the Imperial military, with proceeds from the concert being publicly donated to the Veterans memorial hospital.

Back in the Arena...

As they entered the arena, Krynda stopped, as she could

feel the beat of the music. Tamir gestured for her to follow as he smiled ear to ear.

"It's really getting going, and we still have time..." Tamir shouted. Over the sound of the warm-up act, the atmosphere was full of excitement. He could see a warm-up band playing music. Their seats were closer, as they weaved their way closer to their seats, the temperature increased. Krynda spun around, taking in the entire place. The stadium was packed. As if millions were there, but it wasn't more than 120,000.

Minutes Later, the lights in the stadium dimmed to nothing, plunging the crowd into darkness, the crowd erupted in song as Aerrea songs began being played through the huge speakers scattered throughout the stadium. He started sweating in anticipation as the beat of the music got louder, the whole stage started to shake and vibrate.

Half an hour later ...

"Just wait until It's just the two of us , playing games in this dark room. If you play with me today, , I'll take your breath away," the girls sang after Avéline's solo verse, the crowd going wild.

"Are you ready to play with me?" Nyxcerra sang, smirking,

"Yes..." the crowd screamed,

"I'm not sure girls if they really want to play..." she quipped, playing up to the crowd. She loved having them in the palm of her hand. Jysell shook her head .

"I don't think they do Nyx, I don't think they deserve it, maybe we should send them downstairs to the boudoir..." Jysell added, as the backup dancers moved around the set pieces, changing the set from its current state to the boudoir set. The crowd began to chant and stamp their feet, realising what was about to happen, as Nyxcerra walked towards the back of the set, disappearing into a cloud of fog.

Just before the stage lights went off, plunging everyone into darkness for a moment which felt like an eternity, Tamir and Krynda screaming out into the crowd.

"Boudoir...." They screamed in unison.

Moments later, a row of dark red spotlights kicked in, plunging everyone into a barely lit environment, flooded with red light.

"It's happening, don't you get too excited.." Krynda added playfully, mocking his infatuation with Nyxcerra, especially as he held a Nyxcerra light stick in his left hand.

"Shut up, this is why Nyxcerra is the Empress of my Universe and not you: everything she does is just... perfectly... naughty,"

Krynda didn't have a chance to make a sarcastic comment back to him, because Nyxcerra took to the stage, and the crowd erupted in cheer. Just as Nyxcerra stepped forward, playfully singing,

"*What you doing down here...? Are you lost?*" She coyly sang, knowing she had the crowd already.

"*So, you came along just to take a peek,*" she sang playfully, revealing more of her lingerie from behind the long coat she was wearing.

"*I've seen you lurking around up there...*

Didn't think you were so weak

You never stay, just taking glimpses of the dark" she sang as she grabbed a male dancer by the collar, pulling him close enough to kiss, before she turned his face away, and simulating kissing his cheek, she turned to the crowd who were frantic at this moment.

"*Why don't you stay, get some release*
You come alone, come tell me darling,

What do you seek?," Nyxcerra teased them, dancing now with a troupe of young male dancers. Her outfit completely revealed, gone was the coat from before, it was less of an outfit and bore more of a resemblance to lingerie.

She greeted the female dancers with sass, bringing some of them close, while also sending some away the ones she kept close. She fixed their outfits, adjusting their garter belts, making sure they looked perfect. One of them was covered by a long silken robe, until the crowd realised the female dancers were the other members of 'Aerrea'.

"I think my girls are ready to join me on this one..., don't you think..." she asked the audience as the other girls were introduced wearing outfits similar to hers, except Syala who was the mysterious girl in the long silken robe, which hugged her figure but didn't show much. The crowd going wild at this revelation.

"*Take a journey to the boudoir , follow me, Tell me your secrets, and fantasies...*" Nyxcerra sang, walking toward with the rest of the girls, each of then pulling a male dancer behind them by a different coloured silk tie, in each of their tribal colours.

"*We'll find someone for you, To do as you please, Stay here for a while, or stay for the night...*" they all sang, the atmosphere was electric.

"*Nothings off limits here, for the right price,*" the crowd sang as Nyxcerra gestured for the crowd to take over, as she smiled seductively at the crowd in the front row.

CHAPTER 47

"MAKE UPS...DONE..IT'S JUST THIS.."

Syala leaned forward placing her hands on the small vanity table, she fenced at her pearlescent fingernails, she'd never had them done like this before, it was never a consideration, am she slowly cast her eyes on the tables dark wooden surface which was now littered with an assortment of makeup kits, a selection of sponges and brushes—all of it arranged carefully before her, just in case she wanted to add any more, as she looked up at her reflection in the mirror she sighed, dropping her shoulders. The make-up artist had done a great job. They had always been good at making her look beautiful, in a raunchy and seductive way.

"You ready?"Jysell called out from the other room of their suite at the hotel, yet there was no reply.

"Sy??" Jysell followed up a few moments later, coughing Syala to tut, before replying.

"Make ups... done..it's just this.." she trailed off.

Syala had been surprised that the label had paid for these three suites at the hotel, especially for an award ceremony on Jalan II, Nyx had said it was probably due to the demographics, it was a predominantly Impiri population, on a planet were two out of the three billion watched their traineeship.

Tiiona and Avéline were waiting patiently in the living area, Tiiona's hair was freshly coloured, with a streak of light pink on one side of her hair. Her outfit for the night was typical Tiiona, beautifully shaped and taped trousers with a low-cut and revealing blouse, this all black outfit in stark contrast to her alabaster skin tone.

"It's so nice to be on Jalan II again, hopefully this time I'll get to see Casilas, it's been so long, do you think he got the tickets I sent..." Avéline added as she brushed off her skirt, before checking the hem of the stockings she was wearing, the dark seam ran its way down the back of her legs, leading to her sparkling heels, she lost herself in admiration of the shoes.

"Yeah, I'm sure he did.., your gonna have to introduce me sometime.." Jysell added, pausing to see if it caught Avéline's attention, all while Tiiona openly mocked Avéline's motions as she checked the seams.

"I do hope so, and no. Definitely not interested in introducing him to you. He's mine..." she mocked playfully, blushing slightly.

"He's your brother-in-law..." Jysell questioned openly as she noticed her blushing.

"Widowed brother-in-law... there's a difference, and it's... its complicated..." she trailed off, nervously wanting to change the subject. They wouldn't understand. How could they?

"What's taking her so long?" Avéline added as she fixed her earrings. She had wanted them lower, but the wardrobe had put them higher on her ears, knowing this was a good enough diversion to Jysell's questions.

"It's the outfit, it's always the outfit..." Jysell added,

unable to mask it. She'd sat with her and discussed it. It was only for the red carpet walk, then no one else would see it until the awards ceremony finished.

"I told her it was a compromise. It's longer than they would have given her before, but now it's the fit. She says it's too suggestive of her figure." Jysell added, just as Nyxcerra came in, her skirt was short on one side and slightly longer on the other, topped by an elegantly crafted silk and leather corset, tied with bright turquoise cords at the back. She stepped forwards. Avéline turned to see him and was surprised,

"Geez Nyx, didn't realise you were going as Illara from the show..." she mocked.

Nyxcerra stood there smiling, kicking her right heel back, and she balanced on one leg.

"I mean, I do look kinda special tonight," she coyly giggled,

"Don't I? , I asked for something a-bit special. Especially for our first night here, amongst our own people"

"So, where's Sy?, she still not ready yet? We're getting picked up in ten minutes..." Nyxcerra added, noticing the time on the clock in the corner of the room.

"You ready yet?" Jysell yelled down the suit towards the bedrooms,

"Give me a minute...?" Syala's voice called out:

"You've got 5 minutes... then I'm coming to get you..."

Tiiona looked at Avéline and leaned forward, not wanting to make a scene.

"Have things have been weird between them ever since their fight...? about the clothing again," she exclaimed, exasperated.

"But we've been here for three weeks, and it's still awkward?" Avéline replied, puzzled.

"Yeah, professional, but Sy is shutting everyone out. She's had enough," Jysell added

"Still, here we are, in a row of suites that were already paid for, someone had booked these suites for us at 'dark tower on 108th street'..." Jysell exclaimed as she wandered around the massive, spacious suite, decorated in the finish decor.

"Yeah, have you seen the place, Zabian-rose cream as standard for just washing your face, it's 350 credits for 250ml of this stuff, it's just..." Tiiona added.

"Just look at this place. Seems like the government rolled out the red carpet just for this, some sort of PR angle it must be..." Jysell replied as she walked close to Tiiona.

"Nothing to do with the government, all courtesy of Lady Centych Kalidral Vale...," Nyxcerra replied. As she spoke that name, the girls went silent, remembering the time they had met her that infamous night.

"She owns a majority share in this one as well as the one back on Prim..." Nyxcerra proclaimed, as she folded her arms, she spun on her heels in the living area.

"Now I can see why all her soirées are held there. She's partying in her own home..."

Avéline looked over, feeling the gaze of someone looking at her, before gasping

"Sy.." she spoke, taken aback by the conservative but simplistic beauty of what she was wearing.

Syala leaned in the doorway, showing off her casual white long length dress, ending just below her ankles, by no everyone was looking at her

"What do you think?" Syala added in a matter-of-fact style.

"Amazing. But what about tonight's outfit..., we've got five minutes..."

"It's not about that.." she replied as she wandered playfully from the doorway to the living area.

"It's about me, I'm not coming" Syala turned back and found a low slung chair to sit on. Her long hair was gathered into a low ponytail, emphasising the glamorous length of her hair.

Nyxcerra came forward and took her hands. "You know that you always look stunning. No matter what you wear, but what do you mean, you're not coming.?"

"But I ain't going, not wearing that. Not this time. I'm sick of having to be the one who makes compromises," she sat, arms folded, staring out into the sunset,

"I told Jys if I truly can't wear it, that I'm staying put," Syala insisted. She was staying here tonight.

"Just tell them the back strain has flared up again, you go , enjoy yourselves, it's not like their going to miss me, not with what Nyx is wearing tonight, going to steal all the attention..." Syala added, knowing that Nyxcerra was annoyed, seeing her fold her arms.

"Well, I'm ready" Nyxcerra added,

"The transports on the roof waiting for us should take us a minute to get there, but we have to leave now," Jysell added as she patted Syala on the shoulder before making her way to the suite door.

"But it's not until 7", Jysell replied, forgetting what Nyxcerra had told her already that evening as they sorted out each other's hair.

"Jys, remember I need to be there for 6, was told to head down early, as the host for one of the awards... hence this outfit..." she gestured at her outfit for the night.

———

The entire stay here had been one long tribute to excess and indulgence., and they had only been here for a few days.

Avéline had spoken to Aeryth about the conversation with the girls. Aeryth had arrived with Leix on a private cruiser from another hotel down the coast.

After embracing Aeryth, Nyxcerra cut straight to business, wanting to say it before Aeryth noticed it.

"It's about Syala, so she said she's not coming. It's about the outfits again, and I wasn't going to argue with her or force her, not this time." Not giving Aeryth time to respond, she quickly added.

"Aren't we big enough now to allow her some leeway" Nyxcerra added abruptly. She'd never spoken to Aeryth that way before, but was hoping that she hadn't overstepped the situation.

"Fine, Leix, put out a quick statement. She's been fighting a relapse in her back pain after that fall last winter, so we've taken the precaution to have her rest tonight...." Aeryth scowled. Leix looked at her and nodded his head.

"Already got something similar prepared, I'll get it out to the right channels, should head off any rumours, since no one has seen the girls this evening..." the rest of the girls were guided away towards the pre ceremony press conferences, while Nyxcerra was kept back.

Her hearts raced. She knew she was in trouble. She'd never talked to Aeryth that way before and knew it was about that.

Aeryth smile at her as she brought over a flute of sparkling wine, Nyxcerra taking one.

"Thank you...." She paused.

"Aeryth, it's about..." she was cut off by Aeryth shaking her finger at her.

"The situation with Syala, it's fine, thought it might

happen at some point, but it's you that I'm worried about..." Aeryth spoke, her voice laced with concern. She leaned forward and whispered in Nyxcerra's ear.

"If you ever talk to me like that again, I'll make sure I ruin your career. I'm not just anyone you can talk to like that. You come to me and tell me, in advance. So I can have this covered. The media are bound to have seen you all come here, minus our lovely Syala, rumours will start... and.."

"I see your..." Nyxcerra added, but was hushed by Aeryth.

"Let me finish, and I can't be dealing with rumours, that's it. I hate rumours..." she hissed, before leaning back and smiling.

"Now darling, go and enjoy yourself..." Aeryth spoke, her demeanour totally different to what it was only a few seconds earlier.

As the girls were being handed glasses of wine as they sat in the transport, a tall, muscular Thetan security guard kept his gaze on them, causing Nyxcerra to look at him and smile.

"So, who might you be big boy..., has something caught your attention.." she playfully mocked, the atmosphere in the transport was as if the event itself was just one big cocktail party, and the journey there was a logical prelude to the night to come. This entire night was about public relations, and living to excess, especially if Lady Vale was to be in attendance later that night.

He carefully stood up and made his way towards them,

"Great Nyx, he's coming this way... it looks like you've got what you wanted, yet again..." Jysell laughed, causing him to grin, he knew exactly what they were talking about. As he got in front of them, he crouched down, taking them all by surprise. Before finally speaking, his voice was deeper than expected, but polite and calm.

"Well, ladies, I'll be the head of your security detail tonight until we are all in the venue. You will need to be careful..."

"We have taken all possible precautions. We are still going ahead with the carpet walk, photos and brief interviews."

"So, what's the cause for all this extra security? I've not heard much from our PR contact in a while..." Nyxcerra nervously enquired, as the tone of conversation changed within the transport.

"We must apologise for the anti-local government protests which we will hopefully not have to deal with tonight, terrorist group "the way" have said that want to interrupt tonight's proceedings. Me and my team won't allow that to happen.

CHAPTER 48
"SO WHAT DO I SEE IN FRONT OF ME !..."

A Few Days Later...

As Avéline entered the stage the crowd cheered, she had hoped they liked her dressy casual look of a knee-length skirt, which carefully hugged her hips, with a loose-fitting blouse to finish it off, her hair curled ever so slightly as it rested on her shoulders. 'They like the look' she thought based on their reaction.

A smile crept onto her face as much to her surprise, with the house lights on she could recognise the influencers in the crowd, before pausing, catching sight of a familiar face, bowing her gaze slightly as she recognised Neziphera Zappal, the aide to Lady Vale, standing at the back, how she had gotten tickets without it flagging up to her, she was startled by her attendance she smiled nervously as thoughts ran through her mind, 'was Lady Vale here too' she thought, she shook her head to chase away the thoughts, she had a job to do, if she was there she'd better give her a show to remember.

She tapped her feet to the beat of the music. The atmosphere was full of excitement. She turned around and bowed to the band playing music, before turning around, looking out into the crowd, she could see only fifty in attendance.

"So what do I see in front of me!..." she spoke without amplification

"I wish to thank you all from the depth of my soul and my hearts that you have turned up here tonight, on this hot summers night, unfortunately we're going to have to turn the temperature up a-bit tonight..." she laughed as she like to the crowd who cheered.

The club was hot and stuffy, but it fit the purpose of the night. Avéline started sweating. As the beat of the music got louder, the whole stage shook and vibrated. Avéline tensed up. The nerves had arrived. This was the moment of judgement: she opened her mouth and sang at the hovering microphone.

"I sit here, watch you set my heart ablaze", her voice holding out the last note before the next verse came flowing out of her mouth.

"With such intensity it would burn for days,"

"I don't know how you do it. You got into my bed, my heart in so many ways..." she finished, just as the tone of the song became seductive, slow and bass heavy. As the people at the concert swayed back and forth, left and right, according to the beat of the music, Avéline felt herself swaying with the music as well as she sang the rest of the song, the crowd enjoying every moment of it. As the song finished, she bowed to the crowd, holding the bow for a while, counting the seconds as she bowed to the count of fifteen, before looking up again. The crowd cheered as she arose from the bow.

"Avéline, we love you…" a voice called out from the crowd, causing her to smile.

"I bet that's what you say to all the Aerrea girls…" she mocked as the crowd laughed.

"It's great to be here tonight, to give you, my loyal fans, a sneak peek at what I've been working on. I hope you enjoy what's up next, a song I wrote… 'No Promises'"

Avéline's voice rose high, following the pipped notes from the musician's flute, in time with the beating of the drums. As she sang, a soft silence fell across the club. The key lights dimmed on cue as the spotlights focused on her, not fazed by this. The crowd stood, enthralled by her voice. She'd had a crowd listen before, but this crowd was hers.

Looking out into the crowd, she sang, remembering she had seen some members of the Aerrea fan groups. She had answered their questions, all for the fans, she said, thanking them for their support over the cycles.

As the melody changed, she sang with conviction, always verging on the cusp of breaking down, but as the consummate professional she pushed through, the lyrics started off as joyful before taking a dark turn as they gradually fell into melancholy.

The cacophony of the music, her voice and the adrenaline causing her hearts to beat rapidly caused her to pause, surprising herself she'd never felt this enthralled before, her scales tingled, the open back of her blouse flapped in the breeze from an air conditioning unit behind her. The four rows of scales sent a wave of sensation across her body. She stopped, confused by the reason for such a reaction before continuing again. She'd only ever experienced this kind of sensation when with a partner, never from music.

Then it dawned on her, they were here for her, not Nyxcerra, Tiiona, Syala or Jysell, she was the reason they had come, knowing she was being recorded by the fans and the influencers, she ran her hand through her silvery grey hair, smiling a wide smile to the crowd before forcefully grabbing hold of the hovering microphone and pulling it close in once motion.

"No promise I can ever give. I betrayed you with a smile," she belted. instinctively smiling a sultry smile as she finished the line, shaking her head gently as she sang the last line. "And I knew I did it, all the while"

As she sang, she closed her eyes, her voice ringing out across the crowd.

The crowd grew silent, no one moved, choosing to just stood there in silence, absorbed in the music. For a moment she stopped, the tone of the music rapidly dropping to a more sober but expressive mood. She stopped and looked towards the floor. At the same time, she let out a tear. The music and her emotions got to her. Resigning herself to her lack of control, she sighed and tried to smile.

'Your audience is waiting, give them something to talk about...' the voice in her head rang out, she knew exactly what to do, as she devilishly smiled at the same time as raising her head, staring at the crowd before pulling the microphone towards her lips. The sensation of the pop filter vibrating as it carefully touched her lips. She stood motionless.

The slight sound of her breathing echoed its way out of the speakers. The audience awaiting her next verse; they hanging off every word she spoke. She cleared her throat before she unleashed her voice again.

"I don't know you, no more. I'm not the one that you adore." She sang down the microphone, in a lower register than she was comfortable, only ever having sung that low during those first weeks as a trainee, instantly startling the audience, who were in awe for a moment before they cheered. A wave of emotion cascaded over her. She didn't really know what had come over her. This was a tone she had never sung openly to an audience before.

Sometimes in rehearsal she had riffed off others, occasionally mimicking the tonality of more radical singers within the trainee groups, or her peers at the label, but couldn't get the tone right, she knew she didn't have the lows of Syala or the growl of Tiiona, or the luxurious thick timbre of Nyxcerra's bottom end.

She felt like stopping, but the rush of adrenaline pushed her further. She sang lower again, this time sinking to her knees. She sank, holding her head in her hands. Her crowd stood in amazement, her emotions had taken over.

This experiment was a complete change in the style of music that she normally sang. It made her uncomfortable but also thrilled her, not knowing whether to do it again or to stop. Her sections of songs were usually seductive and upbeat. But this song was different. A departure which she hoped the crowd would enjoy, as well as the reviewers and influencers in attendance. She knew them all by name. This departure could either make or break her solo endeavours. The crowd just stood there absorbing the moment.

Some of the audience cheered and began chanting "Avéline" in a growing succession, following by the stamping of their feet, the vibrations carrying to be felt even on the stage.

They could feel the pain and anguish she had been feeling, the pain they all had felt at some point before.

She turned and faced the crowd. Even though she couldn't see them properly, the stage lights allowing her to only see the first row before the rest faded into darkness. She knew it impressed them. She looked out at them as she sang. The feeling of the audience made her smile a weak smile as she sang, every note allowing her to see them more clearly before she stopped. Her band continuing for a few seconds before they hesitated. She had gone silent.

As a solitary tear slowly made its way down her cheek, she reached over and wiped it away. As she realised she had lost herself again in the music, some news had gotten the best of her.

"I'm sorry all of you, I just cannot continue without letting you know..., someone is missing here tonight..." she added, her voice trembling.

"For Isshi, a close friend of mine who, unfortunately, died during that horrific parliamentary bombing last month. Those of you who knew him, please raise a glass, and those who didn't know him... He was always a supportive friend. He always knew how to make us smile. He was the craziest of us." She paused.

"And I'll miss him dearly." She added the crowd was mostly silent. The crowd didn't know what to say. A few members of the small audience mumbled or took sips of the drinks that were in their hands.

"And May the Goddesses lead him to rebirth, as this existence will not be the same without him....." a voice echoed out, breaking the silence. Avéline's hearts raced. That voice, she knew that voice, but it couldn't be. She dismissed it as quickly as she thought about it. It couldn't be. The scales down her back tingled as she thought about it. The sensation of travelling through her scales became distracting, even slightly embarrassing. The small audience turned towards the voice which stood in the middle of them. Avéline looked over to where the voice was coming from, trying to pinpoint where they were exactly.

"For he was one of my closest friends," the voice added.

Avéline smiled as she heard him speak again, throwing her microphone to the floor with a thud before it whistled for a second before being turning itself off.

"I know that voice anywhere..." she exclaimed.

"Don't leave me in the dark here Masani - brother, come here and help me..." she called out, reaching out towards him. Members of the crowd began whispering,

"Masani? Avéline doesn't have a brother...? "a member of the audience enquired to his friends standing next to him, who looked at him and shrugged their shoulders. It confused them as well.

The crowd slowly parted as a darkly dressed figure made its way towards the stage. It stumbled, tripping over a wayward foot, but managing to stabilise itself before it fell to the floor. It looked up, pulling back its hood, which had been covering its head.

"Of course, Masati - 'sister'..." he spoke as he held out his hand, placing it just below Avéline's. She smiled as she placed her hand on his. She knelt their in-front of the steps leading away from the stage into the audience.

"One and all, this is a special night. Not just as a preview of my solo work. But a personally special night, finally my Masani..." she stopped, laughing to herself as he helped her stand up. She staggered forward a step before righting herself.

"My brother...well, as close to that as can be..., is here to see me after all this time..." she smiled as she pulled him close and embraced him. Her shoulders sank as she felt his warmth embrace her.

"Casilas, I thought I could smell you, but I wasn't sure...it's been so long," she whispered as she took a deep breath.

Casilas looked at her, and wiped a tear from her face.

For a second he stared at her, lost in thought, she was beautiful, the neckline of her blouse was low and very revealing of her figure. He shook himself from his thoughts just before she spoke.

"Surprise Avé..." he replied, his voice deep and calm.

"Casi, I never expected the see you, it's been too long but I cannot deny that it was an amazing surprise" she giggled, her happiness was infectious, making Casilas smile.

"You know what I mean, and I know that look anywhere." She added as she stopped. Casilas' voice was pitched low, but his words were calm and gentle as he levelled his gaze on her, trying to guide her over towards the corner of the nightclub. Trying to hide his growing concern for her wellbeing.

"You know why I stayed away...don't you?" Casilas added, grabbing hold of her by the shoulders. He couldn't fight his emotions, his right eye beginning to fill with tears. She carefully nodded her head, her false confidence dropping for a second.

The two of them were huddled together in the far corner of the nightclub, off from the main stage, seemingly alone in their own conversation, though Avéline could feel the attention of others, staring at her. Beyond their small cluster, the occasional member of the band looked over, just to keep an eye on the unfolding situation.

The security guards and Avéline's personal security detail stood far in the distance, observing everything. Everyone was enjoying the night. A group of young Impiri near the bar laughed.

The laugh causing Casilas to look over and notice a few of them stagger over towards them before catching Casilas' gaze, before making a quick detour away. he pulled up his jacket collar to hide the eagle tattoos on his neck, a giveaway that he was from a Makla-hara household.

Not wanting to bring any undue attention to himself. After a few moments of watching the group slowly pass them before making their way towards the stage, Casilas sighed.

"I miss her too, you know...", she whispered,

"I miss them both, Masati and the little one., still can't believe it's been...fifteen cycles. It still hurts today as much as it did then". Her bottom lip beginning to tremble, she stopped as tears began making their way down her cheeks. She shook her head and forced a smile, trying to distract herself from her own thoughts.

"But enough of that. I'm too sober for that kind of talk. Buy me a drink, won't you?" She implored, looking at him. For an instant, he was lost in thought.

He smiled, that face, that smile. He couldn't shake it. Over the cycles she had grown more like her sister than he expected. His hearts raced as he looked at her, trying to shake the instant attraction he felt. He took a breath. Her scent lingered in the air, she even had the same aroma as her sister.

Avéline looked over at him.

"What's wrong Masani, I got the messages you sent. I'm glad that the family are doing well. You said you had been involved in the uprisings that I've been hearing about."

He grabbed hold of her hand.

"let me show you," he whispered and guided it to his face. She stroked his face gently, first with the back of her hand, followed by her fingers and palm.

"The lighting in here is terrible, but then again, my vision has never been the best in the darkness...I stumble a lot, it's always been hazy in the dark." She stopped. "Still going for that rough look that she liked, I see, but what's this?" She inquired as her fingers caressed his face, making their way to his left eye socket. She recoiled her fingers as she felt its emptiness.

"Is this that they've done to you? They dare to harm those close to me. I never expected them to be as open about their hatred."

Casilas shook his head, noticeably tightening his grip on the arms of the chair, as painful memories came to mind, before quickly disappearing.

"Well, you could say I asked for it..." Casilas joked, shrugging his shoulders playfully

"Luckily, Tala was there to guide me through this, especially in recent days ..." he responded.

Avéline's mouth was drawn in a tight line. Her smile had dropped, her brows furrowed.

"Tala?" Avéline whispered, before leaning away gently. She'd never read that name in their messages, who was this Impiri?.

"Did I say something wrong here??" Casilas enquired, before it slowly dawned on him. He'd never messaged her regarding him moving on,

Avéline blushed as she leaned forward.

"So she's the one that's been keeping you away from me all this time..."

"I never expected tonight to be the night I tell you this..." Casilas muttered, his hearts racing.

"What's wrong?" Casilas enquired, a worried look came across his brow.

"Okay, I'm going to stop being evasive. I owe you that, at least." She replied nervously, shifting uncomfortably on the sofa. She readied herself and sighed.

"... I'll make this easy for you to understand. When my

sister died, I thought you would be alone for a while. To accept her death was hard for us all." She paused, brushing away the tears...

"I thought you remembered the promise you made... did you think that the promise to my family was over? Did you think we, I, had forgotten about you?" Her words cutting through the silence.

Casilas sat there, the words sinking in. Memories flashing back into his consciousness. Flashes of times with Adeline, the brief moments he spent with Ezmé.

Avéline looked at him, hearing his shallow breathing. Knowing the onslaught of emotions he was going through, she reached forward, feeling for his knee, finding it and slowly patting it.

Casilas smiled, trying to force the memories back into the recesses of his mind.

"Well, I thought a lot of things. But that had never jumped to mind." He paused.

"Honestly, I thought that my bond to your family was figurative, not literal," he replied.

"But mostly, I thought about nothing but your sister and our little one for cycles. Not even a second thought about anyone else. My own life coming to terms with it all was much more important to me than anything. Even family. And if it meant that I would never get to think of anyone that way again, I was willing to accept the goddesses' will, it was okay." He proclaimed.

Avéline sat there, absorbing everything, the nuances in what he had said. Trying to block out the external noise from the band still playing to the audience.

"I can understand that. It's a sweet sentiment and everything, but it was like you were not even here sometimes. Times when we." She corrected herself.

"When I needed you," she sighed, faking a smile, pushing back the tears which were still forming.

"It's great that you can listen and be there for someone. I just had hoped. Hope that it would be different, but I got that all wrong. And I'm going to have to accept that" she looked down fiddling with a ring on her finger.

"Do you love her...?"

"What?"...

"Do you love her, this Tala...?"

"Come closer," he whispered, trying to ignore the question. Instinctively she moved herself closer to him, before he sank off the chair and onto his knees, grabbing hold of her hands.

"You know how hard this has been for me..." Casilas whispered, his voice cracking.

"Of course, it's not like I expected you to remain the widower forever." Avéline sarcastically replied, blushing in embarrassment for making him uncomfortable. She instinctively reached over and picked up a glass she had placed on the table hours earlier. She fumbled the glass into her hand.

"It's just that ...I thought you had remembered. "she paused, nervously looking at the ground, her cheeks flushed. She casually bit the left corner of her lip before speaking again.

"I thought you weren't ready, and that if you were you would have told me...". She replied, her voice quieter than it was before, as if she was trying to hide it from anyone else within earshot of their conversation.

Casilas looked over and the band, who were still playing to an audience who were too busy enjoying themselves to pay attention to what was happening.

"It's not like I had feelings for you back then or anything. I mean. I just thought you knew you could confide in me. Since we are still kind of family.." she replied jokingly, as she sipped the drink that she held in her hand. Stopping to savour it's a slightly bitter taste, she sighed.

"Look at me, spilling my hearts out to you. Aren't I worthy of some feelings of my own? I mean, I've done well for myself, haven't I? I've toured the empire for the last cycle and a half. Even sung in front of the Emperor on Prim," she stopped to sip her drink again, Casilas sat there listening,

"So many sponsorship deals, it's driving me insane. I finally come home to preview a new album and make a fool out of myself by confessing my feelings to my windowed brother-in-law. Maybe it's in our genetics. Maybe that is why Adáline found you so appealing." She joked, laughing out loud. It was nice to laugh like this, she thought. It had been difficult over the past few months.

"Is that what she said...?"

"Well, that's the most appropriate thing I could say., as usual, Adá used more expressive words," Avéline joked in response before her smile dropped. She leaned forward, which for an instant concerned Casilas.

"So, you've still not given me an answer... do you love her ... "she whispered after she took another sip of her drink before deciding to finish it in a single go, placing the glass on the table next to her, and wiping a drop off of her lip, savouring every drop.

"Who?" Casilas deflected the conversation, startled by witnessing Avéline finishing the drink so quickly.

"Tala... the one who's captured your hearts" she quizzed, still leaning forward.

Casilas looked at her, reading her concerned expression, and realising that he would have to explain everything at some time, resigning himself to this conversation at this point in time.

"She's been through a lot with me, all the situation with the... incident.," he spoke, his voice trembling. He stopped, shocked by how this conversation made him feel.

Avéline looked at him, her face still full of concern.

"It's not my place to ask, but does she make you feel the way you felt with my sister?" She quizzed again, this time she sat back. The look on her face was stern, all playfulness was gone. This was a serious conversation.

"Don't respond straight away, think this answer over," she added, just as Casilas tried to speak.

He cleared his throat before replying, feeling a lump appear in his throat.

"It's different, your sister..." he stopped, took a breath before completing his thoughts.

"Adá and I shared something special, something that I'll cherish for the rest of my days. Losing her and Ezmé was nearly the end of me. That's why I couldn't face seeing you, it was just messages". He paused, looked at her, trying to force away his emotions,

"You look so much like her. I couldn't risk losing you as well." He sank further to the floor, his head in his hands. Memories of the three of them flashed into his consciousness, the times they spent before it was taken away. These memories were hard for Casilas to hide from. He clenched his hands to his head. Trying to snap himself out of this.

"I know, ridiculous. I just couldn't bring myself to tell you." He added through clenched teeth.

Avéline carefully lowered herself off of the sofa in front of him. Grabbed hold of him and held him close, placing her head on his shoulder.

"You know mother asks for you? Even father did before..." she murmured.

"Avé..." he whispered, a look of shock flashed across his face.

"Last summer while I was away on tour, came down with Canthari Syndrome. He took a drastic turn. Within 6 weeks, he was gone..." she sobbed,

"You should have contacted me, I would have ..." Casilas whispered gently.

"I knew you were still grieving. I knew you kept your distance for that reason." She paused, trying to force back her own tears.

"I didn't want to bring you down with me. It wasn't the best time for me either..."

Casilas looked at her, concerned.

"I had heard about that through the media. Can't believe he betrayed you." He said, turning towards Avéline as she turned towards him.

"Don't always trust what you hear through those channels. It wasn't just his betrayal that ended our relationship. I wasn't always..." she stopped, sighed and tried to force another smile, knowing that it would not work.

"...The most loving of individuals, I always pushed him away..., I didn't know why at the time, but now I know why I did it."

"Because I knew he wasn't good enough for me, he would always hold me back. I was trying to find some-one...someone like you," she responded nervously.

"I wanted to have something like you and Adé had. That's what true love is. That's what I thought a love bonding could be.

"Maybe I had the traditional view in mind, yeah me, the none traditional, having very old-fashioned dreams. I mean, I don't think Adé even knew that much about it before she asked..."

"She asked? What do you mean... when?" Casilas drew closer. He furrowed his brow as he placed his hand on Avéline's knee.

She smiled a gentle smile as she felt the warmth of his hand, the slight roughness of his skin.

"The last time we spoke, in the hospital, while you were on your way. Not long before, she." She stopped, as tears began to trickle down her cheeks again. She nervously looked over as the band stopped playing. Fearful that she had to return to the stage.

Her drummer looked over, noticing that Avéline was still busy. Noticing her posture, he turned to the bass player and whispered,

"Keep it going, she's not ready..."

"She asked me something to take care of you. Tyrrheni , we call it, or commonly called Tyrrhé."

The look on Casilas' face changed from concern to confusion. As what Avéline had just told him, sank in. 'Tyrrhé, Tyrrhé' he mouthed until it stopped him just as he was about to speak. His confused expression changed into a gentle smile.

"Tyrrhé, that word. I knew I had heard that word before. Adé had mentioned it once before. Just in passing. If anything ever happened to her. But I wasn't paying attention as much as I should have," he smirked, before quickly realising Avéline wasn't joking. He knelt there in thought, trying to remember things from the past.

"It was day 3 of our wedding, the rite of Thal....."

Avéline stopped him a mid-sentence.

"Thaldoiset"- 'Rite of Family'. I thought you would have remembered that..." she added exasperatedly.

"Avé, really. You expect me to remember a ceremony which lasted for eight days, in your native tongue. I probably understood ten percent of what the priest was talking about."

"But you..." she snapped back, her brow furrowed and her lips drawn.

"You know what? You don't understand, do you? To us. Tyrrhé still goes on. Within our" she trailed off before starting again,

"Within my community. As small as it is these days. More often since the dark days..." she ranted, annoyed with herself for even bringing this up.

"Avé, it's ..., it's just something that I never expected..."

"To be honest, I never knew you saw me in the same way as your sister..."

"Really?" "I was young, but I know what it meant when Adé asked me, I thought that once I was of age, and had made my own life, that you would be there..." she shyly turned away, she blushed again, as she played with her hair nervously, it had been in the back of her mind for cycles, that he would be there.

She turned back to him slowly as he spoke again.

"I didn't really notice, I ..." he mumbled, looking at her intently. Realising that these words were difficult for her to say.

"I thought you knew what Adé had asked me. I thought you remembered Tyrrhé. I bided my time. That one day you'd allow me to fulfil that promise."

Casilas was about to interrupt, to stop her from pouring out her feelings, but stopped. Allowing her to get these feelings out.

"But now it's too late. My own mistake for not stepping up myself. I should have done this a few cycles ago. Let you know how much you've meant to me, to my family."

"Avé, if I had known, I ... I would have taken it seriously."

She looked at him, a gentle smile appeared through the tears.

"Well, this Tala is lucky. My loss is her gain..." she wiped her tears away with the back of her hand and struggled to stand up, holding onto the chair before standing up.

"Help me to the stage, would you?, I've got a few more songs to sing before the night is out..."

"You're going to stay aren't you..." ask pleaded.

"I wouldn't miss it for anything," Casilas replied as he helped her to her feet.

CHAPTER 49
"I CAN'T STOP MYSELF WANTING YOU..."

6 months later...Euphoria Club, West Quay, Rulian Quarter 23:47pm

"Ryx, why did we end up here again ?" Avéline spoke into Ryx's ear, not wanting anyone else to hear it, the sound of the club's music filled the air, a mixture of dance music and pop, the kind of music Aerrea performed but remixed.

"I told you, Euphoria ,this place is crazy, all the a-listers end up here at some point, I'm surprised we've not been caught by Nyx.."

"Nyx, where?, where?" Avéline said, frightened, looking around frantically, trying to catch a glimpse of her, her hearts racing. She didn't want to be found out, not today and especially not by Nyxcerra, shed never hear the end of the argument.

"She's not here, but you know she frequents this place. Luckily, Vi on the door said he'd let me know if she's coming in tonight..". His voice calming her down while jovially mocking her. He laughed, taking a deep breath. The air filled with the aroma of various legal narcotics.

"And you are a-list. I'm surprised that you've never been invited here... either by Aeryth or Nyxcerra. So I thought I'd surprise you.. looks like some of us need all the help we can get," he added, without hesitation.

"I'm getting a drink." Avéline spoke, her voice becoming slurred, the alcohol over the past few hours had taken its toll on her, she'd been for food hours before, but by now there was no food in her system to soak up the alcohol, her stomach rumbled. Ryx was still completely in control. He'd been pacing himself, surprised by Avéline's ability to keep drinking.

"Hey, I'll get this one, another Caspian Sunset?" He enquired as he tapped a few buttons on a tablet in the middle of the table.

Avéline drained her neck back and smiled, gesturing with two fingers.

"Make it two..." she laughed. She was enjoying herself for the first time in months.

She leaned forward, looking longingly into his eyes. He had changed. He was more attentive this time, seeming to understand her more, she thought.

"I can't believe I'm falling for you again," Avéline playfully whispered as she leaned over towards Ryx,

"You know they still don't know the girls. I mean," she whispered as she picked up a Caspria sunset from the table, just as it was placed there by a server. Before sucking its contents through a golden straw.

"6 weeks and they still haven't noticed that you're happy all the time..., they mustn't be paying attention..."

Nyxcerra's always too busy, she's never at home, most

evenings she at some private event that Aeryth has invited her to, Jysell and Syala, always busy designing something, and Tii , even she hasn't noticed, and we live in the same room.

"I'm sorry for last week, keeping you out all night. Did you get to rehearsal on time...?" Ryx enquired as the music lowered in volume as the DJ was choosing the next part of his set.

"No, 45 minutes late, got a stern telling off, I just told them I had to get a prescription for headache meds.., well I had a headache, that clubs music was way to loud.." Avéline added, well I have nothing until later tomorrow, so I'll be fine."

Avéline adjusted her figure hugging dress, which was shorter than she would normally wear, but she knew the effect it would have on Ryx, pulling it open slightly to allow her legs to be on display. She knew what she was doing, toying with Ryx as she caught him looking, causing her hearts to race. She had missed being confident like this, as she had previously been when she was with him.

She cast him a seductive smile, gently biting the corner of her bottom lip before shyly looking away. She reached for the tray lined with Kaspian sunrise shots on the table, licking her finger as she spilt some of her own drink onto her finger.

She recognised that taste, Kalita syrup, she'd never really been a fan, the first time she had drank it with Nyxcerra they needed up very inebriated and with Nyxcerra flirting with the servers, this memory making her laugh, but now she'd grown accustomed to it.

She loved it here at Euphoria, the right amount of decadence and reserved sexuality. Euphoria was a trendy club, and her people knew who she was. She wasn't just the quiet member of Aerrea; she was Avéline. This place was a haven for the rich and the powerful.

"I thought we were going to have a good night," Avéline spoke as she got distracted by a young Thebian girl. Her light green skin and dark blue hair caught her attention, an attention that Ryx noticed.

"Well yes we will, you deserved a good night out, it's been a while, and I'm sure we both deserve a-bit of fun" he paused to take a quick shot,

"So has something or someone caught your eye my dear?" Ryx whispered into her ear as he gestured for the young Theban girl to come back, as he saw her turn around.

"I might have seen something or someone that I find....appealing..." she joked, I'm sure you couldn't handle me, let alone this..." she stopped as that young girl arrived

"This stunning beauty..." she paused, as she looked longingly at the young woman.

"Your name, my darling...?"

"Illara..."

"Hello Illara..." Ryx laughed as he saw Avéline staring wide eyed at her.

"Welcome back Ryx, haven't seen you in her in a while. What's the special occasion?" Illara replied, causing Avéline to recoil.

"You two know each other..."

"Ryx, he's a frequent visitor..." Illara replied, smiling a knowing smile at Ryx, who nodded his head in acceptance.

"Well, this one here..." he gestured towards Avéline, embarrassing her.

"Had forgotten my birthday last month..." he bowed, causing Avéline to turn to him, quickly placing her palms together..

"Forgive me..." she pleaded playfully.

"I think I can make that up to you later..." Avéline purred, winking at him,

"That's not enough of a present... it is a month late.." he added.

Avéline gestured for Illara to come close so she could whisper in her ear, all the meantime watching Ryx looking at them both, Illara in her silvery corset with short black shirt

"That sounds fine with me..." Illara replied as she fixed her corset.

"" They maybe you can try to have both of us..." Avéline whispered into Ryx's ear before kissing him, as Illara reached into her corset, pulling out a small bag, filled with some small paper looking sheets, taking out one, carefully placing it on her tongue and gesturing for Avéline to come closer.

Avéline looked puzzled but went with the flow, getting closer to Illara, when out of know where Illara pulled Avéline close, kissing her, transferring the paper item into Avéline's mouth via her tongue.

A wild and pleasurable set of emotions and feelings filled her mind, not sure if she enjoyed it, but it had caused her to react, 'is this the sensations Nyxcerra gets, in her encounters with the same sex?' She thought.

Avéline broke the kiss, feeling the paper slowly dissolve on her tongue. A weird sensation traveled its way through her body, at the same time as it affected Illara.

"Then maybe we need to find someone a bit more private..." Ryx spoke, Avéline turning to him,

"Aww, that's a shame, though you were adventurous..." she mocked openly as she started feeling the effects of the drug as it worked its way through her body, part of her screaming out inside as she would have never said that kind of thing before, she would have thought it but never said it. Her worries gradually fading as the drugs kicked in.

CHAPTER 50

"EITHER WE SOLVE THIS TODAY... "

The Next Morning...

Avéline sat sinking into the oversized sofa in the living room, she loved this sofa, where she could hide from the world and feel safe, but now it felt all consuming, but she was powerless to leave it.

She sat staring into the middle distance, her eyes glazed over, even though she was tired her mind was still going at a thousand miles an hour, her hearts racing. She sat there motionless, in a trance while everyone else was busy doing something, Syala was talking with Nyxcerra on the sofa to her left, occasionally either of them looked at her, before going back to their conversation.

"Tiysein, mussa niina häni on keponut mislle, Mettä he toivat seitellä hallassa pitovok loitaksen, mussa toivät toi tehdä suuta, häni mesitti misslle lukaivaa, koko ratkai-semme tämän tämään dai dän telkee päsaksen, olemeko balmiita feitä tädä kailkki tois sänen virhensä tallia... - I know, but that's what she's told me, they can cover up the possession charge, but can't do anything more, she gave me an ultimatum, either we solve this today, or she'll make a decision, are we willing to throw this away all for her mistakes..." Nyxcerra questioned, Syala looked at her, before glancing at Avéline, lost in thought for a moment before replying

"Se on hänen elämänsä, anna hänelle uhkaivaa, se ton joko hohi sänen kanssaan dai se on ohi meille, dän ansaitsee tämän valinnan. jäi dai tene..- It's her life, give her the ultimatum, it's either over with him, or it's over for us, she deserves that choice. Stay or go..,"

"Once she's back to herself, I'll ask..." Nyxcerra replied, they had spoken in Simi, Syala's mother tongue, to hide her conversation from Avéline.

Meanwhile Jysell was trying to catch up on her reading, but her mind was racing unable to focus on the words. She was still in shock of watching Avéline stagger back into their apartment an hour earlier, her hair disheveled, her lipstick had smudged, the heel of one of her high heels had broken which she continued to carry in her left hand.

What had happened that night?, why was she staggering back at 10am? She knew why, Ryx; it had to be. She'd fallen off the rails once she was back with him, she'd warned her, but to no avail. Her thoughts were interrupted by the sound of Tiiona being busy in the kitchen brewing up a concoction, using various roots and powders she had made up over the cycles, a "family secret", to help Avéline recuperate.

The smell from the chopping and grinding of spices made its way into the living area,

"Geez Tii, a-bit strong with the aliac root, don't we think..." Jysell exclaimed as the smell reached her, the warming sensation of aliac root caught the back of her throat. Tiiona couldn't stop thinking about what must have happened the night before, she knew that glazed expression, the inability to think straight, before moments of clarity before falling back into a near catatonic state, Ifruapycin, a highly illegal and addictive drug, banned around most of the known galaxy.

She'd pulled a small bag of it from Avéline's jacket as she put it away. Normally she would have just thrown it, by this was serious, Ifruapycin wasn't just illegal across the empire, a class omega drug. So just even possession was an offence which carried five cycles in prison. In her worried state she had to tell Nyxcerra, who then disappeared at the time upto the management offices on the higher floors, for crisis talks with Aeryth and Leix before coming down to discuss with Syala, who had read her expression when she came back from the conversation, her face white with fear, with tears in her eyes.

Avéline slumped herself in the chair, her hearts racing, feeling hot one moment and freezing cold the next, her breathing was shallow and laboured, telltale symptoms of Ifruapycin the comedown was difficult, she knew Ryx had been there the last time, but he had left her at the building entrance before getting a transport out, Leaving her to fend for herself.

She couldn't remember much but being questioned by security and the capital police in a room on the ground floor, before being allowed upstairs, how long she had been there, she didn't know. Her eyes began feeling heavy as she slowly drifted off to sleep.

She gradually opened her eyes a few hours later, to find nothing a blanket covering her, she looked around, her head pounding, her eyes heavy, needing a drink, her mouth bone dry, the others must have gone out she thought, before realising they were staring off to the corner of the room in heated discussion.

"Well, it's this, or it's over. We can't survive this kind of scandal. Trying to keep the media quiet about this will cause another scandal," Nyxcerra proclaimed before noticing Avéline staring at her.

She sat thinking about how terrible she felt before other memories flooded her mind; the drinks that she'd been drinking, the sickly sweet taste of Kaatk at the club, the following embrace with Ryx — the press of his mouth on hers, the way his hands had traveled over her body not caring that other people were there—and waking up next to him and another girl, who she was eluded her, all she could think about was Euphoria club, and the name Ilara, she must have been from the club, she thought.

She stifled a groan. What had she been doing that night, hoping to the goddess she hadn't let it go too far? But knowing too well that they had spent the night together, the three of them. What had she been thinking, taking Ifruapycin again? She didn't even like it the first time. But here she was recovering from Ifruapycin again.

Well, she decided to take herself to bed, to sleep this off, but struggled to get up., at least not then. She wouldn't have to be thinking of what happened that night. No need to remember it. Except that even now, she couldn't stop her memories from cascading through her mind. In fragments, the fragments came and went instantly, a disjointed mess, out of sequence and intensity. She closed her eyes, trying to surprise them until she could sleep, but that just made them come even quicker—

"Avé," a voice interrupted her, causing her to flicker open her eyes. She gradually pushed herself up on the sofa, seeing Nyxcerra standing in-front of her.

"I thought we agreed you were going to lay off the parties with Ryx, second one this week., and now your coming back wiped out, looking a mess, I mean what the fuck Avé" Nyxcerra proclaimed, with bitterness in her voice, Avéline couldn't help being immediately on the defensive. She was glad the flush on her scales wasn't readable from here, as it would betray what she'd just been thinking about.

Nyxcerra wandered over to her before piercing herself on the edge of the sofa, sighing angrily with the rest of the girls gathering around.

"I'm worried about you," Nyxcerra said, still looking at her. Nyxcerra's expression was distraught. She wore no makeup, her hair tied back, and was wearing loose, casual gym clothes, unusually hiding her physique.

"I've been worried since you got back with Ryx, we all have, which is why I..." she stopped, glancing over at the others

"Why we've got to talk about this"

"We know about the Ifruapycin, Tii found a baggie in your jacket pocket, your lucky you weren't charged for possession of this, Security downstairs reported you for this, as you stupidly dropped the baggie while entering the building, Leix saved your ass from getting put away for five cycles."

"Ave, is he really worth it...?"

She hadn't signed up for this, all she wanted to do was sing, get famous and make her family proud, and get laid on the way, but being a therapist for Avéline, having to give her this ultimatum was difficult, instantly thinking of how Ceres would have done this, would she have tried to smooth this over with Aeryth, or would she be the one sitting here asking Avéline to give up what she had worked so hard for, or to give up someone she loved, even though he was obviously a bad influence on her.

"Get can get over this...little situation. Maybe we should all check-in at Emerald Bay next weekend. Just relax and enjoy ourselves."

"Avéline stared at her. Did she really just tell her they were all concerned about Ryx?

"What? Really Nyx, you're asking me if he's worth it, I've never felt so alive!" Avéline didn't want to discuss it. He was hers and she was happy.

"Nyx, for once, you're wrong. He's not a bad influence. I'm finally be allowed to do as I want..."

"Is he pressuring you??" she asked out of curiosity.

"Pressuring me! Ha!" she exclaimed, running her hands through her hair.

"I'm aware of all of it. I said yes to the Ifruapycin, yes I slipped up earlier, but I'm old enough to look after myself. I'm not the naïve kid you all once knew..."

"Really Avé, I've done stupid stuff in my life, but nothing as stupid as Ifruapycin. You know a bad trip could kill you... he's bad for you," Tiiona exclaimed as she came closer and sat on the other sofa. This revelation shocked Avéline, her eyes welling with tears as she clenched her fingers into a fist.

"Tii, even you!" She exclaimed,

"I thought you at least would be on my side," she hissed, before casting her gaze back to Nyxcerra,

"Well, I'm not doing anything, I love him, he loves me and I'm happy... it's not my fault you're not happy with someone," Avéline mocked, the insult shocking Jysell, she'd never seen Avéline like this before,

"Hey Ave, that's not far..." Jysell spoke before Avéline looked at her with malice in her stare.

"God, Avéline, you have got to stop deluding yourself, he's using you!, can't you see it, you allow him to go places he wouldn't be able to go to, Aeryth...." Nyxcerra wasn't able to finish as Avéline interrupted

"It's me and him! If you can't be happy for me, then just leave me alone, and Aeryth, what does she have to do with this, this is my private life..."

Nyxcerra said nothing, trying to fight her own urges to slap Avéline, to make her see sense.

"See, nothing. It's my private life and I'll do as I see fit..." Avéline exclaimed.

"She said..." Nyxcerra tried to reply but was again cut off by Avéline.

"She said what....?" Avéline replied as she leaned forward, within inches of Nyxcerra's face, this blatant aggression by Avéline pushed Nyxcerra to the edge, without prior warning she slapped Avéline across the face, sending her back into the sofa, in shock.

"If you don't leave him, you're out, not just the group, the label will kick you out, ending your contract..., and possibly ours, see this doesn't just affect you," Nyxcerra cried out, her hearts racing, the room fell silent.

"I don't know about the rest, but I will not allow you to fucking ruin what I've worked so fucking hard to achieve, all because of Ryx..." She took a deep breath and tried to regain a measure of calm.

"You have two hours to decide, him or us." She barked before walking towards the door, Avéline still reeling from the slap, never expecting Nyxcerra to lash out like that. She looked over at Tiiona who turned her head away, ashamed.

"it's your choice..." she said as she got up and made her own way towards the door. Avéline's gaze flicked towards Syala and Jysell,

"You two as well??" Avéline spoke, her voice trembling.

Jysell couldn't bare to look at her and turned around, her eyes full of tears. Syala looked at her.

"I never thought you'd do anything to hurt us. I was wrong..." she spoke before making her way towards Nyxcerra and Tiiona.

"We'll give you time to decide..." Nyxcerra called out as she opened the front door, letting the others go first before slamming the door shut.

Avéline couldn't bear the thought of leaving. She sat there with tears running down her face. She couldn't bare the idea of returning home permanently. Would bring up too many questions. If she went back, she would be forced to confront everything that had happened in the past few months—would have to acknowledge she was the one who was kicked out, that she had broken the law, that she had ruined the careers of the others.

Avéline was afraid, she realised, of what she had done. Her mom's voice rang out in her head, it usually did when she was worried, but this time her tone was firm.

"I can't believe you would do such a thing." He thought.

Avéline's hearts raced. The emptiness of the apartment made it worse, the sound of them reprimanding her in the same disappointed tone that her mother would use.

"I've ruined it all, haven't I" she whispered to herself.

2 Hours Later...

Avéline sat alone, the apartment eerily quiet. She hated the quiet. She sat sinking into the giant silvery sofa, feeling herself sink further into its cushions, wishing it would swallow her whole. Thinking that would be easier than feeling the way she did, she needed to do something. Her mind turned to work. Was there something she could do or prepare for that would keep her occupied?

"System, is there anything else in my schedule, personal or group?" She muttered, getting no reply from the automated system.

"System, any appointments??" she barked, trying to find something to do which would keep her mind off what she had to do.

"Nothing in personal schedule, you've been removed from the private schedule for 52 hours. First engagement is on the..." this revelation caused her to reply quickly, not allowing the system to continue.

"Who removed me from the private schedule?" She added hastily , knowing that the next day she was supposed to appear on the Weekend Preview show.

"Your schedule was erased by Nyxcerra, timestamp 13:42pm today", that was just after they had left her, the severity of what had happened struck her hard, the world feeling as if it was a weight in her shoulders, she sank further into the sofa.

'Had it already been two hours since the girls had called a crisis meeting?' She thought, everything was still a blur, her mind reeling from the heated argument, Nyxcerra's ultimatum still rung out in her mind, "Leave him, or you're out". She knew she meant it, it was no idle threat. She'd never seen Nyxcerra this angry before. Reliving that memory caused her to weep. Her breathing staggered, trying to fight her own urge to break down.

She looked across the room. Everything was left mid conversation. They had let her figure it all out as they went for food; she had to make a decision before they came back, that's what she'd promised, a promise she didn't want to break.

"Or I'll make the decision for you..." rang out, Nyxcerra had threatened to discuss this further with senior management .

As she sat, she began to weep even more. She didn't know what to do. She looked over at the huge clock which covered the far wall. Her eyes widened. The girls would be back within the hour. She never expected it to get this bad. She replayed it over and over as she closed her eyes. Nyxcerra had been silent until she let loose with a scolding that was reminiscent of Ceres, every word carefully thought of, thought of to inflict the most damage, every word hurt.

Even Tiiona had given her the silent treatment. The one individual who she expected to be on her side had made her thoughts known.

"He's a bad influence on you, can't you see he's controlling you" she kept repeating.

"Maybe she's right.." she whispered to herself in between crying out loud.

Avéline began crying heavily, lost in thought as she cast her mind back, remembering when she had told Tiiona that she thought she had feelings for Ryx, which was strictly prohibited by the label, something she had never expected.

"I Don't trust him..," Jysell had said, and she was right, he'd cheated on her, thinking she wouldn't find out, a scandal which Avéline made worse. It leaked photos in compromising embraces with another girl.

She'd spent time with family, who helped her find her way back to some sort of normality. Being home had been difficult, it had been 15 cycles since the death of her sister and niece, thoughts she couldn't get away from.

After keeping herself busy, missing the times when she

felt she had purpose, conversations with her widowed brother-in-law kept her focused.

She was still shocked in how she had managed to put her life back together. Aeryth had even allowed and encouraged her to release a side project, a solo single. Which had been received well by the critics and the fans. The solo album was coming along fine, but now. Her rekindled relationship with Ryx put all that at risk.

But after being reintroduced through a mutual friend and former trainee NieJen a few months after being back home, she had restarted the relationship. She was drawn to him. Even though she knew he wasn't good for her, she felt alive with him.

They had only been back together for a few weeks, it couldn't have been long than six weeks she thought to herself, remembering a whirlwind of events, red carpet award shows, gala nights, having being seen out in loved up photos in private Vip booths at some of the most glamorous clubs in the capital.

That's when it all fell apart, she'd turned up late to rehearsals, had sneaked out during pre award show curfews, had been in a heated argument with Nyx in front of the rest of the girls, and had been caught by the patrols taking Ifruapycin, a highly addictive narcotic, so dangerous it was banned across the empire, that had been the final straw.

"Luckily for your sake, as well as our own, the label has hushed this up"Leix said, supported by Nyxcerra adding that

"your lucky he had favour's to call in."

She remembered the first time she saw him; it was just after they were chosen as the final six. During the torturous time of Ceres death, even though she couldn't think straight, She couldn't keep her mind off him, she'd never been the flirtatious type, but felt drawn to him, everything he said was what she wanted to hear.

"I've known it would come to this," she whispered to herself as she struggled to get up from the sofa, finally being released from its grasp.

She was clearly aware of what she had to do, she tried to hide her intense feelings, however; she wasn't good at it, looking in the mirror, grabbing a small white silken cloth and wiping the running mascara off.

A Few Hours Later...

"Listen" Avéline asked, despite the calm tone of her voice. A serious expression crossed her face. She asked the girls to sit down. They had only just come back from giving her time, but she needed to get this done.

"I need to tell you something." She sheepishly added.

"So you've made a decision....? Nyxcerra asked. Avéline nodded her head gently,

"Ye...." she replied, not giving any further clarification,

I'm going to need your support after this, but I've got myself into this situation, and I'll be the one to get myself out of it"

"I just don't know how I'm going to tell him. I don't want him going off the rails again.."

"Again?, Ave, had he done something before, ha....." Tiiona voice trailed off as she stood up,

"May the goddess spare me their judgement if he's dared to raise his hand against you." Tiiona added.

"No, no he hasn't, he already knows you'd make him regret it" she nervously answered, knowing that she was lying to Tiiona, not wanting to remember the time he had stuck her.

CHAPTER 51
"LISTEN..."

Less Than An Hour Later...

"Listen" Avéline asked, despite the calm tone of her voice, a serious expression crossed her face. She nervously avoided eye contact with him while she spoke, not wanting to look into those eyes, to see his heart breaking.

"I need to tell you something."

Ryx stopped her to say,

"First, let me apologise for getting you in trouble. I just felt like I could lose myself with you, that we could do everything. I wanted to tell you how much you mean to me."

Avéline shook her head.

"That's just it,"–her dark purple eyes finally met his, and for a moment she hesitated

"I don't think we should see each other anymore. I'm sorry, Ryx. It was either us or my career, I... I" She tilted her head, awaiting a reply, Although Ryx said nothing; He just remained silent, a thick, prolonged silence.

"I can't risk what I've worked so hard for, what I've sacrificed for 11 long cycles.

"What she's sacrificed," Ryx thought to himself, his heart racing, the urge to speak his mind, knowing that everyone was against him, they would take her side. It had been three entire cycles... three difficult cycles, the multiple break ups, her shutting him out, the cause of his infidelity. It had always been him who had ended things. "she wants to end the relationship? Fine," he thought.

Before Ryx could even reply, Avéline jumped in, hating the silence which had formed.

"But don't get me wrong. It's not you, it's me. I'm not the innocent girl I was when we first met. I am a changed person. I've finally grown up. I know what I want. I can't just risk it, even though my heart wants to stay. I don't think we're compatible anymore."

Ryx rolled his eyes. "Do you mean to say we're over because of how I'm a risk to your career, really Ave' I'm a risk to your career, you're dumping me because I'm the risk?"

"No... no, not at all, Ryx. You know I don't mean it like that. Please don't put words in mouth."

"I must be hearing it wrong. I thought I was the one ruining my career by falling for a manufactured talent idol," Ryx said, as he reopened the front door, holding onto the door handle as he turned round.

"Look," Avéline tried to reassure him,

"It's not you, Ryx. Really, it's me. I think I need to find myself, you know. I need to discover who Avéline really is before it's too late. I need to..."

Ryx held up his hand for her to stop speaking, but caused her to recoil.

"See, really Ave', I told you that time was an accident,

I'm tired of this, all about you isn't it, Your career, You're done here, go" Ryx replied gruffly,. "This is ridiculous and humiliating."

"Is it something I said? Ryx, you know my hearts beat for you, both of them without hesitation, but this is bigger than us, why don't you believe me when I say this, give me time to find myself, my way, then maybe," her voice trailing off.

"That's it!, your wanting me to wait on a maybe" Ryx shouted, standing with his arm gesturing towards the door. The people walking outside were staring. Those in the communal garden the next to us were staring. For once Avéline didn't mind. There were always witnesses to her misery, usually it was the girls. These residents would do.

"Listen," Avéline spoke again, this time the tears welled in her eyes.

"Please, just wait, let me make something which is just me, then...."

"Don't give me that 'when I've made it we can be together' nonsense," he cursed.

I can't believe you believe that's going to work, are going to dump me on our anniversary! Seriously, maybe it was all my fault. Thought you were different, but I was wrong, your as cold and ruthless as the rest. Even worse, you don't even fucking realise it" "

"Don't say that," Avéline whined as full-blown tears fell from her eyes.

"You're right. I shouldn't say that." he crossed his arms, wondering why was acting this way, shed never refused him before. "Maybe I should say that I never really knew you. You were always a facade. Now I finally found out who the real Avéline is. I bet they warned you about me, the circles I travel in."

"Well, many people warned me about you, but I turned the other cheek because I thought I was in love. Well, I know now I made a mistake. Just go,"

With that last statement, Avéline stormed out into the rain, soaking her. Before turning on her heels and matching back.

A piece of her silvery hair–darkened by the rain–fell in front of her eyes, and she slicked it back behind her ear without a thought.

"I have to think about myself, I just can't... "she added, Ryx replied, but she didn't listen, oblivious. She didn't want to be there. He was skilled at making her come around to his style of thinking.

"Well, I'm sorry you think that," she said, catching the end of his tirade. "My fault... my fault, "she stuttered, her anger and sadness were at breaking point.

"Really, I've just had four of my closest friends, no family, berate me because of how I am when I'm with you, in my own home," Avéline wailed.

"It was pouring outside, my favourite time, the sound of rain, but now that's ruined. Every time I hear the rain, I'll hear their voices, the anger, the pain and the... disappointment." She stopped and tried to wipe the tears away.

"You don't know what it's like. You don't have to live with others who don't even talk to you because of what you've done." She hiccupped massive sobs as she pulled up the collar of her rain jacket as she stepped outside again, the rain still pouring down.

"Just leave me alone," she sputtered. "Give me space..."

Jysell stood in her bedroom looking at the colourful throws and artwork which decorated the room as she tied up her hair in a loose ponytail. She'd style it later, but now it was still a bit damp, occasionally dripping onto her shoulder.

She rubbed her arm, noticing that her skin was dry, cracking slightly under the pressure of her fingers. Causing her to sigh before casting her towel haphazardly to the floor, taking a few steps in just her lingerie towards the shelves across from her bed, searching its levels, looking for something in particular.

She reached for her skin lotion in its crystal dispenser which sat on a self beside other items of makeup, carefully tipping out a small pea-sized amount and began to gently rub it over her bare arms, before making her way into rubbing it across her entire body.

As she rubbed it in it left a faint glittery iridescence to her skin, she loved it, the feeling it gave her, the dry summer air had dried her skin, to the point of it cracking in places, this routine of applying skin cream had been a familiar one.

Especially during the dry part of the summer. She adored

this skin cream it had been a gift from NieJen, she had just got bonded to Kasile, he had worked for the label in the studio as a vocal coach during her trainee cycles, Jysell smiled as the thought about it, she was glad that someone was happy. NieJen had got the cream from Praxus, on special order from a tiny boutique shop in the Praelian sector, the beautiful iridescence made her skin glow. The scent was familiar, the scent of the beaches of home, she longed to go back home, to sit on the black sand beaches, take in the sun and actually relax, she wanted it so painfully much that it made her want to cry, after so long she longed for it, the simpler times.

She knew Avéline would have understood this feeling. She too was far from home. The culture here on the core worlds was different.

Jysell thought about a few things, the sensation of loss and the terrifying emptiness inside her, only Avéline knew the same. The darkness containing the remains of her hearts.

Avéline herself was still tentatively holding herself together after ending it with Ryx, it had been a few weeks but she still broke out into tears when she thought others weren't watching, they all knew about it, but wanted to give her space, to give her the time to heal in her own way.

Jysell knew Avéline would have hugged her, and assured her she would be fine, that soon they would be allowed to relax, She would have sat with her snacking on Boor bread and drinking Khamyr wine, to hell with their diets, they would hide from the world until they both could deal with it again, or until Nyxcerra managed to emotionally black-mail them into doing something productive, which was more likely to happen.

She couldn't stand why Nyxcerra was always busy, off at

some soirées with Aeryth, events where she was the only one from the group invited. She wanted someone to talk to, but she was alone.

Avéline wasn't here. She'd gone for detox treatment, to help remove the last traces of Ifruapycin from her system, and she would be back until the next day, that's what Nyxcerra had said earlier that day over breakfast.

She'd spent days sitting in this apartment, Aeryth had instituted a stay in place order, which excluded Nyxcerra. This omission angered them all. Luckily it ended in an hour, she thought, but she didn't know what to do, where do go once she could.

Jysell had to get out of this apartment if she wanted to avoid sinking into her own depression, until an idea struck her, causing her to lose her balance, giddy at the idea which bounced around her head, rushing over to a pebble, tapping twice on its surface,

"Hey, , send invites marked as priority to Nyxcerra , Syala, Tiiona"—she hesitated a moment—

"and NieJen, and while I remember Soka."

"Recipients list prepared. What message would you like to send..." the system announced, listening out for her reply, but getting nothing.

She'd forgotten to send NieJen a birthday gift last month, and thought this would make up for it. A belated birthday party, she hoped that they all would be able to make it, she hasn't spoken to Soka in ages, she missed her quirky nature, even though she was ditsy she was an amazing lyricist, having written songs for other artists on the label. She didn't normally like big gatherings, a small gathering of a few close friends, that was enough but she wanted a lot of people around her right now, they would be an easy way to distract her from the pressures of life, the constant pressures of being at the top of your game.

She knew without any doubt that Nyxcerra was the type of person you needed on nights like this; she was loud and game for anything, an easy lure for the members of the opposite sex, and usually members of the same, with an unmistakable flair for the over dramatic, she would at least make it interesting and she'd at least make her laugh at something mildly inappropriate, that would keep her distracted and allow her to suppress her longing for home, at least for the moment, until she could go home for the winter solstice festival in a few months.

The system beeped at her again, still awaiting the contents of the message, startling her, she replied.

"Kaspian Sunsets at Zolos at eight, dress up...hope you all can make it..." she paused

"send and flag as urgent..."she added as she wandered up to her wardrobe, before opening it and staring inside, deciding what to wear.

A few hours later...

"So, Jys, what we doing here with such short notice" NieJen asked as she sat herself on the dark leather chair located around the table in the VIP lounge at Zolo's a few hours later.

NieJen sat there beaming with an infectious smile. She'd dyed her hair recently, gone was her black straight hair, replaced now with a rich light blue, tipped with bright pink accents.

This hair in stark contrast to the black velvet catsuit she wore. She held a small glass with one hand, making sure that the others would see the huge sapphire ring on her finger, hoping to be the centre of attention.

Jysell was relieved, even though they hadn't been given more than a few hours notice, they had all managed to show up, she knew the rest of the girls' schedules were empty, Tiiona was at the gym on the lower floors of their building. Syala had been working on her vocals after a bout of Zhulu , - an inflammation of her vocal cords.

Nyxcerra had been asleep, removing from the prior night's event with Aeryth. As always, she was up for a social event.

Nyxcerra adjusted her figure hugging red dress, pulling it open slightly to allow her tanned legs to be on display. She knew what she was doing, toying with the guys sitting across from them. She cast them a seductive smile, gently biting the corner of her bottom lip before adjusting her cleavage, before shyly looking away.

She reached for the tray lined with Kaspian sunrise shots on the table, placing one in front of everyone in attendance. Licking her finger as she spilt some of her own drink onto her finger.

The drink was laced with Kalita syrup, now not just sweet but laced with a highly addictive narcotic, pleasant but dangerous to all other species except their own, an advantageous adaptation in Impiri physiology. She loved it here, the right amount of decadence and reserved sexuality. Zolo was a trendy restaurant, the haunt of the upper class, the young and the powerful, usually advanced booking only.

A waiting list of months. It was an old favourite of Nyxcerra's, her cousin having a controlling interest in the place. It was always busy, but especially tonight being the first night of the Emperor's hundredth Jubilee even table service that night took a while, the restaurant was nestled in the centre of the district.

It was a den of opulence and debauchery; It had no exterior windows, to keep the media out, but that worked in favour of its décor and club atmosphere: dim lighting, techno music, and especially the VIP booths around the outside of the main seating areas.

"I thought we all deserved a good night out, it's been a while, and .." she paused to take a quick shot,

"I might have forgotten NieJen's birthday last month..." she bowed, quickly placing her palms together.. "forgive me..." she pleaded playfully...

"let's have a fun girls' night," she added, flashing a smile.

"We deserve a break like this, it's been ages since we've all caught up.."

"Don't we have a dance practice tomorrow?," Syala pointed out.

"Yeah, but not until after midday, we'll be fine by then...I hope...we have to be on the Emperor's Jubilee Gala at 9 tomorrow night" Jysell chuckled before being interrupted by Nyxcerra, but couldn't be bothered to interject back.

"I'm avoiding having to look at my schedule, even more than that...as well as my parents, are in from Corellia," Nyxcerra decided to admit. She never like it when they visited. She picked up one of the two shorts in front of her and downed one in one swift motion, slamming the glass onto the table with a bang. She bared down as the sour and sweet liquid hit her palate.

"They wanted to have a big family get together at their hotel tonight...you know the typical, concerned parents' conversation, even though they haven't been too concerns in the past six cycles, " she exclaimed.

"But I'm really not in the mood for it, something about me having to set a better example. Especially to the younger generation, I just don't want to get into it not right now, actually, I don't want to get into that conversation for the rest of my career," she added. Tiiona—who looked as if she was about to enquire stayed silent, for once reading the atmosphere and Nyxcerra's body language.

"Well, their loss is our gain..." Tiiona replied, thinly veiled with sarcasm, enough that Nyxcerra looked at her inquisitively before dismissing it.

"Thanks for sorting out the issue with the tables..." Tiiona added as she noticed a slender young waitress dressed in white making their way towards the table., carrying a tray filled with drinks.

Another waiter swooped over with the rest of their drinks and a few snacks,

"Compliments of the house," he added as he put out multiple small plates

"We have a small selection of house specialities, this seasons Taalitian caviar from Taalitan III, poached purple Tori eggs fresh from Pirax , and Trillian chocolate soufflé, done specifically to your liking Lady Jaeihai..." he spoke casting his gaze downwards when addressing Nyxcerra. Nyxcerra smiled before addressing the waiter.

"Thank you Milex...." She paused.

"Tell Kras, that we are humbled by his generosity..." Nyxcerra bowing at the waiter, before adding.

"His front row tickets to the show will be delivered to his home address at the earliest convenience..." she smiled.

"What?" she proclaimed as the others looked at her with suspicious intent.

"A favour for a favour..."

"it's not easy to get a table on a night like this," she added.

"And your drinks, ma'am," a voice proclaimed as they put bright purple drinks at the corner of each place setting. Tiiona looked up in surprise.

"I didn't order these...?" She spoke before realising who was placing the drinks on the table.

"I did," Avéline announced, causing Nyxcerra to stand up. She glanced at her, checking out what she was wearing, a beautiful, elegant dress, not too revealing, cute but not overtly sexy.

She studied Avéline's smile before smiling. Offering Avéline a place next to her, Avéline bowed her head and smiled as she turned to Nyxcerra and Tiiona with a challenging smile.

"Come on Nyx, you know you want one. It's my treat, and an apology"

Nyxcerra thought about protesting. These drinks were her favourite, but Avéline had agreed not to drink for a while, to get it out of her system, but before she could start to protest; she glanced over. Avéline had already passed the drink over to Tiiona. She wasn't in the mood to drink at all.

"I'm not having anything, don't worry. I'm keeping to our arrangement..."

The girls were all looking at Nyxcerra, was she going to accept Avéline's arrival or send her away, she'd been strict with her, limiting her appearance at social events for the last few weeks, to 'try to protect the group' was her frequent mantra. Avéline's hearts raced, she herself didn't know it was too soon, but she had missed them all.

"Okay,"Nyxcerra said, lifting the drink to her lips.

"It's so nice to see you all" Soka squealed,

"it's been so long, not seen you all together since…" she stopped, realising when it was.

"Almost four cycles, the night that Ceres died…" Nyxcerra added, wanting to end the awkward silence, picking up a shot and raising it into the air.

"For Ceres…" she exclaimed.

Avéline started to get comfortable before lifting a glass full of water. She'd always hated to remember that time. She couldn't control how she would react. It was either sadness or a flood of happy memories. She was too embarrassed incase someone in the media got snaps of her crying. She never knew if she was being watched, especially after the incidents with Ryx.

Tiiona picked up hers, lifting it up.

"For Ceres, forever our lead…" she announced without thinking, Jysell and Syala looked up her.

"What..?" Tiiona exclaimed as she saw them stare, Before catching Nyxcerra's gaze, she quickly masked her anger with an open mouth grin, hurt by that simple betrayal, all she had done for them and Tiiona still thought of Ceres as their lead.

"Ceres, always in our thoughts," Jysell and Shaka proclaimed in unison before raising their drinks.

"Ceres…" Soka added, raising her glass. Finally all of them had a glass in the air, knocking them together, trying not to spill their contents.

"Ceres…my love…" Nyxcerra whispered as she knocked back her shot, slamming it to the table afterwards.

Nyxcerra leaned back, taking it all in. This was what she wanted, the club was packed. As she glanced around, she knew everyone here was young and well-dressed. This was the young and successful elite.

She'd been to events with Aeryth, but those were old

money, the elite that she had grown up with her who life, those like her own family, but this young elite, they enjoyed it, their skin bright, their eyes wide, savouring every moment as if it was their last. This is what she longed for, the future she and Ceres had dreamed of.

Wishing Ceres was there brought a small tear to her eye, she knew she had to live her own life now, maybe with no one, but right now she was single and looking for fun, she recalled what Ceres had told her once, that the goddess had created them all, and had spoke to the first couple,

"and I created you in pairs...", now she was one and wanted to seek out another.

She spied the group of Zetoo at other tables glancing their way, clearly wondering about the young women in their short dresses and how they had captured the gaze of almost everyone in the club that night, but no one had yet ventured over to talk to them. She glanced over at them before coyly looking away. She'd let them try first. If they didn't, she'd make a move herself.

"NieJen. Tell me more about you and Kasile Pana, it sounds like a dream bonding. I mean that voice, I gotta be honest, he could sing me to sleep every night," Nyxcerra joked she placed her hand on top of NieJens.

"in the politest way possible..." she added, not wanting to cause any trouble.

NieJen recounted the latest stories from her bonding with Kasile, who was a now a senior producer at a co - owned sub-label with Lady Vale. Nyxcerra forced herself to laugh at the jokes, to enquire about how NieJen and Soka were, Soka annoyed her, too ditzy for her liking, could never get a straight answer, but she was Jysell's closest friend, so she had to deal with it.

If she laughed at the jokes, no one would notice her

strange mood, her mention of Ceres, her parents' arrival and Tiiona's passive aggressive attitude caused her mind to spin. If she laughed and smiled and nodded enough, until a thought came to find, she knew she had the attention of the young Zetoo makes across from them, they would be her attention for the tone being.

She kept taking sips of her drink, which Avéline must have refilled at some point, though she hadn't noticed it. Other trays of food came out, which she picked at,

Their small gathering grew. First of all, it was Xin and Zhiu, their label seniors, then a couple of other girls from their trainee cycles, Wini and Tasa; they'd been meeting with Amillia Tane from Ixius, a rival label and had noticed them and had wanted to join, followed by Roseah, then some of the dancers from AliEliz-Sto arrived.

The gathering kept expanding from the VIP area , down multiple tables, to small clusters located around the VIP bar, ordering Kaspian sunsets and trays of Crystallised Kalita.

Nyxcerra felt like half the club was hanging out with them. Conversations stopped and started as other arrived and some left, some spun off into small groups dancing on the wooden dance floor.

For a moment, a young Khal girl caught her attention. She was tall, beautiful and elegant. She had to look at her twice, her heart stopping for an instant. She looked too familar. She reminded her of Ceres, the same sparkle in the eyes, the same physique and the way she carried herself. She wanted to rush over and see what would happen, but before she could get up and introduce herself to her, a trio of Zetoo from the other tables—they introduced themselves before being offered seating—sat down at their table.

"I was just about..." Nyxcerra was about to speak before Avéline leaned over, giggling.

"Nyx, Chol's just become dangerously single, thought you might want to...you know," Avéline whispered, with a meddlesome wink, gesturing over at Chol. He was tall, handsome, and young.

"He's a friend of Soka's, well, more of a 'close friend' if you get me..." she added, wanting to see how Nyxcerra reacted.

Nyxcerra didn't react to that news at first. She'd been sitting at the table all night and as others had come and gone, she ended up in the middle of everyone at the table, before she felt the tingle of a finger being run up her back. Glancing round, she was surprised by Chol.

"Could I refill your glass tonight....? He whispered, gently grabbing at her hand as she reached back, rubbing his thumb slowly down her fingers.

Avéline did have a point. Chol was single, and now she recognised him. Chol from Kamus, one of the new groups which Aeryth managed. They had just had their first release. Why shouldn't she talk to him? What was left to hold her back? She was 'eternally unattached'. She remembered a reporter calling. her, little did they know. She didn't have Ceres anymore, but she wanted to find someone, someone to make her happy.

Nyxcerra remembered how nervous she had been when she flirted genuinely with someone new, it had been cycles since she had flirted with Ceres, lost in thought for a moment before snapping back to reality.

"Chol!" Nyxcerra exclaimed after a beat, standing up slowly, fixing her dress, while keeping her eyes fixed on him, watching his gaze flicker to her body, she loved this game, trying to keep his attention from staring at her body.

"How've you been?" She added as she bit the corner of her lip, at the same time carefully tracing the back of her finger down her neck, she could feel herself getting aroused, the scales on the back of her neck starting to tingle once again.

Chol seemed startled by her attention; she'd seen him once at a work meeting a few months back, but she'd soundly ignored him, he was still a trainee at the time and had stepped out of line by approaching her,

"Great, thanks," he said cautiously.

"I'm sorry about last time, had a few things on my mind, you know what I mean...let me make it up to you" she apologised before she turned her flirtation on fully, flashing her brightest smile, pulling him close by his black tie and planting a passionate kiss on his lips.

Poor Chol didn't stand a chance. Before he knew it she had released the tie and had pulled away.

"Now Let me really make it up to you....,"She leaned over to him and whispered in his ear, he nodded his head the moment she started whispering.

"Once we are in that room, I'm going to slam the door shut and devour you, I know what I'm doing, you might be new to this, but I'm certainly not" she whispered, causing him to close his eyes briefly.

She remembered how he had glanced at her moments before,

"I saw you watching me earlier. I didn't honestly think you had the confidence to even stand in front of me. I'm glad my first impression was wrong." She whispered again, knowing his kind loved the sensation of a whisper.

"See, I know your enjoying this, the whispers, and I can whisper anything you want, if your willing to help me, especially with these scales... but first you can get me another drink, then we need to find somewhere a-bit more private..." which caused him to smile before whispering back.

"I'll try to do my best. I learnt a few things from Soka over those cycles. You can thank her later." He added.

CHAPTER 53
"... UNTIL YOU CHOSE TO BRING IT UP..."

The Next Morning...

"Where's Nyx?" Tiiona hesitated as she walked through the doorway of the kitchen before stopping. She stood drying her now short blonde hair with a towel awaiting a response but getting nothing. Jysell was sitting at the table alone, leaning over while tapping her fingers absentmindedly on its worn wooden surface, lost in her own thoughts.

"Jys" Tiiona added, causing Jysell to snap out of her daydream.

She glanced up.

"Hey, Tii. I think she's just changing, shed had to have another meeting with Aeryth about the tour. Looks like they are adding more date, again."

"She was having a word with her again. I'm sure she's always agreeing to all these dates. I've had it with the touring. Give us a break. Let us find our creativity again." Tiiona added as she put down the towel and picked up a small knife and a piece of fruit, and began to chop it aggressively.

"The tour, what does that have to do with Nyx, its not like she can say no, she's under contract, she can argue our point, but its still Aeryth's decision..." Syala asked without preamble as she walked in from another room, clutching a small basket of bread with one hand before sitting down, running her ringers through her raven black hair. Syala cautiously ventured inside and pulled out the chair across from her. The table had uneven legs. It rocked occasionally as the weight on its surface shifted.

Nyxcerra walked out into the living room, dressed in casual oversized clothes. Sinking into her hoody she sat herself down on the sofa, putting her legs to her side.

"I think we all need to talk..." she added as she leaned back, awaiting an answer.

Tiiona leaned against the counter in the kitchen and looked across into the living area, seething. Maybe it was the recent conversations, maybe it was the eighteen hours day the day before, maybe the lack of sleep, maybe it was all of them.

She'd not been this angry in cycles, not since losing the race meters from the finish line.

She began clenching her teeth as she tapped her fingers against the stone work surface, before putting down the knife she had been chopping fruit with, ignoring the fruit. She clenched her fist as she thought about it. Without warning, she snapped.

"I'll go first, if you don't mind, clear the air a bit." Tiiona seethed.

'Really Nyx, bringing up the accident yesterday, I've apologised and thought it was done with,' she thought, almost mouthing it to herself.

"What's up, Tii? You seem tense," Nyxcerra spoke as she saw the anger etched on Tiiona's face, not expecting the oncoming tirade.

"I was fine Nyx, until you brought up the accident last night, it's not fair you know that... I thought we'd got over this, but it seems like you want to bring up old wounds..." staring at her, her brown eyes unwavering.

"She's right...," Avéline agreed as she sat off to the side of the kitchen, peeling a ripe green Hysn fruit with her fingers.

"Thanks Avé, but I can fight my own wars" she snapped back, this taking Avéline by surprise , her instant reaction was to get up abruptly and walk off into the living room before sitting on one of the chairs, with a huff.m, she'd never expected Tiiona to dismiss her that way.

"But what else do you expect me to do?" Nyxcerra sarcastically replied, she wasn't

"First it's, little miss toxic relationship over here" as she gestured over at Avéline, Nyxcerra wasn't surprised, if they were going to argue about this, then here was better than anywhere else, at least the media wouldn't find out.

"Close to destroying everything I've worked so hard for us to achieve" she scowled, standing up. The atmosphere between them all had been souring for a while, especially since the crisis talk with Avéline.

"Then you're back out there again, the downhill racing, as if nearly losing you wasn't enough . If your going to keep sneaking around like this without Aeryth and Leix suspecting something—which they might already—then maybe, you should have told us, not have me catch you sneaking out last night, I mean, come on Tii, what the actual fuck...?" She stepped closer to the kitchen, slamming down the glass she had on the work surface, cracking the glass before taking a step back.

Startled, Tiiona didn't answer right away. She stared around the tiny space filled with platters of food their photographer had gifted them.

"You don't know how difficult it is for me, seeing all the work we've put in be eroded by my mistake," Tii said at last.

"I just needed to feel like myself, ever since... Ceres.. left us..." she paused,

"Come on, she died, don't you think I know that, she was the one who kept us focused, I've tried my hardest to do what I thought she would have done..." Nyxcerra replied, she never wanted this, but had done the best she could.

"But you haven't... your not the same as her," Avéline added, piping into the argument.

She resented that. She had tried to look after them all. But they didn't know the lengths she'd gone to, to keep them at the top. It could have been far worse if she hadn't done things, things even she thought against, but had done them, anyway.

"Trust me, I know that. It's not like I wanted this role." She could feel the scales on her back heating up, she clenched her hands, and could feel her hearts racing deep inside her chest.

"No, I don't think you do understand ," Syala chimed in tersely, chiming in on the argument. She'd been biding her time, waiting for the right moment. Leaning forwards she raised her voice.

"She was always here, even during the exercises, but your never here, always off at some Soirée or private event, but we are never invited...it's like we are an afterthought"

Syala added, these thoughts having been running through her mind for months.

"Just because you saw holos of me at a party with Elim, once?, maybe twice. That hardly counts....it's not like I wasn't on the clock, you wouldn't understand...or want to understand the intricacies of what goes on behind doors," Nyxcerra hissed.

"I can't believe that you all think that,", her eyes welling with tears

"How fucking dare you, okay girls..." she preached, scowling at everyone, feeling the atmosphere in the room change. She was tired and not in the mood, but if they wanted this, they would get it.

"I'll make it simple for you all, hit singles, breakthrough first album, multiple awards, we are the top of everything, the sponsorships we have..." making them all silent, she wasn't going to let it go, they needed to know.

"Because I sweet-talked the directors, the fashion brands to even look at us, my acting work in those dramas, all because of the events that I go to with Aeryth, it's not all fun.., but if you still think that, then I'll stop, let you figure it out...our industry isn't all sugar and roses"

"I doubt that, I'm sure sleeping with all these executives is the most fun you've had in cycles...Ceres would have never done it this way," Tiiona mocked. As she wandered across the room, Nyxcerra standing there, being attacked at all sides, feeling her anger rising, noticeably breathing deeply as she clenched her muscles.

"Then you're more naïve that I thought, you have no idea of what goes on behind closed doors, favours, that's all it is, a favour for someone in exchange for a little preferential treatment, Ceres knew this, of course she did, she knew it was favour's and secrets, especially secrets when ..." she stopped, before blurting it out, wanting not to say it but her emotions got the better of her.

"When Aeryth is her mom..." this revelation caused the room to go silent, Jysell shook her head, Tiiona froze mid walk into the living area, Avéline sat up, "Can't be" she exclaimed in shock.

"She would have told us..." Avéline proclaimed, sitting up.

"Would she?, she would have told us that her dad had an affair with Aeryth, while he was betrothed to her sister Coralie and she was the result of that union...so of course she kept it secret." She added bluntly.

"But the scandal would have ruined them, so she went on hiatus at the time Ceres father married her mom, that 3 cycle hiatus of Eternity, was used to cover it up, only the head of BYL and the members of Eternity knew about it"

"She knew everything?" Tiiona exclaimed as she ran her fingers through her hair, shaking her head in disbelief.

"Of course she knew, she was told when she reached the age of ascent, she was brought up as Coralie's daughter, completely unaware. It was lucky that Aeryth and her mom looked so similar..."

"Then how do you know? Wouldn't be something she'd share so easily..." Jysell sat sunk into the sofa, her voice cut through the atmosphere.

Nyxcerra stood, tears welling in her eyes, remembering what had happened that fateful night.

"We shared a lot, more than you'd ever know, She told me this, one night after we had been drinking, swore me to secrecy..., and I kept that promise until today..." she shook her head at the end, realising she had broken that promised, her hearts racing, her palm's sweaty, a feeling of dread descend on her, but a weight has been lifted off her shoulders, it had been six cycles since she had found out.

"I can't believe it. She knew Aeryth was her mom and didn't tell us..." Syala proclaimed, the shock still setting in.

"That's why she was picked...isn't it..." Tiiona added, talking over Syala.

"Maybe, we'll never know, but it's the way this industry works. How do you think 'Eternity' got to the top, favours, it's always been about favours?" She exclaimed, without giving anyone else room to speak she added.

"Ceres knew this and was okay with it, I never wanted to be in charge, I was happy being the visual, her death was harder on me that you could realise, I... I.." she stuttered, could she reveal their secret, the weight of it since Ceres death was difficult.

"I doubt that, you always argued when it was something you felt we should be doing, you coveted the role, I bet you was happy when they offered it to you.." Tiiona added as she stood less than a meter from Nyxcerra, staring at her straight in the eye.

"I bet you wanted her gone, maybe you're the one who caused her death.." she argued as she forcefully poked Nyxcerra in the shoulder, pushing her back, who was dismayed by the accusations.

Without warning, Nyxcerra swung at Tiiona, slapping her straight across the face, causing her to grasp at her face, her right cheek throbbing in pain. The rest of the girls recoiled in shock, having never seen Nyxcerra lash out.

"Me...." She screamed

"How fucking dare you! How dare you say that! You know nothing..." she screamed, before falling to her knees, sobbing.

"Nothing about the relationship we had. I never wished

this..." she sobbed, trying to explain through the tears. Things she had never said before openly bubbled to the surface, the only way she could explain how things really were.

"We were in love and I loved her... truly loved her," she blurted out, her emotions getting the better of her.

"No, no way, we would have all noticed..." Tiiona stuttered, trying to make sense of it all. Avéline was taken back in shock as she tried to work it all out.

"It's true Tii, I've known for cycles..." Jysell proclaimed, putting herself out there, she'd been quiet during this argument, she hated the conflict, but she had caught them in a passionate embrace when they thought no one else was in the apartment.

"Jysell, you knew and didn't say..."

Jysell nodded in response.

"Wasn't my secret to tell, thought they'd say something at some point" she added, after thinking about it:

"Anyone else know about this? Am I the only one who wasn't told"

Syala opened her mouth, then shut it again, before chiming in, unable to silence herself.

"I'm sorry, Tii, I suspected something."

"Yes, you all could have told me. I mean, how can our closest friends be in a relationship with us not knowing?" She quipped, feeling out of the loop.

Nyxcerra's vision was getting blurry, her eyes full of tears. She was a little surprised with herself for bringing that up, but maybe she shouldn't have been. It was always there, a secret that she stubbornly kept nursing deep inside her: the knowledge that she loved Ceres, and wanted the world to know, yes she'd done favours to help them all progress, while she'd only ever been in love with Ceres.

"It's been hard not telling you all the truth, and that's my fault. We both wanted to say, but didn't want management to know, it would affect the fans, loose a demographic, we both agreed, but management found out anyway" she finished, her voice small, resigning herself to the questions they would ask.

"I more than anyone miss her. I can't change the past, I wish I could, I honestly do..." she sobbed as her emotions overwhelmed her.

"I tried to do what I thought was best for us." Nyxcerra started to reach for Tiiona, who was standing puzzled, only to think better of it, and let her hands fall helplessly to her side.

"There's two easy ways to fix everything. We keep going as we are, or I step down," tears running down her face, not caring.

"I never wanted this pressure, and maybe this proves that I can't handle it, I'm sorry, Avéline I'm sorry for forcing you to not follow your hearts, Tii, I should have listened, but I was too focused on my own pain, Syala, I should have stood up for you more, Jysell, I never listened properly..." she apologised before storming off towards room, not giving anyone else the chance to speak.

Avéline shook her head.

"Well, I think she's made a decision —so, someone needs to talk her out of it"

"I'll do it, At least I'll try," Tiiona snapped, interrupting her.

"How's she's managed to cope with all this, as well as all of our personal things... I couldn't do it, could you Tii" Avéline added, half telling her off, half accepting they had all ganged up on her.

"I'm sorry," Tiiona started to say, but she didn't have an answer, and she knew it.

"I think we should do this together, Avé"—Tiiona seemed to falter a little, her confidence failing her as it all sank in—

"I can't do this alone"

She blinked in shock.

"Tii, I think you're right," she insisted.

"It's all gotten complicated."

Moments later they arrived at Nyxcerra's bedroom door, tearing her crying and the clattering of things. She was serious. Avéline popped her head around the open door. Nyxcerra was on her knees, hastily folding things before putting them in a leather weekend bag.

Tiiona peaked around and knocked gently on the door, the sound causing Nyxcerra to stop as she was doing. Without turning around, she spoke.

"What do you want? You've got what you've always wanted. Take it, I'm done," she hissed, angry and disappointed.

Tiiona sighed as she shook her head, hating herself for letting it get this way. She swallowed against the hard, vicious sobs that rose up in her throat. She hated the atmosphere that had been created.

"We need to talk about this..." she added.

"I'm going to leave now. You should probably have a word with Aeryth, so it's not seen as a negative. I'll leave quietly. It's what's best for 'Aerrea'. You know, for appearances' sake," Nyxcerra added, as she had already packed a few things into a suitcase, grabbing hastily whatever she could reach.

"I never wanted this..." Tiiona added as she saw

Nyxcerra place a framed photo of the girls during their selection celebration into her bag.

Tiiona wrapped her arms around herself. She realized that a few tears had escaped, probably running in dark lines down her face. She reached up to wipe at her face. The part of her that was angry and confused felt bruised, and eager to lash out, but knew she had ruined everything.

"Nyx, you don't have to go..." her voice causing Nyxcerra to pause her packing.

"We just need to talk more, be as open as we used to... you know..."

Nyxcerra couldn't bare to turn round, before slowly turning, seeing Tiiona with Avéline standing behind her.

"I miss those days too, when it was the six of us against the rest, but it can't be like that, I'm not Ceres, I don't have her level head, too emotional, always ruled by my own emotions..."

"Well, I don't get it. Maybe I never will, but we are stronger together, the five of us. We...." She stuttered, "I don't want you to go... and..." she started sobbing, unable to stop herself.

"I'm sorry, so sorry for suggesting you had something to do with... you know..." Tiiona replied and she walked over and crouched beside Nyxcerra.

She was right; she didn't get it.She couldn't truly understand all the pressure that Nyxcerra was under. And aside from that one date with Nerys, which anyway had ended with Nyxcerra confessing that she didn't think she couldn't fall I love with anyone, Tiiona had never really seen her with anyone else.

She didn't understand how it was, knowing she'd chosen to stay single to focus on her career, Jysell, Avéline and Syala had been with other people, but Nyxcerra had been torturing herself with mental images of the life she'd had with Ceres, even when she had been performing favours to get to the top.

"Nyx, I'm sorry, I never understood why you were so hard on us, but I think I now know the reason behind it, please don't go..." as she spoke Jysell and Syala appeared behind her at the doorway, "We all want you to stay, we just need to not keep secrets, okay... no secrets..."

CHAPTER 54
"NOT ALL THINGS, ESPECIALLY WITH THE MEN, NOT LIKE US BUTTERFLIES..."

8 Months Later...
   The Excelsior Theatre of the Arts - 20:27pm

Yulian 'Yuli' Kondó walked onto the red carpet for the Gala with Ryx at her side, the late evening sun shining from behind her, the entrance to the theatre was ornately decorated for tonight, Thomas in attendance slowly walked the red carpet from arrivals, through the press pit, past a selected and screened crowd of fans, into the influencers press pit and into the venue.

As she set foot on the red carpet, the music turned down almost instantly. The silence rolled down the carpet all the way towards the influencers' press pit. Everyone stopped what they were doing to see her arrive, conversations ended as they saw her, influencers flocked over to their side of the red carpet, to get a glimpse of her, her dress had been hinted at, she'd carefully teased it through the social platforms, and tonight was the grand reveal.

"Yuli, over here, give us a smile..." a holographer from the sidelines cheekily pleaded, knowing she loved to smile at the camera. She turned towards them and gave them a sultry pose with a cheeky smile.

She was dressed in an elegant and slightly revealing long blue sequin covered dress, hugging her body carefully, in contrast with her rich tanned skin and straight black hair which stopped just below her bust-line, the dress catching the light and reflecting it in little rainbows onto the ground surrounding her.

Ryx spent some of his time introducing her to some of the other producers at the gala, ones that he knew from his time at BYL. She wanted to know everyone, this was her first Gala, she had taken the outer worlds by storm, an up-and-coming starlet, singing was only second fiddle to her acting abilities, she'd co-starred in Nyxcerra in Black Masquerade earlier in her career. She knew their names already, having spent time studying who they were, but she playfully acted as if she didn't know them, a skill she used to her advantage more than once, feigning innocence, she was young and impressionable, at least that was the act that she portrayed.

She welcomed them with flashed smiles, casting her gaze over everyone, giving hugs to those she knew, knowing the drones would capture the details and the photos would be leaked to the media who would create their own narrative about what was happening, all part of the plan.

Yulian knew what to do, and her publicist Kira knew what he was doing. She'd hesitated about being seen out with Ryx, but realising his past relationship with Avéline would hopefully cause a-bit of publicity if she turned up that night.

Yulian paused, she had felt better than expected, her

nerves from earlier had subsided. She glanced over at Ryx lovingly, as he accompanied her. She was in a gloriously expressive mood, even though she delicately embraced others to make sure that she still looked elegant as photos were being taken.

Ryx guided her towards a reporter, who was eagerly waiting for a brief comment, yet she stopped when she nearly bumped into a young Impiri girl.

The young woman's bright blonde hair cascaded over her shoulder and down to her waist, she was getting a huge amount of attention by the media who were busily taking photos of her as she posed seductively.

Yulian paused for a second, trying to work out who it was, Mesmerised by her outfit. The young woman's revealing red dress had caught the attention of almost all the media and influencers in attendance. She turned around slowly, catching Yulian and Ryx by surprise.

She nervously stepped back, not realising who it was, but it was written across Ryx's face. He knew exactly who it was, causing him to try and hide his expression. It was Avéline. She looked totally different that her usual conservative appearance. Her skin looked tanned, her skin was flawless, and her eyes sparkled.

"Yulian, daring.." she half stepped back, smiled as she looked at her,

"Looking fabulous tonight... nice to have you here tonight, we've got a great crowd," she called out enthusiastically, her voice dancing through the air, causing Yulian to relax.

Avéline looked over at Ryx, who looked at her nonchalantly, as if he was looking straight through her. For a moment Avéline stood there.

"Nice to see you too Ryx, it's... been a while.." Avéline

asked, nervously awaiting some sort of response. It had been nearly a cycle since the last time she had seen him.

"Yes, it has.." Ryx finally replied before stepping back as Yulian looked at him scornfully before looking back at Avéline, shaking her playfully before embracing her gently,

"So sorry about that. What can I say? He's not always the best with words..." she mocked,

"Not all things change, Yulian my dear, not all things, especially with the men, not like us butterflies..." Avéline joked, catching Ryx staring at her.

Knowing that they were being watched, Avéline knew exactly what they were concerned about, her relationship with Ryx had been widely publicised, and now his open relationship with Yulian was causing a stir, a young up-and-coming power couple the media had already labelled them.

"Avéline, didn't think you'd make it..." she paused, savouring the perfume she was wearing as it caught her attention, a sweet and airy scent.

"I am so glad you are here. We have things to discuss....", she looked her, her dazzling smile revealed the bronze glow at her cheeks, her skin radiant and smooth, her hair cascaded down to her shoulders before continuing down to her hip, every time she spoke his hair bounced with his movement.

"We do need to talk, but I need to introduce you to someone first" She paused and clapped twice loudly, a young woman dressed in black leather walked over from within the crowd, her hair tied back into a ponytail, her makeup caused conversations to stop, her skin a pearlescent white, in stark contrast to her bright red lips. She carried a small leather handle which was attached to two chains, one on each side. These chains led their way up to her choker, attached at the centre. She carefully walked her way towards Avéline before stopping in front of her, bowing gracefully.

"And who may this beautiful thing be? She is definitely a gift..." Yulian remarked playfully, glancing over the young woman, giving her a small seductive smile causing the young woman to blush, casting her gaze downwards instinctively.

"She's my inspiration..." Avéline spoke as she looked at her, pulling the handle, causing the young woman to come closer. Avéline held her hand out and caressed the young woman's face.

"She definitely keeps me inspired..." she purred, the cameras and drones going wild, recording every moment of it. Avéline knew exactly what she was doing. Nyxcerra's suggestion of doing this had caused a stir, the right kind of stir that she needed for her solo attempt, showing that she wasn't the young girl that they were used to.

"Of course, she's here for the effect I wanted..." Avéline whispered to Yulian, her voice trailing off. She pulled the young woman closer before kissing her on the forehead.

"For those in attendance tonight, are in for a treat... l" Avéline teased as she stood next to Yulian, posing for the cameras.

"Tonight I present my crowning achievement, the first public performance of 'Without you.'" The crowd collectively gasped. Avéline had promised this would happen next month, but had been encouraged by Aeryth to do it tonight, while the entire empire was watching.

This awards gala was covered by the press, but now it was a showcase, it was time for Avéline to shine.

Everyone was nowhere. Even those who were fashionably late had only recently arrived, from her closest friend

Soka to the most influential artists across the empire. Avéline hadn't felt the centre of attention in ages. This all changed the moment she had her inspiration turn up, knowing this was the kind of stunt Nyxcerra would use, but it had worked.

CHAPTER 55
"I WISH YOU HADN'T DONE THAT YOU KNOW..."

A Few Hours Later - 04:27am

"I wish you hadn't done that, you know". Ryx added as he hung up his suit jacket, undid the cravat which was tied around his neck, casting it onto the bed.

"It puts a strain between you and me.' He added as he slowly undid the cufflinks on his short before turning to place when in a box beside the bed, carefully opening the box with his fingerprint, placing them next to a golden ring, a silvery necklace and a single gold loop earring, he longingly looked at the earring, taking it out for a moment, smiling for a moment as he put it back in the box, the earring stained dark red where the loop ended.

"What's that...?" Yulian asked,

"Nothing, just some old things..." he replied hastily.

"And Hadn't done what?", what did I do this time? Yulian enquired as she carefully released the small clasp on the necklace she was wearing, nervously placing the necklace in its leather bound case on the vanity table across from the bed.

"When you said that, I had embarrassed you, in front of her." He looked across the bed at Yulian, reading the confusion on her face, and added,

"You said it's the problem, with all males"

"Her, you mean Avéline, I was fine with seeing her, your the one who ghosted her" she replied turning towards him, as she slowly undid the knot behind her neck where the dress was held up, allowing the top of her back to be exposed, she turned her head and sighed,

"Finally got all that off." She murmured to herself.

"But I've got a little surprise for you.." she added as she slowly peeled the dress down, revealing her white embroidered bra, as she slowly wiggles the dress down to reveal patching panties and garter belt, holding up her tanned stockings and high heels.

"I thought we could have some fun tonight before we go to sleep, all that repressed sexual tension at the gala was palpable, got me going" she added as she walked over to him, her hips swaying as she walked, within seconds she was standing in front of him, as she began carefully running her fingers up his shirt, before grabbing at his collar.

"You should be the one apologising to me" she hissed, "Making me look like a fucking fool in front of the media, I couldn't careless that she was your ex, I'm the one they all wanted to see, but you made it awkward..." she somewhat playfully added, smiling devilishly at him.

"Now I think you need to get on your knees and apologise...to me"

"Of course my queen, I'll apologise for what I did wrong, it was a fault on my part..."

He kissed her gently before slowly grabbing her throat,

"I'm sorry for making you think you had any control over me..."

"I'm the one who made you, without me your nothing, and don't you forget it." He finally released his grasp on her throat.

Causing her to gasp slightly,

"Oh dear oh dear, I am sorry about that..." she playfully replied, with a smile on her face.

Without a second thought he slapped her across the face, surprising her.

"You think I'm joking here, don't you..."

"What the fuck was that, are you insane.." she screamed back.

"Yulian you know that you don't have anything without me, this past year, what's happened to your career, it's skyrocketed, all because of what I do for you...you better not forget that, unless you want to resort to the cheap tactics of Avéline, trying to make herself relevant in an ever changing industry like this, an industry I have shaped to meet my needs."

"So don't you ever question my actions, especially in public again, otherwise I'll end you..." he replied slowly, staring at her, his hands clenched into fists, before slowly releasing them.

"I'm sorry babe, I didn't realise how hard it would be for you, having to see her again. I should have just ghosted her too, but it's Avéline. I was starstruck..."

"Your a star darling, my star, you shouldn't be star struck by anyone, especially Avéline, she pales in comparison to you..." he replied as he pulled her close, kissing her passionately, his other hand running its way over her body on its way toward her panties, causing her to break the kiss.

"Not yet..." she purred.

"Maybe I'm the one that should be getting on my knees..." she winked at him, be smiled a gentle smile as he unbuttoned his shirt, casting it onto the bed.

She stood before him, as she unclasped her bra, casting it onto the bed beside his shirt, playfully looking into his face. Her heart raced as he stood there. He had a broad chest, tight muscles that swelled beneath his sleeves. His hands slowly caressing her naked body, with each touch her body tingled. Her hands shaking with every touch.

"What do you want from me?" She whispered, almost purring as her breathing became shallow.

A devilish look filled his eyes as he pushed her to her knees.

"Please me." He added.

CHAPTER 56
"YOU KNOW WHY I'M HERE..."

An Hour Later - 05:27am

Ryx walked into the entranceway of the hotel suite, knowing that she was staying here alone that night, a perk of performing at the gala, the other girls were staying in different hotels scattered across the capital, each hotel chain trying to gain favourable reviews from its celebrity clientele.

Avéline stepped back nervously, allowing him to enter, she surprise at seeing him there at the door caused her to not think straight.

Avéline's face flushed as she told herself he was not her type, that he was bad for her, that's why their relationship had ended, he was too much of a distraction, when she was with him she couldn't focus, she'd nearly lost everything because of him

She'd let the others down, she'd caused issues for the label, which got him fired, but there she was letting him back inside her apartment, but felt herself being drawn to him again like an insect to a naked flame. His piercing green eyes had always caught her attention.

That look he gave made her hearts race. She shook her head gently, trying to get the thoughts out of her head. Had the label sent him, were they trying to cause a scandal, The typical thing she'd realised the label loved doing, keeping her always guessing about everything, were they trying to force her out from the group, all these thoughts were a mess in her head.

She knew nothing would happen here. She'd just got herself into the right place, but now she had taken a huge step backwards, she expected him to stop but he walked past her without stopping, brushing past her, causing her brows to become furrowed, seaming to ignore her, stopping just behind her,

he muttered,

"I think you know why I'm here" casually, how he always whispered, when he talked with her, a sound she honestly missed.

Her head was on fire, not knowing what to say or what to do. He'd changed a lot physically over the past year, he'd become more athletic, was he more attractive? Most definitely, she thought to herself. She kept thinking about his athletic build. Now he was immaculately dressed in a tan coloured coat, very much in fashion.

Her thoughts moved over to Yulian, he'd been leaving the Gala with her, all loved up, the pictures already busily making their way through all the feeds, overshadowing the tensions when they crossed paths earlier that night, he had ignored her as if she wasn't even there, which still hurt her. Was he still seeing her? she thought. She wanted him to feel the way he made her feel , her hearts raced, her scales tingled, she could feel herself wanting him more.

Would she dare go through with it, with how she felt? She didn't know if she could let herself go. She knew what was at risk if the label found out her career would be over. Not a little reprimand, it would be fully over, she'd be blacklisted from the industry, she wouldn't ever be allowed to work in the entertainment industry, she'd be lucky to get a job working on a star-cruiser singing. That was the reach and influence of the big three, BYL, ESE and YTM, eighty percent of the artists in the empire were signed to one of these labels or a subsidiary label.

He grabbed her arm and turned her toward the wall. He brushed her hair to the side, looked at the pale scales which framed her neck.

She saw a smile flicker on his lips when he whispered the words,

"Seems like you need a good time" Her jaw dropped. She blinked hard. He'd noticed the pale tone of her scales, mockingly disappointed to see that they hadn't turned a light shade of blue, as was normal for their kind when in a state of arousal. She was close, with every fibre of her being she wanted in some way to resist him, to prove that she was over him, that he didn't have any control of her.

Time seemed to stop when she was around him, having it feel like only a second had passed. It all happening so fast she didn't know how she got there and to be honest, she didn't care.

Ryx was there, leaning against her, she could feel the heat radiating from his body, warming her back, his breath tingled her scales as he blew a stream of warm breath along them, the building excitement causing her to lose her composure, feeling her knees getting weak she sank down before realising, it was driving her mad, as she fought against her own desires.

"I've missed you so much. I'm sorry about what happened. Can we just give it another go..." he whispered into her ear. Before placing his hand against the wall. Avéline slowly turned herself around and he was there, close, she could feel his breath on her face, her thoughts erratic, she tried to speak, but couldn't, it was bad enough that she couldn't breathe, speak, swallow or hear anything outside of her own thudding heartbeats. But now she was having trouble with her own thoughts. Would she dare rekindle the relationship with him? Ryx sensed her nerves and leaned forward.

"You wanna let me make that beautiful face of yours glow, like you know I can," he whispered in a low tone that had her hearts racing even more. She instinctively felt her head slowly nodding, surprised by her own reaction. Her own body was betraying her thoughts. She wanted to melt into his arms, to feel the heat from his body against hers.

Swallowing the lump in her throat, Avéline managed to eek out,

"With me, seriously?"

He smiled at her.

"Of course, it's always been you, you know that," he replied. She wanted to reach out and caress his face, to pull him closer. But something stopped her. Her own thoughts pulling her back. She wanted someone, right now, anyone would do. The memories of her last conversation with Nyx flashed into her consciousness, how she scolded her, the same way that Ceres would have, she'd let the girls down, but right now, was the group more important than her own happiness, this fight continued in her every thought.

"I don't know if I can...it's just." She spoke, her voice

breathy and laboured, trying her hardest to resist the urge to take him there and then.

Maybe it was the label, a plot by Aeryth and Leix, to force her out, to shake up the group, doing that would sell tickets, gain interest in who would replace her, would it be another member of the 106.

Even with all this she couldn't shake the idea that it was a hoax, a prank organised by Aeryth herself, something so twisted, a sick example of her sometimes twisted sense of humour, but she couldn't help asking,

"Are you serious?, she didn't put you up to trick me like this"

"She? Who are you talking about, Ave?" He replied,

"Aeryth?" He added as he realised who she was talking about.

"If she found out I was here, I'd be dead. They warned me to keep away, but I can't. That thing with Yulian, it's nothing, just sex. I know I hurt you. I like that to hurt you, to make you realise..."

"But that doesn't matter now. Yulian isn't important. She knew I still loved you... after the way I acted earlier," he replied, almost bringing himself to tears. He looked at her longingly before adding.

"Why would she?, all I want to do is to brighten up your evening, by telling you how much I love you, you know that don't you Avé" he said with a roguish grin that made her dizzy with her own desire, the scales down her back tingled, not all of them, but the primary ones tingled all the way down her spine, she took in a deep breath, a musky scent caught her by surprise, she felt her inhibitions fade, her own instincts take over as his pheromones got to work, she'd never noticed that his kind produced them, but she definitely sensed something different about him.

"I miss the touch of someone, of you, the way you used to make me feel," she whispered, pausing

"I miss you Ryx." she whispered. A wry grin appeared on his face as she gently blushed as she looked at him.

She was actually going to do it, to release the tension that had built up, she looked over and saw her own hand caressing the side of his face, by her own amazement, she was reacting instinctively, her fingertips tracing their way down his neck towards his chest.

"So you've decided..." he murmured. His tone was suggestive. She knew what she was thinking, wanting to take that next step.

She grabbed hold of his collar and pulled him close, and stepped closer to him, her lips close to his.

"I'll let you decide if I have..." she whispered as she kissed him, before pulling away nervously, letting go of his collar and stepping back. 'It was wrong, Wasn't it?' She thought, 'it would repulse the Goddesses'. She was so ashamed, she was afraid her hearts would beat right out of her chest, she couldn't go through with a lie.

"I can't...its..." she shamefully whispered.

Ryx carefully fixed his collar and chuckled to himself.

"Complicated..." he playfully replied. Avéline nodded her head slowly.

"You could say that. I want to physically, but in my hearts I know it's not real, it's purely physical, the joy you make me feel, but that's all it ever was, purely superficial"

"You always enjoy being the tease, don't you?" He replied, a dash of anger peppered his tone of voice.

Avéline laughed nervously.

"What do you mean??. I... I," she stuttered. She was never the tease. She had always followed his lead.

"Don't play so coy with me, I hate it when you do that..." his expression changed as he spoke.

"Really, Avéline, cut the false cute act? you're just as fake as Ceres was..."

He reached out and with his fingers he gently brushed aside her hair, lingering there for a while as he kept it sink in, watching the realisation appear on her face, enjoying it in some perverse way.

"I don't understand..." she replied before adding, as her thoughts stumbled over each other,

"Ceres?, what do you mean? The same as her... how did you??"

"Know Ceres? It's obvious, of course," he paused, mocking her.

"It was our little secret." He smiled as he straightened his collar while not taking his gaze off of her.

"You... and" Avéline stuttered as she tried to comprehend what he'd just said.

He slowly turned around and walked back towards the door, pressing the lock on the door, then looked over his left shoulder.

"Yes, me and Ceres, we were a thing, before that bitch did the same as you, thought you were better than me, that you could make it without my help..." he hissed, slamming his hand against the door, causing it to rattle in its frame.

"I thought you were different, but then it turns out, all you Impiri girls are the same," he smiled. Avéline's heart rate dropped.

"I loved you..." she mouthed,

"I just couldn't think straight when I'm..." she added before he placed his finger against her lips,

"Shhhh..., I've had enough of your goddamn lies. This is over when I say we're over." He replied through gritted teeth, causing her to recoil in fear, her eyes widening as she realised that he would not let her go. He stood there towering over her, mocking her, laughing as she realised what was going to happen., she stood there scared, a look of fear emblazoned across her face.

"That's the same frightened look she gave me that night... before she fell," Ryx added as he reached towards his belt, releasing its clasp.

EPILOGUE

An Hour Later - 06:27am

Avéline gripped the rim of the porcelain sink and tried to steady her hands, failing miserably. Her breathing was shallow, erratic and laboured.

She gripped the sink harder; her knuckles turning white as she tried to control her anger as she stood motionless, staring at her reflection in the broken mirror. The bathroom was a mess, items strewn across the marble surface beside the sink.

Her once perfect makeup was now a complete mess. She looked like a tribal face-paint than she would have wanted. Her hair was dishevelled, she was a shocking sight.

Looking out of the one un-swollen and unbruised eye, She licked the corner of her lip, wincing at the pain, tasting the bitter metallic taste of her own blood, before dabbing it away with a tissue she hastily grabbed from the tissue box.

"One last time," she whispered to herself.

"One. Last. Time..." - she thought, disgusted with

herself, 'he knew you would give him one more chance, he knew he could get to you, you forgave him the last time he lashed out. He knew you would take him back,' the voice in her head screamed out. "He tried to rape you tonight, you know that..." the voice in her head added. Its delivery shocked her into thinking straight.

"I had to do what I had to do..." she muttered, as she re-buttoned her blouse, before wiping the tears away, grabbing the blood-soaked knife off the vanity table as she gingerly stepped over Ryx's body, lying motionless on the bathroom floor, just as the sound of sirens grew louder.

ACKNOWLEDGMENTS

First and foremost: my ever-patient family, who didn't mind me disappearing to "get some writing done". Without this I wouldn't have been able to this done.

Thank you to Assad, Alice, Declan, Paula and Jordan for reading my beta copies or early drafts, or just listening to me discuss it, helping me make it better, your critiquing has helped make it better in ways you can't imagine, so thank you.

I wish to thank anyone who has listened to me prattle on about this book, during its inception and the lengthy process of writing it. I hope it has been worth it.

I'd like to thank Tim from Dissect Designs for making this amazing cover.

I'd also like to thank *you* the reader for picking up this book, from the depth of my heart I thank you.

ABOUT THE AUTHOR

Thomas has been writing stories ever since he was young. Stories have always held a special place in his heart, from the stories told to him by family, especially his maternal grandfather. What started out as an intrinsic love for story-telling, has turned into his passion and creative outlet, creating worlds and characters.

There's nothing he likes better than writing (and reading and listening to) stories, stories that challenge the status quo, to heroic misfits, the rebels with a heart, the crazy ones who will never leave your side and most of all the trouble makers - we all love a little troublemaking don't we.

These characters have always been an inspiration to Thomas, he hopes you will find characters that you love or hate., or maybe a bit of both.

Thomas spends his time working in the technology sector, residing in the United Kingdom.

twitter.com/thomasraiwrites

instagram.com/thomasraiauthor

CPSIA information can be obtained
at www.ICGtesting.com
Printed in the USA
LVHW100050281022
731758LV00002B/22